Richard Allington's first indication of what was happening came in the form of a long airmail letter from Barbara. He read it through twice, hardly able to believe it the first time, and then felt a cold chill settling round his heart. Like a man in a dream he stood up and moved over to his office window, staring out at the familiar skyscraper towers of Manhattan . . .

He tried to imagine it cold and dead, the city, the nation, and the whole planet frozen in icy darkness, and a shiver ran through his spine.

Barbara had to be wrong!

NIGHTWORLD

Robert Charles

CORGI BOOKS

NIGHTWORLD

A CORGI BOOK 0 552 12187 8

First publication in Great Britain

PRINTING HISTORY

Corgi edition published 1984

Copyright © Robert Charles Smith, 1984

This book is set in 10/11 Mallard

Corgi Books are published by
Transworld Publishers Ltd.,
Century House, 61–63 Uxbridge Road,
Ealing, London W5 5SA

Made and printed in Great Britain by
Cox & Wyman Ltd., Reading, Berks.

NIGHTWORLD

1

There was a black spot in the tail of the comet.

Barbara Allington could see it clearly through the thirty-six-inch mirror reflector telescope which was focused on the night sky between Mars and Jupiter. The time was two a.m. on the morning of October 28th, 1985. The weather was fine, the air was crisp and cold, heralding the first sharp ground frost of autumn, and the sky over the southern half of England was free of cloud. At the Royal Greenwich observatory, located in the spacious parkland grounds of Herstmonceaux Castle in Sussex, the conditions for observing the heavens were as near perfect as they could be.

The nucleus of the comet was a bright speck of white light, hurtling toward the centre of the solar system from the vast darkness of outer space. Its orbit would take it in a tight turn around the sun before it would disappear again on another stupendous loop somewhere beyond the far-flung, ice-cold worlds of Neptune and Pluto. The complete orbital journey took seventy-six Earth years, from the fiery heat of the celestial furnace, to the remote, freezing emptiness on the far edge of the star's domain.

The comet bore the name of the man who had first predicted its regular return, although it had been sighted and recorded as far back as 467 B.C. by the ancient Chinese. Probably it had been seen long before that, millions of years ago by the first ape-man gaping upward from the Olduvai Gorge, but then there had been no written records. It was impossible to determine how many times the comet had flashed between the Earth and the sun, for until Edmond Halley had plotted its movements no one had understood the recurring nature of these brilliant and often terrifying streaks of light in the heavens.

Now Halley's Comet was returning for yet another fleeting visit through the inner planets, but this time it was bringing in its wake an unexpected passenger. The dark spot showed up like a splashed stain, or a black hole torn in the streaming, nebulous white tail.

Barbara gazed upward at the spectacle until her eyes ached. The pin-prick blaze of light looked immobile against the countless galaxies of the cosmos, but she knew that as it approached the sun it could be moving at anything up to four hundred miles per second. Already it was hundreds of millions of miles closer than when it had first become visible as a faint, luminous patch in the far heavens some three months ago in midsummer.

The speeds and distances involved were mind-staggering, and difficult to get into perspective. Barbara had to remind herself that what appeared in the telescope as a finger-length vapour trail, was in fact fifty million miles of gaseous mist and dust specks, glowing incandescent with reflected sun and starlight.

The strain of concentration was too much; she found herself blinking and moved her head back reluctantly from the eyepiece of the telescope. She got up from the viewing chair and made way for the white-haired man who waited beside her. Professor Harold Willoughby immediately resumed his own observations.

'What do you think it is?' Barbara asked.

'It's most certainly something new,' Willoughby conceded cheerfully but unhelpfully. 'It wasn't there when the comet made its last appearance in 1910. Not that I'm old enough to have seen it myself,' he added hastily. 'But anything like this would have been noticed and reported.'

'Perhaps it was smaller then, or tilted at an angle to show a smaller profile.'

'Perhaps. Perhaps.' Willoughby had been an astronomer for fifty years, and had learned never to rush to any conclusion. 'We'll check back of course and re-examine the old photographs which were taken during the last visit, but I think we'll find that this is something that the comet has picked up on its more recent travels through space.'

'Like picking up a hitch-hiker along the Milky Way?'

Willoughby smiled. Barbara had been his assistant for six months, it was her first job after leaving university, and he had finally come to like her fresh and slightly irreverent sense of humour.

'You could put it that way,' he agreed. 'Except that in this case the comet didn't stop and politely invite the hitch-hiker to come on board. It probably drove right through the object, or passed so close that it was sucked into the tail with no chance of escape. More of a hit and run, if you see what I mean.'

'Could it be an asteroid?'

'Heavens, no! It couldn't possibly have any solid mass. For one thing a collision between the comet and an asteroid of that size would mean the total destruction of both. Even a near miss would flip the comet slightly out of orbit, and as we both know it's coming back dead on course, exactly as our calculations have predicted. Finally, if it were an asteroid it would be much too heavy for the comet to pull through space. A comet, my dear Barbara, is just a great, insubstantial bucketful of nothing. Even the nucleus is nothing more than a celestial snowball of grit, gas and ice. Like everything else in our tiny corner of the universe, it draws its life and flaming energy from the sun.'

Barbara waited for Willoughby to continue, hoping he would make a more educated guess than some of her own, but the professor lapsed into a thoughtful silence. After a moment he dug into the pocket of his shapeless jacket and produced a cream toffee which he unwrapped and popped into his mouth. He chewed contentedly, and then as an afterthought fished out the bag of sweets and offered it without taking his eyes from the telescope.

Barbara smiled and took a toffee. She was becoming quite fond of Professor Willoughby in his eternally baggy suits. The pockets were always bulging with the tools of his trade: calculator, slide rules, notebooks and pens, plus the odd apple and the inevitable bag of sweets. He had the wisdom of years, the patience of his profession, and the carefree appetite of a twelve-year old schoolboy.

She waited until he had to rest his eyes from the telescope, and then prompted him again.

'Professor, what do you think it is?'

Willoughby shrugged. 'It has to be gaseous — a cloud of some sort. Vapours, dust particles, or some sort of cosmic mist. It's more substantial than the tail of the comet, it has more density, and is probably a little heavier. But definitely it is not solid matter.'

'Where did it come from?'

Willoughby gestured upward, the movement of his hand taking in the entire oblong of night sky visible through the open dome housing the telescope.

'Somewhere out there,' he said calmly. 'The entire universe is filled with vast clouds of swirling gas and dust between the stars. What the comet has picked up is just a diminutive patch of all that cosmic fog and debris. It isn't possible to say where on its wandering the comet managed to suck the little cloud into its slipstream, but the interesting thing is that it is bringing it closer for us to study.'

Barbara knew enough of the mind-boggling magnitude of the galaxies to view an astronomer's concept of diminutive with suspicion. She said slowly, 'Just how little is this cloud?'

'Perhaps as large as the planet Mercury, perhaps

smaller than our own moon. It's difficult to tell at this range, although we should be able to get some measurements from the photographs that are being taken through the Isaac Newton tonight.'

'It's a pity it's not still here.'

Barbara spoke with a note of regret, for she had never had the opportunity of looking through the giant 100-inch Isaac Newton telescope, which had until recently been housed in a ninety-foot-high aluminium dome in another corner of the Herstmonceaux estate. Now the dome stood empty, for the telescope had been moved to a new mountain site at an altitude of 7,500 feet on La Palma in the Canary Islands.

'Not so,' Willoughby objected promptly. 'We're getting much better pictures from La Palma. There's no sky-glare from the cities, much less atmosphere obscuration, and no pollution. At that height they are totally cloud-free for eighty per cent of the time.'

He paused and glanced up at his assistant. 'I do see what you mean. It is rather a shame that we can't use the Isaac Newton ourselves. But look on the bright side. If you stay with us long enough, then perhaps you'll get the chance to work at La Palma. You'll have a nice little paid holiday in the Canary Islands. How about that?'

Barbara smiled briefly. It was cold in the viewing dome, for any form of heating would cause warm air currents to distort the vital sharpness of the mirrored images. To keep herself from shivering she was wearing two thick-knit jumpers and a thick woollen skirt and jacket. 'It would be nice to see some sunshine,' she agreed.

Willoughby moved his head close to the eyepiece again. He was fascinated, even though he was not an excitable man. He had been following the track of the comet for the past ten weeks, watching it grow brighter and closer, but his attention had always been concentrated on the bright glow of the nucleus, and he had failed to notice the black cloud in the tail. It was the detailed examination of a photograph taken through the Isaac Newton telescope two days earlier which had first pin-pointed the new phenomenon, and now Willoughby guessed that astronomers all over the world would be looking at Halley's Comet with new interest.

'We suspect that every star and solar system is condensed out of gigantic swirling clouds of interstellar dust and gases,' Willoughby murmured his thoughts aloud. 'The inner planets, from Mercury to Mars, have had most of their gas and liquid evaporated away, while the outer planets, from Jupiter and onward, are still mostly gaseous in content. Now this cloud that is being pulled behind Halley's Comet could help us to prove or disprove everything we know, or think we know, about the way the galaxies were formed. The cloud could contain samples of the original primordial material.'

'So that could be great-great-grandfather, coming to visit us again after all these trillions of light-years,' Barbara returned wryly. 'I was doubtful when they told me at school that we were all descended from the apes, and even more doubtful when they told me that the apes emerged from a handful of sludge at the bottom of the ocean. Now I have to believe that my first ancestor was just a gas bubble in space.'

'Don't mock.' Willoughby grinned. 'After all, it is quite thrilling really. Do you realize that in a few weeks time Columbus Two will be able to scoop up some samples of that cloud and bring it back here to Earth. We will actually be able to study what could be the original cosmic protomatter in our own laboratories.'

'Can Columbus Two do that?'

'Of course. It is designed for a close, fly-past encounter with the nucleus, but after that its secondary task is to collect samples from the comet's tail. Now the tail includes the cloud, so it must be possible to obtain cloud samples instead.'

Willoughby's voice had risen to its first discernible

pitch of enthusiasm, and Barbara realized that in his own calm and unflappable way he was keenly stimulated by the new discovery. He hunched himself closer to the eyepiece of the telescope and again became silent and absorbed in his own thoughts.

Barbara had to be content with gazing up at the slit of night sky where the telescope pointed through the open roof. The comet was still invisible to the naked eye, and so was the tiny, man-made, comet-chasing satellite Columbus Two. She had to imagine them there against the glittering backcloth of stars, but her imagination was vivid, and the exercise was sufficiently satisfying to push away the small sense of foreboding.

For deep inside her she felt something vaguely ominous in the presence of the sinister black cloud.

Columbus Two had in fact been launched over two years before, in the late summer of 1983. The satellite had been lifted into space in the nose cone of a two-hundred-ton *Ariane* rocket which had soared up from the launch pad of the Europa Space Centre in French Guiana.

Once clear of the Earth, and separated from its parent rocket, Columbus Two had followed virtually the same space path which the imaginative journeys of Voyager One and Voyager Two had pioneered before it. They had all been aimed at the planet Saturn. The Voyager satellites had both by-passed the ringed planet, sending back streams of photographs and data, and were now continuing on to investigate the outer planets. Columbus Two had a different purpose: it was programmed to fly one wide, looping orbit around Saturn, and so use the gravitational pull of the planet to help propel itself back on a return flight to Earth.

The turnaround had been successfully made in the late autumn and early winter of 1984, and the satellite had covered more than three-quarters of the long journey home. Now Halley's Comet was coming up fast behind it. Soon, just inside Mars orbit, the comet and Columbus Two would be travelling on parallel paths, only a few hundred miles apart. The satellite carried cameras to take close-up pictures of the comet's nucleus, together with instruments to provide data on its chemical composition and magnetic field.

After the comet had passed the satellite was confidently expected to go through its long, diaphanous train, taking more instrument readings and pictures, and scooping up small samples of the diffused gas and cosmic dust particles. Finally, while the comet grazed the sun and spun itself round to race back into the cold darkness of infinity, Columbus Two would return to Earth orbit. Hopefully the satellite would be recovered after a parachute drop into the South Atlantic, and with it the samples from the comet's tail.

The days passed quickly as the comet overhauled the satellite, and the long-awaited moment of close encounter in space drew near. On Earth astronomers all over the world were intrigued and excited, most of them far more so than the placid Professor Willoughby, and speculation about the comet's strange new travelling companion was loud and varied.

None of them were particularly worried. They all knew that the comet would miss the Earth by at least fifty million miles, and so would the dark cloud patch which was almost a third of the way down the tail, directly behind the nucleus.

Even if the wide-flung skirts of the main tail passed over the Earth it would do no harm, for in 1910 the Earth had in fact passed through the comet's tail with no ill effects, and nothing more noticeable to the general populace than a faint luminosity in the sky.

Most of the astronomers, gazing through their telescopes from Europe and America, came to the same conclusion as Willoughby. They agreed that the dark spot had to be a cloud mass, composed of black dust particles and swirling vapours. It had to be heavier than the main tail to remain intact, but the tail was a ghost-mane a million times more rarefied than air, so the passenger cloud was probably of no more density than an ordinary earth rain-cloud. After a week of calculations the most widely held estimate of its size put it slightly smaller than the Earth's moon.

There was a ripple of interest in the media, and a few scare reports that the cloud might eclipse the sun. The astronomers quickly scorned this idea. Halley's Comet and the cloud would pass so close to the sun that they would be dwarfed into insignificance by its enormous girth.

The predictions of doom persisted from a few of the Hindu pavement astrologers squatting along the streets of Colombo and New Delhi, but no one whose opinions could be taken seriously could see any real portent of danger.

At Herstmonceaux the debates were lively and gradually approached the levels of elation. The Columbus Two Comet Mission had been jointly financed and launched by the major nations of Europe, and now the unexpected appearance of the cloud had up-graded its potential returns and importance. As the comet came into range of the satellite's cameras and other instruments a steady stream of photographs and data was beamed back to Earth. It was all turning out so much better than had been planned, and there was a definite feeling that for once Europe had pulled off a space coup ahead of the Americans and the Russians.

To those involved the whole event became exhilarating and intoxicating; even Willoughby was affected, and Barbara found herself enthralled by the close-encounter drama. She was an impressionable young woman, keen and intelligent, and with her bubbling black curls, sparkling eyes and bright personality, she had made herself very popular. She was a new girl on the observatory staff, but was quick to grasp the revelations as they were explained to her.

But the feeling of unease persisted. As a child her favourite book had been *Treasure Island*, and even now her subconscious mind could not help associating the black spot with an evil sign. In learning the facts about comets she had also become acquainted with the mythology, and knew that in the past these blazing visitations in the sky had long been considered the heralds of death, disaster, and dire catastrophe. It was believed that the comets had caused kings to fall, empires to collapse, and even the gods to die.

Barbara could understand why these fiery bolts in the heavens had filled the hearts of primitive man with terror, and once mentioned her vague fears to Willoughby. Her superior merely smiled complacently, told her not to worry, and gave her another toffee.

By this time Halley's Comet had become a bright, flashing star which had overtaken the slower-moving satellite. Phase One had been declared a triumph, and the Comet-Mission controllers had made their fateful decision. Radio signals were beamed up from the Europa Space Centre on the north coast of South America which manoeuvred Columbus Two directly into the path of the cloud. They were aiming for a second close encounter, and the black cloud loomed large and menacing behind the whirling silver speck of the tiny satellite.

2

Outside the complex of the United Nations Headquarters buildings in New York the flags of the 156 member states flew bright and colourful in the weak and watery December sunshine. A stiff breeze blowing up First Avenue made the flags strain bravely from the flagpoles, giving a display of stalwart unity that was hardly matched by the tensions and discord that so often filled the council and conference halls within.

The sunlight glinted on the green-tinted windows of the towering, thirty-nine-storey glass and marble Secretariat building. Inside, Richard Allington, the former English Ambassador, rode the elevator down from his office on the thirty-eighth floor to the ground floor lobby. The car stopped three times on the upper levels, letting men and women of all races flow in and out. The conversations they brought with them, and the snatches of talk that were heard briefly from the busy corridors and offices, were as varied as the people who worked here. New rice strains were being developed in Taiwan, another well-digging programme had begun in southern India, the spectre of famine again overhung Ethiopia, and the colossal headache of world inflation still diminished every stretched and straining budget. The people involved were all intense and dedicated, but they found time to acknowledge their new Secretary-General.

Allington was almost sorry when the elevator stopped on the ground floor. In his office he had to contend with the endless paper avalanche of reports and statistics, and outside the Secretariat he was subjected to the interminable pressure politics of the warring delegations. It was only in other people's offices, and in the corridors and elevators inside the Secretariat, that the real work of the United Nations seemed to come alive.

He walked without haste across the lobby, past the stained glass panel that was symbolic of man's struggle for peace. Once outside he paused to watch the fountain splashing into the pool immediately opposite. The breeze rippling the stiff row of flags was fresh on his cheek and tousled his thick, dark hair with its light, distinguishing streaks of grey. He was a tall man, wearing a grey suit that had been tailored in Savile Row. Physically he was in much better shape than most of his fellow diplomats at the UN, and he managed to look much younger than his fifty-seven years.

But that was today, he had told himself ruefully as he shaved that morning. So far he had been Secretary-General for less than six months. Give it another year and he would probably look more like an old man of seventy.

Reluctantly he turned to face the General Assembly building, a white structure of graceful, sweeping curves, glass-fronted on the side which faced the Secretariat, and domed in the centre of the concave roof. He would have preferred to take a quiet stroll in the park-like gardens overlooking the East River, but a glance at the unrelenting face of his wrist-watch showed that he was already late. He squared his shoulders and walked briskly forward.

Two minutes later he was taking his place behind the green Italian marble podium in the vast General Assembly Hall. A few stragglers were still trickling in, but most of the six-member delegations had already taken their seats.

The remaining two seats behind the podium were also occupied. The eternally harassed-looking but capable

Luis Valdez, the Brazilian Under-Secretary-General for General Assembly Affairs, was polishing his spectacles in the right-hand seat. He nodded briefly to Allington. They had found they could work well together, and had already exchanged their views on today's business in a long, private conversation earlier in the morning. Separating them now, his powerful bulk relaxed in the centre seat, was the President for this session of the UN General Assembly, the Ambassador for Angola, Julius Mangala.

'Good morning, Richard.' Mangala half-rose from his seat, his perfect white teeth flashing a cheerful smile of welcome from his smooth, ebony face. He wore a dark suit with a red silk tie. Gold links glinted at his shirt cuffs but they were his only extravagance. He was an African Marxist intellectual who had become refined but had not yet gone decadent.

'Good morning, Julius.' Allington matched the good-natured smile, feeling as bland as a Confucian Chinese. It was one of the quirks of the job, he reflected, that you ended up borrowing all sorts of different racial mannerisms. With the Japanese you bowed, with the Americans you were blunt and pragmatic, with the Arabs you talked in dignified circles and took an age to reach the point. One day, he supposed, he would wake up and find he was no longer British, but some kind of multi-racial human melting-pot that would be a total misfit in any other environment than the UN.

'How is your cough?' he enquired, nursing a secret, fleeting hope that it might be worse than yesterday, perhaps even bad enough to prevent Mangala from any serious and sustained speech-making.

'Much better,' the African answered happily. 'I tried a new throat spray which Doctor Valdez recommended. It seems to have worked wonders.'

They continued to make small talk while they waited for the last few delegates to find their seats. On the surface they were two men in harmony, seated beneath the huge UN emblem of a united world inside a wreath of laurel leaves which was on the wall behind the podium. However, they both knew that their polite words and charade smiles were fooling no one; least of all the hundreds of reporters and TV camera teams crowding the packed press galleries on either side of the long hall.

The media men were here in force and gleeful anticipation of a lively debate, for Richard Allington and Julius Mangala were old adversaries who had frequently crossed swords in the past. Mangala was seen as the champion of the poor Third World, and the undisputed leader of the delegations from black Africa. On the other side Allington was seen by his enemies as the chief representative of the rich First World, and by his friends as a man desperately trying to balance realism with idealism in order to try and hold the rapidly disintegrating organization together.

The whole of this annual session of the General Assembly, which had begun in mid-September, had been highlighted by a series of passionate verbal duels between Allington and Mangala. Today was the last meeting of the regular session, and the thorny subject of Namibia was on the agenda. It was a topic on which Mangala would be at his most vehement, and Allington would be certain to respond.

Another clash of wills was expected, and the press knew they would not be disappointed.

The appointment of Richard Allington as Secretary-General of the United Nations was the last of a series of compromise appointments. They had begun with the end of Kurt Waldheim's second five-year term in the top post, and had been exacerbated by the ever-deepening conflict between the superpowers and the Third World. The Third World countries had been determined that a representative of one of their delegations would be the next Secretary-General, while the superpowers had been equally dedicated to restoring a working balance in an organization already dominated by the sheer weight of Third World votes in the General Assembly.

It was in the late seventies that the gap between the rich and poor nations had become a vast gulf, threatening at the least to make the United Nations unworkable, and at the worst to destroy it completely. In the forty years since the original fifty-one members had founded its famous charter for the promotion of peace and all its related ideals, more than a hundred new nations had emerged to claim their places in the General Assembly. Each country had one vote, which gave the new postage-stamp-size countries which could barely raise an ambassador's fare to New York, exactly the same voting power as China, with more than a quarter of the world's population, or the United States which contributed more than a quarter of the entire UN Budget.

The result was an almost total degeneration of the original ideals. The Third World countries had become a steamroller power bloc, pushing unrealistic and outrageously one-sided resolutions through the General Assembly. At every turn the big rich nations were outvoted by the majority of small nations, which then did not have the means to carry out their grandiose schemes. As if that was not enough, the UN had become a hotbed of anti-democratic hostility, hurling endless abuse at the United States and its Western allies.

The General Assembly had become a Theatre of Farce, where it was fashionable to insult and revile those countries whose co-operation and resources were essential to make the organization function with any effect. In such a theatre, thunderous ovations could be given to the Palestinian terrorist leader Yasser Arafat, and to Idi Amin, the Ugandan dictator and mass-murderer of millions of his own people.

Ironically it was mainly at the insistence of the United States that the one-nation-one-vote principle had been written into the UN charter. Now the imbalance had on several occasions almost brought the Americans to the point of walking out in disgust. If they ever did it would cause financial collapse, and render the whole concept of the United Nations meaningless.

It was against this bitterly divided background that the battle for the position of Secretary-General had been fought. The rules were that the fifteen-member Security Council would nominate a candidate, who would then need a two-thirds majority vote in the General Assembly to be elected. To complicate matters the five permanent members of the Security Council, Great Britain, France, America, Russia and China, each had the power to veto any nomination. Inevitably the election rules had become a formula for prolonged and destructive deadlock.

The struggle had defeated Waldheim and the leading contenders, and made it impossible for any of the following compromise candidates to function effectively. The whole issue had become a perverse shambles, making a mockery of the entire concept and principles of the United Nations. Allington's immediate predecessor had been a Doctor of Divinity from Sri Lanka, elected because he seemed the candidate best qualified to offend no one. After three months the distraught man had resigned, claiming ill-health as the cause, while in reality everyone knew he had succumbed to despair.

The political in-fighting had continued. The African delegations remained pugnacious, the Asian delegations had fluctuated and wavered in varying degrees, until finally the bulk of the Latin American delegations had agreed to support another European candidate. Richard Allington had been proposed and elected with only a one-vote margin in his favour.

To the surprise of many people the United Nations was still surviving, but its reputation as a forum to promote peace and harmony in the world was in tatters, and its intellectual respectability in the eyes of the media had become extinct.

Allington knew that if he stayed the course he would

have a tough fight ahead of him, and there were many who did not expect him to last out. He had landed what had always been regarded as the most impossible job in the world, and after four decades it seemed that now it would be impossible to hold the UN together, much less to further its idealistic goals.

He had inherited every insoluble problem imaginable, and in addition to performing political and economic miracles he was expected at the same time to please 156 different masters. Public opinion and the unsympathetic media confidently expected him to fail. They all knew it would take a philosopher-saint to succeed, and even then the sceptics insisted that he would have to be black!

Despite all this Allington was determined to do the job he had been given. In getting to grips with his new responsibilities he had come to realize that despite the squabbling in the conference halls there was still valuable work being done in the Secretariat. There were black spots and areas of gross mismanagement, but in most cases economic aid was reaching the under-developed areas, many killer diseases and much Third World sickness had been eradicated, and famine relief did reach the starving. The political failures were splashed across the world headlines, but behind the inflammatory speeches and the howling recriminations there were many functions that were doggedly improving the health and living standards of the world's poor.

There was enough good being done to make the organization as a whole worth saving, and so Allington was determined to save it. Even on the shameful political front the UN could still play a useful role. It could not enforce peace, but frequently its machinery and mediations provided enough face-saving to avert an unwanted war. For all its faults it was still the most important international institution yet devised, and even if it took another four decades to iron out its defects and animosities it could still play a positive role in the future of mankind.

In Allington's mind there were two tasks he had to accomplish. First he had to continue the vital groundwork in the various UN activities in the field, and second he had to restore sanity, trust and reason to the opulent debating halls.

To achieve the latter he had to bridge the yawning gulf between the Third World and the big powers. He had to persuade the Third World leaders that their violent rhetoric and hopelessly unattainable resolutions could only be damaging to their own interests. Somehow he had to make them realize that the United Nations could provide a path to hope and progress for them all, providing they could accept its limitations, and work together for aims that were not beyond the bounds of political credibility.

Unfortunately, to persuade them to see reason he had to rise to every verbal challenge. Every debate became a conflict and so far he could see no light at the end of the tunnel. The black delegations of Africa stood solid against him, and so he found himself in direct opposition to their chosen Goliath, the Angolan Julius Mangala.

While he waited for the debate to begin Allington looked among the packed ranks of delegates for a friendly face. The blue, green and gold hall occupied the second, third and fourth floors of the building, and from the circular skylight high in the ceiling a single shaft of sunlight beamed down. There were seats for more than two thousand delegates, of every possible colour and creed, but the face he was most desirous to see was not there.

In the first six seats of the front row he recognized the delegation from the United Republic of Cameroon. They had won the lottery drawn before each Assembly session, and the other delegations were then seated in alphabetical order. This placed the group from Columbia about a third of the way up the hall, but one of their six seats was vacant. The ambassador from Columbia, the beautiful, passionate, coffee-coloured

Lorna Maxwell, was still absent on a fact-finding mission to Indonesia.

Allington noted the empty seat with a twinge of regret. Lorna, and Luis Valdez, were the only diplomats he could count as friends among the multitude of Third World representatives. Together they had been largely instrumental in persuading the Latin American group to support his election. He needed them still, and with Lorna there was more than just friendship and a mutual belief in the preservation value of the UN.

Allington was a widower who had devoted himself to his political career ever since his wife had died ten years before. There had been one child, his daughter Barbara, but circumstances had kept them apart since she had passed her A levels and gone on to university at Cambridge. There was a vast ocean between England and New York, and they each had their own lives to lead.

For Allington it had been a lonely life, although for a long time the pressures of work had kept him from realizing the full extent of his loneliness. Then he had met Lorna. It had been a brief introduction and a short exchange of words on the work of the UN Children's Fund, but the bright sparks of chemical and biological magnetism had automatically flashed between them.

What Lorna saw in him Allington didn't know. Most of the time he was too busy and preoccupied to recognize his own driving power and handsome looks. But what he saw in her was a rare, vibrant woman of great fighting spirit, and a vast depth of genuine human feeling.

Lorna Maxwell carried the mixed blood of the hardheaded, hard-hitting American oilman who had been her father, and an Indian mother who could trace her bloodline back to an Aztec princess. She was a child of the Old World and the New, combining a determination to thrust forward into a positive future, with all the pride and assurance of a cultured past.

She was an injection of sweet, fresh air into his stale, workaholic life, and as time went on Allington found himself enjoying her companionship more and more. She was much younger than he was, with a zest for life he found rejuvenating, and he needed her to balance the stress and strains of his daunting new role.

His thoughts were drifting on to pleasant paths, and reluctantly he came back to the present as he realized that Mangala had at last opened the debate. He steeled himself, feeling like a medieval knight awaiting the harsh slap of a mailed gauntlet, and in the same moment aware that the comparison was slightly ridiculous.

The subject of Namibia came up immediately, as always ignoring the black terrorist raids to the south, but condemning the latest South African counter-moves along the borders. It was a hoary old problem, one that in one form or another had wasted many years of tedious and ineffective debate. It was an excuse for black Africa to scream justified hatred at the political structure of apartheid, but so far it had served no other useful purpose.

Mangala rose to speak, demanding a resolution for direct UN intervention, with United Nations emergency forces to be stationed on the South African side of the border, and all South African forces to be withdrawn from a fifty-mile buffer zone. It was a fine speech with a foregone conclusion. Mangala knew that the majority of the Assembly would support him, but that the resolution would never be implemented. South Africa would never agree to the proposal, and the Security Council would not be prepared to enforce it.

Allington groaned inwardly as he listened to the familiar storm of soap-box oratory, and wished that he could be with Lorna in Indonesia. For a few moments he dreamed of the bliss they might have shared on some lazy, sun-drenched tropical beach on Bali, but then a thunder of applause greeting one of Mangala's more inflammatory remarks dragged him back again to the business in hand.

He told himself that he must pay attention, and that at

fifty-seven he was too old to sit day-dreaming like a schoolboy. Lorna had probably been right when she had said that their relationship was getting too close, and that they needed a break from each other to get their friendship into a proper perspective.

It was ten minutes before Mangala finished his speech and Allington rose wearily to answer. The African had won the bulk of the Assembly and Allington knew he faced a hostile and even contemptuous audience.

In that moment the issue seemed all-important, and no one in that vast hall yet knew that this was the last time that the General Assembly of the United Nations would ever trouble itself with a purely local problem.

Out in space Halley's Comet had left the bleeping satellite that was Columbus Two far behind. Continuing its accelerating journey the comet had plunged down through Earth, Venus, and Mercury orbits to hurtle into its tight turn around the sun. The satellite whirled on through the thin, gaseous mists of the streaming tail, until it was sucked into the black mass of the trailing cloud.

And then the bleeping stopped. All the satellite's signals were obliterated, and all control from Earth was lost.

3

It was immediately after the break for the Christmas holiday that Barbara discovered the horrific truth. She had spent a week in London, staying with two girl friends who had been her boon companions at Cambridge. The festivities had been a continuous whirl of parties and dancing, and as there was no particular man in her life at this precise moment in time she had been free to play the field. She returned to Herstmonceaux feeling exhilarated and exhausted, and with a few promising dates booked up for the coming weekends. She did not know then that she would never keep a single one of those planned romantic rendezvous, or even see any of those old and new friends again.

It was a cold day, but the sun was shining bright in the pale blue sky as she drove her red mini through the west gate into the castle grounds. There had been a light fall of snow on Boxing Day, but so far it had been a mild winter. The massive, brown-brick, crenellated walls of the castle, bristling with towers and tall chimneys, rose majestically before her on her left. Behind the castle the sunlight glinted off the wind-ruffled waters of the lake, and further off to her right it positively gleamed off the tall silver dome that had once housed the Isaac Newton telescope. The equatorial group of domes, housing the telescopes which were still in use here, were hidden from her view behind the castle.

She parked her car and carried her weekend case

across the arched stone bridge that spanned the moat to reach the main entrance. On the bridge she paused for a moment to watch the mallard and other waterfowl on the lake. This was a beautiful place to work. The castle was steeped in history. The estate was a nature reserve of grass and woodlands. And at night there was the close-up study of the distant galaxies in all their star-decked glory. She was happy here, stimulated on every level, and a quiet day like this was even better than midsummer when the tourists flocked in to picnic and view the exhibitions.

The cold nip in the air finally urged her on into the castle. It now housed the exhibition halls, the main administrative offices for the observatory, the library and staff canteen. There were a few bedrooms for night staff, and Barbara's room overlooked the central courtyard. She hurried there to unpack. The drama of Halley's Comet was the most exciting thing that had happened since she had arrived here, and now that the holiday was over she was eager to get back to work.

It was five o'clock when she left the castle to join Willoughby in the thirty-six-inch telescope dome in the equatorial buildings. The dome was already open to reveal a wide gap of the night sky, and Willoughby was blowing on his hands to warm them as he adjusted the focus of the telescope. They were both muffled in extra layers of scarves and jumpers, but it was difficult to work with gloves. On these longer, midwinter nights the astronomers usually worked in two shifts. Tonight Willoughby and Barbara had the use of the telescope from five till midnight.

Willoughby was amiable as always, chatting about the weather and the holiday as they made ready. As far as Barbara knew he had taken only a three-day break, but he seemed to shy away from any mention of the observations he had made without her.

Finally Willoughby settled down to viewing. He became silent for almost half an hour, deep in thought and concentration, but his face was strangely troubled. For a while it seemed that he had even forgotten his favourite sweets. When at last he had to rest his eyes he seemed strangely reluctant to give up the chair. He lay back with his eyes closed for a few minutes and then resumed viewing.

Barbara began to sense that something was wrong. She waited for him to rest his eyes again, the moment when he would normally have offered her the opportunity to look through the telescope, and when he did not she reminded him of her presence.

'Professor, you're not alone tonight. Are you going to let me see what's happening?'

Willoughby looked up at her and frowned. Suddenly he seemed older and uncertain, and she realized with a shock that his grey hair had whitened in the short space of the past week.

'I don't know if I should.' Willoughby chewed uncomfortably on his lower lip and hesitated. 'But then I suppose you'll have to know. I can't keep it from you while you're working with me.'

He stood up with obvious reluctance and moved out of the way. Barbara stared at him. She didn't understand and she didn't know quite what to say. The ghost fingers of an unreasonable and unnameable fear gripped at her belly and she felt the small hairs prickle on the back of her neck. Quickly she slipped into the viewing chair and pressed her forehead to the eyepiece.

She saw Halley's Comet, a bright red fireball where the glowing fuzz of the coma surrounded the core of the nucleus, with streams of sparks glittering in its flowing mane. It was much closer than when she had last seen it, and the star pattern behind it had changed to show that it had moved a vast distance across the heavens. But it was as and where she expected it to be, zooming in towards the sun. In a few days time it would pass in front of the sun, and then be lost from sight until it had circled the gigantic centre piece of the solar system and reappeared from behind it.

The magnified view of the comet was an awesome and splendid sight, but Barbara knew instinctively that it was not the comet itself which had frightened Willoughby. She looked behind the brilliant head, searching the far-flung tail, and then she felt the ghost fingers clawing even deeper into her stomach, twisting at the very roots of her being.

The black cloud had moved. It was no longer immediately behind the nucleus. Instead it had broken free from the tail, and compared to the comet it had grown to more than three times its original size. Or, if it had not grown, Barbara realized with a sense of cataclysmic shock, it had moved considerably closer to the Earth.

She stared at it for a full minute, and then withdrew white-faced to stare again at Willoughby.

'Professor, for God's sake, what is happening?'

Willoughby bit on his lip, and then said slowly, 'Columbus Two is inside the cloud. The satellite is doing exactly what it was programmed to do after it had collected its samples. It is returning to Earth. But it appears to be pulling the cloud along with it.'

'But how?'

'We don't quite know. It would seem that at close range the pulling power of the satellite has proved stronger than the pulling power of the comet. The cloud has broken away from the comet and attached itself to Columbus Two.'

'But can't we stop it? Can't we signal the satellite to change course? Or self-destruct? Or something?'

'I'm afraid not. All those things have been tried from the space centre in Guiana, but the signals are not getting through. The cloud has enveloped the satellite and is acting as some kind of barrier. Columbus Two is coming home, and instead of bringing home a few small samples it's bringing the whole damned thing.'

Barbara was dazed. From the beginning she had felt those small, nagging misgivings about the cloud, but the enormity of what was happening now left her stunned and unable to think. As though she was listening to a small, distant child she heard her own voice say faintly,

'Professor, what does it mean?'

'Even the stars live and die.' Willoughby was evasive, and seemed to find some refuge or comfort in the abstract. 'Our sun was born out of a cloud of gas some five billion years ago. Eventually its nuclear furnace will burn hotter and hotter until it swells into a red giant. Then it will pour out heat and energy and shrink again to a white dwarf. Finally, after fifty billion years or so, it will become a cold, dead, black shell.'

He paused, then concluded, 'That is, if it lives out its normal life-span. But even the stars can have cosmic accidents, and sudden endings.'

And more so the dependent planets. Barbara realized that this was what he was trying to tell her. A planet's ability to support life could be altered by so many things; a shift in orbit, a slight increase or fall in temperature, a collision with some other celestial body, or some kind of permanent eclipse of the sun. The day the black cloud embraced the Earth might well be doomsday for all its life forms.

Like a rabbit mesmerized by a snake Barbara found herself drawn back to the telescope, staring in horror at the sinister, shapeless nemesis in space.

Behind her Willoughby said bleakly, 'They saw it from La Palma four days ago. Most of the big telescopes will have spotted it by now, but we're hoping to keep it quiet for a little while longer. At this stage we can't see any point in creating a world panic.'

In Washington D.C., in the Oval Office of the White House, the panic had already started. The President of the United States, Glenn J. Anderson, was staring at the spread-out litter of photographs and reports with the look of a man who had just seen his world collapse beneath him. The famous square jaw, usually exaggerated by his cartoonist enemies, but always photographed in strong half-profile by his media friends, had now dropped slack and open. His eyes had glazed behind hornrimmed spectacles, and when he took them off to blink at the grey-faced, tight-lipped man on the other side of his desk, his hand visibly trembled.

'Oh, sweet, holy shit,' the President said. 'Merle, are you sure this isn't a mistake, or some kind of sick joke. For God's sake, tell me it's somebody's idea of a joke.'

Merle Forrester, the President's Scientific Adviser, wriggled uncomfortably in his chair. He was not a regular visitor to the Oval Office. The President was a practical man, normally too preoccupied with the more pressing problems of economics, home politics and defence. Forrester wished that he could have left the great man in continued ignorance, but this was something that had to be brought to the President's attention. He mopped perspiration from his balding forehead with a pale blue handkerchief, and at the same time leaned forward to stab a finger tentatively at the large, full colour blow-up immediately under Anderson's nose.

'I'm sorry, Mr. President, but there it is. That picture was taken through the 200-inch telescope at Mount Palomar last night. There's no doubt about it — the cloud has busted free from the comet, and it's following the satellite down to Earth. We're helping to monitor the flight now from NASA, and we've tried to radio signal a change of course, but we're not having any more luck than the guys at the Europe Space centre who sent it up. The damned thing just doesn't respond to anything we've tried so far.'

'Isn't there anything we can do to stop it?'

Forrester shrugged. 'Some of our people think that when it gets closer — when the range gets shorter — then maybe we can push a signal through. The only trouble is that a deep space satellite like this one draws its power from two solar vanes. While it's in the cloud it's not soaking up sunlight, so by the time it gets close enough for a signal to penetrate, the propulsion engines won't have any power. By then the cloud and the satellite will be travelling under their own momentum.'

'How?' Anderson groaned. 'How the heck did all this happen?'

Forrester told him. 'It was just something nobody could foresee,' he finished gloomily. 'Nobody expected the cloud to leave the comet and hitch on to the satellite.'

'But it has, and now we've got to carry the goddamned baby.' Anderson shifted the reports and photographs helplessly around his desk, wondering why the hell his advisers always brought him problems and never solutions. He rubbed his eyes and replaced his glasses, trying to think.

'Damnit, haven't we got a comet-mission of our own up there? Something that can be programmed to go into this thing and change its direction?'

'No, sir,' Forrester was apologetic. 'We did plan a comet-mission at one stage, using the new mercury-ion thruster solar electric engines, but then the Office of Management and Budget cut the project funds. We were pouring too many dollars into the shuttle programme, so the decision was taken to abandon our comet shot, and leave it all to the Europeans and their Columbus Two. We couldn't justify to Congress the expense of duplicating their effort.'

'Columbus Two —' Anderson pushed a photograph of the satellite out of the heap with his finger and looked at it vaguely. He was suffering a brief mental blank as his brain refused to grapple with the catastrophic implications of the main problem. 'Hell, I didn't even know they had sent up a Columbus One.'

'They didn't,' his Scientific Adviser explained. 'It's a kind of European joke. The first Columbus was the guy who discovered America.'

Anderson groaned and covered his face with his hands. Thirty seconds passed in silence and then he squared his jaw and shoulders and faced up to the coming nightmare.

'Okay, Merle, you say this cloud is coming right down on top of us. Maybe it won't. Maybe it'll give us a miss, or maybe we can do something to divert it, but what happens if it hits?'

'If we're very lucky we could pass harmlessly through it.'

'So pray for that, but what's the worst?'

Forrester drew a deep breath to steady himself. 'It could depend upon the composition of the cloud. The gases inside it could be highly toxic, like cyanogen. If it penetrates through our atmosphere it could poison the whole planet. Or it could be highly inflammable, like petroleum gas. Or a kind of acid, sulphuric or nitric. Or it could be electrified. Our Voyager Two space shot passed through a cloud of electrified gases orbiting Saturn, the temperature there was hotter than the surface of the sun.'

'What a choice,' Anderson said bitterly. 'We can choke to death, be eaten up alive in an acid bath, or just plain fried.'

'It probably won't come to any of that. Remember that this thing was towed through space by the comet, and a comet is nothing but a big, dirty ice-ball heated up by the sun. The cloud can't have much weight. Whatever its composition I wouldn't really expect it to sink through our atmosphere.' He paused, then finished gloomily, 'But if it sticks, then we're all gonna freeze to death in the dark. The Earth will be no more habitable than Neptune or Pluto.'

'Merle, you are some comfort,' Anderson said with heavy sarcasm. He knew he was being unfair to a man who was as worried as he was himself, but at that moment he couldn't help it.

The two men were silent for a moment. Anderson's gaze wandered over the desk top and finally settled on the framed colour photograph of his wife and two daughters taken in the rose garden of their family home in Vermont. Lucy was seated on a garden chair, relaxed and elegant as always, and the two girls, Ellen and Claire, aged sixteen and twelve, were sitting cross-legged on the lawn on either side. All of them were happily smiling.

Anderson had started on a headache, and now he felt the anguish of a knife pain to the heart. He and Lucy had shared so many good times. Maybe now, if they had to die together, it wouldn't matter so much. But the girls were so young, so full of life and hope. There was so much joy and laughter in them.

He had to turn away quickly, swallowing the sudden lump in his throat.

'Do something,' he told Forrester forcefully. 'Boost some more power into those signals. Come up with some more facts and ideas. From here on you've got top priority. You can have anything and anybody you need.'

'We're already on to it,' Forrester assured him. 'But there isn't much time. Astronomers have been watching this damned thing for months, but it didn't divert and swing toward us until a couple of days ago. Now we don't have too many days left.'

Richard Allington's first indication of what was happening came a few days later, in the form of a long airmail letter from Barbara. He read it through twice, hardly able to believe it the first time, and then felt a cold chill settling round his heart. Like a man in a dream he stood up and moved over to his office window, staring out at the familiar skyscraper towers of Manhattan. The airmail was slowly crumpling in his tightening fist.

From here he could see it all, the great white block of

Pan Am, the futuristic silver spire of the Chrysler Building, the Empire State soaring up almost twice as high as the rest; and further away the twin square blocks of the World Trade Centre that topped even the Empire State. Down below in the concrete canyons the financial and business capital of the United States throbbed with boundless activity night and day. New York was a vast, sprawling, living dynamo, pulsing with all the raw, thrusting vigour of the greatest and most progressive nation on earth.

He tried to imagine it cold and dead, the city, the nation, and the whole planet frozen in icy darkness, and a shiver ran painfully through his spine.

Barbara had to be wrong! It couldn't be as bad as she feared.

He turned abruptly on his heel and went back to his desk, startling his secretary by cancelling all his appointments for the day. Every other business had suddenly become totally irrelevant and he pushed it all to one side.

He began a series of discreet enquiries by trying to put a telephone call through to the big Hale Observatory on Mount Palomar in California. He figured that if anything bad was happening out in space then the people there must know about it.

He got nowhere. The Mount Palomar switchboard was not answering calls.

He tried the other major American observatories in succession, all with the same result. It was impossible to get a line through to any of them, and that, he decided grimly, couldn't be any kind of concidence.

He read Barbara's letter again. She claimed she had been sworn to secrecy, and that her people were trying to avoid any premature panic. A similar information clamp-down must be taking place in the US. That was why the observatories were all cut off from the outside world.

Before he had been worried. Now he tasted real

fear. It was beginning to look as though his daughter was not exaggerating, and the whole world had good cause to be afraid.

He decided to go right to the top. He had a passing acquaintance with Merle Forrester, the President's senior Scientific Adviser. If he could get Merle to meet him somewhere he knew he could spring the question as a surprise and wring out the truth.

He gave his secretary more numbers to obtain, and again ran into a series of dead ends. Merle Forrester could not be reached.

Allington began to feel slightly sick. His secretary was looking baffled, still hoping for an explanation, but his next demand was a purely personal impulse which only added to her confusion.

'Get me a line to Djakarta,' he told her abruptly. 'The Celebes Hotel. I want to make a person-to-person call to Lorna Maxwell. She's with the working party from the South East Asia Human Rights Committee.'

He waited in growing apprehension as the effort was made. He desperately wanted to talk to Lorna, to urge her to cut short her mission and hurry back to New York before the disaster struck. But after three fruitless hours of trying to make contact he was again frustrated.

Lorna Maxwell was not at the hotel. She had left without telling anyone else in the UN group where she was going, and no one knew when she could be expected to return.

4

While Allington was making his frantic efforts to contact her, Lorna Maxwell was driving a hired Toyota saloon out of Djakarta, heading east on the first lap of a three-hundred-mile journey to the small town of Batang on the north coast of Java. She was embarked upon what she knew could prove to be an extremely hazardous venture, but it was one she was determined to see through. For the past four weeks her committee had been given the official blinker tours, but at last she had the opportunity to find out the truth for herself.

She had to change gear every few seconds, accelerating, braking and swerving as she wove through the swarming chaos of pedestrians, cars, cycle rickshaws, and the reckless youths on their flashy Japanese motor cycles. She had left the city centre and as she approached the ever-expanding outskirts of the Indonesian capital the streets on either side became a maze of red-mud lanes and alleyways leading into squalid shacks and slums. The air was hot, filled with choking exhaust fumes, and all the sweltering human odours that betrayed a definite lack of sanitation.

The poor dwellings got worse, roofed more and more with shreds of sacking or canvas, and the overcrowding became unbelievable. Here was squalor and poverty and every grim symptom of a chronic population explosion. It was far worse than anything she had ever seen in the slums surrounding her home city of Bogota, and she began to bite her lip in anguish.

Modern medicine had worked miracles in Indonesia, and where babies had once succumbed in vast numbers to a wide range of fevers and disease, they now thrived and multiplied. Unfortunately the new wonder drugs had been followed too slowly by the new concepts of family planning, and although heroic efforts were now being made, the entire archipelago of the East Indies had become inundated with human beings. The struggling nation of Indonesia had ground to a halt, and then slid inexorably into reverse, unable to progress due to the sheer deadweight of its surplus people.

The booming Third World birthrate had become a crushing burden, and its attendant evils were the crux of many of the problems the United Nations was trying to tackle in a hundred different parts of the world. However, on this occasion, none of it was Lorna's immediate concern. Instead her committee was here to investigate human rights, and more specifically the plight of the thousands of political prisoners still believed to be incarcerated in Indonesia's island camps.

There were six in her party: herself, Srivaji, the smooth Thai politician who was Chairman of the Committee, and four middle rank diplomats from the UN Secretariat. The Indonesian government had given them a luke-warm reception, and in between trying to distract them with banquets and various other social functions and side issues had grudgingly pretended cooperation.

Most of their time had been spent frustrated in Djakarta, talking to a series of government officials and military men, all of them blandly insisting that the prison camps were being dismantled, and the political prisoners released. Only criminal prison camps remained, and it was politely suggested that the long lists of missing persons might possibly contain the names of some hardened criminals, but were probably people who had died in the mass purges of the late sixties, or who had never existed at all.

Srivaji had played them at their own game, and Lorna had to give him credit for his efforts. She had to acknowledge that Allington had been wise to select another Asian to lead this particular committee, and in Srivaji he had picked the right man. The Thai matched the Indonesians smile for smile, sympathizing with the affront to their dignity, apologizing for his own presence, but all the while politely insisting that his committee must be allowed to visit some of the prison camps. His hosts obviously had nothing to hide, so once the visits had been made he could return to New York with a report that would be satisfactory to all concerned.

Finally the UN party was permitted to visit two separate islands which were used as criminal prison camps. In each case the inmates looked reasonably well fed, and had been issued with new shirts and new Red Cross blankets. The committee were allowed to ask questions freely and had heard solemn confessions from a variety of thieves, rapists and murderers. The confessions sounded genuine. The committee agreed that these were camps for convicted criminals. They also knew that the shirts and blankets had been handed out only hours before they arrived, and would almost certainly be collected in again as soon as they had departed.

The Indonesian officials hoped that the UN officials were now satisfied. Srivaji clasped his hands piously together and assured their hosts that for his part there was no more doubt. But he had been expressly asked to make a report on Buru — he named a political labour camp with the worst possible reputation — if the committee could see Buru it would conclude all his instructions.

There was much lip-tightening, evasion and delay, but Srivaji was apologetically insistent. A week went past in verbal manoeuvring, and then with great reluctance they were flown out to Buru. They were shown an empty penal colony and assured it was no longer used.

The camp showed every sign of being hastily abandoned. The grey ashes of a cooking fire were still warm when Lorna turned them over with her foot, and the smell of fresh urine and unwashed bodies still lingered in the stale, listless air. The camp had been occupied only hours before, and Lorna guessed that the luckless prisoners had been herded out of sight on to some secluded corner of the island; or else packed into ships that were waiting over the horizon. As soon as the UN committee had investigated and departed the prisoners would be returned.

After an hour they were flown back to Djakarta, bitter and angry, but at last conceding defeat. Srivaji had played his last card and there was nothing more to do. Reluctantly they began their preparations to fly back to New York.

It was then that Lorna had been approached by the little Javanese who was now her only travelling companion. She had noticed him several times over the past few days, always hovering uncertainly just outside the hotel. He wore a faded shirt and shorts, cheap sandals and a tarboosh, the close-fitting Muslim cap. His face was wrinkled to the colour and texture of a bad walnut. She had assumed him to be a beggar or a tout, and when his thin fingers had plucked at her sleeve as she passed him in the street, she had turned with the intention of telling him curtly to go away.

'No, miss,' he spoke urgently. 'I am not beggar.' His dark brown eyes flickered nervously, scanning the passing faces along the street, checking back toward the hotel she had just left, and then once again meeting her own. 'You are United Nations Lady — yes? You investigate *tahanan politik*? Maybe I help you. I am *tapol*!'

'You were a political prisoner?'

'Yes, miss. For ten years — maybe twelve — on Tembu Island.'

'Tembu Island?' She repeated the name to make sure she had heard right. Her committee had come armed with hundreds of sworn statements from prisoners and their distraught relatives that had been smuggled out of Indonesia, but although scores of islands had been named as prison islands, this one was not familiar.

The brown face nodded. He looked up and down the street again and then drew her out of the mainstream of pedestrian traffic into the shadow of a shop doorway. Lorna made no resistance. Her curiosity was fully aroused.

'The government show you places.' His mouth curled into a sneer round the word government. 'But not bad places. Cleaned-up places. If you want I can show you Tembu Island — for *tapols*, a very bad place.'

'How far is Tembu Island?'

'Down the coast. One – maybe two – days drive. Then twenty-thirty mile out to sea. We go by bus, then I borrow fishing sampan from good friend.'

Lorna frowned, wondering how much she could trust him.

'What is your name?' she asked.

'Sumo.' He clawed off the black astrakhan hat, revealing an almost bald head with a few short bristles of grey hair as he bowed formally. 'I am called Sumo, miss.'

'And why are you so eager to help me?'

The Javanese straightened up slowly, pursed his lips for a moment, and countered with a question of his own.

'How old you think I am?'

Lorna stared at him doubtfully, noting the thin, wasted frame, the hollow cheeks and deep lines in his temples. He had the worn, creased look of a man in the winter of his life.

'Fifty-five,' she guessed. 'Sixty?'

'I am forty-one.' Sumo replaced his *tarboosh* carefully. His lop-sided smile showed up the gaps in his bad teeth and his eyes were sad. '*Tapols* grow old quickly. The government will not let a man leave a prison island until he is old and useless. But sometimes they forget — we are not always as old as we look.'

'I believe you,' Lorna said quietly. 'But you haven't answered my question. If Tembu Island is so bad, why are you willing to risk being sent back there?'

Sumo shrugged. 'I am free, but because I was a *tapol* I am nothing. I am non-person. No employment, no nothing. I am like political leper. Also, all my friends are still on Tembu. My brother still on Tembu. Maybe I show you — maybe you help my brother.'

Lorna questioned him for another ten minutes, and by then she had made up her mind. It was an impulse decision, but she knew it was the only opportunity she was going to get to dig out the real facts of the situation. She had asked Sumo to wait for her and then hurried back to the Celebes Hotel, stopping only to change into more suitable travelling clothes and to write a brief letter to Srivaji.

She explained that she was following up fresh information, but suggested it might be best if their hosts were allowed to believe that she was taking a short holiday. She kept the note deliberately vague with no details. She had no wish to cause any complications for the rest of her committee, and had decided that if they knew nothing then they could not be held responsible for her actions. She left the sealed envelope with the reception desk, relying on the usual incompetence of the hotel staff to ensure that Srivaji would not receive it until she was well on her way.

She had rejoined Sumo, and turning down his suggestion that they use one of the local buses she had preferred to hire the car. The Javanese had no commitments in Djakarta, his home was in Batang and they had begun their journey immediately.

Driving out of the city was hard, nerve-testing work, and for a while the traffic nightmare and the problem of finding the right road occupied all her concentration. Then gradually the bedlam eased, the squalor disappeared behind them, and the road led out into the rural rice paddies. The flooded green fields reflected the sunlight with dazzling intensity beneath the vivid blue sky, and after a few more miles she pulled up at the side of the road to rest. Already she felt dusty and sweat-stained and her shoulders ached.

She turned to Sumo sitting hunched and silent beside her and asked hopefully, 'Are you sure you can't drive?'

'No, miss.' The shrunken brown moon face was apologetic. 'I am sorry, miss.'

'Okay, don't worry about it.' Lorna pulled a pack of cigarettes from her handbag on the dashboard and offered them. 'I'll take a five-minute break and then drive on. Are you sure this is the right road?'

'Yes, miss. Very sure. This road follows north coast.'

Lorna lit the cigarette for him, then her own. In silence they contemplated the cultivated landscape before them, the terraced fields rising up through lush green palm groves to the jungle-covered slopes of the central mountains. It was a different Indonesia to the noisy bustle of the city they had left behind, an Indonesia of exquisite peace and soft tranquillity. It gave time for reflection. Sumo smoked gratefully with his eyes half-closed, while Lorna was deep in thought.

So far she had not stopped to consider seriously the risks she was taking, instead she had allowed the sheer momentum of her actions carry her forward. Now she had to face up to it. If Tembu was a political prison camp of the worst kind, then it could prove to be a very dangerous place indeed. The camps had been described as filthy, inhuman hells, where prisoners were brutally and sadistically tortured. Most of the camps dated back to the horrific purge following the aborted communist coup of 1965. The Indonesian government claimed that they no longer existed, and many of them probably had been phased out. Those that remained were carefully concealed from foreign eyes, and Lorna knew that if she was to be discovered while prying into one of these still-festering sores, then reprisals might well be painful, and possibly fatal.

A shudder ran through her. She was not yet past the point of no return and she could not afford to proceed blindly.

She turned to Sumo. 'How do we approach this island? We can't risk being seen.'

'We land at night,' the Javanese said simply. 'Hide and watch through day. Then leave next night.'

Lorna rubbed sweat from her temples. 'It sounds dangerous.'

Sumo looked into her eyes, debating something within himself, and then decided to come clean.

'For you, miss, very dangerous. If soldiers catch us — very bad. If sampan wrecked on reef — very bad. Many sharks in Java Sea. Many pirates too.'

'Pirates?'

Sumo nodded. 'Many pirates attack small boats. Especially boats with foreigners. Steal money, rings, watch. They like to rape women.'

Lorna stared at him, suddenly alarmed. 'Are you going to rape me?'

'No, miss.' Sumo looked hurt and shocked. 'I help you. Maybe you help my brother. But you fine American lady. Pirates like to rape.'

Hell, Lorna thought, I bet they would too. She knew the effect she could have on men, and Sumo was right. She recalled now that there had been increasing numbers of reports of petty piracy in these waters. Petty unless you were the hapless fisherman who got hacked to death for a handful of cigarettes, or the screaming woman who was gleefully gang-raped.

She was suddenly so close to panic that she had to start the engine quickly and slam the car into gear. She resisted the coward urge to turn back and let the renewed momentum carry her forward again — on to Batang and whatever awaited her on Tembu.

In Moscow the dawn was breaking, and the lights still burned in the windows of the Kremlin. The Central Committee of the Politburo had been in continuous session for the past twelve hours and the old men were tired. Grigori Komarov looked round the circle of grey, haggard faces nodding owlishly over the polished, dark wood surface of the conference table, and knew that most of them were on the point of collapse. They were all in their eighties now, the shock had been too great, and they were no longer able to cope.

For a moment President Komarov, in title the most powerful man in the Soviet Union, felt horribly alone. He had not been groomed for this great task, and the honour had caught him unprepared. In Brezhnev's time the old guard had refused even to discuss the question of succession. Perhaps they had all expected to live for ever, or perhaps they had hoped that Brezhnev would depart while another of their number was still capable of picking up the reins. In the event Brezhnev had lasted too long. When the choosing of a new leader became inevitable they had to face reality and select a younger man.

Komarov had received the crown. He was sixty-two, a tough and capable administrator, but obviously they did not expect him to rock the boat with any great changes. Also they intended to counter-balance him by hanging on to their own positions for as long as possible. It was this which made Komarov feel so hopelessly alone. He needed younger men, tomorrow's men, to help him breathe new life into the stale ranks of state and party leadership. Instead he was stifled and isolated by yesterday's men, lingering to hold him back when they already had one foot in the grave.

Their minds were set and conditioned by dwelling on a lifetime of familiar fears: the China threat, the

American nuclear threat, and the endless gloom of bad production figures and bad harvests. Now they found it difficult to assimilate this new crisis — the approaching black cloud from outer space which threatened to turn the entire planet into a global graveyard.

'I think I must begin to agree with President Komarov.' The crack in the ranks came at last from the dour-faced Soviet Prime Minister, Andrei Ladiyev. 'Our scientists at the Mount Pastukhov Observatory have been watching this cloud mass for the past two weeks. Every calculation shows that it is on a direct collision course with the Earth. It will impact in approximately forty-eight hours. We must initiate the emergency measures now.'

Komarov felt a moment of gratitude and seized the opening.

'Premier Ladiyev is correct. We do not know what will happen when this cloud strikes the Earth. But it will strike, and we can only hope for survival, and take what steps we can to contain civilian panic. We must bring back army units from the borders to help police our cities.'

'No.' Sukhov, the spokesman for the old guard, was adamant. The possibility that they might not be able to control their own people still would not sink in, and he continued grimly, 'Our biggest danger is still the Americans. The arrival of this cloud could disrupt our communications and give them the opportunity they have always wanted to launch a surprise nuclear attack. What we must do is to order all our military forces to red alert. At this moment we cannot afford to relax vigilance on our borders.'

'The Americans will face the same problems we must face,' Komarov insisted wearily.

'The Americans cannot be trusted.'

'The threat to our security has always come from the West.'

'We cannot take the risk.'

'Enough.' Komarov raised his hands against the flurry of voices and knew that he must concede partial defeat. 'We will order the Soviet Navy and Soviet Air Force to red alert. They are our answer to nuclear attack. But we need the soldiers to protect the cities — there will be panic, civil disorder, perhaps rioting and looting.'

'The Red Army must stay on the borders.' Sukhov pounded his fist on the table. 'We must protect our flanks on the ground.'

'By tomorrow night this cloud will be visible to the naked eye,' Ladiyev said slowly. 'The next night is perhaps the beginning of an eternal night with no end. When it happens there will be panic.'

'The West could use this moment of panic to win a first-strike war.'

'We will maintain our front-line forces on full alert,' Komarov repeated his promise. 'But we must re-deploy our reserve army units to help control the cities.'

'No,' Sukhov said stubbornly, but his eyes were hollow and he was reduced to weakening denials with no new arguments.

Komarov took heart. If Ladiyev continued to support him he knew the old guard would finally yield. They were all dulled with fatigue, struggling out of their depth, and soon their will-power would drown in the dark of the new unknown. The knowledge did not bring any relief, just the return of the great weight of responsibility and loneliness.

God help us, Komarov thought, and it was the first time in fifty years that he had acknowledged even the possibility that there might be a God. Soon it would be less of an acknowledgement and more of a fervent hope.

In Paris and London, and every major capital of the world, the anguished heads of government held similar sessions to thrash out their own emergency plans. They all knew the cloud was coming, and they had to prepare for it according to their resources and abilities.

Washington was no exception, and six hours after the Moscow all-night sitting President Anderson faced another crisis meeting of his own. It was attended by his Joint Chiefs of Staff, his scientific and defence advisers, and all the senior members of his cabinet. It was the most miserable collection of stony, tight-lipped faces the President had ever seen, and he guessed his own was no exception.

A four-star hawk from the Pentagon got up and gave it to them straight from the shoulder.

'Mister President — we just learned that an hour ago the Russians put all their military forces on to a red alert. Maybe that's just a precaution for when the cloud hits. Maybe they're scared that we might take a crack at them when the lights go out. Or maybe they're planning to take the advantage and wipe us out. We have to be ready for anything.'

'Okay,' Anderson had expected something like this. 'We'll match them. Go to red alert until the cloud hits and the dust settles, and we know what the hell is happening. But don't let ourselves get side-tracked by the Russians. Their main problems are gonna be the same as ours, right down at grass roots on our own home ground.'

'You think our people will panic?' The Secretary of State still wasn't convinced that it could happen.

'No more than their President,' Anderson confessed wryly. 'For Christ's sake, the whole goddamned world is gonna panic. That's why I want the National Guard on stand-by from here on. The first sign of trouble — or at the latest a few hours before the cloud hits — I want them moved quickly into key positions in every city. I want this country sewn up tight. We gotta try to keep calm.'

'You mean there's nothing we can do to divert this cloud?'

Anderson looked to Forrester. 'Merle, it's your ball.'

Forrester hadn't slept for three days. He had to make a visible effort to pull himself together and answer.

'We've tried everything. The satellite that's pulling the cloud back into Earth orbit won't respond to any kind of signal. A few hours ago NASA shot a rocket through the heart of the cloud. We had hopes that the cloud might go into reverse and follow the rocket back into space. But that didn't work either. Maybe some of the cloud tore away and went with the rocket. We're not sure. Maybe if we could send up enough rockets, all at the same time — but there isn't enough time left to get them ready. The whole damned thing has happened too fast.'

'But if the satellite is bringing it down — surely the rocket should have taken it back up?'

'That's what we figured. But the cloud has picked up speed. It's got a hell of a lot of momentum. It's already getting an additional gravitational pull from the Earth. Or maybe the one rocket we tried just busted through it too fast. We don't know. NASA is still working on it. Probably the Russians are too. Maybe somewhere the computers will come up with something.'

The four-star hawk had an aggressive mind. He stuck out his jaw and said bluntly, 'The satellite is causing all this trouble. Why don't we just send up a missile and blast it?'

Forrester sighed. 'Maybe we could, if we knew where to target the missile. Right now it would be like shooting needles blind into a haystack, and hoping to hit a fly's eyeball.'

Anderson could see that his scientific adviser was on the point of cracking up, and decided to take off some of the heat.

'Let's leave it that the space boys are doing all they can. In the meantime we have to prepare for the worst. So far we've kept speculation out of the media, but the story has got to come out. I'm going to Capitol Hill this afternoon to address a Joint Session of Congress. I have to give them the straight facts. Later tonight I'll make a TV address to the nation.'

The Secretary of State spoke reluctantly. 'I can see it has to be done. Our people have to be warned. But what about the rest of the world? Allington, the Secretary-General, has been trying to nail down some of my senior staff. I think he already has a pretty good idea of what is happening. He wants to break it to the UN.'

Anderson hesitated, then nodded. 'All right, give him the full story. I guess the Third World governments have the same right to know, but God knows how they're gonna cope with all this. Brief Allington, and try and get him to time his speech at the UN with my speech to Congress.'

They talked for another hour, and then the meeting broke up as grim-faced as it had begun.

At Herstmonceaux Barbara watched the Army arrive. They came in three trucks with a major in a command Land Rover, and quickly established themselves in one of the large exhibition halls which had been cleared to receive them. Immediately the major had posted armed guards at the east and west gates to the grounds, and at the main entrance to the castle.

It was happening at every observatory in the world. Just a precaution, the astronomers were told, but Barbara could not help feeling deeply apprehensive as she watched the military men going efficiently about their business. The prominent display of well-oiled automatic weapons seemed to indicate that they had every expectation of being attacked by a fear-crazed mob.

Already the first batch of scare stories had appeared in the sensational press. The professional astronomers were all disciplined groups who had succeeded in keeping their own counsel, but there were many irresponsible amateurs who had inevitably noticed that something was amiss. In the past two days there had been rumours of a Black Hole eating up the stars, and of a Satan Cloud looming out of a hostile universe. So far these unsubstantiated reports had stretched public credibility and had been briefly denied, but the clamour of doomsday voices was fast rising and demanding to be heard.

Impact was only thirty-six hours away. The Prime Minister had at last been forced to explain the bitter truth to Parliament, and the authorities were taking no chances.

'Do you think people will hold us responsible?' Barbara asked Willoughby as they sat together in the staff canteen.

The professor raised listless eyes from contemplating his cup of half-cold coffee. He had lost three stone in weight and his hair was now totally white. His lips barely moved to answer. 'Does it matter?'

Barbara bit her lip and said no more.

They all knew there was no escape. Perhaps the Earth would perish quickly, poisoned by the great mass of swirling vapours from outer space. Or perhaps the planet would survive only to die a delayed and lingering death, trapped for ever in the dark eternal winter of a new ice age.

Either way they faced a bleak future, and there was nothing to be gained by blaming themselves for launching the ill-fated Columbus Two.

What was done was irrevocably done, and what was to be was destined to be.

5

On Java Lorna Maxwell was still unaware of the awesome, unstoppable menace bearing down with horrendous finality upon the Earth. She had her own mundane problems, beginning with an over-heating engine in the hired Toyota car. She had covered some two hundred miles before the first clouds of steam boiled out of the radiator and she had been forced to a halt. Sumo had found more water to get them going again, but after a few more miles the radiator had boiled dry for the second time. A group of village boys had pushed them to a dilapidated garage, and there they had to leave the car until it could be fitted with a new thermostat.

It was a time-consuming business and Lorna groaned over the delay. There was no way to continue except by public transport and the next bus was not due to pass through until the following morning. The small coastal town where they had stopped boasted one fifth-rate hotel, with resident cockroaches in all the rooms, and rust-stained cold water in some of the taps. The alternative was to sleep on the beach, so reluctantly they stayed for the night.

In the evening Lorna walked to visit a small Hindu temple that overlooked the sea. The courtyard was crowded with men and women arguing with an ancient holy man who squatted cross-legged beneath the shade of a palm tree. The old man wore nothing but a dirty loincloth. His beard and hair were grey straggles and his forehead was daubed with streaks of vermilion powder. He shouted back at his audience in a high-pitched, screeching voice.

The noisy clamour spoiled the peace which Lorna had hoped to find. She backed away and then went down to the beach, searching for a secluded spot where she could strip down to her bra and panties and bathe.

As she swam through the milky froth of white surf the conflicting voices from the temple still drifted in the warm night air. They were in a strange language and Lorna had no way of knowing that the old holy man was also an astrologer and a visionary. She ignored the voices and floated lazily on her back.

She noticed vaguely that there was a large patch of the heavens where there were no stars, but the moon was low on the horizon, throwing the tall shadows of the palms across the silvered sand, and for the moment it was all very pleasant.

It was mid-morning before they were able to board the battered local bus. It was a museum piece with wooden seats, brightly painted but with no glass in the open windows. It was packed inside with people, and on the roof with livestock and luggage. Lorna squeezed inside with Sumo, and after a babble of debate and the shunting re-deployment of bodies a space was cleared for them to sit.

The bus took off in a cloud of dust and the frightened squawking of a crate of chickens somewhere above their heads. It was a slow, dusty journey, painful on the bottom, but made bearable by the cheerful resilience of their fellow-passengers. The road stayed with the coastline, revealing mile after mile of palm groves, white tropical beaches, and the dazzling blue sea. Inland were more unending miles of terraced rice fields.

They reached Batang by mid-afternoon and disembarked, stiff and bruised. The heat was oppressive and Lorna needed a large glass of iced tea from a nearby stall to revive herself. Then Sumo led her to his mother's house, a small, sparse stone dwelling with a corrugated tin roof. He left her there to rest while he went out to arrange for the hire of a sampan.

He came back two hours later, full of smiles and assurance, and at sunset they went down to the beach. The sampan was waiting for them, anchored to the sand by a rope secured to a large stone. It was there for the taking, with no sign of the owner. Sumo explained unhappily that his friend had no desire to meet her. If anything went wrong the fisherman would claim that his sampan had been stolen.

'That's some friend,' Lorna complained bitterly. 'If we do get caught it means the police will have a genuine civil crime they can charge us with.'

Sumo hung his head a little lower and squirmed his feet uncomfortably in the sand.

Lorna hesitated a moment, but knew that if she hesitated too long she would never pluck up the courage to get into the sampan at all. She picked up the stone anchor and staggered with it as she walked into the waves and heaved it on to the deck of the sampan.

It was a flat-bottomed craft with a crude shelter of old canvas and sacking stretched over arched bamboo poles. There was a single mast at the prow and a collapsed sail, and at the stern an ancient auxiliary outboard engine. The stench of dead fish wafted up from a jumble of wet nets and Lorna wrinkled her nose in distaste. She had paid an exorbitant price for the dubious privilege of borrowing this boat, and it was definitely no bargain.

'Come on,' she ordered Sumo brusquely. 'Before I change my mind.'

The little Javanese helped her to push the sampan into thigh-deep water and steadied it while she climbed aboard. He walked out a few more yards and then Lorna pulled him up behind her. Sumo found a bamboo steering pole for her to use and hold the sampan off the shore while he worked with the pull cord to start the engine. After a few minutes of grunting effort the outboard spluttered into life, and Sumo grinned broadly as he steered a course for the open sea.

It was a calm night, the waves were a gentle swell, and to the north-east the sky was jewelled with silver stars to guide their course. Behind them was the growing patch of starless sky, now swollen to a much larger area than the night before, even though there was no visible cloud. Again Lorna was too preoccupied to notice this unusual phenomenon. She was remembering that Sumo couldn't even drive a car, and was having sudden doubts about his ability to navigate.

'Are you sure you can find Tembu Island?' she demanded.

Sumo nodded. 'Sampan slow. Take five, maybe six hours. But we be there before sunrise.' He smiled at her concern. 'You okay, miss. My father was a fisherman. I know all the islands. Long time since I fish with my father. He dead now. But I remember.'

Lorna relaxed, somewhat reassured. Sumo was sitting cross-legged on the deck beside the tiller, and after a moment Lorna made herself comfortable beside him.

She had learned a lot about her new friend during the past two days. Sumo had told her that he had been a minor civil servant, working in the Batang post office, before the bloody upheaval that had torn apart the whole of Indonesia in 1965. He had been married then, and he and his young wife had been arrested together. Someone had denounced them as communist sympathizers, although Sumo insisted they were not. They had been sent to separate island camps, and Sumo had not seen his wife since. He believed she was dead, but could not be sure.

Lorna guessed that it was the remote chance of finding his lost wife, as much as the hope of freeing his brother, that was driving the Javanese on this crazy adventure. United Nations efforts and the weight of world opinion had already been instrumental in freeing thousands of Indonesia's political prisoners. Only a few secret camps remained, and perhaps they too could be opened up if enough pressure could be brought to bear. Lorna could promise Sumo nothing, but with the evidence she hoped to uncover, it was just possible that something could be done.

To pass the time she asked him to tell her more about the camps, and soon began to wish she had remained silent. Sumo's stories corroborated much of what she already knew from the written reports, and most of them made her shudder. The interrogation techniques practised by the Indonesian military men were crude and invariably applied to the sexual organs of the victim, thus adding maximum degradation to maximum pain. Sumo's toneless voice went into detail after revolting detail until she told him to stop. They were past the point of no return and she had heard enough.

The rest of the night passed slowly. Sumo did not attempt to hoist the clumsy lateen sail, but relied upon the steady chugging of the auxiliary engine. The creaking of the sampan and the splash of the waves were the only other sounds. The time crawled by, but it was still an hour before dawn when at last the dark hump of the island emerged from the thickening line of the far horizon.

'Tembu,' Sumo said, and there was a tremor in his voice as he pointed toward the sinister place where he had been held prisoner for twelve of the most despairing years of his life.

The island loomed closer and Sumo shut down the throttle on the engine, reducing their speed to a crawl, but also reducing the noise. Lorna felt her heart beat faster as they were able to distinguish the white curl of surf breaking on the beach, and further up the black, feathered silhouettes of the palm trees. There was nothing else, and for a moment she prayed that the island might prove as deserted as it seemed. Right now the secondary dangers of sharks and pirates had paled into insignificance.

Sumo turned the prow parallel to the beach while they were still some two hundred yards off the shore and began to circle the island. He seemed to know exactly where he was heading, for after a few minutes he gave a grunt of satisfaction, and changed course to make directly for the island again. The water foamed suddenly white in dangerous, hissing swirls on either side, and Lorna realized they were shooting a gap through a submerged reef. The sampan rocked wildly and she gasped with fear as the spray spat in her face. Then just as quickly they were through, and into smooth water beyond.

'We lucky,' Sumo whispered. 'Sea very calm.'

Lorna nodded dumbly. Her heart was still in her throat, making it impossible for her to answer.

Sumo switched off the engine and tilted it inboard so that the propeller could not be damaged. Then he used the steering pole to push them close to the beach. He was in a hurry now, fearful of being caught in the open, and he did not pause until he had poled the sampan deep into a narrow, salt-water creek with thick banks of reeds and foliage on either side.

When the sampan came to a stop Sumo wasted no time. He dropped the stone anchor over the side and shortened the rope, and then helped Lorna to climb out on to the bank. He reached back to pick up her bag which was heavy with the weight of binoculars and a camera.

'Quickly now,' he urged. 'Soon sun come up.'

Lorna's legs were stiff and unsteady from squatting for long hours on the sampan's deck, and she moved reluctantly behind him. Sumo returned to the beach and began to follow the line of the palms. Lorna floundered in the soft sand and was glad when after half a mile he turned inland again. The path Sumo had found immediately began to rise steeply. Lorna's legs ached and she began panting for breath. The dawn was beginning to break, and in the dim filtered light she saw the shapes of strange ferns, jungle plants and small trees thrusting out of the undergrowth on either side.

At last Sumo called a halt and she sank gratefully down to rest. The sun climbed higher and as the light brightened she realized that they were on a ridge, in a hollow formed by a bowl of rocks. Sumo signed to her to be quiet and then crawled to the edge of the hollow. Lorna followed him on her hands and knees and peered over the screen of rocks. Below the ridge she saw the spartan huts of the penal settlement spread out on a cleared plain.

She went back for her bag and pulled out the cine camera. She had a telephoto lens and plenty of film, and she laid the camera close to hand ready for use. In the meantime she began observation through the binoculars. Sumo knelt beside her, pointing out the salient points of the camp as she made the first sweep.

The sun was already hot on their backs and Lorna realized that by midday they would be baked in their exposed vantage point. But the discomfort could not be helped. They had food and water, enough to survive the day.

She did not know then that this was the last day on which the sun would shine.

In New York Allington was watching the sun set for the last time. It was a blurred red disc in a steel grey sky, balanced on the far rim of the horizon above the twinkling lights of the vast sprawl of Queens and Long Island behind the East River.

He stood on the roof of the Secretariat Building with Valdez and a large group of the Secretariat staff. They stood in silence, like men and women at a funeral too tragic for words, each one listening to a dread litany of death in the privacy of their own minds. The wind blew cold at this height, slicing through Allington's heavy overcoat like a blade of ice. Its mournful sigh cut a raw nerve, and suddenly Allington could not bear to watch the sun sink all the way. He turned on his heel while the dying orb was still only half-submerged and went back to his office.

It had been a hard day, beginning early in the morning with the bleak news from the President's office. All efforts to divert the cloud had failed, and now he had the unenviable task of announcing to the Third World the fact of its imminent arrival. At this stage it was no surprise, but he had never been forced to swallow a more bitter pill. Immediately he had called for an emergency session of the full General Assembly.

The majority of the delegates had been shocked and stunned, but before he had finished speaking there had been pandemonium. Some of the delegates were incredulous, others outraged. Only a few of the Asian groups, those with home cultures more deeply rooted in astrology, were not totally surprised. There was a clamour for more information, and ferocious tirades of blame and abuse were hurled at the advanced space-probing nations who were held responsible.

Allington found it impossible to quell the fury of hysteria. Valdez had added his desperate pleas for calm to no avail, and it was Julius Mangala, roaring like a bull to make himself heard, who had finally restored a brief semblance of order.

Inevitably the battle shifted to its usual focus, another clash between the African President of the Assembly and the English Secretary-General. Mangala had picked out the major points from the babble and fired them at Allington in quick succession. This was no time for political defence and parry, and Allington answered as honestly as he was able.

For perhaps five minutes the delegates listened, and then Mangala pitched their main cause for grievance.

'Why were we not told earlier? Why were we not given time to prepare?'

'There was hope that the danger could be averted,' Allington shouted over the swelling hubbub for the twentieth time. 'While that hope remained we tried to avoid a world-wide panic.'

'The Western nations have given themselves time to prepare,' a voice screamed from the assembly floor. 'The rest of the world has been abandoned."

The accusing cry was taken up on all sides and the storm broke anew. Arguments flared in a hundred languages, and the delegations from America and Europe found themselves besieged by hostile neighbours. The delegates were all on their feet and the noise was deafening. Fist fights flared in several parts of the vast hall, and Allington and Mangala shouted themselves hoarse in their efforts to bring the situation back under control. It was no longer possible, and a shower of missiles, from shoes to wrist-watches, were hurled angrily at the rostrum.

The ugly scenes grew more and more violent, and in the end the security staff had to rescue Allington, Mangala and Valdez from the rostrum. As they made their exit the once proud concept of a peaceful and progressive gathering of the united nations of the world was virtually at war within itself.

They were scenes Allington had no wish to remember, but they were scenes he could not put from his mind as he sat alone at his desk at the end of the day. He was surrounded by the paperwork of unfinished business, which no longer had any purpose. He was the world's political pope, but like his spiritual counterpart in the Vatican he was powerless to aid the world in its greatest, and probably final, crisis.

Above Tembu the sun was still a white-hot core of blistering power. It was directly overhead and for Lorna and Sumo there was no shade in their ridge-top hollow of rocks. The cloud was coming in from the dark side of the Earth, and there were still a few more hours of grace for the side which faced the vital solar furnace.

Lorna had shot most of her film during the morning, while the sun was still behind them. The prison camp was a large sprawl of primitive, palm-thatch huts, with no visible sign of washing facilities or lavatories. It was surrounded by a fence of barbed wire and patrolled by guards with long, heavy riot sticks. The soldiers were billeted in drab brick buildings outside the fence, where the red and white colours of Indonesia hung limply from a flagpole in the stifling heat.

The prisoners were overcrowded and undernourished, and few of them had anything more to wear than a pair of tattered shorts. The camp was half a mile away from their hiding place, but viewed through the binoculars or the telephoto lens of the camera, the poor wretches behind the wire showed up as emaciated skeletons. Sumo told her in a whisper that there were no medical facilities for *tapols*, and often very little food. In his time on the island many of his companions had died of tuberculosis, or starved.

By midday, with all her film exposed, Lorna had seen enough, but they could not leave the island until night fell. They were sipping sparingly from their water bottles, and Lorna was beginning to feel dehydrated. The sun seemed to be boiling them alive. She felt more and more drained and lethargic, and eventually allowed Sumo the uninterrupted use of the binoculars. He was searching the camp repeatedly for his lost brother, and by mid-afternoon his anxiety had given way to a dull, fatalistic misery. He had to accept that his brother had either been moved, or that sometime during the past two years he had died.

Perhaps it was the erosion of hope that made Sumo careless, but suddenly Lorna was startled awake by loud, distant shouts of alarm. In the same moment Sumo scrambled back to her side, pulling at her arm in agitation.

'Miss Lorna! Wake up, Miss Lorna. Bad trouble!'

Lorna crawled quickly to the edge of the hollow and peered out. The guards were running and shouting around the barrack block buildings, picking up rifles and pointing towards the ridge. With a sick lurch in her stomach Lorna realized they had been spotted.

'Must run,' Sumo wailed. 'Back to sampan.'

There was no other choice. The guards were already sprinting toward them and flight was their only hope. Lorna sprang to her feet, pausing only to snatch up the cine camera with its precious film, and stumbled after the Javanese who was already diving down the seaward side of the ridge. There was a sharp crack in the still air, and then a harsh, automatic stuttering sound, and in terror Lorna realized that the soldiers were shooting at them.

The ridge protected their backs as the bullets whined high, and they plunged down the slope like rabbits bolting into the undergrowth. For the next few minutes they were lashed, tripped, and buffeted by greenery as they hurtled at breakneck speed down to the beach. Twice Lorna fell, rolling heavily and covering herself with dirt and crushed fragments of fern and grass, but each time she held on to the camera and picked herself up again. Birds screeched in fluttering panic in the palm trees above them, marking their trail for the soldiers to follow. Then abruptly they were clear of the jungle and palm trees and back on to the white sand.

They ran along the beach, floundering and gasping for breath. Lorna felt the sharp pain of a stitch in her side and longed desperately to stop and hide. But Sumo was racing ahead of her, she didn't want to be left alone, and there was no air in her lungs to cry out to him to stop. She had to keep going, even though her heart felt like bursting and her legs threatened to fold up beneath her.

She was on the point of collapse when they reached the sampan, but somehow she was able to help Sumo push it clear of the reeds and back down the creek. As they neared the deepening channel that cut across the sand to the lagoon, the first of the soldiers emerged from the tree line half a mile further up the beach. More shots rang out, and more long bursts of automatic fire.

The two fugitives scrambled aboard the sampan. Sumo tipped the engine back over the stern and began to pull frantically on the cord. Lorna grabbed the steering pole and thrust hard for deeper water, sobbing now, and expecting at any moment to feel the tearing impact of a bullet rip through her cringing flesh.

Mercifully the engine fired on the second pull. Sumo gave it full throttle and Lorna lost the bamboo pole and almost fell overboard as the sampan roared for the gap in the reef. She crouched low on the deck, making herself as small a target as possible, and stared mesmerized at the soldiers running up the beach. More gunfire crackled and the bullets whistled past on either side, and it seemed a miracle that neither of them was hit.

Then the sea swirled and foamed, a boom of spray broke over her hunched shoulders, and they were through the reef. The sampan skimmed onward over the blue waves, and the frustrated soldiers on the white beach fell further behind.

Lorna rolled face down on to the deckboards and let relief turn her into a shaking jelly. For how long she lay there she did not know, but when Sumo groaned and cursed aloud she made the effort to struggle up on to her elbow and look back.

A mile of open sea separated them from the island, but still they had not escaped. From behind the island a sleek grey shape had emerged to continue the pursuit, and she recognized an armed patrol boat of the Indonesian Navy.

6

When the cloud arrived Barbara and Willoughby were again taking it in turn to observe through the telescope. The heart-broken professor had for days refused even to look at the heavens, finding the fast-growing image of the swirling black cloud mass too painful to contemplate. Then at the penultimate moment he had discovered an anguished urge to see magnified for the last time those stars that were still visible.

The sun had bowed out during the late afternoon, its grey light fading miserably behind a curtain of pale English drizzle, as though too distressed to say goodbye. However, by mid-evening the weather changed for the better, and the sky over Surrey, Kent, and the greater part of Sussex became clear of any Earthbound cloud. Willoughby knocked on Barbara's door to announce his change of mind, and after some hesitation she decided to accompany him. They left the castle together and walked over to the equatorial domes housing the telescopes.

To the north and west there were no stars, for already the approaching space cloud had blotted out more than half the night sky. Willoughby was suddenly in a hurry and Barbara twice had to break into a trot to keep up with his long-legged strides. Her heart began to thump against her breastbone and she knew it was not caused solely by exertion. Every glance upward filled her with inescapable fear.

They reached the dome and went inside. They had

use of the thirty-five-inch reflector as before, and Willoughby busied himself with opening the shutters and focusing the telescope. After his panic spurt to get here he seemed to have a relapse, and became uncommunicative, dull-witted and slow. He was an old man who had already accepted his sentence of death from remorseless Time. Barbara began to wish that she had stayed in the castle, but then she felt a deep pang of pity for him. Before the coming of the cloud Willoughby had been like a favourite uncle to her, and she knew she would never have forgiven herself if she had allowed him to stand this last vigil alone.

For ten minutes Willoughby gazed upward, then he moved away from the telescope, rubbing his eyes, shaking his head and biting his lip. Barbara took his place and saw that he had the telescope fixed on the southern half of the sky where the familiar constellations were still clear. For a while she too stared at this last glimpse of the distant galaxies.

'The comet has gone,' she ventured at last.

'It's between us and the sun.' Willoughby's voice was disinterested, because Halley's Comet didn't matter any more. 'It will soon reach perihelion — that is its nearest point to the sun — then it begins the return journey. In spring it would have been visible again —'

His voice trailed off into silence. He had relayed the information mechanically, like a computer, but unlike a computer he had a soul, and the hurt in his soul had dried up the dispassionate words.

The rest of it Barbara knew anyway. After tonight nothing would be visible. They would never see the return flight of Halley's Comet, and when it passed again in seventy-six years time it would pass a dead planet, no different from any other in the lifeless solar system.

She moved the telescope and found the heart of the black cloud. It was a picture of infinite evil, the dark whirlpools of gas and dust churning together in malevolent fury, seeming so close now that she felt as though she could be sucked up through the barrel of the telescope and drowned in their cruel embrace. She felt icy cold, frozen and suffocated at the same time, but she could not tear her gaze away. It was as though the cloud had already attained a complete hypnotic control over her mind.

They knew its composition now: mainly hydrogen with ice droplets, ammonia and methane, with particles of iron dust, nickel and magnesium. In essence it was very similar to the composition of the comet and its tail, except that it was concentrated into a greater and more dangerous mass. The cloud looked black to the human eye, but in fact it was emitting enough reflected light to allow a spectrum analysis of its chemical parts. The analysis of the cloud's radio waves conducted at Jodrell Bank had also determined that it was strongly magnetic. The latter quality was no surprise, due to the fact that the cloud had glued itself so firmly to the homecoming satellite.

Columbus Two was now presumed dead inside the cloud. The dark nebula had used the tiny man-made machine to give itself new impetus on its long journey through space, but in doing so it had engulfed its unwitting benefactor and starved it of life-giving sunlight.

Soon it would do the same to the Earth.

The thought swelled huge and monstrous in Barbara's mind, like the cloud itself, and suddenly she tasted blood inside her mouth. She had bitten her own lip and the sharp pain helped her break free. With an effort of will she tilted the telescope down and forward until she found the magnificent blue-glowing galaxy of Andromeda more than two million light years away.

For the few hours that remained they observed Andromeda, but the cloud was now on the last lap of its fateful journey. It was speeding down upon them at more than three hundred miles per minute, like a huge expanding mouth steadily devouring the stars. In ones, twos and handfuls the fiery specks blinked out, and at last the outer edge of the cloud was biting deep into Andromeda. Again she could not tear her gaze away, and with chilling finality Barbara saw the whole galaxy engulfed. It was snuffed out like so many candle flames by what appeared to be a vast fog of thickly-banked black smoke and choking fumes, as though somewhere behind it were the unseen, infernal fires of hell itself.

Willoughby tilted the telescope forward and as far down as it would go, aiming for a last despairing glimpse of Pisces. Then one by one the four bright stars of the last visible constellation slowly disappeared.

There was nothing left. No matter which way they tilted the telescope there was only the seething black cauldron of cloud.

'That's it,' Willoughby said bitterly, and there were bright tears of infinite sadness in his tired eyes.

He was choked with emotion, but Barbara felt flat and drained. She put out a hand to comfort him, holding his arm.

'I'm sorry, Professor.'

'Don't be sorry for me.' The pain made him sharp and angry. 'I've had my life. I've seen the miracle of the stars. Be sorry for yourself, Barbara, my dear. For your own generation. For all the future generations that might have been — but will never be.'

Willoughby had surrendered to fate, but something in his matter-of-fact dejection sparked the opposite pole in Barbara. She was young and alive and she couldn't accept the Day of Judgement and the End of the World quite so readily. Her fighting spirit flared and she answered defiantly:

'We're not dead yet, Professor. Let's go outside.'

'Why?' Willoughby saw no point, but when she dragged at his arm he followed her like a lamb. He no longer had the will to resist.

They went outside to watch the last few minutes of the fast-spreading blackout that had already filled the telescope and the viewing slit between the open shutters of the dome. The far-flung glimmer of a few pale stars low on the horizon flickered bravely for a few more seconds and then vanished.

The darkness of the night sky was absolute.

The cloud had arrived.

For several minutes Barbara and Willoughby stood close together in expectant silence, but nothing happened. There was no shock of impact and no sound of collision. The Earth did not vibrate or jerk out of orbit. The sky did not burst into an inferno of flame generated by friction. There was no bang, and no whimper.

Just black, silent nothing.

Barbara breathed fearfully, wondering how long it might take for the suffocating gases of the cloud to sink down through the thickening layers of Earth's atmosphere.

Five minutes passed. Ten minutes — and still the air was cold and fresh, and unchanged. It did not burn in her lungs. She was not choking. There was no sensation of being poisoned.

Fifteen minutes passed. They were still alive, and the Earth seemed unharmed and in one piece. It was almost an anti-climax.

Barbara turned and looked back at the blaze of electric light spilling out of the open doorway to the dome. It was a reassuring comfort in the unnatural darkness.

'We're not dead yet,' she repeated firmly to Willoughby. 'And while there's life — there's hope.'

It was an old adage, but she clung to it as though it was a bright new beacon of truth, willing herself to believe it. While there was life, surely there must be hope.

It was in Asia that the full horror of the cloud's arrival was immediately experienced. The time was six a.m. in England, but further round the globe, over the huge sub-continent of India, it was midday with the sun blazing down from a searing blue sky. For the millions of people living there, going about their daily business in the swarming, overcrowded towns and cities, in the small rural villages, or ploughing the red earth fields, the shock was as brutal and as terrifying as it could possibly be.

In one moment life was normal, and in the next the rolling black tide of the cloud had poured over the western horizon. Like a pot of black paint that had been tipped carelessly over a tennis ball the swift-spilling flood enveloped the earth and extinguished the sun.

With unbelievable speed and suddenness the last day had been transformed in a matter of seconds into endless night.

In Indonesia, almost four thousand miles to the southeast, the day was a little further advanced. The time was late afternoon and Tembu Island was a bright green splash of jungle and palm trees, ringed by white beaches in the tropical blue of the Java Sea. The grey patrol boat sliding out swiftly from behind the island cut a creaming bow wave as she turned to run down the fleeing sampan. The red and white flag streamed proudly from her masthead, and sailors in smart white shirts and shorts ran quickly to man the heavy machine-gun mounted on her foredeck.

Lorna watched it approach with her heart sinking like a ton of lead into her constricting stomach. Sumo had the throttle wide open on the straining engine, but the sampan was slow and clumsy and all hope of escape was now futile. The patrol boat was bearing down upon them like the steel fin of a tiger shark that had scented blood.

Lorna groaned and cursed and almost wept. All her good intentions and all her fine ideals were collapsing beneath her. All the risks and all her efforts had been for nothing. Instead of being able to help the poor wretches she had so recently filmed in their misery, she would now be condemned to join them.

The injustice of it filled her with frustration and self-pity, but then she saw Sumo's white, frozen face. Whatever might happen to her, he would fare ten times worse, and he knew it. He sat rigid at the tiller like a staring corpse.

'Oh, God,' Lorna sobbed aloud. She buried her face in her hands and hugged her elbows tight to her trembling breasts. For a moment she could not bear to look at the terrified Javanese.

Time stood still, and another face appeared in her mind: a strong face with steady hazel eyes and dark hair distinctively streaked with grey. It was the face of the man who was slowly falling in love with her. The face of the man she knew she already loved. The face of the Englishman, Richard Allington, the Secretary-General of the United Nations.

She wondered whether Allington would ever know what had happened to her? What problems she would cause him if he did discover that she had been arrested and thrown into a political prison camp by the Indonesians? Or what inner grief he would suffer if she was just to disappear and her fate never be known.

Oh, Richard, she cried silently to the man who would never hear. *I only meant for us to part for a little while. . . . For both of us to have time to think and be sure. . . . For me to try and do something positive instead of just shuffling paperwork and talk, talk, talk at those endless, pointless conferences. . . . But not for ever, Richard. . . . Not like this. . . . Not like this. . . .*

And the words seemed to echo and re-echo through the distraught corridors of her shock-numbed mind.

The powerful, swelling roar of the patrol boat forced her to open her eyes. The miniature grey warship was almost on top of them, and with a sudden jolt of new panic she realized that it was not slowing down to stop.

The patrol boat was aiming to smash into the sampan and plough it deep under the waves.

In the same instant she realized something else. The sailors on the patrol boat were not planning deliberate murder. Instead the object of their pursuit had been suddenly and totally forgotten. Every man on the looming foredeck was staring with mouth agape at the western horizon. They were like men turned to stone, struck dumb, deaf and blind by some awesome spectacle. What was happening was simply happening, and the patrol boat was surging on under its own momentum with no human hand or mind in control.

Sumo yelled in terror and threw his weight on the tiller. The sampan swung to one side and slipped past the cutting steel bows. They were almost overturned as the patrol boat rushed past, and then the sampan was bobbing wildly in its disturbed wake. Lorna threw herself flat, digging her fingers desperately into the cracks between the deck planks. A wave crashed over the low gunwale and drenched her, and her body slid helplessly to and fro as the sampan continued to rock violently from side to side.

Slowly the motion abated and Lorna was able to sit up. And then she saw what had startled and stunned the wide-mouthed Indonesian sailors.

The western horizon was no longer blue. It was a thick black line where the sea met the sky, and growing thicker and blacker with every second. Like a tidal wave of ink the foul cloudspill rushed toward them, blotting out the blue of the sky while its equally insidious night shadow pulled a black shroud over the sea. It poured over their heads in an instant eclipse of the sun, swirling on to the eastern horizon to devour the last shrinking ribbon of fading daylight.

The patrol boat was lost behind the abrupt curtain of stygian darkness. The same darkness veiled the island they had just left, and everything else. Even the crude shelter tacked on to the sampan was no longer visible, and Lorna had to crawl forward and feel for Sumo, touching him to be sure that she was not wholly alone.

They were safe from the patrol boat, but in the aftermath of this horrific black apocalypse Lorna would have preferred to be its prisoner.

7

America woke up to accept reluctantly that there would be no dawn. The TV announcement by their President had given them eight hours warning. Time enough to argue over it, refute it, scorn it and reject it, but also time to sleep on it. When morning came the sky remained pitch black, and then they had no choice but to believe it. Unless they chose to believe that the Earth had stopped dead on its axis and was no longer making its regular twenty-four hour revolutions, there was no other alternative.

There was some anguish and some despair, and a surge of spontaneous praying as the churches filled for impromptu services. However, there was no mass panic and wailing hysteria to match the events that were endemic to Africa and Asia and the less advanced corners of the globe.

The peoples of Europe and North America were not unaccustomed to short winter days and long cold nights, so for a while, they told each other, they could manage without the short hours of daylight. They bought up all the available supplies of candles, torches, batteries and light bulbs and prepared to survive. They kept the electricity burning and in America some two-thirds of the working population went on about their normal daily business.

Soon after midnight Richard Allington had taken a cab out to New York's La Guardia Airport and boarded a plane for the short, thirty-minute flight to

Washington. On arrival he took another cab to the Washington Hilton on Connecticut Avenue where he had booked a suite. He slept for a few hours, and then continued the series of determined telephone calls he had begun in New York. By midday he had what he wanted, an appointment at the White House.

A large black, bullet-proof limousine called to collect him, even though it was only a few minutes walk. As he left the hotel to get into the car Allington could not prevent himself from looking up. The street lights, the coloured blaze of neon advertising and the bright shopfronts all combined to give a picture of an ordinary evening. It was difficult to believe that this was noon and not midnight, without looking at the unrelieved blackness overhead. In that moment Allington would have given ten years of his salary to see just one pale star.

He climbed into the back of the car with the young White House aide who had come into the hotel foyer to meet him. They had said hello but were both too tight-lipped to speak further as the car moved smoothly away from the kerb. The traffic was normal, but Allington noticed large numbers of people on the pavements. There were queues outside the food and liquor stores, so far orderly, but a sign that hoarding had begun. On every street corner were steel-helmeted National Guardsmen, called out to reinforce law and order, but so far their mere presence had been sufficient to maintain calm.

But how long could it last, Allington wondered. The guardsmen were only human, they had their family commitments to wives and children. When society began to break up, the cracks would start to appear in their morale and discipline. In this situation nobody was going to be safe or immune.

The limousine passed through the iron gates to the White House, the bright sweep of its headlights illuminating the long curve of the drive. Posted at every

few yards on both sides of the drive were men of the
Third United States Infantry, the Old Guard, responsible for security and ceremonial duties in the capital.
They stood stiffly to attention, and Allington noted that
their numbers exceeded the usual limits for mere ceremony. There was a large crowd outside the gates,
clamouring for the latest bulletin on the cloud, and the
White House was prepared for anything.

He was kept waiting for ten minutes in an ante-room,
and then escorted into the Oval Office. Glenn
Anderson sat in the high-backed chair behind the massive desk, flanked by the Presidential flag and the flag
of the United States. Merle Forrester was the only
other man in the room. He was standing to one side of
the desk, his right elbow supported by his left hand,
and his right hand pulling nervously and repeatedly at
his jaw. The stance had once been an occasional sign
of agitation, but now it had become an almost permanent habit.

Anderson took off his horn-rimmed glasses, stood up
and moved round the desk, extending his hand. He
dragged up a smile but his jaw moved slowly with the
effort.

'Hello, Mister Allington. I'm glad to meet you at last.
I guess we should have got together before, both of us
being comparatively new boys in top jobs. I've been
meaning to invite you to a White House dinner, but
somehow over the past few months the right opportunity didn't seem to come up. Then, over these past
weeks, things have got pretty hectic.'

'I fully understand, Mister President.'

As he spoke Allington tried to calculate the strength
of the handshake and the man. If anything could be
done about the black cloud then it would have to be
done through the advanced space technology of the
United States. That placed an awesome weight of
responsibility on the broad shoulders of the man
before him, and Allington felt with relief that

Anderson would not collapse too quickly under the load.

'I'm sorry I had to keep you waiting,' Anderson continued. 'But I've only just escaped from a press conference. They gave me the worst media-mauling I've ever had. Worse than the TV cameras last night. Hell, they chewed me up worse than Congress.'

'I can appreciate that,' Allington said with feeling. 'I almost got torn to pieces when I broke the news at the UN.'

'I heard.' Anderson pulled a sour face. 'I guess that's why you were so persistent in seeing me. I guess that gives you a right to see me, so now we're here. Let's sit down.'

Allington nodded. He pulled up a chair as Anderson went back behind the desk. Forrester still watched them uncertainly.

'Merle, for Christ's sake, will you sit down too please. You're driving me nuts standing around like that.'

The Scientific Adviser reluctantly pulled up a third chair and Anderson looked back to Allington.

'You know Merle, I think.'

Allington smiled wryly. 'Not so well as I thought. I've been trying to nail him down and talk to him for the past week, and got stalled all the way.'

'I'm sorry, Richard.' Forrester was embarrassed. 'Really I am. But I've been so goddamned busy. I just wasn't taking any calls.'

Allington looked at the worn-out shadow of the man he had known, noting the deep, dark caverns under the sleepless eyes, and again he nodded understanding.

'It's okay, Merle. No hard feelings.'

They were silent for a moment. Anderson put on his glasses again and fixed his gaze directly on the Secretary-General of the United Nations. It was his way of demonstrating that he was ready to get down to business.

'Okay, Richard. You're here. So fire away. How can this office help the UN?'

'By keeping me better informed,' Allington told him bluntly. 'You did a magnificent job on TV last night. It was informative, calming, reassuring, and well-timed — for the American people! For the rest of the world — it was a sell-out.'

Anderson seemed to rear forward in his chair, ready to explode. He had enough people griping and complaining and he didn't need any more. Allington checked him with a staying movement of his hand.

'Just one minute, Mister President. Please let me finish. I know you gave me the facts to inform the UN at the same time that you were talking to Congress. But my delegates then had to pass the information back to their respective governments. Those governments had to be assembled, and they needed time to plan what needed to be done, and time to prepare their populations. They didn't get fair warning. In fact, the great majority of people in the Third World got no warning at all. The Assembly was right to shout me down in disgust. We did abandon them.'

'Sir,' Anderson said heavily. 'I am the elected President of the United States of America. My first duty is — and always must be — to the American nation.'

'I agree,' Allington said calmly. 'But the American nation has always been great enough to accept a vital and necessary responsibility for helping to maintain peace and stability in the rest of the world. This crisis affects us all. I don't think twenty-four hours prior warning would have harmed the United States, but it might have eased some of the sheer terror and total collapse that's taking place in parts of Africa and Asia.'

Anderson frowned, and then squared his shoulders. He was a direct man who believed in moving forward and not looking back. 'Okay, I take your point. But time is short and there's nothing to be gained by going over what's done. What do you expect me to do now?'

'I think I've already said it,' Allington smiled briefly. 'I need to be better informed. As I see it my job is to try and hold the rest of the world together, and to do that I have to restore some level of credibility to the United Nations. If there's any more bad news to come, I want it in good time, so that my delegates can give their governments time to prepare. If there's any good news, I want to pass that on quickly. It might check some of the panic. At the moment the Third World is literally in the dark, in every way imaginable.'

Anderson looked to his Scientific Adviser. 'Merle, give it to him straight.'

Forrester coughed to clear his throat. 'At the moment it's not good. The cloud wasn't heavy enough to penetrate very far through the Earth's atmosphere, but it was big enough to completely envelop the Earth. It hit us, and just flowed all round the planet, sealing us in. It's formed another thick black dust and vapour layer of upper atmosphere. We're inside it and we're not passing through it. The cloud has stopped moving and Earth gravity is holding it all around us like another skin. We don't know exactly how far out into space it now extends, but it's too dense for the sun's rays to pass through.'

'The satellite,' Allington said hopefully. 'It's been on target all the way, so it should be dropping back to Earth. Maybe the cloud samples will tell us something.'

'The satellite hit sea level two hours ago,' Anderson said gloomily. 'There were three French ships and two British ships waiting for it, and we sent in six US Navy ships to widen the net. The problem was they couldn't get a fix on the damn satellite until it fell through the cloud. Then there wasn't enough time. In the darkness they all missed it. It sank somewhere in the depths of the Atlantic, about three hundred miles off the coast of French Guiana.'

'Maybe it won't matter too much,' Forrester said.

'We've already got a chemical analysis of the gases and dust particles in the cloud. I don't think the samples would have given us any more.'

'So what are our chances of getting rid of it?'

Forrester stalled. 'Everybody's working on it.'

There was silence for a moment, and then Anderson said grimly, 'All we can do at the moment is leave it to NASA, and try to buy time. I'm making another TV announcement this afternoon. I'm gonna tell my fellow Americans that we expect the Earth to pass through this cloud, but that it will probably take a few more days. I suggest you give the same message to the United Nations. We have to aim to keep up morale and minimize panic. Then maybe in a few days time we can give a more positive progress report.'

Allington reflected that for much of the Third World it was too late. Morale was shattered and panic was widespread. But he saw that for the moment nothing else made sense.

'I'll call another General Assembly,' he promised, although he shuddered at the thought.

Anderson nodded. He had very little faith in the United Nations, where Third World venom had almost totally alienated the United States, but he was an astute politician and he saw a possible ally in the English Secretary-General.

'Keep in touch,' he advised. 'From here on I'll make sure a line of communication is kept open.'

Forrester had the last solemn word.

'Don't fly back to New York, Richard. Since the cloud arrived air traffic control and communications have been a mess. It could be safer to go by train.'

In England Barbara was at a loss, suspended in a limbo of helpless waiting. With the stars blotted out it was no longer possible to observe the heavens, all research work at the observatory came to a dead end, and technically she was out of a job. She stayed only because there was nowhere else for her to go. With her mother dead and her father absent in New York the family home in Surrey was empty for most of the time. She had no close relatives, and was reluctant to impose herself upon girl friends for more than short holiday periods.

For the first two days she did not step outside the castle, trying with the rest of the permanent staff to glean something hopeful from the reports coming in from NASA, Jodrell Bank and elsewhere. None of it offered any long-term future. The sun's rays were incapable of penetrating the thickest areas of the new layer of cloud, although reports had come in of patches of bleak, grey gloom where the darkness was not absolute. Overnight the Earth had become a doomed planet, with only a few fading glimmers of twilight.

Barbara spent most of the third day brooding in her room, and then told herself to snap out of it. She needed a drink. It was technically mid-evening, a time when the pubs would be open, and she saw no reason why she shouldn't drive out in the mini. She knew the local roads well enough not to get lost.

She needed a change of company, but the pricking of her conscience made her invite Willoughby. She was worried about the professor, who had slumped into a deeper depression than any of them, and seemed incapable of getting himself out of it. In the circumstances an evening at the Red Lion seemed an ideal prescription.

Willoughby objected, arguing that it might not be safe to leave the castle, but after some perseverance Barbara talked him into it. She pointed out that three days had passed, and no demented mobs had yet tried to storm the castle. The soldiers had proved to be an over-reaction and an unnecessary precaution. So far there had been no riots anywhere in England, which meant that ordinary people were behaving sensibly and calmly in the crisis.

To appease her, and partly because he didn't like the

idea of her going out alone, Willoughby finally put on his hat and coat and joined her. The armed guards on duty at the west gate pulled dubious faces, but they allowed the mini to pass through. They had no orders to stop anyone from going out.

Barbara drove slowly, taking comfort from the bright beam of her headlights lancing down the road before her. The mini was a reliable little car and she had ample petrol for the short journey she intended. On either side was a seemingly solid wall of blackness, but she kept her gaze on the tunnel of light ahead. She drove into Herstmonceaux village and found the pub. Light and noise spilled out on to the forecourt and there were several cars already parked. Barbara nosed the mini into a vacant space and stopped.

She locked the car and they went inside. The lounge bar was quiet and almost empty, but the public bar was busy with a flock of young people round the juke-box and fruit machines, and a group of older men in the corner. Barbara wanted the noise, and to be able to lose herself in the crowd. She smiled at Willoughby and led the way in.

They went up to the bar. Barbara asked for a gin and tonic. Willoughby chose a pint of bitter and insisted on paying for both drinks. They sipped and tried to relax. The latest pop tune blared from the juke-box and Willoughby put one hand to his ear and winced.

Barbara laughed. 'At least it's a change.'

'Indeed it is,' Willoughby forced a rueful wisp of a smile and tried to match her mood. 'I'm surprised to see so many people here. It's almost as if nothing unusual were happening.'

'The British always stop for tea at three,' Barbara reminded him. 'By the same token they don't allow anything to interfere with their social life at the pub. It's got something to do with Dunkirk, and the Battle of Britain, and all that.'

'The Bulldog Spirit,' Willoughby agreed. 'Although

I'm not sure whether it really does come from nobility of character, or just dim, squinty eyesight.'

Barbara felt better. It was the first joke she had heard him make for several weeks. It made her feel sure she had done the right thing in bringing him here.

She kept the conversation going, darting from subject to subject, anything to draw him out, and anything to steer away from the cloud. Unfortunately the cloud was dominating many of the conversations around them, and was a difficult topic to ignore.

'What's going to happen to the harvest?' one of the farmhands asked through a lull from the corner. 'Seed's in — but the corn won't come up if the sun don't shine.'

Willoughby's face paled and he looked down at his glass. It was empty and Barbara took it from his hand.

'Let's have another,' she said too brightly, and too quickly.

She pushed up to the bar, bumping elbows with the group of youths at the juke-box. They had just begun to argue among themselves about the cloud, and suddenly a hand shot out to grab tightly at Barbara's wrist.

'Here,' a girl's voice insisted. 'She'll know. She'll tell us.'

Barbara turned in alarm. The hand which had stopped her belonged to a girl of about seventeen. She was plump and blonde and her tone was loud and accusing, causing most of the customers in the bar to pause and listen. As far as she could remember Barbara had never seen the girl before.

'She works at the observatory,' the blonde girl announced. 'I've seen her there. I worked there myself last summer, in the tea-rooms. But she's got a proper job there — a posh job.'

'Is that right?' One of the young men in the group moved aggressively to block Barbara's path to the bar. He wore a black leather motor-cycle jacket and leather boots, and apart from his scowl the most noticeable thing about him was his thick, dark curling sideburns.

'What's it all about then?'

Barbara groaned inwardly. She had not expected to be recognized and she could willingly have kicked the girl who was holding her. At the same time she saw the futility of denial, or of losing her temper.

'You all know as much as I do,' she said with forced calm. 'It's all been in the papers, and on television. I honestly don't know any more.'

'You must know more.' Sideburns refused to move and the blonde girl wouldn't let go. 'If you work there, you must know more.'

'I'm sorry,' Barbara insisted. 'Please let me go.'

It was too late. She was the centre of attention now and the whole crowd was pressing round her with questions, most of them determined, some angry, and a few quickly becoming ugly.

'What is this cloud? Where has it come from?'

'How long is it going to stay here?'

'It's a bloody war game that's gone wrong —'

'When's the sun going to shine?'

'What about the harvest —'

'It's a new weapon, I tell you — something to do with the bloody Yanks.'

'Please,' Barbara begged, struggling to disentangle herself. The questions were coming too fast and most of them were hostile. She was beginning to realize that under the seeming normality of the pub atmosphere there were deep under-currents of fear, and like a dam burst they had been abruptly released. Most of the men here had been drinking heavily, and as their faces pushed close she could smell the beer and whisky fumes on their breath.

She felt fear and panic, and then Willoughby tried to break through the circle that surrounded her.

'Leave her alone,' Willoughby was shouting. 'Leave

her alone! It's not her fault. I'm the one who is responsible.'

The words registered. There was a moment of hushed silence. Heads turned slowly to stare at the flushed, white-haired old man. Then the circle broke to draw him roughly into its centre. Immediately it closed and the onslaught began again.

'How, Grandad?'

'What are you talking about?'

'Who the hell are you anyway?'

'My name is Harold Willoughby. I'm a professor of astronomy at the Royal Greenwich Observatory.' Willoughby had to shout again to make himself heard. 'I'm one of the team which was making a study of Halley's Comet. We sent up the satellite which brought back the cloud.'

'You sent up that satellite?'

'Not me personally.' Willoughby fumbled as he realized he had made a mistake. 'It was a joint European effort. I'm only a small part of the British team.'

'But you caused it — your lot sent up that bloody satellite.'

'You brought this bloody cloud thing down on us.'

'I'm sorry.' Willoughby pushed away an accusing finger. 'Please. We have to go now. Please —'

He tried to free Barbara from the blonde girl's grip, pulling hard on the other girl's wrist. But it was another mistake.

'Here, hang about.'

'Don't start pushing me, mate.'

'Get your dirty hand off young Wendy.'

Sideburns broke Willoughby's grip and pushed him back. Willoughby tried again and suddenly the whole crowd was clawing at him, pulling and pushing. Willoughby flailed helplessly and struck one youth a glancing blow on the shoulder. Instantly the youth punched Willoughby hard in the face. The older man flew backwards, arms waving to regain his balance.

He knocked into other side of the circle and then they were all hitting him.

Barbara screamed, pushed the blonde girl off and tried to help the professor. She clawed both hands into Sideburns's eyes from behind and dragged him back. He roared with fury and his elbow drove back into her stomach, slamming the wind out of her. She let go to double up in agony and then the blonde girl was punching her from behind.

The whole bar room was a pandemonium of screams and curses, struggling bodies and flying fists. Barbara saw Willoughby slip down on to his kness but she couldn't get near enough to help him. Then a kick to his shoulder pitched him flat on his face. Another boot drove into his ribs and his body jerked. Now he was only moving under the impact of the blows. His body was limp. His face was deathly white and his eyes were closed.

Barbara screamed again, this time with all the bursting power of her lungs.

It did the trick. The kicking and the punching stopped. The ring of men and youths began to back away, leaving Willoughby lying still and silent on the floor.

'The old bugger's snuffed it.'

'We didn't hit him that hard,' Sideburns complained.

'He must have had a weak heart.'

The voices were softer, apprehensive and ashamed, and nobody stopped Barbara as she stumbled forward to kneel at Willoughby's side. He was not breathing and she tore open his coat, struggling to get through the layers of scarf, necktie and pullover to feel for his heart. There was no beat. Willoughby's lower lip was cut but there was practically no blood, and the corners of his mouth were tinged whitish blue.

Barbara choked back her sobs as she recognized the signs, and tried hard to remember the instructions of a half-forgotten first-aid course she had learned at school. She had to check his mouth to make sure there was no obstruction.... Tilt his head back to ensure a clear airway.... Cover his mouth with her own and breathe into his lungs.... See the chest inflate.... Let it fall.... Repeat....

She went through the movements mechanically, tasting his blood as his lips touched her own. It was as though she was watching someone else do it all, while the real part of her was still shocked and sobbing. She remembered suddenly that she had to give heart massage as well. Heel of the left hand on the breastbone.... Right hand over left.... Push down hard with both hands.... Repeat, fifteen times.... Then mouth-to-mouth.... Two inflations.... Heart massage.... Push down hard, fifteen times.... Back to mouth-to-mouth.... Two inflations.... Back to heart massage, fifteen times....

She worked desperately for what seemed an eternity, and then became aware of a hand touching her shoulder. She turned her head and saw two uniformed policemen kneeling beside her.

'You've done your bit, miss,' one of the officers said gently. 'We'll take over now.'

Barbara moved aside. She was drained and exhausted and found she could hardly stand. Someone guided her into a chair. She watched the two policemen continue working on Willoughby; one of them taking over the mouth-to-mouth resuscitation, the other the alternate massaging of the heart.

It was all to no avail, and when a doctor and an ambulance finally arrived, Willoughby was pronounced dead.

After an hour of questions and statements Barbara was escorted back to the observatory by the police. One of the young constables drove the mini for her, and before leaving her to rejoin his companion in the following police car he advised her strongly not to go into the village again.

Barbara was left feeling stunned and deflated. The shock of Willoughby's death had hit her badly, and the policeman's parting words were yet another body blow. She stood beside the mini and stared up at the lighted windows of the castle. Suddenly it had become a prison — but for how long?

She looked to the dreadful black sky. It was like being struck blind, and she shivered. It was very cold, the temperature was dropping, and her mind plunged down the icy slope to despair.

'*What about the harvest?*'

It was an echo from the nightmare in the pub, but it was a valid question. No sunlight meant no warmth. Without warmth and sunlight food crops could not grow. The spectre of a new ice age was beginning, and the peoples of the Earth were facing swift starvation in freezing darkness.

At the observatory, and in the village, all the lights were burning, but again Barbara wondered for how long could it go on. The rich nations could for a short time burn electricity night and day to light the streets and buildings, but there was already an energy crisis and inevitably the power sources must fail, to plunge village after village, town after town, and city after city into total darkness.

If the cloud stayed, then how long could the Earth survive? In the West the answer could perhaps be measured in a few months. In the rest of the world it was probably only a matter of weeks.

8

Indonesia was one of the few dark grey twilight areas where the sun was able to give a glimmer of relief for a few days before the cloud finally settled to an equal thickness all around the planet. Impact had been over Europe; from there the cloud had surged in all directions over Asia, Africa and the Americas, colliding with itself over the South Pacific Ocean. It piled up in mountainous swirling masses over the Fiji Islands, and then began to wash back to fill up the shallow patches where the first rush had passed too quickly. Like water it found its own level, but having less weight it took more time. Parts of the Third World were given a few hours, or at the most a few days grace, but it meant only a lingering death instead of a swift one.

For Lorna and Sumo it meant eighteen hours of pitch blackness in their tiny sampan, drifting helplessly with the whim of the invisible sea. They sat close together, holding hands for mutual comfort, trying to comprehend what had happened, and wondering whether they were doomed to starve, or freeze, or drown.

It had been late afternoon when the sun had been extinguished, and they waited without hope for the next dawn. When the time came there was no relief, and Lorna closed her eyes with weariness and silently wept. An hour passed, perhaps two, and then she became aware of Sumo pulling tentatively at her arm.

'Look, Miss Lorna,' his words were hushed and choked. 'Open eyes and look.'

She hardly dared to obey, but slowly she blinked open her eyes. There was still no sunlight, but at least the blackness was no longer total. She could faintly distinguish the outline of Sumo's head and shoulders, and the shape of the prow of the sampan.

She jerked her head back and stared upward. She could see nothing, but unless all the planetary laws had changed the Earth must have partially revolved on its axis, which meant the sun must again be positioned over their heads.

They waited anxiously but the light did not improve. Day had become something between dusk gloom and night, and night had become something too terrible to contemplate.

However, they could see each other in dim silhouette, which gave them hope that whatever had happened might not be permanent. It restored their will to live, and a strengthening breeze stirred Sumo into action. He crawled forward to set the sail and the sampan moved with the wind.

'How do you know which way we're going?' Lorna asked.

Sumo shrugged. 'This time of year, wind most times blow from north. If blow from north, will blow us on to Java. What else can we do?'

Lorna realized he was right. Java was to the south. Borneo to the north. Sumatra to the west. In addition to the large islands the whole of the Java Sea was dotted with hundreds of small islands and islets. If they were lucky the wind would blow them on to land, and with no compass, sun or stars to steer by, they could only pray and trust to the wind.

Six hours passed before they heard waves breaking on the shore. Sumo cried out with elation and steered into the sound. Lorna clung on to the bamboo archway supporting the sampan's crude shelter and peered desperately ahead. The sampan lifted beneath them, dropped, lifted again, and abruptly they were in the booming surf. There was not enough light to reflect the salty whiteness of the spray, and it was eerie to be caught up in tar-black waves that leaped and tumbled against the greyness.

The sail cracked, slapping and swinging wildly as it lost the wind. But it didn't matter now, the waves were carrying them forward in a last rush that threw the sampan on to the unseen beach. There was a jolt, the suck and hiss of the retreating sea, and then the next wave broke over the stern of the stranded craft and pushed them a little higher.

Lorna cried Sumo's name and grabbed for his hand, afraid that they might be tipped out and separated, perhaps never to find each other again. Together they scrambled over the side and ran up the beach with the waves chasing at their heels.

When they had rested and gathered their wits they went cautiously forward. They kept the sound of the sea behind them and after a few minutes blundered into a palm grove. They felt the rough trunks with their hands and dead fronds crunched under their feet.

'Keep going,' Lorna said, and still holding Sumo's hand she pulled him on.

She had the fear that they had landed on one of the small islands, and that having escaped from the sea they might now be equally hopelessly marooned. If so the palms would soon give way to thick jungle and that would be the end. She had to find out quickly because it didn't bear thinking about.

They groped their way through the palm trees, and then almost tripped over a low earth bank. Lorna staggered on her heels down the far side, still towing Sumo behind her, and then they both splashed into ankle-deep water. It was Sumo who recognized where they were.

'Rice field,' he cried out with relief.

Lorna stooped and felt in the muddy water around

them with her hand. Her fingers traced the path of the young rice plants in orderly rows. The discovery was the nearest she had ever known to a miracle and her heart soared. She grabbed Sumo and hugged him tight.

'We're on Java,' she shouted joyously. 'We're on Java! It must mean we're on Java.'

They pushed on with renewed vigour, wading through the flooded rice paddies until they eventually climbed out on to a hard road. Lorna instinctively turned to the right. If they were on Java they were on the north coast, and her sense of logic told her that this way the road must lead back to Djakarta.

They walked for a mile before stumbling into a small village. Fires burned by the roadside and dogs barked at them out of the darkness. Suddenly there were people on either side of them shining flashlights into their faces. They began jabbering with Sumo and Lorna had to wait for him to translate.

The upshot of it all was that they were indeed on Java, but the local population had only the faintest idea of what was happening. A big cloud had come from beyond the stars to shut out the sun, but they could only argue vaguely but vehemently about the details.

For the moment Lorna was too hungry to bother. She had clung on to her shoulder-bag through all their ordeal, and had enough local currency to buy them a meal of rice and fish, washed down with hot tea. Only then did they begin to make plans.

They were a hundred and fifty miles from Djakarta, and approximately the same distance from Batang. Their sampan had clearly drifted a long way west before being washed up on the beach, which was helpful to Lorna, but disappointing for Sumo. He was worried about his mother, his only surviving relative, and wanted to return to Batang. Lorna understood his problem and did not press him, but he still felt some responsibility for her safety and finally made a compromise decision. He would accompany her as far west as the next town, where hopefully he could put her on a bus bound for Djakarta before he made his own way back to Batang.

After they had rested and eaten they continued their journey, determined to cover as many miles as they could while the few brief hours of twilight remained. They were on the main road now, and began to meet more and more people hurrying to and fro. They were men and women struggling to rejoin lost families, or whole families on the move in the vague hope of finding somewhere where the sun might still be shining.

The streams of refugees thickened, some pushing east and some pushing west, mingling rivers of ghost people and lights bobbing in the grey gloom. The turmoil was gradually increasing and Lorna realized that the whole of Java was like a giant ant heap that had been kicked apart, the ants running everywhere because they were too stupid to know that there was nowhere better to run to. It was happening in slow motion at first, as though the ants were drugged by the monumental shock, but like an unwinding spring the movement was getting faster, more threatening and more dangerous.

As the groups passed each other they shouted for news, searching for lost friends, or just trying to find out what was ahead. At first the exchanges were friendly, then an edge of fear and uncertainty crept into the voices, and finally menace. Lorna could understand none of it, but Sumo grew more and more agitated and clung tight to her arm. Twice he pushed her off the road and shushed her into silence as large groups went past, and the third time she demanded to know what was happening.

'Killing, miss,' Sumo said unhappily. 'Killings have started.'

'Killings?' Lorna felt wretched and filthy, she was crouching up to her thighs in rice plants and mud again, but most of all she was baffled. 'What do you mean — killings?'

'Hindus kill Muslims. Muslims kill Hindus.' Sumo was ashamed and hung his head. 'They say that in one village the *Iman* of the mosque has named this devil cloud the Wrath of God. It is God's Punishment. The *Iman* has called the Faithful to wage *Jihad* and kill the unbelievers. In that village the Muslims have killed all the Hindus. In the next village there were more Hindus than Muslims, so the Hindus killed all the Muslims.'

'Oh, no!' Lorna groaned with dismay. 'A *Jihad*? A Holy War! I can't believe it.'

'The people are confused.' Sumo tried to excuse them. 'They turn to their Holy Men for advice. Sometimes even Holy Men are not very wise.'

Lorna wanted to shrink deeper into the rice paddy and hide, but instinctively she knew that no matter how bad things were now, they could only get worse. She had to push on.

'This next town,' she asked. 'What is it?'

'Town called Indramaju, miss.'

'No, I mean the people. What religion?'

'Big town, miss. Many people. All religions.' He bit his lip nervously. 'I think, maybe more Hindu than Muslim.'

And he was a Muslim, Lorna remembered. For him Indramaju might well be more dangerous than for her. She said slowly, 'If you like, I'll go on alone.'

Sumo hesitated. He wanted to turn back, but he could not abandon her yet. He shook his head.

'No, Miss Lorna. I come with you. Put you on bus for Djakarta first.'

Lorna didn't argue. When they parted she would be friendless in this nightmare situation, totally dependent upon her own stamina and resources, and she was not looking forward to that moment. She took his hand and they climbed back on to the hard road. The large group of loud-voiced Hindus who had alarmed Sumo had passed by, but the two-way flow of unidentified humanity continued unabated. They moved with it toward the uncertain temper of Indramaju.

An hour later they were in the town. It was large enough to have its own electricity supply and the bare bulbs gleamed in pools of yellow-white light. They were in a street of poor, tin-roofed shacks and cheap shops with refuse-filled gutters, and angry voices argued all around them. Now there was nowhere to hide except in the jostling crowds and they had difficulty in pushing their way through.

Sumo found the breath to explain that the town was being swamped by the peasants from the fields and the countryside. The outsiders were being drawn by the town lights, but they were seen as a threat and they were not welcomed by the already frightened townspeople. The crush was adding to the rising religious tensions which had been fanned by the rumours of what was happening elsewhere. It was all fuel for fear, and violence was smouldering just below the surface.

Sumo headed directly for the bus station. They had passed this way four days ago and Lorna remembered that the buses stopped beside the vegetable market in the centre of the town. They were almost running now, and Lorna was praying that there would be a bus.

It was a vain hope, for they were not even destined to reach the bus station. A high-pitched scream rang out somewhere ahead of them, followed by loud shouting, the pound of running footsteps, and then more screams. The whole commotion was blood-curdling, swelling louder and closer with every second, and Lorna froze with terror.

Sumo changed direction and hauled her bodily into a narrow dirt side street. Lorna found her wits again and ran fast beside him as they tried to avoid the sounds of the disturbance. They came out on to another main street and Sumo instantly skidded to a stop and backed up again into the alley. There was still more screaming and shouting from the direction they needed to turn.

'What is it?' Lorna gasped, although with dread in her

heart she already knew. Sumo's actions were unmistakably those of a hunted animal.

'It has started.' Sumo was trembling, his voice was almost a whimper. 'I have seen it before. In the big purge, when the communists were murdered. In Indonesia there are many old hatreds.'

Fierce shouting and more death shrieks echoed from the centre of the town. It was enough for Sumo and he made up his mind. He pulled Lorna on to the main street again, but he no longer had any intention of trying to reach the bus station. He turned in the opposite direction. Panic was driving him back to the dubious safety of the darkened rice fields, and in fear and despair Lorna could only hurry beside him.

Faces whirled past them, a turmoil of agitated men, women and children, but for the first hundred yards no one tried to stop them. Then they had to pass a walled courtyard, and an arched entrance that showed a glimpse of a fire-lit temple. A temple, Lorna realized with horror, not a mosque — but by then it was too late. A gang of Indian youths spilled out from the courtyard, armed with bamboo sticks and flaming torches. Each one of them had the bright red paint mark of *Shiva* daubed on his sweating forehead.

They had whipped themselves into a frenzy. They were hunting — and Sumo still wore the little black Muslim tarboosh cap that marked him instantly as prey.

Sumo stumbled to a stop and turned again. Lorna automatically parallelled his movements, like a dumb, mindless shadow, and together they fled back the way they had come. The street was in sudden uproar with people shouting at them; hands grabbed to stop them and fists struck at them in passing. The mob was in full cry behind them, swelling with every moment, and missiles and rubbish from the gutters were pelted at them from both sides of the street.

They covered sixty yards. Lorna's heart was

hammering, her lungs were bursting, and her legs were failing beneath her. The yelling clamour of pursuit was overhauling them fast, and then a lump of rotten fruit struck her in the face. She staggered and in the same moment Sumo's hand was torn from her grasp.

She ran a few more steps before she faltered and turned. Sumo had been bit by a thrown stone. It had cut open his ear and sent him reeling as the bright blood splashed down the side of his neck. The mob howled in triumph and Sumo was given no chance to regain his balance. One of the long bamboo sticks lashed out and knocked him sprawling. He screamed as he went down and then a dozen of the improvised clubs were smashing down over his head and shoulders as his face hit the dirt.

Lorna took a half-step forward, but against the animal fury of the beating sticks there was nothing she could do. The tail end of the mob surged round those who had fallen upon the quivering, shrieking thing that was Sumo, and continued to rush toward her. They were a horde of dark brown faces, all with mad glittering eyes and the bright paint mark of *Shiva*.

'No.' Lorna screamed. 'I'm not a Muslim. I'm a Christian. *I'm a Catholic Christian.*'

She spoke in English, and for a moment the tableau froze. The hostile faces stared at her, the sticks and fiery torches hung poised to strike, like a hundred Swords of Damocles over her head. They had realized that despite her dark, coffee-coloured skin, she was not another native of Indonesia like themselves, and they wavered. Then one of the older faces answered her, also in English.

'*Yes, but you are not Hindu.*'

The words were harsh, and he repeated them in their own language. The mob emitted shrill howls of approval and flowed in for the kill.

Lorna spun on her heel, trying to protect her face with her hands and her stomach with her elbows. The first blow thwacked hard across her left shoulder and knocked her down. The sticks thrashed at her back and buttocks as she fell and she curled up screaming into a foetal ball. In that moment she was sure that she was going to die, and prayed that she would lose consciousness swiftly.

She did not hear the crack of the first revolver shot or the high-revved snarl of the approaching jeep. She was drowning in her own sea of overwhelming pain, and the second and third revolver shots penetrated only faintly. Slowly she became aware that the beating had stopped, that she was still alive, and the mob was running away.

She was lifted to her feet and only then did she open her eyes. The glare of the jeep's headlights dazzled her. She blinked a few times, and then saw that she was being helped by a lieutenant and three soldiers of the Indonesian Army. She was limp, a dead weight of jelly in their hands, and all that really registered at first was the lifeless body of Sumo which was still sprawled face down in the now empty street.

The lieutenant was named Ichsan, and his patrol was the forerunner of the troop trucks which were being moved into Indramaju to restore order. He was able to tell her that there were no longer any bus services, all organized transport throughout Indonesia had already broken down. The countryside was virtually out of control, but martial law was being imposed on the capital and all major towns.

He talked in struggling English as he drove her back to a military post outside the town. Lorna sat slumped in the front passenger seat of the jeep beside him, and barely absorbed anything that he was saying. She was bruised and battered, bleeding from a dozen superficial cuts, but most of all she was stunned and sickened by what had happened to Sumo. They had left her faithful little companion sprawled in the street where he had fallen, and as they drove through the town and the scattering crowds the jeep's headlights picked out more broken bodies lying in the gutter. Lieutenant Ichsan remarked casually that they would be collected up and decently buried later, but Lorna did not believe him.

At the military post she was questioned by the major in command. She gave her name and added that she was a member of the United Nations Commission for Human Rights. Fortunately her passport was still in her shoulder bag, so there was no difficulty in proving her identity. The major handed it back after a brief glance and asked how she came to be in Indramaju.

It didn't seem to matter any more, but the truth was a long and involved story. It was easier to say that she had been visiting a friend in Batang, and that her friend had been helping her to return to Djakarta.

The major did not disbelieve her. He had too many worries on his mind in this time of crisis, and he saw her as yet another problem to be disposed of as quickly as possible. He pursed his lips for a moment, frowning as he wondered whether he dared spare any of his resources, but then made his decision.

'Lieutenant Ichsan found you,' he said simply. 'So Lieutenant Ichsan will have to escort you to Djakarta.'

Ten minutes later, still dazed and helpless in the fast swirl of events, Lorna was again sitting in the jeep and heading west into the darkness. Lieutenant Ichsan was at the wheel beside her, and two armed Indonesian soldiers sat in the cramped rear seats with their rifles upright between their knees. Her changed circumstances seemed unbelievable. Less than twenty-four hours ago she had been trying desperately to escape from the Indonesian Navy, and now she was under the protection of the Indonesian Army. It made her realize that in the present state of chaotic flux anything could happen, and nothing could be expected to remain unchanged.

The roads were still packed with refugees, many of them pushing handcarts or bicycles. They were in a state of milling panic, like blind sheep, not knowing where they were going or what they were hoping to achieve. Some were still searching for a rumoured oasis of sunlight, others were fleeing from religious strife. The aftermath of the cloud was worse than the aftermath of any war.

The crowds made driving slow and difficult, and even when the surrounding darkness became absolute again, signalling that it was technically night, the hordes of struggling people still clogged the way ahead.

At the outset Ichsan had tried to engage her in conversation. He was a slim, handsome young man with a pencil line moustache, and his flashing smiles told her that he clearly fancied himself as a ladies' man. He was also obviously intrigued by this beautiful raven-haired woman which the generous fates had so unexpectedly placed in his charge.

Lorna found herself unable to respond. She was close to the point of exhaustion, and she was still grief- and guilt-stricken over what had happened to Sumo. She blamed herself, because she knew that if she had had the courage to go alone, she could have persuaded him not to enter Indramaju. He had wanted to return to Batang, where the widowed mother he had worried about must now be doomed to starve without him.

After a few unsuccessful attempts to draw her out, Ichsan gave up. He knew she had been through a traumatic experience, and although he was visibly disappointed he soon found that he needed all his concentration for the task of driving. Progress was slow, sometimes a crawl, and with the rare spurts never exceeding thirty miles per hour. Most of the time he was honking his horn to clear the way.

After the first hour fatigue took over, and despite the bumping and the jolting and the noise Lorna nodded into sleep. The rest of the journey took on more and more the ill-defined, eerie qualities of a nightmare. Half-awake and half-sleeping she was conveyed along the endless river of lost souls, seeing brief glimpses of their tortured faces in the weaving splashes of torchlight. She heard their sobs and moans and banshee wails, and the scenes that were shrouded in darkness were all the more exaggerated in her fevered imagination. It was a voyage through Hell, and all the pity that was in her flowed out to the poor wretches on every side, until she was left drained and weak and emotionally empty.

It lasted for eight hours, although it seemed like eternity. Ichsan stopped twice, but only to let one of his soldiers take a turn at the wheel. When the jeep entered Djakarta he was again driving, and as they neared the city centre the human traffic flow eased. They passed more military vehicles and roadblocks with troops, and it was immediately obvious that the capital was under a tight curfew and martial law.

When the familiar frontage of the Celebes Hotel appeared Lorna was too stiff and stupefied to make any immediate move. Ichsan stopped the jeep, switched off the engine, and then got out to walk round the bonnet and help her. He walked with her up the steps and into the foyer, and there, reluctantly, he said goodbye.

'My duty is in Indramaju,' he apologized. 'I must return to my unit. I wish you a safe journey back to New York.'

Lorna thanked him. He gave her another of his flashing smiles, a smart military salute, and then he was gone.

Lorna watched the jeep drive away before she turned to the reception desk and learned that the rest of her UN party had left two days ago without her. It was bad news, but not totally unexpected.

She went up to her room, showered to wash off the mud of the rice fields, and then treated her livid collection of welts and bruises with antiseptic cream and surgical sticking tape. She dressed carefully in clean clothes and then packed her smallest suitcase with the things she considered essential. She saw no point in wasting time and left immediately for the airport.

The hotel reception desk could give her no information about flights, but they did manage to call up a taxi. She endured another ghastly dream journey, struggling to stay awake, but at last she was deposited at the airport.

More bad news awaited her. The world air routes were in chaos, all out-going schedules were cancelled, and no one knew when they might be restored. Most definitely there were no known connections to New York, or even the United States.

'There must be something,' Lorna argued desperately. 'There must be a plane of some kind going somewhere!'

The harassed young woman behind the departures desk conferred with a colleague, and then offered a faint ray of hope.

'Perhaps there will be a plane. A Japan Airlines Flight is due in from Colombo in ninety minutes. Perhaps in these conditions it will not land, but it may have to take on fuel. It is bound for Tokyo. We think if it does land it will try to take off again.'

Tokyo was one step nearer to New York, and the Japanese were more efficient than the Indonesians. Lorna decided that if she could get to Japan then she might be able to get an on-going air connection, or perhaps a ship across the Pacific. Any move was better than staying here.

'Please,' she said without hesitation, 'book me a seat on the flight to Tokyo.'

Two hours later she was watching through the plate-glass window of the departure lounge when the red and green landing lights of the JAL flight appeared above the far end of the main runway. The plane was late. She had almost given up hope, and she watched with indrawn breath as the lights glided slowly down toward her. The aircraft took shape as its flight and passenger cabin lights became visible, and she recognized the huge, hump-backed silhouette of a jumbo jet.

It occurred to her that the plane was coming in rather fast.

Afterwards she could think of a hundred reasons for what had happened next. It seemed that only half the airport staff had reported for duty, and so the airport was functioning with only partial efficiency. Whole sections of the runway lights were out, and the control tower was operating under some reduced form of emergency lighting.

Probably the pilot was confused, possibly he was not receiving adequate landing instructions from ground control, and certainly he was under the most terrible strain.

Whatever the reason, the giant aircraft badly miscalculated its approach. Lorna recoiled with horror as it hurtled out of the blackness, coming in too high and overshooting the misleading, broken pattern of the runway lights.

For a few seconds she thought it was going to crash straight through the departure lounge and land on top of her, and then at the last moment the pilot swerved. She saw the monstrous silver underbelly slide up and away to her right, as though she was underwater and watching the sideways flip of a great whale, and then it hit the control tower.

The jumbo jet exploded in boiling wreaths of red and orange fire, crushing the control tower beneath its blazing steel breast. It had belly-flopped, and broke its back with a deafening, grinding roar. The flight deck seemed to slide back into the fuselage as it folded up, the whole aircraft crushing itself like a concertina. Then two more secondary explosions scattered the wreckage over the runways in a shower of shooting fireballs.

Lorna had thrown herself flat in the nearest corner a split second before the windows of the departure lounge caved inward from the fearful blast. It was as though an atomic bomb had been dropped and the whole building swayed and shuddered. The plaster cracked and crashed down from the ceiling and the lights went out. Lorna's head was reeling from the sound and she felt as though her eardrums had burst.

When she was able to pick herself up she moved gingerly over the piles of broken glass and debris. The heat from the inferno hit her in the face as she stared out through the jagged opening where the window had been. The scene of fire and carnage was a glimpse into Satan's abyss, and left her numb with despair.

God alone knew how many people had just died, and it was obvious that no more aircraft would be able to land or depart until the wreckage had been cleared away.

Djakarta International Airport was closed.

She was trapped on Java.

9

Three days had passed and there was no longer any hope that the cloud would pass over. The scientists everywhere were agreed that it was being held like an outer envelope above the atmosphere by the gravitational pull of the Earth. The only life-bearing planet in the solar system was locked in a bubble of black gas, and there was no way the bubble could be made to burst. The planet was already dying, and the countdown of its last days had begun.

'One fart from space —' Glenn Anderson had commented bitterly, off the record and for the ears of Merle Forrester alone.' — One million years of evolution, but that's all it takes to wipe us out. Just one stupid, little aimless fart from outer space.'

'We're not wiped out yet.'

Forrester was reduced to skin and bone, hovering on the edge of a complete mental breakdown, but he still shared the President's Crisis Control room with direct links to NASA and every other major space agency.

'We've established that the cloud has a strong magnetic field. Some of our people think that could be the key.'

'How, for Christ's sake?'

'We don't know yet.' Forrester was nearly in tears. 'But we're working on it. It's gonna take time.'

'We don't have much time.' Anderson didn't want to see his Scientific Adviser crack up, he didn't think anyone else could handle the job any better, but he had to pile on the relentless pressure. 'We have to disperse this thing. Or get it moving. We need a breakthrough.'

'If you whip some of these boys too hard they go to pieces.' Forrester defended the whole scientific brotherhood. 'You screw them up too much and they can't think at all.'

Like I'm screwing you up, Anderson realized, and he turned away and sat down heavily behind his desk. He couldn't look at Forrester for a moment and his gaze settled instead on the framed portrait of Lucy and the kids. He hadn't seen much of them since the cloud had hit, and every time he looked at the picture a goddamned lump came up in his throat.

'Merle,' he said firmly, 'we gotta solve this thing. There's gotta be something we can do.'

In New York, as in Washington and every other city in the developed world, the lights had been burning nonstop for more than eighty hours. The big neon displays above Times Square and Broadway had been switched off to compensate for the continuous hours without daylight, but it wasn't enough. Maintaining the power supplies had become a massive headache for every electricity generating company, and the problems multiplied. So far New York had been lucky, but elsewhere the overloaded power lines had failed and caused blackouts. Soon it was inevitable that the companies would have to enforce selective cuts.

Allington had already initiated power-saving measures at the UN. His staff was international, its technicians and diplomats drawn from every country in the world. Many of them had already left to go home, and so he was able to shut down whole offices that could no longer function. Most of these were on the middle and lower floors. The upper storeys still blazed with light.

The office of the Secretary-General was never empty. Since his return from Washington Allington had put in twenty hours each day, eating and catnapping on the job. When he did go home for a change of clothes and a few hours uninterrupted sleep, Luis Valdez took his place. They now had a hot line to the White House, and they ensured that there was always one of them available to take a call.

While they waited between bulletins from the Crisis Control Room they had to cope with the flood of reports pouring in from hundreds of other sources all over the world. Each one was a plea for help, a cry for some urgent action to be taken before it was too late. Allington tried to answer them all, if only to let the embattled governments and relief agencies know that they had not been forgotten, that efforts were still being made to combat the cloud, and that the UN was still in existence.

When he considered the difficulties of communication, the weight of reports getting through was staggering. Every communications satellite in orbit was now inside the cloud, and they had all gone dead immediately on being engulfed. The information arriving on his desk was travelling by more old-fashioned methods, and at least half the world was totally cut off anyway. Still the paperwork, the cables and the telephone calls flowed in.

Allington tried to keep up with every new development. There was little he could do about any of it in the short term, but if NASA could find a way to get rid of the cloud there would be a vast task of reconstruction in every corner of the globe. He had to believe that NASA would succeed, that somehow the Earth would survive, and so already he was calculating priorities and resources. It was the only way to keep going.

He was working at his desk, talking with Valdez, when one of his staff knocked on the door and announced that Julius Mangala wanted to see him. Allington stifled a groan. He had not eaten for five hours and he had not slept for eighteen. He had just been on the point of handing over to Valdez and taking a break, but he knew he could not afford to offend the African.

'Send him in,' he said reluctantly.

Mangala appeared a moment later, his broad shoulders almost filling the doorway. Today he wore a dark blue suit, but with the inevitable red silk tie and the discreet gold cuff links. Communist red and capitalist gold — they were the symbols of his belief in a fundamental Marxism that was not intended to go hand in hand with poverty. It made Allington realize with sudden insight and some surprise that in his own way Mangala was also an idealist.

'Hello, Richard. Hello, Luis.' Mangala's tone was sombre, his face serious.

'Hello, Julius. Come in and take a seat.'

Allington got up and moved a third chair over to his desk. Valdez shifted to make room and Mangala sat down heavily. The African wore the mantle of a man who had come with grim purpose.

'Is there any more news?' he demanded.

'Not since yesterday,' Allington said as he returned to his chair. 'The space scientists are still studying the cloud, but so far they haven't thought of a way to remove it.' He paused. 'You know that I will inform you — and the entire General Assembly — as soon as I learn of any new development.'

Mangala nodded briefly, as though the promise was immaterial. 'Yes. Yes I know that. But I have decided that I wish to call another full meeting of the General Assembly as soon as possible.'

Allington stared at him. The alarm bells were instantly jangling and he knew that he was about to be faced with yet another package of trouble.

'Is that wise, Julius, after this morning?'

He stressed the words gently, for it was less than ten hours since they had addressed the assembled delegates with the bleak news that the cloud was here to stay. It was left to the individual governments to decide whether they would be equally frank with their populations, or whether they would continue to maintain the belief that eventually the Earth would emerge from the cloud. The people needed hope, but Allington was determined that the governments would have facts. As usual the session had ended in an uproar, verging on to another riot.

'It is necessary,' Mangala answered him flatly. 'This morning, and ever since this cloud arrived, the delegates have listened to nothing but you making weak excuses for the Western space nations. It is time they heard something else. It is time to do something positive!'

'What do you mean?'

'I mean that the Third World is suffering too much — and the rich world is not suffering enough. The West has all the big stockpiles of oil and coal for creating electricity. And the rich nations are selfishly burning up the power supplies night and day to create their own light — while the rest of the world disintegrates into pagan darkness. There is no justice! The West is responsible for this situation, but, as always, it is Africa and Asia which suffers the greatest hardship.'

It was a fine speech and Allington could not deny it. He was tense and he tried to answer calmly. 'I agree, Julius. The reality is harsh and there is no justice, but what can we do about it?'

Mangala leaned forward. He was excited and a sheen of sweat gleamed on his black face. 'I will call for a resolution. The United Nations will demand an immediate and equal redistribution of all the world's energy resources.'

'Electricity can only flow through cables,' Allington reminded him patiently. 'You can't ship it out to where there are no grid networks.'

'It is the coal and oil which fire the power stations which must be shipped out,' Mangala retorted angrily.

'And the gasoline to drive transport. The foodstuffs, and blankets and warm clothing, it all must be shared out where it is needed most.'

'We are doing everything we can —'

'We are not doing enough. The peoples of Africa and Asia are starving. It is getting colder without the sunlight. They are freezing. Where there is electricity the power stations are running low on coal and oil. Soon there will be no light, even in the cities. The West must give the Third World an equal opportunity to survive. All the food and energy resources *must* be fairly distributed. Those who have plenty *must* give to those who have nothing. I will propose this resolution to the General Assembly.'

'It will be a popular demand,' Allington said wearily. 'And, of course, you will win a majority vote. You'll get the resolution passed, but once again the United Nations will be voting for something it cannot possibly hope to see implemented.'

'This resolution must be implemented. It must be enforced. It will carry the whole moral weight of world opinion.'

'And when has the moral weight of world opinion served any purpose?' Allington asked frankly. 'Except when the governments we try to bring together are both looking for a way of saving face.'

'This is not a petty border dispute between two nations. This is a catastrophe which affects the whole world.'

'Precisely. And it is simply too catastrophic for the United Nations to go on repeating its past mistakes. You can get your resolution passed, but we both know the rich nations will ignore it. There is no way we can make them share out their reserves. You'll only succeed in what the General Assembly has been doing for the past ten years, which is widening the gulf between rich and poor. Surely it must be better to wait until we can see a real solution where we can all pull together.'

'What solution?' Mangala snarled bitterly.

'At the moment I can't see any —'

'Of course not. You are blinded by your stupid paperwork.' Mangala grabbed up handfuls of the reports and letters littering Allington's desk and hurled them about the room in a fury of emotion. 'Is this all the United Nations can do?' His voice rang with contempt. 'To sit at desks and read reports. And then make more reports. And then read reports about reports. This gets us nowhere.'

'Julius, please!' Valdez was shocked but moved quickly to intervene. He grabbed the African's arm with both hands before it could sweep more papers to the floor, and then his gaze switched rapidly back to Allington who had jumped to his feet.

'Richard,' I think you should know that in Angola things are very bad. The power station outside Luanda has already broken down. The city is totally without light.'

Allington understood, and slowly he sat down.

'I'm sorry, Julius, but the facts still remain. If you pass this resolution you will only pull the United Nations even further apart.' He paused, and then made an effort to reach the man, choosing his words with infinite care.

'Julius, I think we both want the same thing, you and I — but we have to recognize the limitations of the organization in which we serve. It is easy for me to make the compromise, because my country is one of those which enjoys the best of it. For you it is much more difficult. But somehow we have to work together, and wait until the direction and moment is right, if we are to achieve anything at all. Please try to bear with me.'

Mangala was silent for almost a minute, struggling to control himself and glaring at his own big hands pressing down on the edge of the desk. Then he looked up and spoke stubbornly.

'I will call a meeting of the General Assembly and propose my resolution. It is my right.'

Valdez left with Mangala to attend to the details, and Allington remained alone to tidy up his disrupted office. He gathered up the strewn papers and dumped them in the centre of his desk. He stood over them for several minutes, frowning, and wondering whether his actions were as futile and meaningless as Mangala's, and then he sat down to sort them slowly into order.

Most of them he had already read. America, Europe and most of North Africa were in total darkness, and over Asia the twilight patches were slowly disappearing as the cloud found its own level. From inside Russia and the Soviet Communist Bloc there were no reports at all. The iron curtain had been clamped down tight and no information was getting out.

Many of the reports showed that the advent of Doomsday had done nothing to improve the historical stupidity of mankind. In a score of places familiar disputes had flared again as opportunist military regimes had attempted to mount sneak attacks on old enemies under the freak cover of darkness. Syria had launched a surprise strike on Israel over the Golan Heights. Guatemala had invaded neighbouring Belize. In Taiwan Red Chinese landing craft had stormed the beaches.

Behind the veil of continuous night, free from the restrictions of superpower satellite surveillance, the war-hawks and dictators were pursuing their petty ambitions of revenge, greed or conquest. The fighting was fast and furious, as the instigators hoped that before the sun shone through they would be able to present the world with a successful coup d'etat, or a fait accompli.

As if the calamitous evil of the cloud was not enough it seemed that every political, tribal and religious jealousy in the world had been revived and inflamed. The old troublespots of Beirut and Belfast, and virtually every capital city in Latin America, were involved in orgies of sectarian killings. Hundreds of wild-eyed prophets, priests and cult-leaders, were crying that this was The End of the World, and advocating some kind of Holy Slaughter to appease their gods. Tribal blood feuds and purges had erupted all over Africa, the Middle East, India and Indonesia —

Shock stopped Allington reading as he came to the accounts of the Hindu-Muslim massacres in Indonesia. As far as he knew Lorna Maxwell was still stranded somewhere on Java, and the thought that she might already have been killed by some rampaging mob was like a cold axe-blow to his heart.

He pushed the reports aside and stared at the three telephones on his desk. They were useless instruments, for over the past few days he had made a dozen attempts to contact the Celebes Hotel in Djakarta, and all had been in vain. He knew that the main group of the UN Human Rights Commission was on its way back to New York, but that Lorna had been left behind. And that was all he knew. Thirty-six hours ago Lorna had still been absent from her hotel, and since then all telephone links with Djakarta had broken down.

Hundreds of thousands of people had died in one way or another since the cloud had arrived, and for the first time Allington faced the fact that Lorna might be among them. It was a frightening thought, as frightening as when he had first learned of the coming of the cloud, and he was stunned by his own sense of sudden loss. He had been happy with his wife, and after she had died he had believed that it would not be possible to fall in love again.

But the years had passed. Lorna had come to fill the empty void, and now he felt all the acute grief of losing another loved one.

Blackness swept over him, a blackness of mood that exceeded even the blackness of the cloud. He felt desperately lonely, as though already he was the last man on Earth. There was no way he could reach Lorna, but on a sudden impulse he picked up the nearest telephone and asked for a line through to England.

He could not speak to the woman he loved, but he had a daughter he loved as dearly. Barbara was his only child, and his own terrible loneliness made him feel suddenly guilty. He had neglected her over the past two years because their careers had pulled them apart. Now she was alone in England, just as he was alone in New York, and that was wrong.

He could not go to her, his place was here at the UN, but perhaps she could come to him.

He waited anxiously for the connection to be made, praying that it was not already too late. Transport and communications were breaking down so fast that many places were already as remote as other planets.

He had to wait for an hour and thirty minutes, but then with infinite relief he heard her voice.

10

For the first time in her life Lorna was glad that both her parents were dead. Her father she remembered fondly as a big man who made visits, always bearing presents, always smelling faintly of crude oil, and always wearing an open-neck shirt and a wide, infectious grin. The visits made her mother bright and cheerful, and Lorna had shared those concentrated bursts of happiness. They came to an end when Lorna was twelve years old, and big Joe Maxwell was killed in a drilling accident in Alaska.

The oilman left his wife and daughter with a healthy insurance policy which cared for all their material needs. It was enough to put Lorna through university in Bogota where she gained degrees in sociology and economics. Through her mother she felt a close affinity to the Indian people who formed most of Columbia's poor. From her father she had inherited the strong streak of American determination which was dominant in her character. Together with a crusading compassion that was wholly her own, these qualities had led her into social work for the Columbian government where she had quickly become a driving force of considerable impact.

Her efforts to re-house the slum dwellers, and to give them better schooling, sanitation and health facilities had not always been welcome. There were other government officials, most of them in posts above her head, who preferred to bulldoze the squalid shacks out of the way, hoping that the occupants would then disperse back into the countryside and conveniently cease to exist in the cities. She had tried to do too much, and become a thorn in too many entrenched flanks, and so perhaps it was mostly to get her out of the way that she had been appointed Columbia's youngest ever Ambassador to the United Nations.

Lorna's mother had not lived quite long enough to see her move into the arena of international diplomacy. It was a loss which had saddened her deeply at the time. But now — as she stumbled away from the ruins of Djakarta airport — she was glad they were both at rest. If they had been alive, they would have been apart, as they almost always were. Her mother would have been alone in Bogota, and her father isolated on yet another drilling contract in Africa or Arabia, or some other God-forsaken spot on the Earth's surface.

Now the whole world was a God-forsaken place, and she would not have wished her present anguish of loneliness upon her worst enemy, much less those she had loved.

She had been running, her chest was heaving and the weight of her suitcase was breaking her arm. The bright red glow from the fiercely burning jumbo jet was fading behind her, and the terrible darkness was closing round her once more. She was moving blindly down a road she couldn't see and at last she came to a gasping stop.

Ahead was the black unknown. She was running to nowhere, and slowly she turned to look back towards the airport. In her panic she had fled from the scene of disaster, but now a part of her was being drawn back to the warmth and the light.

She was so wretched and confused that part of her wanted to give up and die. She had already been through so much that her strength and courage were at their lowest ebb. She felt that she couldn't take any more.

Yes, she was very glad that both her parents were at

peace. Now that the black cloud was slowly killing off the whole planet it was easier to have no one to worry or care. It was better to have no home to go to. She was glad she had no close relatives, and few close friends. She had no one really important, and that was good. No one — except Richard.

Richard — his face loomed large in her memory and the tears ran down her cheeks. She remembered the earnest dinner conversations that had gradually become more relaxed, in restaurants that had gradually become more candlelit and intimate. The evenings at the theatre and ballet, the touch of his hand, and the warmth of his kiss. It had unlocked something which surged so powerfully within her that she had been afraid of it. Her head had been in such a whirl that she couldn't be sure if it was right, for him or for her. So she had put them both to the test of parting, and lived to regret it.

She cursed herself for a fool and wished that she had never left New York. Her emotions tumbled and she could no longer think straight, and she had never felt so helpless in her life.

She did not know how long she stood crying, but slowly she became aware that she was not alone. Something that rattled and creaked had moved up behind her, and when she turned her head she saw a *betjak*, one of the thousands of tricycle rickshaws which were normally as thick as flies in the streets of Djakarta.

The *betjak* driver had rigged up an oil lamp which swung dangerously from the hood of his rickshaw. In its light she saw him standing patiently by the tricycle. He was a thin man, with spindly, muscle-knotted legs and arms. When she turned he smiled hopefully.

'Where you go, miss? I take you — where you want to go?'

'To America,' she said bitterly, even though it was impossible.

The smile became a frown, and there was a long silence.

The *betjak* driver looked towards the burning airport, and finally summed it up.

'No airplane now, miss. Perhaps ship? You want go to docks? I take.'

Lorna stared at him. It was as good as anywhere, and she could see no other alternative. She certainly could not stand here for ever, crying at the roadside. She nodded dumbly and the *betjak* driver hurried forward to take her suitcase and help her into the rickshaw. Quickly he turned the whole thing round and climbed on to the saddle of the tricycle. He had found a fare and feared that if he hesitated she might change her mind.

The *betjak* bumped slowly back into the city. They were not a swift mode of transport at any time and now the driver had to take extra care. The oil lamp jerked and swayed on its piece of string, throwing a small, moving pool of light, dazzling Lorna and threatening to spill hot oil into her lap at every pothole. She cowered away from it, clutching her suitcase beside her, and then she rested her head back and closed her eyes. She could only trust in the good intentions of her driver.

It took two hours to reach the docks, and by then the streets were again filled with *betjaks*, motor cycles and people, most of them carrying some kind of torch or handlamp. Lorna guessed that the curfew hours were past, and people were again hunting for food, or to fulfill their other needs. Fear gripped her again as she remembered Indramaju, but here there were plenty of soldiers and military vehicles in evidence, and the whole weird atmosphere was wrapped in a tense, almost brittle calm.

As they entered the dock area her driver began shouting to other *betjak* drivers and the people passing by. She guessed he was questioning for information and he made several false stops and turns before he brought her to a lighted office building with a sign proclaiming THE DUTCH EAST INDIES STEAMSHIP COMPANY. He pulled to a weary stop, twisting on his saddle to face her.

'No ship for America, miss,' he said unhappily. 'But this company have ship sail for Singapore. Only this one ship sail from Djakarta.'

Lorna bit her lip, but Singapore was on most of the main Far East shipping routes, and the airport there might still be functioning. At least she would be off Java.

'I'll check it out,' she decided. 'Will you wait for me?'

'I come with you, miss.' The *betjak* driver did not want to lose her any more than she wanted to lose him. He picked up her suitcase and trailed behind as she went into the shipping office.

The room was crowded, with half a dozen loud-voiced arguments in progress, and it was some minutes before she could force her way up to the counter and attract the attention of one of the two sweating clerks. Her voice registered over two or three others because she spoke English, and the man was obviously seeking escape from the babble of his own kind. He turned to her with some relief, but his answer to her query was a flat disappointment.

'I am very sorry. The only ship we have sailing is the *Java Queen*. She is due to leave in two hours. All her passenger cabins are fully booked. Most of them were booked many days ago.'

'I must get a passage of some kind.' Lorna saw her only chance of escaping from Indonesia slipping from her grasp and her pleading became desperate. 'I'll sleep on deck if necessary.'

The clerk shook his head. 'I am sorry. The *Java Queen* already has more than her full complement of deck passengers. That is why all these people are arguing. They all want to go to Singapore.'

'Please,' Lorna begged. 'I must get away from here. I must get back to America.' In her despair she launched into the anguished tale of her misfortunes, but the clerk's face only hardened and he shrugged helplessly. She was on the point of giving up, but then she was interrupted by a deep, cheerful voice with a thick Dutch accent.

'So what's the trouble, hey?'

Lorna turned. The voice belonged to a man of about thirty-five who had moved up to lean one elbow casually on the counter beside her. He wore seaboots, tough cord trousers and a seafaring jacket. A tousle of blonde curls showed under the pushed-back peak of his cap, and there was an easy grin on his suntanned face.

It was on the tip of her tongue to tell him to mind his own business, but she needed every friend she could get. She told her story again and the blonde man looked her up and down with speculative eyes. He clearly liked what he saw.

'It's okay,' he told her when she had finished. 'My name's Carl Drekker. I'm Chief Officer of the *Java Queen*. We can squeeze another one on board. I'll fix it for you.'

He waved aside her thanks and turned to the booking clerk, speaking in a language which she guessed was Dutch, although she didn't understand. There was another argument, the clerk was protesting, but Drekker had a way of over-riding all objections. He reached over the counter to pick up a blank ticket, borrowed the clerk's pen, and scrawled in a cabin number. The man took back his pen and the ticket, staring doubtfully at the latter, and then suddenly a sly, knowing grin spread over his face.

'It's all settled,' Drekker told Lorna. 'Just pay the man your money. I have business to attend to, but I'll see you on board later.' He gave her another grin, a parting wave, and then he was gone through the crowd as suddenly as he had appeared.

Lorna stared after him and frowned. She was far from being stupid and warning bells were already ringing in the back of her brain. However, when she turned back to the booking counter the clerk had filled out the rest of the ticket except for her name. It was that or nothing so she opened up her shoulder bag and paid.

Her *betjak* driver took her the rest of the way to the ship. It proved to be an old freighter, streaked with rust like some ancient zebra of the sea. Pools of light spilled down from her mastheads, but the smokestack was grimed so black it was invisible against the night. Lorna had even worse misgivings as she looked it over, but still there was no choice.

The *betjak* squeaked to a stop at the foot of the gangway and the driver dismounted and looked at her hopefully. It was his turn to beg.

'Please, miss, very long way from airport, and I have six children. Give me ten dollars.'

He had done his best for her and Lorna was grateful. She gave him a twenty-dollar bill and wished she could have afforded more.

Then, slowly, she carried her suitcase up the gangway.

Lorna was fast asleep when the *Java Queen* cast off her mooring ropes and moved slowly out to sea. A lascar steward had shown her to a single cabin on the upper deck, grinning lewdly as he let her in. She had ignored the grin, just as she had ignored the smile of the man who had checked her ticket, and the leers of some of the crew. She knew there was trouble coming but for the moment she was too tired to care.

The cabin was clean and tidy and it was a relief to close the door and be alone. Except for dozing briefly on the sampan and in Lieutenant Ichsan's bouncing jeep she had not slept for over seventy hours. She was on the point of collapse and there was neither strength nor will in her to unpack. She pulled off her shoes, skirt and jumper and crawled into the single bunk. Immediately she fell into the deep sleep of total exhaustion.

Carl Drekker spent the first six hours of the voyage on the bridge. Without sun or stars to fix their position it was not going to be an easy trip, and the ship's captain was relying entirely upon his compass, and careful chart plotting of their speed, direction and distance covered.

Their course was due north-east for the first 260 miles, which would place them in the Karimata Strait midway between Borneo and the large islands off Sumatra. There the *Java Queen* would swing her bow through a ninety-degree turn to head due north-west on the next 700-mile tack up to the Singapore Strait. Hopefully there would still be shore lights to guide them up the narrow waters of the strait to the sprawling island port that was their destination.

The captain had a wife in Singapore, which was his main reason for making the scheduled run. Chief Officer Drekker had a mistress in Singapore, but he also had a mistress in Djakarta and another in Bangkok. Any port was much the same to him and any woman was a challenge. He was a born seaman and the ship was his home. As yet he had no urge to find a wife, for he had found that his rank and his blonde good looks attracted a plentiful supply of women to slake his powerful sex drive.

It was quiet on the bridge. Spooky was how Drekker would have described it. The sea was calm and the *Java Queen* was like a spectral steel coffin sliding through the unnatural blackness. Drekker could not help thinking of Wagner's Flying Dutchman, doomed to sail his phantom ship for ever until the Day of Judgement. The only difference was that for the *Java Queen*, and all the world around her, the Day of Judgement had already arrived.

When the ship's bell signalled the change of duty

watch Drekker was relieved by the Second Officer. He was glad to get away from the morbid atmosphere of the bridge, but that was not the only reason for his cheerful whistle as he strode back to his cabin. He had waited in keen anticipation for this moment, and already his thoughts had made him randy.

He stopped whistling as he opened the cabin door, turning the handle quietly. The light was on inside, and he paused with a feeling of deep, warm satisfaction as he saw the woman sound asleep in his bunk.

She was lying on her back, her rich dark hair tossed carelessly across his pillow, her eyes closed and her breathing slow and heavy. Her hand was clenched tight around the edge of the sheet, and in her dreams or nightmares she had pushed the covers below the level of her breasts. She was not wholly naked as he would have wished, but the white silk cups of her bra were an exciting contrast to the smooth, delicious, coffee-coloured breasts.

Jesus, he thought, this one was really beautiful. He had tried them all, Chinese, Javanese and white, and all shades in between, but this one promised to be definitely something special. She had it all, in all the right places, and she had class. Even in her sleep she had class. He licked his lips and realized that already he had a king-sized hard on.

He flipped his cap into the corner, sat down on the only chair and quickly pulled off his boots. His jacket and shirt he tossed after the cap, but then he hesitated. He was tempted to strip off his pants and dive straight into bed on top of her, but that was a bit too fast, even for Carl Drekker. To be polite he would at least have to wake her.

For almost a minute he just sat and watched her. She looked so vulnerable, and was so heavily asleep that he began to feel guilty at the thought of disturbing her. But she was irresistible. The more he looked at her the more he wanted her, and at last he reached forward with one hand and gently eased one coffee cream breast from its silk cup. Still she did not wake, and he leaned down to kiss the ripe, dark nipple.

Lorna jerked as though she had been stung. For a moment her body thrashed wildly in the bed, and then her eyes blinked open and consciousness came back to her in an urgent rush. She clasped a hand to the violated breast and screamed.

'Easy, easy now. It's okay.' Drekker smiled at her. 'I'm your friend, remember?'

Lorna sat up in the bunk, clawing the sheet around her and shrinking back until her bare shoulders pressed against the cold steel of the bulkhead. She had to fight to control her own hysteria, and when she spoke her voice was cracked and shaking.

'Just what the hell do you think you're doing?'

Drekker shrugged and sat back in the chair. His naked chest was a lush forest of tight blonde curls and he still expected his hard physique to prove attractive. His easy smile was only briefly apologetic.

'Perhaps I make a mistake, hey? I rush you too fast. I should have kissed you first on the cheek, more like a gentleman than a rough sailor.'

'You have definitely made a mistake,' Lorna snapped at him. 'Please get out of my cabin.'

'Your cabin?' His smile became incredulous.

'My cabin,' Lorna repeated. 'I'm a fare-paying passenger, remember.'

Drekker looked down at her suitcase still standing in the middle of the floor, and her outer clothes dropped on top of it. He realized then that she had made no close inspection of the cabin and decided it was time to enlighten her.

He stood up and opened the wardrobe door, revealing a row of shirts and jackets, most of them with the three gold bars of a Chief Officer on the shoulder.

'My clothes,' he said calmly. He pulled open drawers

and stirred up layers of socks and underclothes. 'My socks.' And then looking back at her with final emphasis. '*My cabin!*'

Lorna felt trapped. She said weakly, 'The steward brought me here. There must have been a misunderstanding.'

'No misunderstanding.' Drekker smiled and sat down again. 'There are no other cabins available. You are my guest. It is okay.'

He reached out to touch her hand and Lorna flinched. 'It is not okay. I don't know what you expect, Mr. Drekker —'

'Carl. You can call me Carl. And you must know what I expect.'

'Mr. Drekker, I'm sorry —'

'Carl,' he repeated. He moved again, faster than before, and caught her hand and held it. 'Look, I am sorry if I rush you. But in three days we will be in Singapore, and much of my time I must spend on the bridge. You can share my cabin with pleasure, but I am not a saint or a charity. Don't expect me to sleep on the floor.'

'Please,' Lorna said as firmly as she could. 'Will you go outside for a minute and let me get dressed?'

'Why get dressed?' He jerked her to him, still smiling but with some exasperation. 'Haven't you noticed the World is coming to an End? So why be stupid? What is the point? Let us enjoy ourselves while we can.'

'Please — ' Lorna struggled furiously, but his grip was strong and the more she fought against him the more she inflamed him. She lost her grip on the sheets and he swept them away, leaving nothing but the flimsy material of her bra and panties between her cringing flesh and his hard, groping hands.

'Take it easy. Relax,' Drekker gasped breathlessly, and when she screamed again he tried to cover her lips with his own. With one hand he was clawing at his belt, and as he pulled the buckle open the terrified Lorna knew that he intended to rape her. She couldn't escape his hungry kiss and so she did the next best thing. She opened her mouth and sank her teeth hard into his lower lip.

Drekker yelled with the pain and lurched back. Lorna quickly squirmed to the bottom end of the narrow bunk, but she was still trapped in the cabin. Drekker was on his feet and blocking the doorway. He held one hand to his mouth and when he looked down at his fingers they were smeared with blood from his cut lip.

'You bitch,' he snarled at her. 'You want to play like a whore, hey? Okay, that's what you are — a whore!'

He pushed his trousers and underpants down over his hips, kicked them away, and then threw himself at her again.

Lorna had a few split seconds to prepare herself as he cleared the last garment from his ankles, and she used them to look desperately for a weapon. She found one in the port key, the large, open-ended spanner that was used to bolt down the steel porthole covers in bad weather. It was hanging beside the porthole and she grabbed for it as Drekker landed on top of her.

The impact flattened her, crushing the air out of her lungs, but he only succeeded in pinning one of her arms. The hand wielding the spanner was free, and for the moment his whole mind was concentrated on ripping off her pants. Lorna knew she would only get one chance, one blow, and she would have to make it count. She flung her arm back, and then with all her strength brought it forward again to smash the port key against the back of Drekker's skull.

The Dutchman went limp, slumping against her. He was unconscious and it was another minute before she could summon up enough effort to roll him over on to the floor.

She was shaking like a leaf but she dressed as quickly as she could. Then, with one last fearful glance at the sprawled, naked body of Drekker, she picked up her suitcase and hurried out of the cabin.

She found her way down to the lower decks at the stern of the ship where the steerage-class passengers were huddled in groups in the alleyways and in the open. She chose a patch of black shadow behind a ventilator shaft where the ship's lights did not reach, and lay down beside her suitcase on the bare deckboards. She still had the steel port key clenched tight in her fist and she was determined not to lose it.

She had left Drekker alive, and she wondered if he would leave her alone now, or whether he would come looking for her once he had recovered his senses.

11

Barbara had automatically agreed to join her father in New York, but afterwards, when the immediate excitement of hearing his voice had passed, she found the very thought of the journey terrified her. She desperately wanted to see him again, and making the promise had been easy. Putting it into effect meant leaving the warm and lighted safety of Herstmonceaux Castle, to brave the cold and hostile darkness of a frightening new world, which was altogether a different matter. The idea of *being* with her father was wonderful. The difficulties in actually *getting* to him were daunting, to say the least.

They were still receiving the radio and TV news, so she knew that in most parts of the country the trains had already stopped running. Rail travel was a thing of the past, and road travel was slowly slipping and sliding to a halt. The weather had tightened its icy grip, and the English were never well prepared even for an ordinary winter. Over the past few days some six inches of snow had fallen, and Scotland and the Yorkshire moors were predictably cut off by blizzards. In the south most of the main roads were still passable, but only just.

Allington had advised her to hurry while there was still time, but already Barbara had the horrible feeling that it was too late. All the flights out of Heathrow Airport were severely disrupted, if not grounded, and even if she could get there it might prove impossible to find a plane with a crew still prepared to face the dangers of flying blind across the Atlantic.

She began making telephone calls, but even where she could get a connection and a reply very little updated information was available. The AA and the RAC were both vague on whether it was still possible to drive a car up the A22. The Meteorological Office, for long dependent upon satellite photographs to aid in making their predictions, would not hazard any kind of a weather forecast. The information desk at Heathrow was continuously engaged for three-quarters of an hour, but when she finally got through the answering voice was equally unhelpful. She could not book a flight to America and nobody knew whether there would be any more flights. However, there were passengers waiting hopefully in the departure lounge, and she was welcome to come and join them if she wished. There were no fixed schedules any more. It was all a matter of chance and luck.

Barbara put the telephone down and spent ten minutes thinking it over. Obviously the situation was not going to improve, it could only get worse. The bad road conditions were not just another January cold snap, with a comfortable thaw soon to follow. And soon the airports would be shutting down altogether. She had to choose — go to her father, and face all the dangers involved, or stay here in safe, comfortable, lonely, miserable frustration. And it was a now or never choice.

The last time she had ventured outside the castle it had ended in disaster. She shuddered as she remembered the incident, but it also had the effect of helping to make up her mind. She couldn't just sit here for ever brooding about Willoughby. She had to get up and do something, and the only thing to do was to go to New York. Or at least make the effort. If it didn't work out and she couldn't get a flight, then she could always come back again.

Quickly she began to pack, hurrying in case she lost

her own momentum and with it the determination to go on. She put on her warmest clothes, bearing in mind the bitter cold outside, and as an afterthought she raided the kitchen for sandwiches and a large flask of hot coffee to take on her journey.

Finally she said her goodbyes. They were not many, for everyone who had a home and family had already left and the castle was almost deserted. It was another reason for going and helped to strengthen her resolve.

She was in a blind man's world outside the castle; a world of bitter cold and unrelieved darkness. She needed a flashlight to find the mini, and the snow that lay all around gleamed stark white in contrast in the small pool of artificial light. The wind had drifted the snow up against the back wheels of the little car and she realized she would have to find a spade to dig it out.

Searching, even on familiar territory, was like groping her way around the bottom of a coal mine, but at last she located the building where the gardeners stored their tools. She borrowed a spade and spent half an hour clearing the snowdrift from behind the mini. She paused to get her breath back and after a moment's thought decided against returning the spade. The gardeners would never need it again, but to her it might well prove as invaluable as the flashlight. She put the spade in the boot with her suitcase, then climbed into the car and started the engine.

If the car had not started first time she might have turned back. But the mini had always been reliable. It had never let her down yet. She drew a deep breath, switched on the headlights, backed up slowly, and began her journey.

A few vehicles had been up and down the road before her, and she followed their wheel ruts where the snow was packed hard. She used second gear, her foot resting only lightly on the accelerator pedal, and the mini rolled gently toward the west gate. There were no longer any soldiers at the gate, they had all withdrawn sensibly to the castle, and she passed through without hindrance.

She got stuck after another hundred yards and had to get out and dig a path through a two-foot snowdrift. She felt scared again, realizing that although the mini was a faithful old friend it was still far from being the ideal vehicle for this particular adventure. However, she worked vigorously to clear away the snow and banish the nagging fear. It was not much more than a mile to the main road, and then only five or six miles to the Boship roundabout and the A22 to London. If she could get that far then surely the A22 must be open, and if not she could always walk back to the castle.

Provided the weather did not blow up a blizzard. . . . She shivered and paused in her digging to aim the flashlight up into the black void of the endless night. The beam wove slowly to and fro, but there were no falling snowflakes. Reassured, she grimly resumed digging.

She got the mini moving again and covered another half-mile before the back wheels began to spin and slid helplessly to another stop. Again she got out and cleared the snow to allow the back wheels to grip and get her moving once more. She had to repeat the operation three times before she at last turned on to the main road, and by then she felt exhausted. Doubts plagued her more forcefully and she knew that without the spade she would not have got this far.

From here the road improved. There had been more traffic on it and other drivers had cut passages through the drifts before her. She tried once to speed up into third gear, but the car skidded and whip-lashed on the ice and slush surface before she could regain control. After that she stayed down in second gear and continued her slow crawl.

It took her an hour to reach the roundabout. There she turned north on the A22, following the road signs for London, and mercifully there was a further improvement in the road. Until now she had not passed another vehicle, but on the A22 there were more headlight beams flashing up and down. Each brief, dazzling encounter gave her a moment of comfort. It meant that she was not entirely alone in the world. Also the increased traffic flow meant that the snow had been cut up and flung away from the road which was reasonably clear.

She eased up into top gear, still driving carefully, and at 35 mph the miles flashed by in comparison to her previous painful progress. It was only fifty miles to London and the worst was behind her. Her confidence began to climb. Then she noticed that the needle on her petrol gauge was dropping down towards empty.

It was a shock, and she swore with frustration. Normally the mini was very economical with petrol, and she had hoped to have enough to reach London. Now she realized that all the idling and slow second-gear driving had heavily increased her fuel consumption. Somewhere she would have to find a garage and buy a gallon at least.

She slowed down, staying in top gear but keeping her speed as low as possible to conserve petrol. She was looking out for a garage now, but every one that showed up in her headlights was closed and in darkness. The fuel gauge needle dipped into the red and she bit her lip with apprehension. If she had to abandon the mini she would be in bad trouble. The car was providing her with warmth and light. Without it she would be lost.

Suddenly she saw lights up ahead, a mixture of red tail-lights and white headlights. She slowed into second gear as her own headlights threw some added illumination on the scene, and saw that about a dozen cars had gathered on a garage forecourt. The garage was again in darkness, but the lead vehicles were pulled up close by the petrol pumps. Muffled figures moved threateningly in the glare of lights and voices were raised in anger.

Barbara stopped the mini and wound the window down to listen. The men were arguing and the atmosphere was ugly. Normally she would have avoided such a scene, but there had been no sign of life at any other petrol station along the way and she was desperate. She knew there could hardly be more than a cupful of petrol left in the mini's tank.

'I'll pay double!' a man was shouting. 'Treble if you like. Just for a couple of gallons!'

'I tell you there isn't any petrol.'

'We know damn well there is.'

'He had a tanker delivery a week ago — and he hasn't sold a bloody drop. He's hoarding it.'

'You don't know what you're talking about.'

'You're a bloody liar.'

'Treble. I'll pay treble!'

'There isn't anything to pay for — '

'Liar — you're a bloody liar!'

The argument gained in volume, with tempers swiftly deteriorating and the language swiftly growing more foul. There were three main antagonists: a large burly man in a fur-hooded, thickly-padded, arctic-style anorak, who was obviously the garage proprietor; a smaller man in a dark overcoat who was accusing him of hoarding; and an equally large man in a heavy brown sheepskin coat who was offering to treble the fixed price.

Barbara blushed at some of the names they were calling each other, but she decided to stay and await the outcome. The man in the arctic anorak was heavily outnumbered by the determined car drivers, and she hoped that he would quickly see reason. She heard another car pulling on to the forecourt behind her and moved her mini forward to secure her place in the queue.

'Go somewhere else,' the man in the anorak snarled

stubbornly. 'There's nothing here.'

'We know there is.'

'And there's nowhere else to go — all the other garages have sold out.'

'So they say.'

'Dammit, man, you can name your own price now. Why keep holding back?'

'I've nothing to sell. Fuck off, the lot of you!'

'Right then — ' The big man in the brown sheepskin lost his last shred of patience and pushed the garage owner out of the way. 'We'll serve ourselves and to hell with you.'

'Oh no you fucking don't!'

The man in the anorak defended himself quickly, kicking out at the sheepskin coat and aiming a punch at the other's face. Instantly everyone else pitched in. Fists flailed and the garage owner was driven back. Cursing, he fled for the safety of his kiosk and slammed the door behind him.

There was a ragged cheer from the frustrated group of motorists. The man in the sheepskin coat shook a fist at the kiosk and then began to help himself. He swung out the rubber arm of the petrol pump, thrust the steel nozzle inside his car and squeezed the pistol grip trigger. Nothing happened. The electric motor of the petrol pump was switched off.

'He switches it on inside the kiosk,' the man in the dark overcoat informed the others loudly. He was obviously a regular customer here, but no friend of the proprietor.

'Right, we'll switch it on then.' The man in the sheepskin coat balled a determined fist and led the grim march upon the kiosk.

Barbara watched in horror. She knew she was about to witness an act of violence, but even so she was not quite prepared for what came next. It was a ferocious reversal of what they all expected. The door to the kiosk was flung open again and the burly man in the arctic anorak came out to meet his tormentors. In his hands he carried a double-barrelled shotgun and he wasted no time on words or warnings. He simply levelled the weapon and pulled the first trigger. The shot boomed out and the man in the sheepskin coat was blasted backward into the arms of his supporters.

For a moment they held him, their faces white and startled, their mouths agape, and then they let him fall and backed hurriedly away. The dying man buckled to his knees, and then half-turned and pitched sideways on to his face. The echoes of the gunshot were still ringing as his blood seeped out to stain the snow.

'Now will you all fuck off.' The garage owner was breathing heavily and his voice was harsh. 'If there is any petrol here it's mine, and I'm not selling. That's my right — and it's my right to defend myself.'

'Jesus Christ — there was no need for that.'

'It's my business — and I've got another barrel here for anyone who wants it.'

He glowered from side to side, looking for the man in the dark overcoat, but his Judas had wisely vanished into the night. The other motorists began to follow his example, retreating cautiously to their cars, getting back inside, and quickly driving away. No one seemed to care any more about the man who had been shot.

Barbara didn't drive away. It was pointless because she didn't have enough petrol to go anywhere. Instead she found herself getting out of the mini, and as though in a daze or a dream she walked tentatively forward. Alone she faced the man with the shotgun, trusting blindly in the fact that she was no physical threat, and the hope that old-fashioned chivalry would prevent him from shooting down a defenceless woman.

'Please,' she said quietly. 'I only need one gallon — just enough to take me to Heathrow Airport. That's not much, and you can name your own price.'

Pale eyes stared at her over the shotgun. The facial muscles twitched, as though some kind of struggle was taking place inside, and then what might have been a grin briefly warped the tightened lips.

'I could be tempted, miss — but it's bloody cold for taking your knickers off out here. Besides, it don't seem right with him still warm and bleeding.'

Barbara flushed. 'I meant money,' she snapped quickly. 'I'll write you a cheque for anything within reason.'

'Cheques are no good now, love.'

'Cash then. Just one gallon! How much do you want?'

The man did not answer. The fact that he had actually killed another human being was slowly sinking home, and his gaze strayed back to the body in the sheepskin coat. He began shaking with the reaction and the shotgun wobbled dangerously in his hands.

'Please,' Barbara persisted. 'My car is empty so I can't leave without petrol. Just one gallon to get me to Heathrow. I have to catch a plane to New York. It's terribly important.'

Her urgency penetrated. The man remembered her and pulled his attention away from the body. His pale eyes were dull and his face was bloodless. He was suddenly afraid of what he had done.

'Piss off,' he told her bluntly. He turned away and went back inside his kiosk, shutting the door with slow finality behind him. Through the glass Barbara saw him sit down behind the cash register. Locked in his own state of shock he stared blankly at the wall.

Barbara went back to the mini and slumped behind the wheel. There was nothing else to do and she didn't know whether to curse or cry. She felt tired and helpless and closed her eyes.

A minute passed and she heard a foot crunch in the crisp snow. She jerked fearfully and opened her eyes, but it was not the garage owner with a lustful change of mind. The man who leaned down to speak to her through the open car window was a stranger. His face was rugged, pugnacious almost, but the easy, clean-cut smile made it attractive. His voice was softened by the slow Louisiana drawl.

'Excuse me, ma'am, but I think maybe we can help each other.'

Barbara blinked at him, noting the expensive, belted black leather raincoat, and realizing that he must have come from the wide American car which had pulled up behind her.

'How?' she said doubtfully. 'What do you want?'

'Well, ma'am, it just happens that me and my partner are also headed for Heathrow Airport. If we can we want to get back to New York City, same as you. We got plenty of gas, but we're kinda lost in this country. We only pulled in to check if we're on the right road for London.'

He paused and smiled. 'Seems to me, ma'am, that if you travelled with us it would solve both our problems. You'll get a ride to the airport, and we'll have someone English to show us the way.'

'You are on the right road,' Barbara offered cautiously. 'This is the A22. It will take you right into London.'

'London City is a big area. We heard yesterday they had power cuts, so some parts could be blacked out. We may still need a guide, so the offer still stands.'

Barbara hesitated. 'What about my car?'

The American shrugged. 'I guess nobody is buying return tickets any more. If you're going to New York you'll have to leave the car at the airport. If there's no gas in it then it makes no difference if you leave it here.'

Barbara bit her lip. She was fond of the red mini. It was the only car she had ever owned and she was still paying for it. Also, at the moment, it was her only form of security. She didn't want to leave it, but without petrol it was dead — as dead as the man in the sheepskin coat who still lay where he had fallen. The sight of him lying there reminded her that this was a horribly different world, and all its values were changed.

Where life itself was cheap the payments made or due on a motor car were simply irrelevant.

She studied the face of the American. She liked the look of him and instinctively decided she could trust him. That was all it boiled down to now: whether she wanted to face the long, defeated walk back to Herstmonceaux; or chance her luck with two strangers.

'Okay,' she decided reluctantly. 'I'll get my case out of the boot.'

There was something about the tough-looking but soft-smiling young American that struck a faint chord in Barbara's memory, and when he introduced himself it suddenly became clear.

'I'm Johnny Chance,' he told her as they got into the big American Chrysler. 'This here is Lou Haskins.'

Haskins was an older man, sitting behind the wheel and almost hidden between a thick fur-collared coat and a cowboy-style stetson hat. He grinned and raised a hand in acknowledgement.

'I'm Barbara Allington.' She stared more closely at Johnny Chance. 'You're the country and western singer?'

'You just saved my ego,' he grinned. 'I thought you couldn't recognize me. Lou here is my manager. We had just started a six-week tour of England when this goddamned cloud hit town. We tried to keep going, played our dates at Brighton and Eastbourne, but less than half the audience turned up. I guess they were afraid to come out in the dark.'

'So we're headed home,' Haskins said as he started the car and turned back on to the road. 'We don't like letting folks down, but the only thing made sense was to cancel the tour.'

'I got a wife and a son in New York City,' Chance added quietly. 'Seems that right now the only place for a man to be is with his family.'

'I'm going to my father,' Barbara told them. 'He's in New York.'

As the talk continued she was careful to make no mention of her job at the observatory. She had learned that lesson the hard way in the pub with Willoughby.

Haskins drove faster than she had dared to drive the mini. The big American car held the road better and its headlights threw a longer and more powerful beam. The towns they passed through were brightly lit, with pits of deep blackness in between. Now that she did not have to concentrate so hard on the road dead ahead Barbara saw that there were many more abandoned vehicles on either side. Either they had stuck fast in the snow, or run out of petrol like her discarded mini.

It seemed that in no time at all they were entering the outskirts of Greater London. Here the fears of the two Americans proved groundless. All the buildings and street lamps were lit and they encountered no black spots. Barbara leaned forward from the back seat and played safe by directing them up to the south circular road and then turning west to the M4.

When they came on to the motorway she concealed a small sigh of relief. She was not all that familiar with driving through Greater London and was glad that she had not lost them or led them astray. Heathrow appeared ten minutes later, and by then she had begun to relax and enjoy the company of her new friends.

There was only one thing wrong, the nagging, deep-belly feeling that this latter part of her journey had been all too easy. They carried their bags and suitcases into the airport, and then she and Johnny stood guard over the pile of luggage while Haskins went to make enquiries about flights. He disappeared for half an hour, and every minute that he was away the doom feeling grew heavier in Barbara's stomach. Finally he returned, grim-faced and shaking his head, and her worst fears were confirmed.

'Nothing,' Haskins said. 'An Air Canada flight took

off for Montreal an hour ago, but it doesn't look as though anything else is gonna try and fly the Atlantic. The guy I talked to said a hell of a lot of planes have crashed since the cloud hit. The airports at Chicago, Denver, Sydney Australia, and a whole list of other places, are all burned out. Plus a lot of planes have crashed or just disappeared in flight. Especially the international flights. Seems they've only just figured out that if a plane flies too high the cloud starts screwing up the compass and other instruments. Then it's just lost. When it runs out of fuel it comes down with a bang.'

'So maybe it's a good thing we missed that flight to Montreal?'

'The skipper on that one thinks he'll make it. He plans to fly low, no more than ten thousand feet all the way. But that doesn't help us any.'

'So what do we do?' Johnny smiled lazily, with just a hint of concern. 'You're my manager, Lou. I get kinda used to you making all our arrangements.'

'We could stick around,' Haskins said doubtfully. 'It's just possible another plane will fly in and out again — but it isn't likely. The way it looks the international services are just drying up. Whenever an aircrew gets back to its home town they act smart and stay there.'

'So we're stuck here in England?'

'Maybe not. I heard talk that there's an American cruise ship docked at Southampton. The *Pennsylvania*. She's sailing for New York some time tonight. We've got enough gas in the car, maybe if we drove down there fast enough we could get on board.'

The singer thought about it for a moment, then shrugged. 'Okay, Lou, the cruise ship sounds like our best bet.' He turned to Barbara. 'How about you? You're welcome to stay with us.'

Barbara was doubtful. 'It will be expensive, more than the plane. I might not be able to afford it.'

'Don't worry about it. If we lose time finding the road for Southampton we could miss that ship altogether. Stay with us, Daniel Boone, and we'll take care of any cash-flow problem.'

Barbara hesitated for another second, but then decided she still trusted them.

'Okay,' she agreed. 'Let's go and catch the *Pennsylvania*.'

12

In New York Allington was trying to hold together a rapidly sinking ship. More than half the UN delegations had already gone home, and the remainder, and the Secretariat itself, were only skeleton staffed. He could not blame the deserters for trying to return to their native countries while there was still time. The basic functions of the United Nations were winding down and daily becoming less relevant to reality. The field work had stopped as the field workers struggled to return home to their families, and the voice of the General Assembly had become more hysterical and impotent than ever before. There was only one major issue now, dominant above all others, and the problem of the cloud was insoluble. The continuation of the United Nations had finally become meaningless.

Allington was only bitter on one point. Julius Mangala had called the last General Assembly and won his last hollow victory. The Third World delegates had voted unanimously for the African's proposal that all oil, coal and food reserves should be shared out equally among the nations of the world — and then they had all given up in disgust when the United States and Europe predictably refused to donate more than a token share of their precious stockpiles.

The terminal scenes in the vast green-carpeted hall had been more savage recriminations. The insults and anguish had echoed high in the great vault of the dome, and Allington had steeled himself for another riot. The grim-faced security guards had tensed, ready to form another protective human screen around the green marble podium, but this time it had not been necessary. The delegates who had stayed this far were widely scattered, over a thousand seats were already empty, and the depleted ranks of Third World diplomats hurled their final curses and walked out.

It was the first mass walkout from the UN, the ultimate gesture of anger and despair, and afterwards Allington wondered if it were a fitting end. The representatives from the Western nations departed more slowly, some in sorrow and some with shrugging resignation. In less than five minutes the huge hall was empty except for the three men behind the podium.

Mangala stood up slowly, glanced at Valdez, and then addressed Allington.

'This is the result of Western self-glorification, and Western greed.' His tone was sour and petulant. 'To glorify themselves the scientists of the West sent up the satellite to chase the comet and brought this abomination down upon the whole world. And Western greed is allowing the poor countries of the world to die first. The actions of the rich space nations are despicable and disgraceful.'

Allington said nothing. Mangala was deaf to reason and except for Valdez there was no one left to listen. Argument had become a waste of time, and he no longer cared if the African succeeded in having the last word.

Mangala waited for a moment, then he scowled, descended from the podium and walked away.

Allington sat for a few more minutes, staring at two thousand empty seats, looking up at the empty press galleries, and then higher to the great dome where no ray of sunlight would ever fall again through the single skylight. The silence was absolute, held in place by the fluted wooden battens which formed the gold-coloured walls.

At last he remembered that Valdez was still there. They looked at each other, separated by Mangala's empty seat, then still in silence they rose together and left their places behind the podium. They walked out of the abandoned hall, and in that moment Allington believed that he would never enter it again.

A few hours later Allington sat alone in his office high in the Secretariat building, and wondered why he bothered to stay when most of his staff had already left. If he returned to his apartment suite in one of the twin tower blocks overlooking the United Nations Plaza he would still have been alone, so perhaps that was the reason.

He had just learned that the four junior members of the Human Rights Commission to Indonesia had returned safely to New York, but it gave him no comfort. Their team leader, Doctor Srivaji, had travelled with them only as far as Thailand, stopping at his home in Bangkok, and of Lorna Maxwell there was still no news. Being reminded of Lorna made Allington even more disconsolate.

He toyed with the stack of reports on his desk. He no longer wanted to read them. He was weary of the unending panorama of misery, ruin and collapse. He was glad when his solitude was disturbed, but the relief was short-lived.

His visitor was Valdez, but the Brazilian was uncomfortable. He made no attempt to sit down, and carried his hat and overcoat as though he intended to leave the building.

'Luis?' Allington ended the uncertain pause, putting greeting and enquiry into the tone of his voice.

'Richard — ' Valdez sounded awkward. He came closer and rested his hat and coat on the edge of Allington's desk. 'I am sorry, but I have come to say goodbye.'

'You're leaving?' Allington didn't want to believe it,

for Valdez was possibly the only man here he could count as a friend.

'There's a Brazilian ship at one of the passenger terminals on the Hudson River.' Valdez sounded embarrassed and a little ashamed. 'She sails tomorrow for Rio de Janeiro. I have booked a passage. I am going to my apartment now to pack.'

'Because of what happened this morning?'

'Because this may be my last chance to get a passage home to Brazil. All over the world ships and aircraft are trying to get back to their home port, and then they do not sail again.'

Valdez spoke sharply, but then he was honest with himself: 'It is also because of what happened this morning. Richard, I am the Under-Secretary-General for General Assembly Affairs. But there is no longer a General Assembly. There are no longer any Assembly Affairs. I no longer have any role to play!'

'Luis, I still need you,' Allington said quietly. 'There may still be a role for us to play here.'

'What role?' Valdez asked bitterly. He touched the red telephone on Allington's desk, the direct hot line to Washington and the White House. 'There has been no call on this for three days. The American space scientists can do nothing to rid us of this black cloud. The American President has nothing to say to you. And even if he had — what difference would it make whether one of us is here or not?'

'I don't know,' Allington admitted. 'Perhaps the Americans can't solve this thing on their own. Perhaps they'll have to pool their technology, and everything else they've got, with the other space nations, with Russia, Europe and China. Perhaps then we'll have a role to play. The one skill the UN has developed to a fine art is that of compromise mediation. We devise the face-saving formulae that enables governments of opposite creeds and politics to find solutions where they dare not be seen working together. When they hook themselves on their own rhetoric, we can smooth-talk them off the hook. When they back themselves into their own corners we can bale them out with their dignity intact. Sometimes it is nothing more than the condescending moral bow they make to the mere concept of the United Nations that enables them to back down or step sideways. In one of these ways we may yet be needed.'

'Richard,' Valdez cried hopelessly. 'It is already too late! The Third World is dying, and the concept of the United Nations is for all practical purposes already dead. In Africa, South America and Asia there is almost total darkness. Only a few of their major cities still have electric power. Even in their capitals it is being rationed to a few hours per day, and in some cases to hospitals or government buildings only.'

'I know, Luis.' Allington spoke softly, trying to inject a note of calm.

'Then you know that people are killing each other for scraps of food! They are burning their homes and furniture for a few flickers of light! Civilization is crumbling to extinction in this terrible darkness! They are doomed, and they know it. I know it. You must know it too!'

'Are you blaming me — like all the others?'

'No, Richard. I am trying to make you see that what is happening in the Third World is a prelude to events that the rich nations can only delay for a very small period of time. Inevitably it will happen here. There is nothing to stop it. Our planet has been swallowed up by a black hole of darkness, and all life is coming to an end.'

Allington rose to his feet and moved slowly around the desk. He had never seen Valdez so distressed and he realized now how hard the Brazilian had fought to keep his emotions under control. He touched his friend on the shoulder.

'I'm sorry, Luis. Perhaps it was wrong of me to try

and persuade you to stay. You must have friends and family in Brazil.'

Valdez nodded. 'My wife is dead, but I have two sons at school in Sao Paulo.' He was silent for a moment, struggling within himself. 'Here there is still light and food. Some of the delegates are saying that only the rootless and the cowards are staying in New York.'

'I know that wouldn't apply to you.'

'Sao Paulo is in total darkness. All the power lines have broken down. I may not find my sons.'

Allington said nothing. He understood and he could not influence his friend either way. Valdez drew a deep breath and squared his shoulders.

'But I must go. I must try. I am sorry, Richard.'

'Luis, you don't have to apologize.'

Valdez hesitated, then offered his hand. Allington took it and held the grip tight. Neither of them wanted to break it.

'You have a daughter,' Valdez sounded awkward again. 'Perhaps you should go to her.'

'Perhaps, but I have already asked her to come to me. I believe she is on her way. It would be too cruel if we were to pass each other in the night.' He smiled sadly. 'So I have burned my boats. I must stay here.'

Valdez sighed. 'Goodbye, Richard.'

'Goodbye, Luis.' Allington released his hand. 'Have a safe journey. I hope you find your sons.'

Valdez nodded his thanks, picked up his hat and coat quickly, and hurried out of the room.

Alone again, Allington switched on the TV. All the usual entertainment programmes had been cancelled now to save power, and broadcasts were limited to twice daily news reports and the occasional government speech to maintain calm. Watching the news was easier than reading the paperwork on his desk, and sometimes more enlightening.

There was no outside film any more. The sombre

face of a grey-haired newsreader filled the small screen and his only aids were maps and diagrams, and old clips taken before the coming of the cloud.

There was no mention of any attempt to move the cloud, or to free the Earth from its suffocating embrace, which meant that the space scientists with their batteries of brains and computers were still at a loss. Instead the flat voice of the announcer could only list the ever-lengthening catalogue of deepening gloom.

Throughout the United States of America law and order was rapidly breaking down. Cities like Los Angeles, Cleveland and Detroit, with traditional black ghetto trouble spots, had virtually destroyed themselves in a fury of arson and looting, and everywhere crime was on the increase. Where the power supplies had failed, or power cuts were in force, rape and mugging had become endemic.

Industy and commerce had floundered to a stop. People were reluctant to go to their place of work and leave their homes and families unprotected, and even without the mass absenteeism there was no power to run factories and offices when street lights and home lights had to be continually burning.

The cities and major towns were all patrolled by National Guard and Army units, but these emergency forces were gradually weakening as men abandoned their posts to return to their loved ones. For most of those with wives and small children protection began at home. The defence lines were being drawn small and tight. There was no point in guarding a distant street when your gun might be needed at any moment on your own front doorstep. Looting was rife, and apartment blocks and other small communities were forming their own vigilante groups.

There were many people who had turned to God, the Church and prayer; but many more who had surrendered their souls to a last pleasure whirl and the Devil. In the desperate darkness Satanic cults and witchcraft covens had multiplied, while on a more popular level debauchery had run wild. Morality had degenerated and in the swinging night-life centres of the Western world there were scenes of fantastic, drunken orgies. Close to home, group sex was free in Times Square and parts of Greenwich Village, and nothing was barred.

In the Third World life had become frighteningly cheap. There were food riots everywhere, and cannibalism had returned where there was no more food. Mob law was inflamed by agitators and fanatics and aimed wherever a stockpile of food or fuel was suspected. Self-survival had become the only rule, and millions of uncounted human beings were not surviving. Mankind, east of Moscow and south of the Tropic of Cancer, was becoming extinct.

The military actions which had flickered briefly under the cover of darkness had just as swiftly fizzled out. Either the old scores had been settled quickly, or the rank and file soldiers involved had mutinied as the days without sunlight continued. The armies had deserted en masse to flee back to their homes.

The great refugee treks that had pushed to and fro across Asia were also stalling to a halt now that the cloud had stabilized at an overall level. There were no longer any grey twilight patches where a glimmer of diluted sunlight could filter through, and the milling populations had at last accepted that there was nowhere to go. Many of the columns had simply sat down and died, while others formed roaming packs to attack and rob each other in their endless search for fuel and food.

All over the globe anything that would burn was being consigned to flames to provide light and warmth. Many of the fires blazed out of control. Whole towns and sections of cities had been gutted and razed to the ground. Soon, where there were no large forests, there would be nothing left to burn.

When Allington could stand no more of it he switched the set off. The screen went blank, the shrinking bar of white light lingering only briefly in the centre, and that too seemed symbolic of the fate of mankind.

He walked slowly to the window and stared out over an unrecognizable Manhattan. The apartment blocks still blazed light, but most of the office blocks and the towers of Empire State and World Trade were invisible against the darkness. The world-famous skyline had changed, its silhouette was shrinking into decline. Far below the street lights and traffic signs were still lit, but all unnecessary advertising was extinguished.

Although he could not see it Allington knew that most of the Secretariat building beneath him was also blacked out. As the building emptied and his staff decreased, the lights were going out on floor after floor. The line of darkness was creeping steadily upward. When it reached the thirty-eighth floor he would be marooned. He would be truly alone, on his own tiny island of light high above the city.

Perhaps Barbara would arrive before then.

And then he began to worry about Barbara, and whether she would ever be able to reach him.

13

Allington no longer worried about Lorna Maxwell. When he thought about her, which was often, he grieved, for he had long since given her up for dead. But Lorna was still very much alive. While Allington stared out over the dwindling lights of Manhattan, Lorna was checking the tightness of her seat belt in the passenger cabin of an Air India jet making a cautious and dangerous approach to Calcutta's Dum Dum Airport.

It was twelve hours since the *Java Queen* had docked at Singapore. The old freighter had inched her way slowly and blindly up the straits, and with a precarious combination of seamanship, experience, instinct and sheer luck her captain had steered her clear of shores and sandbanks and finally berthed her against Clifford Pier. Immediately the gangway was down Lorna had hurried ashore. There were no customs or immigration formalities; the dockside was almost deserted, with all the buildings in darkness and only the street lamps throwing small pools of light. She had stood helpless with her suitcase, biting her lip and wondering where to go next, and then the headlights of a taxi found her in the darkness. With a sigh of relief she had asked to be taken direct to the airport.

She was glad to escape from the ship. The entire three-day voyage had been one of fear and hiding. She had found that most of the deck-class passengers carried their own provisions, so she had been able to buy food. Her ticket entitled her to eat with the other cabin-class passengers in the ship's dining-room, but that meant eating with the ship's officers and the risk of another encounter with Carl Drekker, which she was determined to avoid. Instead she stayed in the pitch blackness of the tiny corner of refuge she had found behind the ventilator shaft.

If Chief Officer Drekker had searched for her he had failed to find her. Perhaps he had not bothered to try. She didn't know and had no intention of finding out. For six hours on the second day the ship had run through a violent tropical storm. Huge seas had crashed over the bows, driving the deck-class passengers down into the alleyways and stairways below. There they had huddled in frightened groups, with Lorna squashed against a bulkhead between two families of trembling Chinese. Drekker might have found her then, if he had been free to search the lighted interior of the ship, but while the storm lasted he had been needed on the bridge.

The storm had been the worst experience of all. Most of the Chinese had been sick and the smell of vomit was all around her. The ship had pitched and rolled and dived through the thundering seas, as though at any moment she must capsize or dash herself to pieces against the mountainous waves. Through it all Lorna had wondered how it would ever be possible for the captain to keep a check of his position, and how he could hope to find his course again if the storm ever abated.

Somehow they had survived the storm, and somehow the *Java Queen* had found her home port. Lorna was thankful, and as the taxi carried her from the dockside she wasted no more thought on the problems that were behind her. There were too many problems still ahead.

The taxi crossed the Singapore River, where oil lamps and candle flames still flickered on board the packed but invisible mass of junks and sampans. They passed the impressive City Hall and then Parliament House. The illuminating floodlights were switched off, but in the high office windows lights still burned. Driving on into the centre of the city they had to slow for the sullen crowds. The street lights were burning, but most of the shops had either been looted or were boarded up. Lorna felt scared and expected that at any moment the cab would be attacked. The city had the atmosphere of a jungle, where predators stalked in the blackness, or hunted boldly in lawless wolf-packs.

As the taxi left the city on Serangoon Road they passed the Buddha Gaya Temple, where the courtyards and precincts were packed to overflowing with people, many of them monks in their bright yellow robes, all bowed in silent, submissive prayer. The temple was lighted by thousands of flickering candles and the cloying scent of incense wafted strong and sickly on the cold air. Soon after that all glimmers of light ended, and beyond the beam of the headlights there was nothing but the awful, absolute darkness until they reached Singapore International Airport.

There were no planes in or out for the next nine hours, but at last she was able to board the Boeing 707 bound for Calcutta. The Air India plane had landed at Singapore just before the arrival of the cloud, and the crew had stayed stubbornly on the ground for a week, hoping that eventually the sun would shine and the nightmare flying conditions would return to normal. Finally they had decided that there would be no change for the better, and that to delay any further would be to stay for ever.

For Lorna it was a lucky break. Her fellow passengers had been waiting for most of the seven days in the hope that eventually the Indians would fly home. All the other passengers were also Indians, for no one else had any interest in going to India. Lorna was the only exception. For her Calcutta was just another hop on the way, but she had become resigned to making this seemingly endless journey in short stages.

'Please fasten all your seat belts.'

The polite but seriously spoken request had caused Lorna to double-check the tightness of her belt, even though she had kept it fastened all the way through the three-and-a-half-hour flight. She had heard that of the thousands of military, civilian and private aircraft that had been airborne all over the world when the space cloud hit the Earth, more than fifty per cent had crashed in the sudden blackness. Since then many more had come to grief, as she well knew from her experience at Djakarta, and so she was taking no chances.

The air hostess who had come back from the flight deck to give the passengers their landing instructions was a slim girl in a blue sari. Her dark face was composed, her voice level, but she could not fully hide the nervousness behind her eyes.

'In a very short time we shall be landing at Dum Dum Airport,' she continued bravely. 'We are in radio contact with the control tower and we have been assured that most of the landing lights and other landing aids have been switched on to guide our approach. In the circumstances, however, I must advise you to please remove all your false teeth and spectacles and all sharp objects from your pockets. This is just a precaution, you will all understand. I will give you a cushion each to protect your faces.'

There was a jabber of questions, which the girl could not, or did not want to answer. Lorna refrained from adding to the clamour. *Most* was the word that echoed in her mind. Most of the landing aids were functioning, but not all. The other vision which burned in her memory was the picture of the crashing jumbo jet at Djakarta.

She accepted the cushion which the hostess gave her

in passing and rested it on her knees, ready to bury her face against it when the plane touched down. Behind her the hostess was trying to soothe the panic in an old man and his wife, and further down the aisle a man was sobbing. Lorna stared through the cabin window beside her, seeing nothing but blackness, and trying to calculate the odds on survival. Fifty-fifty seemed a fair bet, and she felt her stomach tighten and her heart beat faster.

The plane dropped lower and lower. The pilot and flight deck crew all stared intently forward through the cockpit windows, and then suddenly the runway lights materialized and hurtled up to meet them. The visual approach indicator lights on either side of the runway glared red, a warning that they were coming in too low. The pilot cursed, pulled back on the stick and took the big aircraft up again in a tight turn to circle for a second attempt.

In the passenger cabin there were screams as they were jerked back in their seats and then flung sideways. Above the shouts of alarm the shaking voice of the hostess in the blue sari called desperately for calm.

Lorna had automatically hunched forward and pulled the cushion against her face. After the jerk and twisting movements nothing happened and she pulled back slowly. She was sweating, her throat was dry, and she decided that she wouldn't bet on their survival at all.

On the flight deck the pilot was sweating just as profusely, but now he knew what he had to contend with. None of the marker beacons or the radio beams of the instrument landing system were in operation. The control tower was obviously undermanned, and he had to rely upon his own skill and the runway lights alone.

He took the aircraft down for the second try. Again the runway lights appeared. He coasted down slowly. The visual approach lights flashed white. Too high, but there was time to compensate. He eased the stick forward. Then he had it right, one red and one white light on either side of the runway lights. The visual approach lights were fitted with reflectors and slats and carefully aligned. At a narrow low angle they emitted red light, and at an equally narrow but higher angle they emitted white light. The combination of one near white and one far red on each side of the runway meant a perfect line of approach.

But it was too fast. The pilot had a split-second decision to make: to circle again, or to trust to the full power of his brakes as soon as the wheels touched down. He chose the latter course while his nerve was still holding out.

The 707 hit tarmac with a fearsome bump, skipped up and then slammed down again. Then she was tearing down the runway with all flaps down and brakes full on, the tyres shredding and shrieking. At the far end of the runway the pilot had to slew her round to the left to avoid crashing into the blacked-out radio beam antennae. It was too much and a tyre burst in an explosion of rubber to drop the port side wing. There was a howling scrape and then a cannon-boom crack as the wing buckled. The aircraft slid shoulder-down for another fifty yards and then lurched to a stop.

The passengers and crew disembarked in a fear-crazed scramble. *Fire* was the one dominating, collective thought, and for Lorna the vivid mental image of the blazing jumbo at Djakarta gave an added edge of terror. As soon as her feet hit the runway she was running as hard as her legs would carry her, and she did not stop until they collapsed beneath her.

No fire trucks or ambulances rushed out to meet them: the emergency services were no longer functioning, but mercifully they were not needed. When Lorna looked back she saw the rest of her fellow-passengers labouring towards her, but behind them the crippled airliner lay dark and silent. The engines and cabin lights had all been switched off and there was no fire.

She had arrived in Calcutta, but it was another dead end. Dum Dum Airport was closing down and only a handful of officials had remained to bring in the last Air India flight from the East. No more flights were expected, and definitely there would be no onward flights to America.

'You must go to Delhi,' she was advised. 'Delhi International Airport is now the only airport in India which is still open. Perhaps there you will be fortunate.'

'Can I get an internal flight from here to Delhi?' Lorna asked hopefully.

'I am very sorry.' The Hindu clerk behind the Air India reception desk shrugged his shoulders and made hand-washing movements with his fingers. His sadness looked genuine. 'This airport is closed. Perhaps if you go to the railway station? Perhaps there are still trains? Our Air India bus will take you into Calcutta.'

Lorna was frustrated and weary. It seemed that every step she made brought her to another black wall. She wanted to curse and cry, but that would have got her nowhere, and finally she murmured bitter thanks to the reception clerk and went to join the other passengers waiting for the airport bus.

There was more frustration and delay. It took an hour for a bus to arrive with a driver, and a further two hours before all the luggage was retrieved from the broken 707. Finally they were ready to leave, and then Lorna realized that the entire skeleton staff of the airport intended to accompany them into the city. The lights in the reception buildings and the runway lights were abruptly switched off. The world plunged into stygian blackness once more, and the bus was as isolated as the aircraft had been in the night sky. The last stragglers came running behind hand-held torches, and the overcrowded coach began the drive into Calcutta.

Lorna was crushed into a window seat with one of the babies from the family beside her overflowing on to her lap. Through the window there was nothing to be seen, while the interior of the coach was a mass of human bodies, packed tight like dark-skinned sardines in a multi-coloured sari sauce. The bus moved slowly and Lorna endured. It occurred to her that she was slowly becoming as stoical and fatalistic as the Hindus all around her. She had no direct control over her own destiny, but like a pebble caught up in the human tide she had to go wherever the flow carried her.

After some thirty minutes had passed Lorna realized that the bus had entered the city. Through the window she could see pale street lamps and the lights of buildings, but they were all diffused and weakened by a thick, swirling fog. She became aware of people filling the streets, catching glimpses of turbans and faces in the thick gloom. It was eerie, and suddenly the faces came into startling focus, hundreds of them pressed close against the glass as the coach slowed to a stop.

The coach was an island in a seething ocean of humanity. To Lorna it seemed that there were thousands of people, men, women and children, blocking the road ahead. Most of the men wore white shirts or white robes, as if they had risen in their death shrouds from their graves. Their faces were twisted in anguish, their mouths were open, and their sobbing, wailing voices were pitiful, deafening, and terrifying.

Lorna cowered back from the window, uttering an involuntary gasp of fear, and feeling her heart hammer with the sudden shock.

'They are Jains,' an unknown voice informed her from behind. 'Their religion is very strong here in Calcutta. They have two very rich temples in this part of the city. I think they must be making a procession from one temple to the other.'

Lorna fought to control her nerves and for the next ten minutes the coach inched its way through the weeping multitude. The ranks of faces passed slowly, men and women, young and old, some wide-eyed and staring, others blindly crying. Some beat upon their breasts, others tore their clothes or hair. They were the ghost faces of lost souls, with rotting or red-stained teeth. Her nightmare memories of Indonesia paled. These were the same images, magnified and multiplied, and made a hundred times more spine-chilling by the continuous, deathly wailing.

She was relieved when the coach at last turned away from the winding route of the procession, shaking itself free of the last fringe groups of white-robed devotees and picking up speed. She closed her eyes and tried to relax, but all too soon the coach had stopped again and the Air India clerk from the reception desk was calling her name.

The Indian was standing in the road outside the open door, and uncertainly Lorna descended from the coach to join him. She looked around, seeing mostly darkness with only a few faint pools of light from distant street lamps on either side. The clerk led her round the front of the bus and pointed into the unrelieved blackness to the right.

'There is Howrah Bridge. On the far side of the Hooghly River is Howrah Railway Station. There you can get a train for Delhi.'

'I can't even see the bridge,' Lorna protested. 'I can't see anything.'

'Bridge is there,' the Indian assured her. 'For Howrah Railway Station you must turn left on the other side of the river. It is not possible for you to get lost.'

'Can't the bus take me over there?'

'I am very sorry.' Again the inevitable shrug and the shake of the head. 'This bus goes to Chowringhee, that is city centre of Calcutta. All other people on this bus go to Chowringhee.'

The clerk's face was apologetic but self-righteous, the Indian mask of justifiable non-co-operation. Lorna knew that if she tried to argue he would only quote a rule book at her. The coach driver materialized from the rear of his vehicle and handed over her suitcase. Then with shrugs and smiles both men returned to the bus. Lorna was left standing as it moved off again into the eternal night.

Fear welled up inside her: fears of the dark, fears of the unknown, fear of the distant wailing, and fear of the thousands of unseen pavement-dwellers; the homeless, the diseased beggars and the thieves, who smothered Calcutta like flies on a human rubbish dump.

She swallowed her fears with an effort, and while she could still remember her sense of direction she turned to her right and walked gingerly forward where the clerk had pointed. She tripped on the edge of the pavement and almost fell. Regaining her balance she stepped up and continued forward, feeling her way now with one hand outstretched and one foot probing before she made each step.

After a few yards her feet found a wooden walkway, and she realized she had crossed the pavement and was on the bridge. She vaguely recalled that the Howrah Bridge across the Hooghly was the third largest of its kind in the world. It was a massive, steel girder suspension bridge, 270 feet high at each of its two tower points, and spanning five hundred yards. It carried a road, with walkways on either side.

Tentatively she began to walk across. She was blind, but she knew the huge network of steel towered above her, and after a few minutes she bumped into a shoulder-high safety rail on her left hand side. She kept going and a few seconds later she tripped over the first body. It did not move or cry out and she could not tell if it was dead or alive, but she knew instinctively that it was a human form.

She stepped over it quickly, lifting her suitcase high, and hurried on. She stumbled over more still or slumbering forms. Some were silent, some twitched or groaned, and some reared up and shouted at her. They were all invisible in the darkness, but she could feel them and frequently fell over them. Several times her feet became tangled up in the blankets or scraps of sacking they used for covering, and twice she screamed when skeleton hands clutched at her legs. She couldn't tell whether this was technically night and these people had laid themselves down to sleep, or whether they had simply laid themselves down to die.

Suddenly a light flashed in her face. It was some kind of hand-held torch that dazzled and blinded her as effectively as the solid darkness it had briefly replaced. She was pushed violently against the safety rail, her suitcase was torn from her faltering hand, and then the light and her attacker were both moving away fast. The light bobbed only for a few seconds and then was extinguished as abruptly as it had flared.

She slumped trembling against the railing. She was bruised and breathless and the whole incident had happened too swiftly for her to scream. All around her she could hear whispers of breathing, and a mutter of voices from roused sleepers who were equally bewildered.

Her suitcase was gone, and now she used both hands to hold her shoulder-bag tight to her breast. It contained her traveller's cheques, credit card and passport, and without those she would be truly lost. Gritting her teeth she continued her slow, groping, stumbling progress across the bridge.

She was afraid that her attacker would come back, or that another would find her, and afraid that in addition to being robbed she could easily be raped or murdered. No one would see, no one who cared would ever know, and her body could easily be tumbled into the deep waters of the Hooghly somewhere below.

That walk across the bridge was the longest she had ever made, the worst nightmare yet in a succession of worsening nightmares, but after what seemed an eternity the thick wooden planking ended and she felt pavement once more beneath her feet. She had crossed the river, and over to her left she could just distinguish a gloom-shrouded oasis of lights.

Left, the Air India clerk had said, and so she hurried left, aiming for the lights. A few minutes later, sobbing with relief, she was inside the partially lighted main concourse of Howrah Railway Station.

The station was swarming with people. How they had ever found their way here Lorna could not imagine, but it seemed as though the whole of India was on the move and hoping to find a train. She realized later that the entire sub-continent had always relied heavily upon its railways, and that trains, which followed fixed steel tracks, were in present circumstances still the most sure transport for finding their destination.

She fought her way through the crush and eventually found a uniformed station superintendent who could give her the information she needed. The next train for New Delhi was the Upper India Express which was due to leave in two hours and thirty minutes. There was plenty of time for her to book her seat, and the superintendent pointed out the ticket office over the turbanned heads of the crowd.

Again she struggled through the mob to join the long, disorderly queue. Immediately in front of her was a huge Sikh with massive squared shoulders packed into a tight, dark business suit, and wearing a large, dark-blue turban. His back was all that she saw for the next thirty minutes as the jostling, pushing and arguing line crawled slowly forward.

At last she was at the ticket window and the clerk punched the first-class ticket she requested and pushed it toward her. 'Nine hundred and sixty rupees,' he demanded curtly.

Lorna offered him her credit card.

The clerk shook his head and pulled the ticket back. 'Rupees only. Credit cards no good now.'

'But it's American Express. Everyone takes American Express.'

'All credit cards, no good,' the man behind the glass insisted. 'You pay me nine hundred and sixty Indian rupees.'

'I don't have any rupees. I have American dollar traveller's cheques.'

'Traveller's cheques no good any more. You go to bank. Bring me rupees.'

'But the banks are closed.' Lorna did not know that for certain, but even if there were banks still open she knew it would be an almost hopeless task for her to find one.

The clerk shrugged and stared over her shoulder. The man behind her shouted for two first-class tickets for Allahabad and Lorna found herself pushed out of the queue.

For a minute she stood there, not knowing what to do next. She could try to push in again and argue, or she could go over the clerk's head and plead with the station superintendent, or she could embark on the almost impossible quest to find a bank. She decided to try the station superintendent first and turned away, only to collide with the huge Sikh who had been in the queue ahead of her.

He had been watching and listening as he carefully checked his own ticket, and now he frowned down upon her. He was about fifty, his nut-brown face creased behind a magnificent grey beard. His sharp brown eyes were uncertain and thoughtful.

'You have trouble, Memsahib?'

'You could say that,' Lorna conceded bitterly.

The Sikh nodded gravely. 'You are American, yes?'

'I'm from South America. Columbia.'

'Why do you go to Delhi?'

Lorna had been through this scene before. She said cautiously, 'I hope to get a plane to New York. Calcutta Airport is closed.'

The Sikh stroked his beard, considering, and then made his offer. 'I have booked an air-conditioned compartment, but I am travelling alone. If you wish you may share it with me as my guest.' He smiled. 'You will be quite safe.'

Lorna remembered Carl Drekker and the *Java Queen*. On the train it might not be so easy to run away and hide. And the Sikh was a bigger and more powerful man; if he had the same intentions it would not be so easy to fight him off. She hesitated, but every move she made was a desperate gamble, and her options were very limited.

'Thank you,' she said awkwardly. 'Thank you very much.'

White teeth flashed behind the grey beard as her benefactor smiled again, and he offered her a hand to shake that was twice as large as her own.

'If we are to be travelling companions, then we must introduce ourselves. My name is Chandra Singh.'

When the Upper India Express rolled out of Howrah Station only thirty minutes later than the advertised departure time Lorna was seated in one of two chintz-covered armchairs in the small private compartment. Chandra Singh occupied the second chair. He had taken off his jacket, loosened his tie, and generally made himself comfortable. On one side of them was the sliding door to the corridor, and on the other two narrow sleeping berths discreetly screened by matching chintz curtains.

During the long wait to board the train they had eaten in the station restaurant and Lorna had learned a little about her new friend. He was the sales manager of a firm which manufactured bicycles, and he had been engaged on a routine twice-yearly tour of regional sales offices when the sudden nightfall descended from outer space. He had reached Hyderabad in Central India, but misled by the hope that the Earth would soon pass through the cloud he had continued his planned journey. He had gone south to Madras, and then north again to Calcutta. Now he was headed west on the last lap to his home city of Amritsar in the Punjab.

Chandra Singh continued his story as the train rumbled through the night. His journey had been wasted because the sales offices in both Madras and Calcutta had been closed. In the southern city the telephones were not working so it had been impossible to contact the regional sales manager there. In Calcutta he had been able to get a line through to the home of the regional sales manager, but the man's wife had informed him tearfully that her husband had been drunk for six days. The rest of the family were devoting themselves to constant prayer.

'That is all there is now,' the Sikh finished sadly. 'On the one hand much drunkenness and wickedness, and on the other hand much weepings and the saying of prayers.'

Lorna had told him most of her own story, and could only nod in agreement.

The hours passed slowly to the swaying rhythm of the train. A dining-car steward served them with coffee, and Chandra Singh told her more about India, and especially about Amritsar, and the Punjab and the Sikhs. He was insisting that when conditions returned to normal she must visit him in Amritsar to see the magnificent golden temple of his religion when the train slowed to make its first stop.

'This must be Chittaranjan,' Chandra Singh guessed, and they moved into the corridor to see if he was right.

The train had travelled through a black void, like some forgotten, starless corner of the outer universe, but now there were lights ahead and people. Lorna stared through the window glass and then flinched back as she saw that there were thousands of people, filling and overflowing the platform in a tight-packed, struggling mass, and surging forward to meet the train. Their shouts and screams were pandemonium as they fought to get on board.

'Get back into the compartment,' Chandra Singh ordered grimly as the carriage doors burst open at each end of the corridor.

Lorna saw the flood of people storming towards them on either side and quickly backed up. Chandra Singh stepped backward to join her, but a dozen desperate Indians were trying to push into the compartment before he could shut the sliding door.

The big Sikh blocked the way, shouting indignantly at the smaller Hindus who begged, pleaded and argued back. Their sheer weight forced him to give way and they poured inside. They were pushing or dragging their assorted bags and bundles and Lorna feared that they must be swamped. There seemed no way that they could escape sharing their once private compartment.

But she had under-estimated Chandra Singh. Until now his every word and action had been courteous, friendly, and often jovial, but he was a Sikh and his pride and dignity had been affronted. He stopped arguing and with a roar of anger he began to act. He balled his two enormous fists and using his great arms like clubs he struck out left and right to knock the intruders sprawling. The fight was fast and furious, but as the front ranks fell those at the rear began to panic and scatter.

In a few short minutes the doorway was clear, and then Chandra Singh began to pick up the bruised and bloodied fallen, and one by one threw them out.

He stood guard in the doorway until the train began to move again, breathless and dishevelled, but bellowing angrily and menacingly at any who dared to come too near. The other private compartments had been breached and occupied by sections of the mob, but the big Sikh was not seriously challenged again. When the train lurched slowly forward Lorna saw that those who had not been able to get on board were still fighting and screaming on the platform. The train gathered speed and the hysterical scenes passed from view, and only then did Chandra Singh close the door and turn to face her.

'I must make apologies for those Indians,' he said sadly. 'But this train will pass through Benares, and most of them were trying to make the pilgrimage to bathe in the Sacred Ganges. All Hindus must do this once in their lifetime, and now the world is ending they do not have much time.'

'Is this going to happen at every stop?' Lorna asked anxiously.

'I fear it is possible.' Chandra Singh straightened his tie and carefully checked the balance of his turban. 'But I shall endeavour to protect you.' He paused, and then made a small confession. 'In some parts of India the Sikhs have been murdered by their old enemies the Muslims, and the Hindus. In times of trouble there is always religious war. Perhaps I should have told you before you agreed to share my compartment, but in spite of this I think you are safer with me than you would be alone.'

Lorna groaned. It did not seem possible that she could be caught up in yet another Holy War.

'That is why I had to throw those people out,' Chandra Singh continued gravely. 'I could not trust them behind my back.' He misunderstood her groan and added more reassurance. 'Please, Lorna, do not permit this incident to alarm you. I am a Sikh. My name is Singh, and Singh means Lion. All Sikhs are Lions! You have an old lion, but still a lion, to defend you!'

Lorna smiled faintly. After the ferocious demonstration she had just witnessed she could not doubt Chandra Singh's ability to defend her. Unfortunately,

Carl Drekker was still in the background of her mind, and fearing a repetition of that experience she could not help wondering who could possibly defend her from Chandra Singh?

They settled down in the armchairs again as the express train resumed its shuddering top speed, but Lorna could not relax. It was difficult to keep track of the passing days. Midnight was for ever and time itself had become confused, and she could not remember the last occasion when she had slept properly. She realized she was very tired, and after all she had been through she was very strained and tense. She could hardly keep her eyes open, but she did not dare to look toward the two curtained bunk beds.

Chandra Singh was still keeping up a one-sided conversation, telling her more about the Sikhs and their history. The Sikhs had fought against the Moguls, and then against the Muslims, and then against the British. They were a fighting race and still formed the backbone of the Indian Army. Chandra Singh was proud of his heritage, and took pleasure in telling his tales.

Lorna's head began to nod, and all she could think of was that Delhi was still more than thirty hours away. She could not hope that Chandra Singh would keep talking throughout the entire journey, and nor could she possibly stay awake for all that time.

She yawned. It was involuntary and Chandra Singh noticed before she could stop it or cover up.

'You are sleepy,' he apologized. 'I am talking too much. It is time to go to bed.'

'No,' Lorna countered hastily. 'It's alright. I'm not tired.'

The Sikh stared at her closely, noting the large dark patches under her eyes. 'You are tired,' he insisted. 'You must sleep.'

Lorna bit her lip and looked away from his glowering eyes. The Sikh seemed to swell as he breathed deeply.

His beard bristled and his face became grim. He was angry.

'I have told you that you are safe. I am a Sikh, and a Sikh is a man of honour. It is safe for you to sleep.'

Lorna looked back into his eyes, uncertain, but wanting desperately to believe him. His tone was stern, and made her feel like a small child who was being silly.

'Perhaps I should tell you something else.' His tone softened and a flicker of understanding showed in his eyes. 'I have a daughter, perhaps a little younger than you. She is in the United States of America, where she is studying medicine. Like you she is far from her family and her home. She is a stranger in a strange land.'

He smiled sadly. 'When I saw you in difficulty at Howrah Railway Station I thought of my daughter. She is beyond my reach. I cannot help her. But I can help you. I am a religious man. I believe that if I do my duty to God, then he will do His duty to me. If I help you, an American lost in India, then perhaps God will take care of my daughter, who is an Indian lost in America. Do you understand?'

'I think so,' Lorna said slowly. 'Chandra Singh, I'm sorry — '

He raised a hand, cutting off her apology. 'It is alright. Now we can both go to bed. You will take the top sleeping berth, and I will take the bottom sleeping berth. Sleep in peace, and do not be afraid. I shall not harm you.'

Lorna felt a huge sense of relief, and five minutes later she was wrapped in blankets on the upper bunk. She was sound asleep within seconds of her head touching the pillow.

14

Launch complex 41 at the Kennedy Space Centre in Florida was illuminated by batteries of powerful arc lamps, creating a dome of artificial light on the blacked out planet. In the centre of this dazzling glare a Titan III launch vehicle stood ready on the pad. The rocket was a three stage monster with strap-on boosters, a combination of two stages of massive thrust Titan technology with a high-performance Centaur stage on top. It stood one hundred and sixty feet tall, and the main core and the strap-on boosters on either side were each ten feet in diameter.

Other rockets of its kind had launched the Viking space craft to Mars, and the Mariner probes to Jupiter and Saturn. They had carried the driving ambition of mankind toward the stars, uplifting his greatest hopes, and exciting his wildest dreams.

The Titan III which was now on the last minutes of countdown carried much more. It carried mankind's last hope for survival.

This would be the third launch in the desperate, frantically rushed NASA programme to investigate the cloud. The first and second launch had both been accomplished using the smaller Scout, the first NASA developed launch vehicle, which was still the quickest and most reliable method of putting a low orbit satellite into space. The two Scout shots had put their relatively small payloads of data-gathering intruments into orbit at heights of 250 and then 300 miles above the

Earth surface. Nothing had beamed back.

The American space scientists and their computer banks could not tell whether their satellites had orbited inside the cloud or above it. The cut-off point for the satellite signals in both cases had been just below 200 miles. After that there had been silence. They could not calculate how far the new layer of black gas and dust might extend beyond the cut-off point. Perhaps both satellites were in dead orbit inside the cloud, or perhaps one or both satellites were bleeping away healthily in alternating sun and starlight, they just didn't know.

And they were no longer trying to find out.

Time was short, too short to spend on wasted efforts to gather data. Instead the Titan III was being used to make a test run for what seemed to be the only possible solution.

The Titan carried no satellite and no high technology instruments. Its computer guidance system was not targeted for Earth orbit, but for an Earth escape mission aimed into the emptiness of space. For a payload the nose cone carried nothing more complex than a magnet, horseshoe-shaped like a child's toy, but developed from an alloy of iron, nickel, cobalt and copper which made it many times more powerful than any ordinary steel magnet of the same weight and size.

As the countdown reached zero the booster rockets were ignited and the Titan III achieved lift-off on twin columns of thundering flame. Pushing up from the pad it rose slowly into the air, leaving the glare of white lights, and vanishing except for the twin trails of fire into the darkness.

In the mission control rooms at Kennedy and Houston hundreds of scientists and technicians watched the accelerating climb on their TV screens. All of them were grim-faced and tight-lipped, suffering under an agonizing mental and emotional strain.

Space rockets were normally launched in bright

daylight and perfect weather, but these were abnormal times. This launch had to take place in pitch darkness and its success could prove vital to the very survival of the planet. It piled merciless pressure on every man present, no matter how minor his role.

The double-barrelled red flame began to fade as the fuel in the booster rockets was burned up. As acceleration slowed ignition of the Titan stage one engines occurred and twelve seconds later the boosters were jettisoned. The main core of the rocket continued to ascend and accelerate. Stage one burned for exactly 262 seconds before the ignition of stage two. Stage one separated and was cast off in its turn.

Stage two boosted the vehicle until it was exhausted, its fuel tanks useless and empty, and it too fell away. The onboard guidance system of the Centaur top stage ignited the Centaur main engine and carried the payload into the cloud.

The TV screens went black. No more signals returned. The watchers at Kennedy and Houston waited in nerve-mangling suspense. The atmosphere in both control rooms was electric, super-charged with human anguish.

Then the screens came alive again, not with data from the silent rocket, but with pictures from the ground cameras monitoring the invisible flight path. The speed of the Centaur had punched through the cloud and its magnetic payload had pulled off a large patch of the cloud and carried it back into space. Behind it the sunlight was streaming down through the large, gaping hole.

It was the wide shaft of sunlight which showed on the monitoring TV screens and the observers went mad with delight. They laughed, cheered and danced, shook hands vigorously and repeatedly slapped one another on the back. It was the sunlight they had not seen for many days, the sunlight which most of them had never expected to see again, and which all of them now knew was the very Light of Life Itself.

But the moments of euphoria were soon over. Slowly, relentlessly, the cloud repaired itself. The hole grew smaller. The single shaft of sunlight was strangled without pity, shrinking, faltering, weakening, until it finally vanished altogether. The merciless, all-enveloping blackness had returned once more.

At Kennedy and Houston the cheering faded. It was followed by a long, apprehensive and thoughtful silence.

In the depths of the Florida Everglades, where the one ray of sunlight had briefly touched the gloomy swamp waters, a few baffled alligators were dimly trying to comprehend what was happening to their world. Except for the fish they were the only creatures still alive there.

The results of the Titan III launch, together with the considered conclusions of the best scientific brains in America, were rushed to the White House within a matter of hours. They were put to President Anderson by Merle Forrester, his Chief Scientific Adviser.

Glenn Anderson wasted no time, and it seemed to Forrester that he had barely got his breath back before he was required to speak his piece all over again. This time he had to face the President's entire Crisis Cabinet, which included the Vice President, the Secretaries of State and Defence, the Joint Chiefs of Staff, the President's National Security Adviser, and, somewhat to Forrester's bewilderment, the Director of the CIA.

'Tell them,' Anderson instructed Forrester. 'Exactly as you told me.'

Forrester stood up and wiped his balding forehead with a handkerchief. For a few seconds he fiddled awkwardly with the handkerchief as he looked up and down the waiting faces around the table. Then he stuffed it hastily in his pockets and began to explain.

'Gentlemen, today we believe we have achieved a

breakthrough with the problem of the cloud. We have known for some time that the cloud is strongly magnetic. This was self-evident from the way in which the cloud was initially attracted to the Columbus Two comet mission, and has since been confirmed by radio telescope observations here on Earth. Because the cloud has this high magnetic quality we believe we have now discovered the means to hurl it back into space.'

'Thank God,' the Naval Chief of Staff murmured softly.

No one else interrupted. They could see that Forrester was in a state of high nervous tension and waited for him to get on with it.

'Earlier today NASA launched a Titan Three from Kennedy Space Centre,' Forrester continued. 'The payload weight that can be carried on an Earth escape mission with this vehicle is eight thousand pounds, and on this trip the payload consisted of one huge magnet. The rocket tore a hole through the cloud. We calculate that for some ten minutes approximately fifty square miles of the Florida Everglades enjoyed a brief return of real daylight.'

'And then what happened?'

'The hole closed up.'

There was a doubtful silence, then the Air Force Chief of Staff said slowly, 'We put a rocket through the cloud before it hit the Earth. The idea then was that the cloud might hitch on to the rocket and go back where it came from. It didn't work — so why is the same principle working now?'

'We can't be sure that it didn't work the first time. Before the cloud hit us it was one dense mass. The rocket went through but then we lost all track of it. Most scientific opinion now believes it is highly probable that the first rocket did tear out a chunk of the cloud and carry it back into space. It just wasn't enough to reverse the entire mass once it was caught in the gravitational pull of the Earth.'

'So now the cloud has spread thin, and with a bit of extra help from a magnet in the nose cones, we can shoot holes through it. We can throw it back into space one little-bitty piece at a time. Is that what you're saying?'

Forrester nodded. 'That's about it.'

'So how many rockets do you figure we need to clear the whole of North America?'

'All of them. The whole damned shooting match.'

'You mean every single NASA launch vehicle?'

'I mean *everything*!' Forrester swallowed hard and spelled it out. 'Not just NASA vehicles. I mean every military missile we've got that's capable of Earth escape. We're gonna have to strip the nuclear warheads off those rockets and fit them with a magnetic payload.'

'We can't do that!'

'You're crazy!'

'We'd be wide open to the Russians — '

'Let me finish!' Forrester shouted. He pulled out his handkerchief, quickly mopped his face, and plunged on. 'Don't you see that we're not just talking about clearing the sky above North America? Even if we did shoot a hole that big it would just fill up again. The cloud would find its new level, not quite so thick, but perhaps still thick enough to keep out the sunlight, and we'd be right back where we started.'

He had their attention again and he paused to let it sink in. Then he hammered his message home. 'This isn't just an American problem, it's world-wide, and it has to be tackled on a world-wide basis. The only thing that is going to work is as near-as-possible a simultaneous launch of every rocket vehicle on the face of the Earth. That means us, the French, the Chinese and the Russians. Like I said before — the whole Goddamned shooting match!'

The idea staggered them. They stared at Forrester, then at each other, and finally at the President. Glenn

Anderson was hearing it for the second time; he had recovered from his first reaction and given it some thought. Now he shrugged and broke the strained silence.

'What Merle is saying does make sense.'

'Not all of it,' his Vice President argued. 'Merle just said we have to clear the cloud world-wide, otherwise what's left will just find its own level again. As I see it we can't do that. Even if we can get agreement with the other space nations, all our launch facilities are in the northern hemisphere. There isn't gonna be time enough to build additional launch pads on the ice caps and south of the Equator.'

'We don't have to,' Forrester answered. 'There are enough missile-carrying submarines in the US, British, French and Russian navies to deploy where necessary in Third World waters. Those submarine missiles will have to be fitted with magnetic payloads and targeted for Earth escape, exactly the same as the land-based missiles.'

'We have to keep something back for defence.' The Naval Chief of Staff who had thanked God was now torn with doubt.

'We can't afford to hold anything back,' Forrester insisted. 'Everything we have may not be enough, but it's the only chance we've got.'

'We can argue the final figures when we have more data,' Anderson cut in quickly. He didn't want any obstructive nitpicking at this stage. 'For the moment you are in the picture. What I propose to do next is to get on to the hot line to Moscow. It's time for some straight talking to compare our findings with the Soviets.'

There were slow nods of agreement all round the table.

Anderson looked to the Director of the CIA. 'Bill, if there's anything you can tell me before I talk to Komarov, I'd sure like to hear it.'

Bill Clifton frowned. He was a professional who had risen through the ranks at Langley, and a vast improvement on previous political appointments. He ran a tight operation and they had succeeded in getting Congress off his back, but even the best in the business could not run an effective intelligence-gathering machine in total darkness.

'Our two listening posts in Western China are still functioning. We know that during the past week the Russians have launched three Soyuz launch vehicles from the Tyuratum Cosmodrome just east of the Aral Sea. What their purpose was, or what they discovered, we don't know. There is nothing coming out from behind the iron curtain at all. Virtually all of East Europe could all be dead for all we know.'

'There's only one way to find out,' Anderson said. 'I'll call President Komarov.'

It was another hour before the connection was made. The usual modern technology link-ups through orbiting telecommunications satellites were dead, and the call had to be routed through the almost obsolete undersea telephone cables. Finally a line was established to the Kremlin, and the President of the United States and the President of the Soviet Union were able to converse. They exchanged pleasantries, and then Anderson got down to business.

'President Komarov, I'm sure you can guess why I'm calling. My space experts have been working on the problem of getting rid of this cloud, and we think they've come up with something. I'm sure your people have been working on the same thing. We're all in this situation together, so an exchange of information must be helpful.'

'I agree,' Komarov answered smoothly. 'Our Soviet scientists will be most interested to evaluate what your American scientists have discovered.'

You crafty old bastard, Anderson thought, but there

was nothing to be gained in niggling over who opened up first. The hard bargaining could be done later. He got directly to the point and outlined the findings of the three NASA cloud probes.

'Our Soviet space scientists have arrived at the same conclusion,' Komarov cautiously confirmed. 'The new cloud mass does have positive magnetic properties.'

Anderson waited. Komarov waited. Anderson silently cursed the stubborn reticence of the Russian and spoke again.

'We calculate that the space cloud has pressed Earth atmosphere down to a ceiling of about two hundred miles. What we don't know is how far the new layer goes up above that level. Can you help us there?'

There was a pause. They could imagine Komarov looking round the attendant faces of his Politburo, counting the signs of assent or disapproval. Finally the answer came.

'The Soviet Union has launched three manned space capsules in the past week. Two were put into low Earth orbit. Neither of these has transmitted any message since passing into the cloud. The third spacecraft was sent into a six-hundred-mile high loop and then piloted back to Earth. It crashed on landing. However, the cosmonaut commander had enough time between emerging from the cloud and the moment of impact to transmit a brief message. The cloud layer appears to be between twenty and thirty miles in depth. Six brave Soviet cosmonauts have died to bring back this one small piece of information.'

Anderson flinched. NASA had not even contemplated the almost certain sacrifice of lives in manned ventures into the black cloud, and he could hear the note of censure and contempt in Komarov's tone.

'Perhaps they have not died in vain.' It was the only consolation he could offer. 'Now we know the rough extent of the cloud our computers will be able to calculate how many magnetic payloads will be needed to displace it.'

'The use of magnetic rockets could be a solution. We will watch your American efforts with close interest.'

'President Komarov, I think you missed the point. My people believe that if this solution does prove feasible it will have to be a joint effort by both our nations. Plus we'll need back-up from the British, the French, and the Chinese. It's going to take every launch vehicle all our countries can muster.'

'President Anderson,' Grigori Komarov responded tersely. 'You must remember that it was a Western space mission which brought this cloud back to our planet. Therefore it must be primarily a Western responsibility to remove it. The Western space nations must use their rockets first.'

'We can't afford to split hairs on this. We have to work together.'

'My government will consider this — after America has fired all her rockets and proved that this theory will work.'

'It has to be simultaneous. For God's sake, the Soviet Union is in darkness. Your people must be freezing and starving a damn sight quicker than ours. It's not just an American problem.'

There was another long silence. Then Komarov said carefully, 'This must be discussed by a full meeting of the Soviet government. We will talk again.'

The line clicked and went dead. The Russian President had hung up, and after a few disbelieving seconds the American President opened his hand to let the red telephone fall back heavily on its cradle in a gesture of disgust.

His Vice President, Secretary of Defence, and Chief Scientific Adviser were all in the Oval Office with him. They had watched and listened in total silence. Now the Secretary of Defence was the first to speak.

'There's no way, Glenn. If we try to go it alone our nuclear arsenal will become temporarily useless without the launch vehicles to deliver the warheads. Even if we could clear the cloud away the US would be left defenceless. We'd be stark naked — and the Soviets would have total nuclear supremacy. They could destroy America and conquer Europe at will. That price is unthinkable.'

'The alternatives are unthinkable,' Merle Forrester croaked hoarsely. His face was grey and he was perspiring again.

Glenn Anderson took off his horn-rimmed glasses and rubbed wearily at his aching eyes.

'Let's keep our heads,' he counselled. 'And our nerve. Komarov will call back. We just have to make him see reason.'

15

The *Pennsylvania* was five days out from Southampton, fighting her way westward through icy, hurricane seas, far out in the pitch blackness of the mid-Atlantic. The 27,000-ton cruise liner was rolling heavily, despite her stabilizers and despite her size. She was 650 feet from bow to stern, ten decks high, with a breadth of 86 feet amidships. Her service speed was 20 knots, but the head-on storm winds and the huge, battering waves had cut her speed by almost a third.

It was without a doubt the worst voyage Captain James Bradley had ever known in all his fifty years at sea. He had started his long career as a cabin boy on a rust bucket hauling sugar up from Cuba, and since then he had sailed on every ocean on practically every kind of ship. He had seen it all, typhoons, waterspouts and tidal waves, but nothing to match the freak weather on this trip.

He knew it had to be the cloud, shutting out the sun, cooling down the planet, lowering air temperatures, and generally playing havoc with the weather.

He turned away from the rain-streaming, plate-glass windows of the bridge and scowled as he moved to check the compass. He was a large, broad-shouldered man, looking every inch a seaman with his neat-clipped grey beard and weather-creased eyes. The compass needle was steady on eighty degrees, west-by-south, exactly where it was supposed to be. With no possibility of taking a sextant reading to confirm his position, Bradley could only hope that the compass reading was true. He had heard that high-flying aircraft were being thrown off course by wild compass fluctuations, but so far as he knew the magnetic disturbance from the cloud was not extended down to sea level.

The helmsman at the wheel was careful to avoid the captain's eye. First Officer Ed Kubrick stood back a pace to give the sailor room to work, and he was not so overawed. His mouth twisted with the faintest doubtful grimace, his shoulders moving with an almost imperceptible shrug.

Bradley understood and returned the shrug. They had both kept up a casual, joking front for the benefit of the 500 crew members and more than a thousand passengers. North America is a big continent, ran the stock reassurance, it was only on the other side of the Atlantic so if they kept going they couldn't miss it. The line had won them some laughs, but now the joke was wearing thin.

The sun and the stars had guided sailors for centuries, whenever they had ventured out of the sight of land, and now even Bradley and Kubrick, with all their modern navigational aids, felt more than a little lost without them. They could plot their supposed position on expensive paper charts, but without the familiar star charts of the heavens there was still room to doubt. In private they were honest enough to admit this to each other, and the atrocious weather was adding to their misgivings.

They would hit North America, they still believed, somewhere between Newfoundland and the Bahamas, providing the compass wasn't playing tricks and leading them round in circles.

The deck rolled again beneath their feet as Bradley glanced at his wristwatch. The time was seven p.m. Dinner was served at eight. He had already overstayed the end of his watch and it was time to go below and change. He was expected at the head of the captain's table in the dining saloon. His presence kept the passengers calm and happy.

'You have the bridge, Mr. Kubrick,' he told his First Officer. 'Call me if you need me.'

Ed Kubrick nodded, and watched the captain go below. He reflected that the old man was getting worried: the last remark had been out of character.

Nothing could happen to the *Pennsylvania*, not even with a hurricane howling over her decks. She was a modern cruise ship; this was only her third round-the-world voyage. She was not as big as the giant *Queens* of the past, but she was big enough and built with every up-to-date feature for passenger comfort and safety. Most of all she had been built in Baltimore, which was Ed Kubrick's home city, and he had great trust and pride in anything which came out of Baltimore.

In the past 24 hours they had witnessed some of the most spectacular lightning displays Kubrick had ever seen. The passengers and crew alike had been terrified by the tremendous jagged forks that had split open the black heavens. The thunderclaps had sounded as though the whole planet was being blown asunder. Twice the crack of doom had occurred immediately overhead, and it had seemed as though the blazing streaks of fire were the fingers of a monstrous electric hand that intended to pluck the ship right out of the ocean.

The *Pennsylvania* had sailed through it all unharmed, just as she had sailed through everything else the crazy, disrupted weather machine had been able to throw into her teeth during the past five days. She had entered the hurricane and now she was riding out of it again. This ship could survive anything. They might have a few navigation worries, but that was all.

Kubrick didn't know it, but his confidence was only a few short hours away from a rude and violent shock.

* * *

Barbara Allington was enjoying herself. The meals served on board the *Pennsylvania* were superb. There were five comfortable lounge bars, a full size dancing hall, a cinema, an enclosed sports deck, a sauna, and an enclosed swimming pool. Everything had been provided to give the pampered passengers their promised holiday-of-a-lifetime. In present circumstances the promenade and sun decks could not be used, but life inside the ship was still one continuous round of rich, spoiled luxury. Captain Bradley had insisted upon a full entertainment programme as usual to keep his passengers and crew from brooding too much over the endless darkness, and the attendant new dangers.

After their desperate race from Heathrow to Southampton it had seemed to Barbara almost too good to be true to find the *Pennsylvania* still in port. Even more good fortune awaited them, for there were still a few vacant cabins. The ship had sailed fully booked from New York ten weeks earlier, passing through Panama to Los Angeles, Honolulu, Tokyo, Hong Kong, Bangkok and Colombo, and then through Suez to the Mediterranean. There the black cloud had descended and the planned itinerary of pleasure ports had been cut short. The European passengers who would normally have flown home from New York at the end of the round trip recognized the needless risk of making two crossings of the Atlantic, and had petitioned the captain to be put ashore. Bradley had obliged, putting his ship into Southampton so that the English, French and German tourists could disembark. The normal rules no longer applied and he had permitted the empty cabins to be filled up again for the final lap of the journey.

Barbara and her two companions had been given three adjoining first-class cabins on C deck. They were only just in time, for the only remaining cabins were quickly filled by a group of Brazilian army officers who had followed them down from Heathrow, and an hour after their arrival the *Pennsylvania* sailed.

Now Barbara considered herself very lucky indeed. It was true she had initially been scared stiff by the bad weather and the lightning, but she had proved a good sailor and the magical atmosphere of the cruise ship had prevailed. She had wined and dined and danced in lavish, glittering splendour, until finally the most wonderful thing of all was happening.

She was falling in love with Johnny Chance.

She knew it was wrong. Johnny had been completely honest with her and she knew he had a wife and child, but at the same time, provided she didn't tell him, she couldn't see where her own feeling could do any harm.

Civilization was collapsing all around them, the Earth itself was dying, and this last unexpected fling of self-indulgent decadence might be all the romance that she would ever know. She was here, she knew it couldn't last, but in the meantime she had a handsome, good-humoured, fine and generous man to share the voyage with her. Common sense told her to make the most out of each precious, passing moment. All too soon they would have to say goodbye, the fleeting hours abroad the *Pennsylvania* would be gone for ever, and only the memory would remain.

On that fifth evening out from Southampton Barbara was feeling supremely happy. Despite the hurricane the interior of the huge liner seemed inviolate and she had spent another dream day. In fact she almost welcomed the violent seas because they slowed the ship down and were making the delightful journey even longer.

She had spent the morning with Johnny and Lou, in Johnny's cabin, listening while he played his guitar and practised singing some of the country and western numbers that had made him famous. He had just the right rugged voice to go with the tough, masculine face and the unruly black curls, and the songs he sang were wry love songs and gunfighter ballads of the old West. Millions of impressionable young women had swooned over them at concerts all over the world, but this time, Barbara knew, the songs were for her alone.

They had finally drifted down to the ship's Mayfair Lounge for pre-luncheon drinks, and luncheon itself had been another wine-accompanied banquet. Afterwards Lou Haskins had excused himself on the grounds of middle age, and ambled off grinning to his cabin to sleep it off. Barbara and Johnny had gone instead to the enclosed swimming pool to play water games and get themselves a fit appetite for dinner.

Johnny Chance in bathing trunks was no disappointment. He was hard-muscled and athletic, showing no trace of soft living. On his right thigh was a bullet scar he had picked up in the last days of the Vietnam war. He had been drafted just before the end.

Barbara was proud to be with him. She had bought herself a sexy little bikini from the ship's boutique, and she knew she made a shapely female figure to match. Swimming was one of her favourite sports and she found she could just keep ahead of him in a race. They had chased each other around the pool all afternoon, and finally confessed themselves exhausted and ready to face another six-course gourmet menu as prepared by the *Pennsylvania*'s palatial kitchens.

To dinner that evening Barbara wore a new white evening dress with a rose-shaped sparkle of red sequins on the left breast, her dark hair piled high to reveal diamond ear-rings. She was certain she looked ravishing, and because Johnny had chosen and paid for both the dress and the ear-rings she knew he approved.

She was flanked by Johnny and Lou, both of them smartly turned out in black dinner suits, with white-frilled shirt-fronts and bow ties. Their other table companions were three American tourist couples and the ship's Second Radio Officer who played host. They were a congenial group, and Lou had an easy, wise-cracking personality that kept the conversation flowing.

As they studied the menu Barbara noticed Captain Bradley enter the saloon and take his place at the head of the central table. In some ways he reminded her of her father, and his presence made her feel safe and secure. If the captain saw no need to be on his bridge then all must be well with their insulated world, despite the foul temper of the elements, and regardless of the gentle swaying of the magnificent cut-glass chandeliers.

At the table behind them Lieutenant Jesus Diego and his five companions ate a silent, almost sombre meal, and left the saloon immediately after the coffee had been served. The six young Brazilians had all attended an officer's training course at the Royal Military Academy at Sandhurst, and had boarded the *Pennsylvania* as their only means of getting back across the Atlantic. They had revealed this much to their fellow-passengers, but otherwise they kept themselves very much to themselves.

Barbara barely noticed the close, reserved atmosphere at the table behind her. In fact she paid very little attention to the general cross-flow of joviality around her own table. She had eyes and ears only for Johnny Chance. She knew she was being silly, like a teenager with her first love affair, but she couldn't help herself and she didn't give a damn.

She had known puppy-love, brief flirtations, and a number of half-fearful skirmishes with the opposite sex, but nothing really intense or abandoned. Now she desperately wanted to surrender herself to love, before it was all too late.

Every course of that meal was delicious, a culinary masterpiece, but afterwards Barbara could not remember the name of any one of the rich parade of palate-tickling dishes that passed before her. Her full attention was elsewhere, and what she did remember was Johnny Chance; his smiles, his gestures, his every word. The wine had flown quickly to her head, and she was bewitched by the oldest rapture of all.

Lou Haskins pretended to notice nothing, and when the dinner party broke up he left them to join a regular poker school he had found in a corner of the Mayfair Lounge. As he watched the cards being shuffled for the first hand he was not entirely happy. He had known Johnny Chance for a long time, and like Johnny he had taken to Barbara immediately. He didn't want to see either of them get hurt, but it wasn't his business and he couldn't interfere. He could only hope the ship would hurry up and get to New York. He picked up his cards and tried to concentrate on the game.

Barbara and Johnny had gone dancing to the six-piece orchestra in the Ocean Ballroom. There was room for five hundred people to dance, but the floor was not crowded. The ship was still rolling steadily from side to side and the movement was keeping many of the passengers in their cabins. Barbara was used to it by now, she had found her sea legs and she had the stomach of a good sailor. She gave herself wholly to the mood and the music, and the strong arms of Johnny Chance.

In England Barbara had drunk only the occasional gin and tonic, but on the *Pennsylvania* she was experimenting in a fascinating new world. During the short course of the voyage she had tried vodka, brandy, and champagne, and a whole variety of liqueurs. Tonight Johnny had again bought champagne, and Barbara was feeling as sparkling and bubbly as the drink inside her.

They danced until she was dizzy, making a laughing mess of the foxtrot and the tango, falling over their own feet in the cha-cha-cha, but performing as well as anyone else at the disco numbers in a style which Johnny defined cheerfully as, "Scratchin' and twitchin'." At frequent intervals they broke off to catch their breath and drink more champagne, but Barbara insisted on dancing every waltz. The slow numbers, when she could feel Johnny's arms close around her and snuggle her face close to his chest, were the ones she enjoyed most of all.

When the dance ended they wove a zig-zag course back to their cabins on C deck. The rolling of the ship had them bumping into first one bulkhead and then the other as they moved through the long corridors between the cabins and they were chuckling and holding each other close for support. When they arrived they were reluctant to part.

'My cabin,' Johnny proposed. 'A nightcap to round it off.'

Barbara smiled and nodded. She was already tipsy and she wanted this evening of paradise to go on for ever.

They went into the cabin. Johnny closed the door and locked it before he took off his jacket and tie and moved to pour two drinks from his private stock. He chose bourbon for himself. Barbara asked for a brandy.

They tasted the drinks, toasting each other, and after all the body signals that had already passed between them there was no mistaking their mutual need. They put the glasses down and Barbara moved closer. Her arms slipped around Johnny's waist and her hands moved up to pull at his shoulders. She raised her face to be kissed, her heart was beating fast in her breast and her eyes and lips glistened with desire.

They had kissed before, brief little friendly kisses, goodnight kisses and thank you kisses, but never yet a fully aroused, sensual, sex-seeking kiss. Johnny knew that this one was going to be different, the kiss of no-return, but he couldn't stop himself. He gathered her into his arms and kissed her.

It was everything he knew it would be. Everything it should not have been. Everything they wanted it to be.

Johnny could feel himself growing hard. Barbara could feel it too and pressed herself more tightly against him. His big hands caressed her, stroking her hair, moving over her shoulders. Barbara moaned and parted her lips as she continued to kiss him. His fingers touched the zip of her dress and eased it down the small of her back. His shirt was open and she nuzzled her face against his bare chest. He leaned over her and kissed her bare shoulder as the dress dropped into a white pool at her feet. He lifted her out of it, swinging her up into his arms in her bra and panties. Still kissing her throat, her face, her lips, he carried her softly moaning in ecstasy to the bedroom.

Afterwards she lay in his arms, trembling, feeling small and vulnerable and exhausted, and just a little bit guilty. She was not ashamed of the passion they had shared, even though it had been wild and erotic, exquisite and agonizing all at the same time, but now she could not help remembering what she had tried so hard to forget.

In two or three days time, four at the most, they would reach New York. And in New York he had a wife, and a son.

She moved herself to look at him. Her eyes brimmed with tears and she bit tentatively at her lip.

'Johnny. Oh Johnny, I'm sorry.'

'Sorry?' He looked confused. 'Sorry for what?'

'For making you.' She blinked and a tear escaped. 'It was all my fault. I threw myself at you. I seduced you.'

'Hey, now, you can't take all the blame to yourself.' He pulled her to him and kissed the tear away. 'This is one old dog you're talking to, and you weren't teaching me any new tricks. Let's just say I let myself be seduced.'

'You must think I'm awful. You're a married man.'

'Then you must think I'm awful, for the same reason.'

'Oh Johnny — '

He closed her mouth with a kiss, and held her until she became silent, still and submissive.

'Barbara, you're a sweet girl,' he said at last. 'So let me tell you one thing. This has never happened before. Ever since I've been married to Mary my career has meant long separations, and a whole lot of temptation. But I've never been unfaithful before — not until you came along.'

He stroked her cheek with one finger and smiled sadly.

'I guess we're just victims of circumstances — not knowing how things are gonna turn out in this crazy night world. Maybe that's just me trying to make excuses for myself. Or maybe I'm trying to tell you that I don't tumble all my little girl fans. You are someone really special. The important thing for you to know is that if there is any blame to be shared, then I should get most of it. After all, I am old enough to know better.'

'Johnny, you're not old.'

'Experienced then. Not quite as young as you.'

He kissed her again, and desperately she kissed him back. Then, when the little wave of anguish had ebbed and flowed, she lay with her face pillowed on his chest. She closed her eyes and felt his fingers gently teasing her hair.

Mary. It was the first time he had mentioned his wife's name, and it echoed over and over again in Barbara's whirling brain. Mary ... Mary ... Mary ... it throbbed, burned and accused ... Mary ... Mary ... Mary ...

After all the high excitement there had to be a reaction, and the large, hot tears forced their way out through her tight-squeezed eyelids in a bitter, inconsolable flow.

On the bridge Ed Kubrick was still in command. Ben Grant, the *Pennsylvania*'s Third Officer, had come to relieve him with the change of watch at midnight, but Kubrick had stayed. They were through the hurricane, but the seas were still rearing high and the winds were still at storm force. Grant was a capable junior officer and Kubrick could have gone below, but this was an abnormal voyage. The weather wasn't playing by the normal rules, and after freak lightning and an out-of-season hurricane there was no telling what might come next.

Kubrick wasn't tired yet. He told himself he wasn't ready for sleep, and taking a leaf out of his captain's book he was overlapping with the junior officers, cutting down as much as possible on their hours of solo responsibility.

If there was to be another emergency he expected it to come from the disturbed elements. An undersea earthquake perhaps, or some violent upheaval of sea and sky. Perhaps the compass would go crazy, or there would be a desperate *Mayday* from some other lost vessel in distress. He had the feeling that since the arrival of the cloud anything could happen, but he wasn't expecting any danger from inside the ship. It didn't occur to him that the next threat could come from behind his back.

He heard the door open and a cautious footfall on the deck. He turned lazily, expecting to see a steward with mugs of coffee, or the duty sparks with a radio message, and instead he looked into the dark, tense eyes of Lieutenant Jesus Diego.

'I'm sorry, sir,' Kubrick said calmly. 'Passengers are not allowed on the navigation bridge except by invitation. If you want to see how we work there'll be another guided tour — '

He broke off as the young Brazilian slowly raised his right arm. In the brown, knotted fist was a Webley service revolver and the black muzzle pointed directly at Kubrick's chest.

'I am sorry, Chief Officer,' Jesus Diego said grimly. 'But this is not a visit out of idle curiosity. My friends and I are taking over your ship.'

Kubrick stared at him. For a moment he couldn't

believe it. From behind the lieutenant his five friends appeared, three of them filtering to the left, two to the right. All of them looked smart and efficient in full army uniform. All of them looked deadly serious, and all of them carried levelled revolvers. Apart from Kubrick and Grant there were three other crewmen on the bridge, the helmsman and two duty seamen. There was a gun trained on each of them, and one to spare.

'What the hell is this?' Ben Grant moved belligerently forward, but Kubrick's hand on his shoulder restrained him and probably saved his life.

'We are taking control of this ship,' Diego repeated. 'My friends and I have discussed this over and over again, and now we are all of one mind. We wish to go home to Brazil, but our hope of getting to Brazil from New York is no better than it was in England. Therefore you must change course, and sail this ship to Rio.'

Kubrick had been slow catching on, but now his mind raced. 'That won't be possible,' he said reasonably. 'The *Pennsylvania* is bound for New York. To turn south for Rio would add another five thousand miles to our voyage, and we don't have that margin of fuel. We'd end up adrift with dead engines somewhere in the South Atlantic.'

Jesus Diego frowned. His thin, dark face was stubborn and angry. 'I do not believe you,' he decided at last. 'You will order the change of course.'

Kubrick shrugged. 'I'm telling you the truth. That's why I won't order a change of course.'

There were two revolvers aimed at Kubrick. Diego moved his away and pointed it instead at Ben Grant's right eye.

'This man is your friend,' he guessed. 'You will order the change of course or I will shoot his head off.'

Kubrick stared at Diego. The Brazilian would no longer meet Kubrick's eye, instead his gaze was locked on to Ben Grant. The Third Officer went pale, he began to sweat. Diego's knuckle began to tighten on the trigger.

'Helmsman,' Kubrick snapped. 'Make a change of course two degrees to southward.'

'Aye, aye, sir.' The sailor at the helm deftly swung the wheel over two points.

Diego looked back at the Chief Officer. 'I am not a sailor,' he said softly. 'But neither am I a complete fool. Two points of the compass is nothing. Turn this ship through forty-five degrees. Sail due south, or this man will die.'

Kubrick clenched his fists but had the good sense to keep them at his sides. The words of surrender were wrenched bitterly through his gritted teeth.

'Helmsman, set the new course, due south.'

'Aye, aye, sir.' The response was subdued, but the sailor turned the wheel. Slowly the big cruise ship came round on to her new heading.

Jesus Diego relaxed and smiled. He lowered his revolver slightly and looked back at Kubrick.

'Thank you, Chief Officer. Now I suggest you call your captain and bring him to the bridge. He will have to know.'

16

The cable that had brought Richard Allington down to Washington was brief and urgent, and it was unsigned. He had read it through a dozen times and been tempted to dismiss it as a hoax, but at the same time it had invoked a deep gut-feeling that it might indeed be important.

Come back to Connecticut Avenue. Will contact you there. Extreme Urgency.

That was all. Eleven words and no clue to their author, except that Connecticut Avenue was in Washington, and no ordinary practical joker would know that he had recently stayed there at the Washington Hilton. Allington had puzzled over the message, and then stared doubtfully at the red telephone that was supposed to be his direct link to the White House. There had been no recent calls, and he had to lift the instrument and listen to the faint humming sound to be sure it was not dead.

Either nothing was happening in Washington, or the President was not maintaining his promise to keep the United Nations fully informed. The cable suggested that perhaps something was happening, and Allington was weary of sitting alone in an empty office feeling obsolete and useless. He checked that Amtrack was still running and made his decision.

He managed to call a cab to pick him up at the Secretariat and take him to Pennsylvania Station underneath the Madison Square Garden Centre. The driver chose to head down Second Avenue and then turn west on thirty-fourth. At street level the city was only partially lighted, with many patches of gloom or darkness. The recent snowfalls had been heavy and the sidewalks were piled high. There was very little traffic and the cab had to drive slowly over the hard-packed ice that covered the road.

He was shocked to see the number of broken shop windows that told of systematic looting, and where the windows were intact they were heavily boarded up. Many of the shattered shopfronts showed signs of having been gutted by fire, and at one point they had to back up from a blaze that was still in progress. A large crowd of spectators had gathered to watch two fire trucks fight the flames. The air temperature was killing cold and they had been drawn by the firelight and the radiated warmth.

'It gets worse every minute,' the cab driver muttered nervously. 'Looting, burning, mugging — whole world's gone plumb crazy. I reckon you're gonna be my last fare, mister. These streets aren't safe to ride any more.'

Allington didn't answer, but at the end of the ride he tipped generously. With a warning from the cab driver still echoing in his ears he hurried into the station. The Big Apple was maggot-ridden with muggers and it wasn't wise to loiter.

The train departed half an hour late and the journey took double time, almost six hours. North American winters could be severe at the best of times, but since the dark nebula had arrived and eclipsed the sun, the Arctic had definitely moved south. The train had barely left New York before it was hit by a raging blizzard. Through the carriage window Allington could see the grey-white curtains shrieking past on the wind, and without the snow plough preceding them to clear the piled-up drifts off the track the journey would have been impossible.

He finally had to walk from Washington's Union Station. There were no cabs running, and like New York the city was under snow and siege. It was the same picture of reduced street lights and looted shopfronts. He strode briskly up Massachusetts Avenue, keeping to the centre and avoiding the pavements and shadows on either side. He was stopped three times by steel-helmeted infantrymen patrolling in groups of four. Each time his credentials were checked and he was advised to get off the streets. The capital was under martial law.

It was a relief to reach the Hilton. The vast hotel was almost empty. Only the staff who lived in and had nowhere else to go were still in residence. There were very few guests, and Allington had no difficulty in booking the suite he had occupied on his previous visit. He took a shower, ordered a meal to be sent up, and then settled down to a long wait.

He had arrived just before noon and all through the rest of that day nothing happened. He slept restlessly for eight hours and then the waiting dragged on as before. He began to get frustrated and angry with himself. He was ready to give the cable up as a hoax and was cursing his own stupidity in making the difficult and unnecessary journey. Then, after he had been twenty-four hours in the hotel room, the telephone rang.

Allington picked it up and identified himself. The voice at the other end of the line was familiar, but strained almost out of recognition by some intolerable pressure.

'Richard, I must talk to you. Stay where you are and I'll be with you as soon as I can.'

Allington tried to get in a question but the line clicked dead. He frowned and hung up. The waiting continued for a further ten minutes before he heard the tentative rap of knuckles at the door.

Allington opened it. His visitor was alone, a frightened

man who looked pale as death. He was glancing over his shoulder towards the elevator like a man on the run from the law, or the KGB, or something infinitely worse.

'Come in, Merle,' Allington said quietly.

Merle Forrester came inside and Allington closed and locked the door behind him. Forrester was wearing a felt hat, gloves and raincoat, but he did not attempt to remove anything. He was shivering and he sat down and huddled in an armchair facing the artificial glowing log effect of an electric fire. Allington recognized the need and poured him a stiff bourbon.

'Why all the cloak and dagger stuff?' he asked when his guest had begun to thaw out.

'I'm sorry, Richard,' Forrester took off his hat and began to maul it in his lap. 'Maybe I shouldn't have dragged you down here like this, but I have to tell someone or I'll go mad.'

'Why couldn't you just tell me over the phone?'

'Because this is top secret. Outside the White House I'm supposed to keep my mouth shut. That's why I couldn't come to New York — why I have to be so careful just coming here. I checked the room you were in over the telephone, so just now I was able to by-pass the reception desk and come straight up. I don't think anyone saw me to recognize my face.'

Allington poured himself a drink and pulled up another chair. 'Take your time,' he encouraged Forrester gently. 'But come to the point and tell me whatever it is you want to tell me.'

Forrester took a long pull at the malt whisky. He seemed surprised to realize that he was still wearing his leather gloves and paused to pull them off. He breathed deeply and then spilled out the whole, confidential story. He described the recent Titan Three cloud probe, with full details of the hopeful plan to break up and remove the black cloud with a mass launch of similar magnetic payloads. Finally, gulping more whisky as his tone became increasingly angry and bitter, he revealed the present total impasse that existed between the White House and the Kremlin.

Allington listened with surging excitement, and then growing disbelief. At a dozen points he wanted to interrupt, but he held back with a firm effort of will. Forrester was a man of cruelly torn loyalties and emotions and he was long overdue for a breakdown. It was better to let the words pour out of him, and put the picture together slowly without any cross-examination.

Finally it was over. Forrester was silent and spent. His bald dome was gleaming again with a wet shine of perspiration. Allington fixed him another drink and then sought to bring it all into fine perspective.

'Merle, what you've told me is that there is a way to save the Earth from the black cloud. That we can get rid of it, or at least enough of it to give the Earth some chance of survival — but that cold war politics are standing in the way?'

Forrester nodded. 'That's the size of it. Moscow doesn't trust Washington, and Washington doesn't trust Moscow. For years now we've been tied up in arms limitation talks, all through the sixties, seventies, and the eighties, and neither side has budged a real nit-picking inch. Now we've got this new problem of the cloud, and the only way to solve it is to fire all those arsenals of inter-continental ballistic missiles into space. So we're back on the old vicious circle. Negotiations, negotiations, and still more goddamned negotiations, all leading nowhere. Neither side can believe the other. They're both certain the other side is gonna cheat, hold back on a few ICBMs, and then catch them naked with their pants down.'

'But, Merle, the cloud isn't just a problem — it's a final death sentence on the whole planet.'

'That's exactly what I keep telling Glenn Anderson and the others, but I can't get through. Moscow is disputing our figures on the total number of rockets needed to clear the cloud. The whole thing is getting bogged down in mutual fear and argument. Up to now the hawks are shouting with the loudest voices on both sides. Christ, Richard, if you stick your head out of the window you'll probably hear the generals howling all the way from the Pentagon.'

'It's madness,' Allington said. 'Insane.' He looked Forrester square in the eyes. 'What do you think I can do about it, Merle?'

Forrester looked down at his hands, they began shaking and whisky spilled from the glass he was holding.

'President Anderson and his cabinet don't want this leaked,' he said slowly. 'They figure they are under enough pressure. They don't want the whole country — the whole world — breathing down their necks to force them to accept a solution. I happen to feel different. While they're passing the buck back and forth in secret with Komarov and his Politburo, the rest of the world is disappearing for ever into chaos and darkness. Every day is too late for another million of the world's population. This solution must be made public. It must be forced through as quickly as possible by the sheer weight of world opinion!'

'I'll do what I can,' Allington promised.

Forrester looked at him, his eyes were blinking. 'I guess I'm passing the buck to you,' he apologized. 'But I'm a scientist, and only a pretty poor politician. You're the Secretary General of the United Nations. You have the voice and the prestige.'

'In theory,' Allington murmured wryly.

'Richard, I only know that I can't do this, but maybe you can. You know how to fight them, and I think you've got the heart and the strength for it. I'm already washed up, finished. It's only a matter of time before Anderson fires me or asks me to resign.'

Allington looked into the distraught face of the

Scientific Adviser to the President and felt a moment of deep compassion. Then he got up and fixed them both another drink.

He caught the next train back to New York and endured another long, gruelling journey through the frozen night landscape. There were more delays, more heavy snowfalls, and soon after passing through Philadelphia the heating broke down. The carriage became bitterly cold and on the last lap he was walking up and down and beating his arms across his chest to keep warm.

When at last he came out of Penn Station on to Seventh Avenue there were no cabs, and he had to walk back to UN Plaza. During his absence the City Council had finally decided that to conserve dwindling fuel supplies all electric power would have to be switched off between eight p.m. and eight a.m., and he had only an hour to beat the curfew. Already there were no lights in stores or office blocks, all inessential lighting had been disconnected. The streets of the city were canyons of gloom, soon to become pits of abysmal darkness.

There was a double incentive to hurry, although in the blinding snowfall he hoped that even the muggers would have the sense to stay in shelter. It was difficult to read the street numbers, but he reached the UN Headquarters without getting lost or attacked, and with ten minutes to spare. There was no point in spending the night in a blacked-out office in the Secretariat, so he struggled past the complex to the twin tower blocks overlooking the north end and went up to his apartment suite.

He had just enought time to boil a kettle for a hot coffee before the power went off. He used a flashlight to find his way to the bedroom, but it was a long time before he slept. He lay wide awake, thinking over what Merle Forrester had told him, and wondering how to make the best use of the information.

He left the light switch down so he awoke automatically when the power came back on, and by then he had decided on his first move. There was at last a positive role for the UN to play, and so he had to rally his dwindling supporters. He guessed that more than seventy per cent of the foreign delegations had already left, but he had to call a General Assembly for those that remained.

Now, more than ever, he needed Luis Valdez. The Under Secretary-General had always been his one sure source of support, always able to balance his own judgement with sound advice. But Valdez was long gone, and to set in motion the call for a meeting of the General Assembly Allington had to go to its President, Julius Mangala.

When he tried to use the telephone it was dead. The breakdowns in all the services were getting more frequent and taking longer to repair. There was no time to waste and so he ventured again into the dangerous, frozen streets and walked the few blocks to the offices of the Angola Mission.

It was several minutes before a suspicious African answered the bell. Allington identified himself and asked to see the ambassador. The manservant hesitated but then let him in and immediately locked the door. He used the house phone to make a call and then told Allington to follow him up the wide staircase to the upper floor.

Mangala was in his private suite. He emerged from a bedroom with two packed suitcases and dumped them on the floor as Allington was shown in. The two men who had always been antagonistic faced each other showing signs of mutual awkwardness. The manservant tactfully withdrew.

'Hello, Richard.' Mangala spoke first, straightening up slowly and squaring his big shoulders as though preparing for another battle.

'Hello, Julius.' Allington looked from the wary black face to the suitcases on the floor, and although they had never been friends he felt strangely betrayed. He concluded bitterly, 'I see you've decided to leave.'

'There is no reason to stay. Most of the delegations have gone home. All my own staff left five days ago, except for Simon — the man who opened the door to you.'

'Yes, I know. I can't blame them — or you.'

'I intended to call at the Secretariat to say goodbye.' Mangala stared at the Englishman thoughtfully. 'But you didn't know I was leaving, so why are you here?'

'I wanted you to call another General Assembly.'

'For what?' Mangala's face twisted into a thick-lipped grimace of disgust. 'Another quarrel? To reach another resolution that the rich powers will ignore? In any case there are not enough of us left to fill one small corner of the Assembly Hall.'

'Julius, there is a way to remove the black cloud. But there are problems, and possibly a vital, mediating role for the United Nations. Or, if we cannot mediate, then we must use our voice, the united voice of world opinion, to push this solution through.' He saw doubt in Mangala's face and gripped the African's arm. 'Please, listen to me. Give me five minutes of your time.'

Mangala shrugged, and then gestured to the large four-seater settee that formed part of a creamy gold fur fabric suite. Allington released his grip and they sat down. Mangala folded his hands in his lap and waited. Allington told him everything, except the name of Merle Forrester.

Mangala became more and more thoughtful, and he noticed the only omission. 'Who gave you this information?' he asked. 'Was it President Anderson?'

'No.' Allington realized he would have to protect Forrester and produced a passable lie. 'It was one of the NASA scientists at Cape Kennedy. He asked me not to reveal his name.'

Mangala frowned, but did not push that question any further. 'What do you expect me to do?'

'Stay,' Allington said firmly. 'Stay as part of the

United Nations and help me. We've been enemies in the past, fighting on different sides, but there is only one side now. We've got a common cause and we must unite — and somehow we must unite Anderson's cabinet and Komarov's Politburo.'

'It is useless,' Mangala complained. 'Let me say that it does not surprise me that the Americans and the Russians are still playing at stupid power politics. They make me angry. They disgust me. They make me angry and disgusted with myself because there is nothing I can do. If I could lead a column of tanks into the White House or the Kremlin, then that would be worth trying. But to talk, to beg, to pretend that they will ever listen to the voice of the United Nations — that is a useless waste of time.'

'We must try,' Allington insisted. 'In the past I have always felt that although injustice has sometimes blinded you to reason, your intentions at heart were always for the universal good. Don't prove me wrong, Julius. Please, prove me right. At this moment the world needs the voice of the United Nations more than ever before. This is our last and greatest chance to make it work.'

Mangala wavered, and then said slowly, 'Richard, I must give you back your own words. Once when I spoke of the United Nations as the moral weight of world opinion, you asked me when has the moral weight of world opinion served any useful purpose. The answer is that it never has — and it never will.'

'You are wrong. If you remember the rest of my words I said there were exceptions — like now, when both governments must be genuinely trying to find a formula that will enable them to work together.'

'Perhaps.' Mangala was unconvinced. 'But I have come to see the United Nations as nothing but an impotent sham, because the rich nations of the world will never bend to give up their positions of power and privilege. If Washington and Moscow come to an agreement it will be because they have no other choice, and not because of anything the United Nations might be able to say or do to persuade them.'

He sighed and stood up, signalling that the discussion was at an end. 'So you see, Richard, there is no reason for me to stay. You know that I have a wife and child. They are with my mother in Luanda. Simon has two wives and six children in Angola, and so we are both going home.'

'You've left it too late. There are no more air flights or ships going to Africa.'

'Perhaps you are right, but we are going to the airport to find out. There is nothing more to do, nothing left to lose.' He held out his hand. 'Goodbye, Richard. I wish now that we had been able to work better together, and I wish you luck.'

Allington accepted the handshake, and for a moment he wondered regretfully what sort of a team they might have made together. Now it seemed that he would never know.

He went back to the Secretariat, a ghost building now, invisible without lights. The doors were locked but he had his own key, and he used a flashlight to find his way to the elevator. He was surprised to find it working and rode it up to the thirty-eighth floor. He went into his office and switched on the light, then slumped wearily behind his desk. He was alone on top of the silent, empty monolith.

There were a few ambassadors to the UN left in New York, and with a real job to give them it might be possible to round up a handful of his senior secretariat staff, but his failure to recruit Mangala left him disillusioned. Mangala was a fighter, the Third World champion. With Mangala he could have presented a united front, a truly United Nations. Now he was back to what he had always been, a cardboard figurehead who couldn't even paper over the gaping splits and chasms in his own camp.

Here was the opportunity, here was the moment, and

there was no longer a United Nations to stand up and speak. The babble of conflict was silent at last, only because the voices had given up and gone home. He was still Secretary-General, but he led no troops. He presided over a dead monument and empty conference halls.

His spirits plunged to their lowest ebb. He felt sour and bitter, reflecting for a moment that perhaps the world deserved the black cloud. He stood up and went over to the cocktail cabinet that was never opened unless he had to show hospitality to VIP guests. He opened it now, breaking his own rules, and taking a bottle of bourbon and a glass back to his desk. He splashed a generous helping into the glass and slowly began to drink. 'To hell with the world,' seemed a fitting toast.

It was his darkest hour, and he had lowered the level in the bottle by several inches before he was interrupted. He became aware that the door had quietly opened. It was almost too much trouble to look up, but after a moment he raised his head to see who had entered.

'Hello, Richard,' Lorna Maxwell said, and her voice was husky with emotion.

Allington stared in disbelief. He was seeing a ghost, or the next best thing to a bolt of precious sunlight bursting in through the doorway, and for a moment he didn't know which. She looked tired and cold, despite the borrowed man's overcoat that was several sizes too big for her. She smiled at him, a small trembling smile, and a tear trickled down her cheek.

Ghosts don't cry, Allington thought crazily, and then he lurched to his feet and moved round the desk. Lorna ran to meet him and collapsed into his arms. She was warm, alive, kissing him hungrily and crying tears of shameless joy. Allington hugged her and kissed her back, feeling his heart soar, his spirits and courage flying high as he too came alive.

'Lorna, Lorna —' Her name was jubilation on his lips. 'Oh, Lorna, I was so sure you must be dead.'

'Richard, my darling, there were times when I thought I would never see you again. So many times when I almost gave up.'

'But how? How did you get here?'

'A Trans World Airlines flight from New Delhi. I got into Kennedy Airport a couple of hours ago.'

'New Delhi, that's India.' He was baffled. 'You were in Indonesia?'

'It's a long story, Richard, and it seems as though I've been to every airport in Asia trying to get a plane home. At Djakarta a jumbo crashed and burnt out the control tower. I got a boat to Singapore, but from there I could only get a plane as far as Calcutta. I had to take a train all the way across India, and I met this fantastic Sikh named Chandra Singh who became my protector.'

She laughed at the shocked expression on his face. 'I mean that in the most honourable way, Richard. Chandra Singh was the most magnificent gentleman I have ever met. He treated me as a substitute daughter, because his own daughter is somewhere in America. I shared his private carriage, and at every stop between Calcutta and Delhi he fought like a lion to keep the rest of India out.'

'Thank God you found a friend.'

'He was a good friend. I was sorry to leave him.' Lorna bit her lip at the memory. 'I had a terrible job getting from the railway station to the airport at Delhi, and all the time I was sure it was going to be another wasted effort and that I should have stayed with Chandra Singh. But then I had another stroke of incredible luck. This Trans World flight had been grounded for several days with engine trouble. The American crew wanted to get home but they had to wait for a spare part. They finally cannibalized another aircraft. I arrived just in time to hitch a ride.'

They kissed again, making up for lost embraces, and

no longer feeling any doubts in the intensity of their love for each other. Allington plied her with more questions, but she made him wait for the details.

'What about you, Richard? What's been happening here?'

He gave her a brief outline, and felt her heart beat fast and saw her smile radiate with relief when she learned that there was one possible way to reverse the catastrophe of the space cloud. He hated to dampen her hopes, but he had to tell her the rest, about the present deadlock between the White House and the Kremlin.

'Then we have work to do,' she decided firmly. 'Somehow I felt all along that if anything could be done then there might be a role for us to play here at the UN. Apart from wanting to be with you, my darling, it's the only other reason that made me determined to get back.'

Allington stared at her, and felt rejuvenated. He didn't need Julius Mangala. He didn't need Valdez. He didn't need the General Assembly. With Lorna Maxwell he had heart and hope. She was his army.

'You're right,' he agreed. 'There is work to do. We'll go back to my apartment and get you a bath and a good meal — and then we'll plan our campaign.'

He took her arm and led her out of the office, leaving the whisky bottle abandoned on the desk.

17

Barbara was deep in blissful sleep and did not hear the light but persistent knocking on the cabin door that awakened Johnny Chance. The American blinked open his eyes, wondered who the hell would want to disturb them this late at night, and wished whoever it was would go away. The knocking came again and reluctantly he disentangled himself from Barbara's arms. Her leg trapped his own and he had to tug himself free, but still she did not stir. She slept like a child, her face tear-smudged, but calm now and contented. He smiled at her and covered her naked shoulders with the sheet before he left her.

He pulled on a dressing-gown and closed the bedroom door behind him before he opened up the day cabin to his unexpected visitors. Lou Haskins stood outside, fully dressed and looking grim-faced. Beside him was the grey-bearded captain of *Pennsylvania*, steel-eyed, unsmiling, and equally bleak.

'This is one hell of a time to come calling,' Johnny complained with feeling.

'It's one hell of a time to be hi-jacked,' Lou answered quietly. 'Let us in, John. We've got problems.'

'Hi-jacked —' Johnny gaped at them. Then he stood back to let them pass inside. Lou closed the door. Bradley nodded to confirm what had been said.

'Yes, Mr. Chance, hi-jacked. I had a telephone call fifteen minutes ago from Chief Officer Kubrick who is on the bridge. The group of Brazilian army officers who came on board at Southampton are up there now, all of them armed with revolvers. They have ordered the ship to change course for Rio.'

'Rio?' Johnny's brain was still dulled by sleep and booze. His comprehension was slow.

'They want to go home,' Bradley explained. 'I can understand that feeling. For myself and fifteen hundred others on this ship home is America. We want to go to New York.'

Johnny stared at him, then at Lou. 'Where do we come in?'

Lou shrugged. 'I volunteered our services.'

'The leader of the hi-jack group ordered me to come up to the bridge.' Bradley resumed his story. 'I decided that first I had to hold a war council with my officers. We all agreed that whatever the risk and the cost we must regain control of the ship. It's not just a question of losing an extra ten days to sail down to Rio and back. If we try it we'll use up all our fuel and supplies. At best we'll be stranded in Brazil. At worst we could get hopelessly lost in the South Atlantic.'

He paused, then got to the point. 'It should be a job for myself and my officers, but we're not professionals in that particular field. It was suggested that we seek help from some of the trained ex-servicemen among the passengers. My second sparks — he's the host at your dinner table — mentioned your names. He'd heard one of you say that you were both with the US Marines in Vietnam.'

'Sure, way back in '74. Lou was an old sweat, a sergeant with eight years behind him. I was just a greenhorn, nineteen years old and too dumb to dodge the draft. It was all a long time ago.'

'About twelve years.' Lou agreed. 'But we haven't aged too much. And, John, you did win a couple of medals.'

'One was the Purple Heart,' Johnny snorted. 'I just walked into a bullet.'

'And the Silver Star — you did a little bit more for that.'

'Gentlemen,' Bradley stopped them. 'I apologize if I've asked too much. Mister Chance, you have every right to refuse, and I certainly can't hold it against you.'

'Easy now.' Johnny looked surprised. 'Just don't take any notice of this. I always argue with my manager, that's what he's paid for. You can count on me to back you up in any way I can.'

Lou coughed uncomfortably. 'John, I volunteered you for more than just back-up. It's kinda the front line.'

'How's that?'

'Well, Captain Bradley has a plan that involves somebody climbing up the outside of the ship. And I just happened to mention the way we used to relax between tours. You know, the backpacking hikes, the fishing — the rock-climbing.'

There was silence. Again Johnny stared from one man to the other.

'There's a way of getting a line up from D deck to the bridge,' Bradley explained. 'A man coming up that way could surprise the terrorists from behind. I'd do it myself, but I have to go the easy way. Lieutenant Diego is expecting me to surrender, and it's the only way I can get up there to fix the line. Two of my officers have volunteered, but neither of them have had any experience at this sort of thing.'

'We have,' Lou said flatly. 'I'll do it myself if necessary. But, John, you were always the best man on a rope on any rock face that I ever climbed.'

Johnny scowled at him. 'Lou, you are one hell of a manager. Of all the weird engagements you've ever booked for me, this one sure takes some beating. But you're damned right. If it has to be you or me, then it's me! These days you run out of wind climbing on to a chair to reach a poker table.'

Lou grinned, and even Bradley cracked a relieved

half-smile. Then Barbara spoke from behind them.

'Please, Johnny — please don't.'

The sound of their voices had at last disturbed her and she stood in the bedroom doorway wrapped in a crumpled sheet. The magic had broken and she was shocked and dismayed.

Her entrance caused an awkward moment. Johnny groped for words and looked embarrassed. Lou Haskins sighed softly and turned his head away to study a completely blank section of the panelled bulkhead. He was wondering now if he should have interfered before it had got this far.

Bradley frowned and tugged uncertainly at his beard. 'We'll wait for you outside,' he decided.

'Sure.' Johnny was grateful for his tact. 'I'll be with you in a minute.'

Bradley and Lou went out, and closed the door behind them. Barbara came forward, her face anguished.

'Please,' she repeated. 'Johnny, I don't want you to kill yourself.'

He took her in his arms and kissed her lightly. 'Barbara, honey, there's no need to worry. Like Lou said, I am a damn good rock-climber. D deck to the bridge can't be more than fifty, maybe sixty feet. With a rope in place it's an easy uphill walk.'

'But it must be dangerous. And these terrorists —'

'Captain Bradley was overstating a bit. These aren't fanatical, die-hard terrorists. It's that bunch of army cadets, still wet behind the ears. They're just scared kids who want to go home. When the heat's on they'll surrender.'

She said stubbornly, 'I still don't want you to go.'

'Barbara, don't you see, I have to help. Otherwise this ship will never get to New York. And I *have* to get to New York! I've got Mary and John Junior waiting for me.'

Barbara's face was suddenly crushed. She looked

away and Johnny knew immediately he had said the wrong thing. He quickly changed the subject.

'If I don't do this, Lou will — and I owe that guy a lot. We came out of the army at about the same time after Vietnam. Then we bumped into each other again in a bar on Fifth Avenue. I was at a loose end, picking a guitar, writing a few songs, playing just for beer money. It was Lou who saw what I could be. He taped a few of my songs and took them round to a record company. He got me my first contract and he's been shaping my career ever since. It was Lou Haskins who made the Johnny Chance legend.'

She wasn't really listening and he had to stop. His minute was up and he kissed her again before he got dressed and left her.

On the bridge the tension was mounting, and Lieutenant Jesus Diego was an angry and frustrated young man. He was realizing too late that he had made a mistake. Instead of allowing Kubrick to telephone the captain he should have sent two of his men to fetch Bradley from his cabin. Forty-five minutes had passed and Bradley had not responded. Already it was going wrong and his companions were looking nervous.

There were three approaches to the bridge, the port and starboard companionways leading up from the open boat deck, and an interior stairway. There were also port and starboard doorways on to the open wings of the bridge, where the officers could get an all-round sweep with their binoculars in fine weather, but there was no way up on to the wings except through the navigation deck. Diego had posted a man to guard each approach, and when Bradley finally appeared it was from the interior stairway.

They faced each other, a few paces apart. Bradley had climbed the last flight of steps with his hands slightly raised, empty palms outward above his shoulders. He wore his full uniform, and his eyes were cold beneath the heavy gold braid of his authority. The Brazilian army lieutenant was equally stiff and smart. His black leather boots and belt and the peak of his cap were highly polished. His belt buckle, cap badge and silver buttons flashed and gleamed. His eyes were smouldering in the dark, thin face.

'You did not come immediately,' he accused. 'You have been planning something!'

'I had to consult with my senior officers,' Bradley answered evenly. 'I had to ask my Chief Engineer whether we do have enough fuel oil on board to run the extra distance to Rio. And only my catering officers could work out whether we have enough food supplies and fresh water.'

'And now you are going to tell me that we do not have enough fuel and supplies?'

'No,' Bradley said calmly. 'We can do it with a safe margin to spare. Once we had checked out the figures we voted on the issue. The general view was that a detour to Rio would not endanger the ship, or give any hardship to the passengers. I had the deciding vote, of course, but the safety of my ship and passengers must be my first consideration. To fight you will probably cost lives, so we will go to Rio.'

Diego was suspicious. He had expected resistance, at the least a storm of argument and protest. This was too easy and he feared some kind of trickery.

'Rico,' he said sharply. 'Search him.'

Rico was the heavyweight of the group, a solid young man with a moustache. He moved up behind Bradley, poking him between the shoulder-blades with his revolver, and using his free hand to make a clumsy search. Bradley stood motionless as he was patted and groped.

'No weapon,' Rico said at last. 'Nothing at all.'

'I don't want any blood-letting on my bridge,' Bradley said firmly. 'In any case the only weapons on board are locked up in the chart-room. You must have found them by now.'

Diego frowned. He had examined the entire bridge deck and he had not failed to notice the locked case with two rifles and two revolvers in the chart-room. He had left them there, believing that his men were adequately armed. Now he wondered if the captain of the *Pennsylvania* was being honest with him. Was it possible that Bradley had conceded defeat?

He did not notice the brief exchange of glances between Ben Grant and Ed Kubrick. The two deck officers both knew that since the era of international terrorism there had always been additional weapons stored discreetly in the captain's cabin.

'Can I bring my hands down now?' Bradley asked innocently, and without waiting for an answer he lowered them anyway.

'Captain, you are being very sensible,' Diego said uncomfortably. 'Perhaps I should apologize for all this, but you understand that there is no other way — no other hope for my friends and I to return to Brazil.'

Bradley smiled. 'It's okay, lieutenant, I do understand. We all have homes and families. We all want to get back to them.' He moved closer to the helm. 'Mr. Kubrick, what course are we following?'

'Due south,' Kubrick said slowly. 'As Lieutenant Diego has ordered.'

'That's hardly a straight line for Rio. We want to get there and get turned around again as quickly as possible, so the first thing we have to do is to plot a direct course.'

'Yes, sir,' Kubrick agreed, wondering just what the hell the old man had up his sleeve.

Diego shot warning glances to his friends, but they were all watchful and alert. Bradley moved into the chart-room and Kubrick followed. Diego took up a position in the doorway where he could watch every movement and listen to every word. The revolver was steady in his hand and only his face was uncertain.

For the next five minutes Bradley was busy with a

pencil, callipers and slide rule, debating his calculations aloud with Kubrick. Finally Diego was invited to inspect the new line drawn across the chart, and a correction of four degrees to westward was notified to the helmsman.

Most of the young Brazilians looked happy and relieved at the display of peaceful co-operation. They were all smiles as the sailor at the helm made the necessary turn of the wheel.

Only Jesus Diego restrained his smile. It was too soon to relax. He did not quite trust the too-helpful captain, and he determined not to relax his vigilance.

An hour passed. Bradley suggested casually that Kubrick be allowed to go below, as he had already overstayed his duty watch. Diego feared some action against him and refused. Bradley shrugged and did not push the issue.

Another hour went by, almost in silence. The worst of the storm was over, the wind had dropped and the *Pennsylvania* was ploughing steadily through long, swollen seas. Bradley stood with folded arms, deep in thought. As yet he had made no effort to speak privately with either Kubrick or Grant. Diego had watched him like a hawk, and could swear that no sign had been made to the two officers.

From time to time Bradley stirred to check the compass, the radar screen, and to stare out through the bridge windows. Diego did not know what the captain hoped to see in the stygian darkness, but assumed it was force of habit. During one of these seemingly ritual inspections Bradley suddenly frowned, and moved closer to the window. After a moment of peering out he turned to pick up a pair of binoculars and moved to go out on to the port wing of the bridge.

'What is it?' Diego demanded.

Bradley paused. For a moment he seemed surprised, as though he had forgotten that he was no longer in complete command on his own bridge. 'I thought I saw a flash of light,' he said stiffly. 'Probably another vessel out on the horizon.'

Diego looked doubtful; his gaze flickered towards the radar screen. Kubrick stood beside the screen. He looked down and saw that there were no blips within the five-mile radius of its sweep.

'Nothing here,' the Chief Officer admitted. He was not sure how to play this but added casually, 'It's probably just outside our radar range.'

Bradley nodded agreement. He opened the door and went out on to the open wing of the bridge. An icy blast of wind whipped over him, carrying a few drops of rain, but he ignored it. He raised the binoculars and gazed out into the blackness.

Diego moved into the doorway to watch. The knife edge of the wind made him shiver and he ventured no further. There was nothing the captain could do out there, nowhere he could go, no one he could speak to.

Bradley swept the glasses from south to north. He lowered them and moved out to the far end of the bridge, his tall figure becoming blurred in the gloom as he passed out of the limited reach of the superstructure lights. Diego saw him with his hands resting on the bridge rail as he gazed forward. Bradley lingered for a minute, used the binoculars again, then turned to face directly out to the far horizon. It seemed that his hands were again resting on the rail in front of him, although all Diego could see was his turned back.

Bradley's hands were touching the rail, but they were not resting. This time they were feeling for the thin aerial wire which he knew was tied to the stanchion.

Five decks below were the crew's quarters on D deck, and immediately below was the open porthole to a cabin shared by two of the cooks. One of the cooks was a fat, jovial Italian-American named Firelli who was also a radio enthusiast. He had brought on board his own stereo hi-fi system with record deck, tape deck, and four-waveband radio. To get a reasonable reception on the latter he had approached the captain and requested permission to run the aerial up to the bridge. Bradley had raised no objection, and so on the first balmy day at the beginning of the voyage Firelli had appeared on the bridge to lower the aerial wire down to his cabin-mate. Now, despite the adverse weather of the past few days, the aerial wire was still in place.

Firelli sat on his bunk and gloomily contemplated the invasion of his privacy and the abuse of his equipment. In addition to his cabin-mate the small room was now crowded with two passengers, the ship's Second Officer, and the Chief Engineer. The aerial he had so painstakingly fixed up had been disconnected from his precious radio and secured instead to a line of nylon rope. Most disturbing of all, the intruders were all armed with rifles, and a Colt 0.45 automatic had been tied to the head of the nylon rope.

They had been waiting for over two hours when suddenly the rope jerked. The automatic was whisked off the table and clanged on the edge of the porthole as it disappeared into the night. Firelli winced and recoiled against the bulkhead. Johnny Chance grinned at Lou Haskins and the two ship's officers and let the vanishing rope snake out smoothly through his hands.

Ed Kubrick was mystified, but he knew Jim Bradley was no tame pushover, and he was certain there was no other vessel out there on the horizon. The old man was up to something, and that polished punk soldier was watching him too damn close. Some small distraction seemed in order and he moved over to speak softly to Grant.

'Ben, isn't it about time we had some coffee up here?'

Diego heard the murmur of the Chief Officer's voice and turned sharply away from the open doorway.

'What are you saying?'

'Nothing.' Kubrick looked startled. 'I just reminded Ben that we haven't had any coffee lately. Is it okay with you if we send down to the galley and ask them to bring some up?'

Diego hesitated. He shot a look to Rico who was standing near to the two Americans.

His friend shrugged. 'That's all they said. I heard it.'

'It's mid-watch,' Kubrick explained. 'At this hour of the morning a cup of coffee helps to keep us awake.'

'Coffee!' Diego echoed the word with some amusement. Coffee was of minor importance. He could afford to be magnanimous. 'Okay, you can ask for coffee.'

Bradley had reeled in the line, praying it would not break. Fortunately Firelli had used the strongest wire that was suitable, to ensure that it would not be torn away too often as the ship passed through inclement weather. The wire held and within a matter of seconds Bradley had the Colt 0.45 in his fist. He concealed it under his jacket, thrusting it firmly into the waistband of his trousers. Still working swiftly, with a seaman's sure touch and skill, he lashed the heavier rope securely to the rail. He made sure the hanging rope was close against the stanchion where it would not be noticed from the wheelhouse.

Without haste he changed his position and used the binoculars again for another leisurely sweep of the invisible horizon.

When he returned to the wheelhouse his jacket was neatly buttoned. He had slightly lengthened the strap on his binoculars and was holding them low to hide any bulge that might have betrayed the fact that he was now armed.

'There was a flash,' he justified his lengthy search. 'But it must be well below the horizon by now. It won't pass near enough to cause us any concern.'

In the crew cabin of D deck Johnny Chance was alone

except for the two apprehensive cooks. He had ten minutes to wait while Lou Haskins and the ship's officers moved into position. He spent the time checking over the self-loading Armalite M16 rifle they had left with him. It was the basic US infantry weapon he had used in Vietnam, lightweight for easy carrying over rough terrain, and chromium-plated to resist rust in wet jungles. He had never expected to handle one again, but even after twelve years it all came back to him like yesterday.

Your rifle is your best friend. Maybe your only friend. Your life is gonna depend on it. His drill sergeant had hammered that into him, and it had proved true. He had never forgotten. There were some things a man didn't forget, like his first rifle, his first woman, his first dead Viet Cong. . . .

In the absence of both Bradley and Kubrick the senior officer was the Chief Engineer. However, the chief was overweight, short-winded and near to retirement, and in this situation he was at a loss. He had passed over command to the second deck officer, a tough, aggressive man in his forties named Kemp. Second Officer Kemp had a stiff right leg and walked with a slight limp, which had prevented him from taking on the job that was about to be performed by Johnny Chance, but he was still a man to reckon with. He led Lou and the puffing Chief Engineer quickly up to A deck and the Mayfair Lounge where the rest of their small assault force had assembled.

The weapons that had been removed from the captain's cabin had already been distributed. Johnny, Lou, Kemp and the Chief Engineer each had one of the four Armalite rifles. Of the four handguns one had been passed up to Bradley and the others were carried by the Second Radio Officer and two more ex-soldiers who had been recruited from the passenger list.

'All set?' Kemp asked briefly.

There were nods all round. One of the two electricians who had been working quietly for the past half-hour said confidently, 'We can pull a fuse and black out the boat deck any time you give the word. The spotlight is fixed to a trolley so you can roll it forward and dazzle them right in the eyes.'

'Okay.' Kemp looked at his watch. 'Five minutes and Chance starts to climb. That's when we take up position.'

'One thing,' the Radio Officer said. 'The Chief Steward just called up from the galley. The bridge has asked for coffee. I told him to tell them yes, but do nothing.'

Kemp looked thoughtful.

Lou recognized the same opportunity. 'You got a steward's jacket that would fit me?'

Kemp hesitated, then nodded.

'Then let's do it.' Lou tossed his rifle to the Radio Officer. 'I guess I'll swap you for a handgun. This thing's too damn long to hide under a coffee tray.'

It was time. Johnny handed his rifle to Firelli and said briefly, 'Pass this to me as soon as I'm on the rope.'

Gingerly the cook accepted the rifle. Johnny climbed up on to the top bunk and wriggled his head and shoulders out through the porthole. The wind clawed him with icy fingers but he hauled himself upward on the rope until he was standing on the lower rim of the porthole. He shouted down to Firelli and the cook returned the rifle. Johnny slung the strap over his right shoulder, settled the weapon comfortably, and began to climb.

It was not quite as easy as he had expected. He had tackled sheer, vertical climbs and tricky overhangs in the Rockies, but when climbing for pleasure he had always had the sense to choose fine weather, and even the toughest rock-face could always be relied upon to stay still. Now there was a gale-force wind blowing, and the *Pennsylvania* was still rolling steadily from side to side. One minute he would be hanging out in space, feet flailing for a grip, the rope burning through his hands, and the next he would be slammed against the hull as it leaned away from him. A glance down showed the sea thundering past in racing black waves, and a glance up showed that the bridge was further away than he had hoped. It was at least seventy feet above him.

He made a couple of false starts, going up hand over hand, slipping back as the ship heeled to port and dangled him away from the hull, cursing and at the same time thanking God that he had remembered to anchor the rope inside Firelli's cabin. If he hadn't tied the bottom end of it he would have swung far out, and then dashed himself off the rope when the ship rolled to starboard and flung him back against the steel hull.

He learned fast, making a quick walk up the hull when the ship rolled away from him, and then just bracing himself with his feet planted firmly on a porthole or window ledge each time the pitch was reversed. Once he had got the hang of it he was able to move up one deck at a time, timing each upward spurt of progress with the favourable slope of the ship.

The ordeal only lasted for a few minutes, for he knew he would have to climb fast or he would never make it. He had to fight against the sideways force of the wind that was trying to tear him off the rope, and by the time he reached the upper decks his strength was failing. His arms felt as though they were being torn out of his shoulder sockets and his palms were raw and bloodied.

He gritted his teeth as he reached the level of the boat deck, hanging on desperately for the last time as the *Pennsylvania* made another long, slow roll to port. Then again the ship heaved away from him, he was slapped against her steel side, his rubber-soled shoes found another grip, and he made the last scrambling, backward-leaning walk up to the bridge rail. He swung himself over the top, dropped into a crouch, and unslung the M16 all in one fast fluid movement.

Kemp had been watching for his arrival from the stern end of the boat deck, and all the superstructure lights suddenly went out, plunging the deck and the wings of the bridge into total darkness.

During the past few minutes Bradley had casually manoeuvred himself to where he wanted to be on the starboard side of the wheelhouse. There had been no way of warning Kubrick and Grant without also arousing the suspicions of the hi-jackers, so the captain was still the only man on the bridge who knew what was about to happen. He was waiting for the outside lights to go out; what he did not expect was for coffee to be served, because that had not been part of the original plan.

The young Brazilian guarding the head of the interior stairway was alert and spoke abruptly in Spanish, causing his companions to tense. Bradley stiffened with them and swore inwardly as he saw the white-coated steward appear with a tray of steaming coffee-cups. He thought somebody had slipped up, but then the steward turned his head and Bradley recognized Lou Haskins. The Brazilians began to relax, but Bradley didn't.

'Coffee, guys?'

Lou spoke amiably and Bradley groaned. Good stewards were polite and always said sir. However, the Brazilians didn't seem to notice and Diego grinned and moved to help himself to the nearest mug.

In that moment the lights went out on the boat deck.

Diego backed off as though he had been stung, the revolver in his hand instantly levelled to seek the ship's captain. His companions also reacted with varying degrees of apprehension, and Rico moved quickly to the doorway leading on to the port side companionway to peer down into the sudden darkness.

'What is this?' Diego demanded harshly. 'What is happening?'

'How should I know?' Bradley looked blank and shrugged his shoulders. He saw an opportunity to move one of his officers out of the line of fire and added calmly: 'Mr. Grant, please telephone the engine-room and ask the chief why the lights have gone out on the boat deck.'

Ben Grant looked puzzled but he went over to the telephone on the bulkhead to obey. Before he could dial, the blinding beam of a searchlight lanced out of the darkness beneath one of the lifeboats to dazzle those looking back from the bridge. Rico swore angrily in Spanish and shielded his eyes.

The silhouette of a ship's officer moved into the edge of the beam, staying just long enough for both Rico and Diego to see that he was armed with a rifle. Then before either of them could aim a revolver he had retreated again into the blackness.

'You on the bridge,' Kemp shouted. 'You have one chance to surrender. Otherwise I've got six armed men out here. We'll take you by force!'

Diego swung angrily on Bradley. 'You said your officers were all agreed. There would be no bloodshed. We would go to Rio!'

Bradley shrugged. 'My Second Officer has always had a mind of his own. I guess he changed it.'

'Then order him to back off — or I will kill you.'

'Alright,' Bradley agreed, but he didn't move.

From the boat deck Kemp shouted again. 'You rats on the bridge! I'll fire one volley into the air — just to let you know we mean business.'

There was a ragged crash of gunfire as he kept his word, enough to let them know that there were at least half a dozen weapons ranged against them on the boat deck. The six young hi-jackers looked at each other with white faces, and while their attention was diverted several things happened simultaneously. An unwatched door crashed open and Johnny Chance burst in behind their backs from the port wing; Bradley pulled out his hidden Colt 0.45; and Lou Haskins hurled his tray of coffee-cups into the cursing face of Lieutenant Jesus Diego.

'Hold it!' Johnny roared. The M16 in his hands backed up the command and after one startled look four out of the six hi-jackers had the sense to freeze. They dropped their revolvers as though they had suddenly become red-hot.

Rico was the impetuous one; he spun away from the window overlooking the boat deck and aimed his revolver at the new threat. Johnny fired a short burst and cut him down. Rico reeled back to hit the door behind him which burst open with the impact and he was blasted out on to the boat deck.

Diego was scalded by the hot coffee, and either pain or frustration made him mad enough to start shooting blindly. His first bullet hit Lou Haskins in the chest before Lou could draw his own weapon. The next two went wild, one smashed through a window, and the other ricocheted off two bulkheads and finally hit the compass. By then Bradley and Johnny had fired together and the young lieutenant was hit from both sides in the crossfire. The revolver tumbled out of his dead hand as he fell.

It was over. Kemp came charging up the companionway from the boat deck but he was not needed.

They had recaptured the ship, but the price was high.

Lou Haskins was critically injured, unconscious and bleeding profusely.

And the vital compass, their only means of navigation in a world without sun or stars, was shattered beyond repair.

18

The atmosphere in the White House crisis room was thick enough to slice. Some of the faces gathered there were hard-set and angry, a few uncertain, and most of them pale and afraid. President Anderson had a headache. All of them were trying to grapple with the unknown elements of the most agonizing crisis they had ever experienced.

'NASA calculates that planet Earth has a total approaching 7000 available launch vehicles,' the harassed Merle Forrester spelled it out for them. 'The USA can muster 1000 Minuteman ICBMs, plus 54 Titan Two ICBMs, 200 Anti-Ballistic Missiles, and 42 nuclear submarines loaded with a further 670 Polaris and Poseidon missiles. NASA can add to that a launch vehicle for every launch pad at Kennedy and Vandenberg.'

He drew a breath before plunging further down the list. 'Our intelligence services credit the Soviet Union with 160 land-launched ICBMs, something like 1300 of the two-stage SS 20 Intermediary Range Ballistic missiles which are aimed at Europe and China, and 200 ABMs protecting Moscow. They have 90 nuclear submarines which gives us a rough calculation of 1260 sea-launched ICBMs. Again we can add a Soyuz space rocket for every launch pad at the three cosmodromes at Plesetsk, Kasputin Yar, and Tyuratam.

'Next comes France with 18 ground-launched ICBMs, and five nuclear submarines carrying a total of

80 missiles. Great Britain has a fleet of four Polaris-carrying submarines with 64 missiles. We think China may have as many as 20 of their CSS X-4 rockets, either as ICBMs aimed into Russia, or as potential satellite launchers at their Inner Mongolia test centre.'

He mopped perspiration from his forehead and concluded: 'Japan can probably put up a couple of satellite launchers from their Kagoshima Space Centre, and the Europeans have two launch pads at Kourou in Guiana. And that's about it.'

Bill Clifton nodded agreement. As CIA Director he had the same list in his briefcase, because it was mainly his experts at Langley who had compiled it.

'We may be a missile out either way with the Russians and the Chinese,' he said quietly. 'But 7000 is a hell of a lot of rockets and missiles. Do we really need to fire them all to get rid of the cloud?'

'Yes,' Forrester insisted. 'Because each rocket is only going to tear away part of the cloud. NASA has been working overtime on this, and even if the scheme is feasible we have a major problem. That problem is time. If we attempt to exchange the warheads for magnetic payloads on all our military missiles, including calling in the submarines that are thousands of miles away at sea, then the whole job could take months. By then there will be hardly any human life on this planet left to save.'

'There's also the production problem,' the Secretary of State said bluntly. 'We have a total shut-down in industry. We could give emergency power to the factories needed to produce your magnetic payloads, but even then we have to find and persuade the workforce to come back and do the job.'

'Exactly.' Forrester was grateful for some support. 'And our allies are going to have all the same problems. We've had to face the fact that it isn't going to be possible to remove all those warheads and replace them with magnetic coils. We'll work on as many as we can, but if we are to act in time then most of those military rockets will have to go just as they are.'

'Will they still do the job?' Anderson demanded.

'The cloud itself is magnetic,' Forrester reminded him. 'That means that some of it is going to stick to any metallic object that passes through it. NASA launched another Titan Three yesterday with no payload of any kind. It was fifty per cent as effective as the previous launch with the magnetic payload.'

The four-star general who was Air Force Chief of Staff said slowly, 'So if we could substitute enough magnetic payloads, we would only need to use half as many missiles.'

'We haven't the time,' Forrester said angrily. 'That's why we have to shoot the whole lot into space. We have to get an international agreement and tear the cloud apart and outward with everything we've got. And we'll only get one chance. If there's enough of the cloud left to form a layer still thick enough to keep out the sunlight, then the Earth will be an iceball of frozen corpses long before we can build enough rockets to try again.'

There was a long silence, then Anderson said grimly: 'I have to agree with Merle. Already we have to think of the Third World countries as mostly dead. At first we heard screams from them, then whimpers — now nothing. We'll start getting as many magnetic payloads fitted as we can, and we'll push again for full co-operation from the Russians and the rest.'

There were majority indications of assent, but the Navy Chief of Staff wanted to hedge his bets. He cleared his throat with a loud cough. 'Mister President, my people at the Pentagon have been doing their own homework with the missile figures, and we still figure it's too great a risk to fire them all. The Russians will sure as hell hold something back. We have to do the same. My people calculate we can keep back two missiles on every submarine, and still fire enough to clear the cloud.'

'My guys see it much the same way,' the Air Force General butted in quickly. 'We figure we can safely hold back on at least fifty Minuteman ICBMs.'

'Sweet, suffering Jesus Christ!' Merle Forrester howled at them. 'What do I have to do to get through to you fucking morons?'

His outburst briefly shocked them, but it didn't stop them from pushing their revised figures forward to the President.

In Moscow the thirteen-man Politburo was gathered around the conference table in the Kremlin, and Grigori Komarov was also faced with two conflicting sets of figures. One had been handed to him by the distinguished professor from the Soviet Academy of Scientists who had just made his report and left the room. The other had immediately been thrust forward by the Red Army Field Marshal who was the Soviet Minister of Defence.

The Academy of Science was in general agreement with the American conclusions and proposals, and advocated cautious co-operation, holding back only ten per cent of the land and sea-based ICBMs. It was as far as they dared go after two of the loudest dissidents among them had disappeared, presumably into one of the remote mental hospitals favoured by the KGB.

The military assessment, which Komarov was reading now, insisted that at least forty per cent of Soviet missile power must be retained for defence. Even that was a huge climb-down from their initial stand, and showed that the military men fully realized how desperate the world situation had become.

Privately Komarov agreed with the scientists, but there were two powerful figures at the table for whom the hardline concessions of the military went too far. One was the thin, hatchet-faced Chairman of the KGB, whose twisted genius was so steeped in mistrust and machinations against the West that he could not ever conceive of the two superpowers working together. The other was Sukhov, the patriarch Keeper of the Faith, who still dreamed his stubborn old man's dream of the eventual, total Marxist domination of even this gasping corpse of a world.

'The document prepared by the Academy of Science is absurd,' Sukhov said with contempt. 'And frankly I am surprised that our Comrade Field Marshal should consider throwing away as much as sixty per cent of our defence capability. I still maintain that this space cloud is a Western responsibility. The Soviet Union should only launch the minimum number of rockets and missiles necessary to clear Soviet air space. Let the Americans, the British and the French, use their submarine missiles to save the Third World. The Soviet Navy must not fire a single missile.'

There were nods of agreement from the old men around the table. They supported Sukhov out of force of habit, because their minds were conditioned, and because he was one of them. They were vicious, ruthless old men, and Sukhov provided the intellectual whitewash that had justified their decades of absolute power. They trusted Sukhov. They did not wholly trust Komarov or Ladiyev. Even the Field Marshal was a young upstart who had only just reached seventy.

'Why must we hold the submarine missiles in reserve?' Komarov asked mildly.

Sukhov stared at him. The answer should have been obvious to a child. 'To defend the Soviet Union.'

'If this cloud remains there will be nothing left to conquer or defend,' Komarov said flatly. To further emphasize his point he turned to the Minister of Defence. 'Comrade Field Marshal, I put to you a question. Let us assume that international efforts can clear the cloud, and that the Soviet Union can retain enough missiles to devastate a defenceless United States of America. What would be the point? Could the Red Army then take advantage of the situation to advance and occupy Europe?'

231

The Field Marshal shifted uncomfortably on his chair. To have given a negative answer at any other time would have ended his career, but now Armageddon was approaching. He said honestly: 'The Red Army is no longer a valid fighting force. The chains of command have broken down. Most of the soldiers have deserted and gone home. Millions of them are probably dead, starved or just frozen.'

The old men were struck dumb. They wanted to bay for his defeated head, that was the custom, but slowly it was all coming home to them.

'If the Red Army is broken, then every army is broken.' Komarov had won his point. 'The Americans cannot attack us. We cannot attack them. Even if the cloud can be removed then everything that is left to us will be needed for continued survival and reconstruction.'

'The Americans are not insane.' Ladiyev agreed with Komarov. 'We must find a way to work with them.'

'We can never trust the Americans,' the Chairman of the KGB snapped quickly. 'They have never had the capacity to match us in a ground war. They have always relied upon a nuclear strike superiority. They will retain enough of their missiles to do the job — and there are a thousand million Chinese who will take advantage from the South East to finish us off.'

'There are no longer a thousand million Chinese,' Komarov said wearily. 'I would be surprised if a mere fifty million are still alive. Except for Peking, all of China has been silent for the past week. We have not heard anything from our own people in Siberia. I fear that east of the Ural Mountains almost everyone is dead.'

'We must have safeguards.' Sukhov was adamant. 'The cloud must be removed, but let the West bear the biggest burden. We must ensure the future defence of the Soviet Union, and the continued glorious forward march of world Marxism.'

*   *   *

In Peking, Paris and London, there were more anguished debates on the same basic themes. The five superpowers were all searching for safeguards, and a formula that would enable them to hold back enough of their rocket armouries to maintain their superpower status. The scenes of conflict and heart-searching turmoil were gradually getting bogged down in disputes over the minimum or maximum number of rockets that would be required to disperse the cloud, with every government and every government department contradicting the other's figures.

There were hawks in each of the five capitals who favoured a limited effort, and the lowest contribution of weapons possible. And, facing them, the scientists and humanitarians urged that every launch vehicle available must be used to ensure success.

While the fierce and bitter wrangling continued between politicians, scientists and generals, the black cloud remained, the sun did not shine, and millions of lesser mortals perished.

In New York Richard Allington took the determined step that made the whole issue public. He appeared in a TV news interview that was shown nation-wide from the NBC studio in the RCA Building at the Rockefeller Centre.

During the preceding 24 hours he and Lorna had worked non-stop to canvass support for their campaign. They had talked face-to-face with every ambassador to the UN who was still in New York, and in telephone calls to Washington they had tried to recruit every Senator, Congressman and government official who would listen.

They had found their first ray of hope in the fact that all five permanent members of the UN Security Council were still in residence. The nations they represented were the same five space nations whose cooperation was essential to launch Forrester's survival plan, and so he had a ready-made mediating team. With some reservations they had all pledged to help him as much as they were able.

That one step forward had been counter-balanced at the end of the day by his failure to make any direct contact with Anderson at the White House. He had made four attempts, and each time he had been told that the President was too busy to talk to him.

Finally, as a matter of courtesy, Allington had made his TV intention known to a White House aide. He had been told in return that a TV announcement would be against the national interest, and warned against it. Angrily Allington had pointed out that he was not trying to put pressure on the United States alone. The filmed interview would be flown out to London, Paris, Moscow and Peking, and hopefully screened in all four capitals.

There had been more argument, but by then Allington had only twenty minutes to get from the UN Secretariat to the Rockefeller Centre. He had made his apologies and hung up.

He felt bad about it as he faced the cameras, for the last thing he wanted was to get too far out of step with the White House. However, it was too late now. They were live in the spotlights, microphones reached out on booms, holding back just short of camera range, and he was being introduced.

The interview lasted ten minutes, with only the minimum of leading questions. Most of the time Allington talked directly into the camera to get his message across. He knew exactly what he wanted to say, and it broke down into four basic aims. The first was a passionate plea to the superpowers to bury their ancient differences and act. The second was to offer the services of the United Nations in any mediating role where they could be helpful. The third was to open the eyes of the church, and any other powerful lobby that could operate any sane and moral influence. And last, and by

no means least important, to offer some ray of hope to
the millions in deep despair. He had to stem the tidal
waves of suicides, to let the damned and the dying
know that something could be done — that something
would be done — and urging them not to give up too
soon.

Hang on to life, for there is still hope, was his message to the masses. No matter how the storm broke, sending it had to be the right thing to do.

One man who watched Allington's speech with mixed
feelings was Julius Mangala. He saw the broadcast on
a TV set in the passenger departure lounge at Kennedy
International Airport, where he had waited in growing
bitterness and frustration for the past thirty-six hours.

When he had arrived with Simon there had been
more than a hundred people waiting for flights. Now
most of them were gone, but they had not departed by
air. Instead they had finally grown dispirited, tired
of hanging around and waiting for something which
wasn't going to happen. They had walked away, broken inside, many of them crying silent tears.

No planes had landed or taken off during those
thirty-six hours. There were no scheduled flights
posted. The airport might have been dead, but it was
not yet shut down. There were lights in the control
tower and lights marking one of the main runways.
These facts kept the would-be passengers hoping that
a plane might land, and if it landed it might take off
again.

It was a slim hope, against all the odds, but it kept
them waiting until the will inside them collapsed.

The restaurant and bar were closed. Mangala was
hungry and angry, and he knew he had left his attempt
at departure too late. He had to accept the fact, but
before he could give up and go back to Manhattan he
went in search of one of the few remaining airport
staff.

He found the airport manager's office and heard movement inside. He knocked on the door. No one answered. The room beyond was silent. Scowling, the big African banged furiously on the door until at last it was reluctantly opened.

Mangala faced a grey-haired man in a crumpled suit. His tie was pulled loose from his collar, his jaw was grey with stubble, and his eyes blinked over heavy grey pouches that indicated long hours without sleep. Behind him were three more tired-looking men who sprawled in chairs around the room.

Mangala contained his temper and introduced himself politely. He was a diplomat, and when the occasion required it he knew how to be diplomatic.

'It is very important that I return to Angola,' he concluded calmly. 'Is it possible that there will be a flight to Luanda, or to anywhere in Africa?'

'Africa?' The grey-haired man looked at him with pity. 'Africa is the Dark Continent, my friend, darker than it has ever been before. So is South America. So is Asia. All those continents are dead. Nothing goes there any more.'

'All commercial flights are now finished,' one of the seated men added. 'Nothing is going anywhere.'

'But the airport is still open,' Mangala argued. 'The control tower and the runway are still lighted. You are still here!'

The grey-haired man nodded. 'Sure, Kennedy is still open. As far as we know there are four other airports still open; that's London, Paris, Moscow, and possibly Peking. They're being kept open to fly VIP government officials between the major capitals. Maybe if you wait long enough there'll be a flight to London or Paris. We could squeeze you on board, but you won't be any nearer to Africa.'

'Then why do you let those people wait?' Mangala found his anger returning. 'There are people in your departure lounge who have sat there for days — waiting for nothing!'

'They've been told,' the grey-haired man said wearily. 'At first we kept telling them, every few hours, but they don't go away until they get sick of the waiting. Some of them argue, some get abusive, a few get violent. We got tired of telling them. Now we just stay out of the way.'

Mangala drew a deep breath. 'I will tell them again,' he offered. The grey-haired man just nodded, and slowly closed the door in his face.

The African went back to the departure lounge, called loudly for attention, and explained what he had learned. His announcement created a stir of argument, but he quickly backed out and left them to make their own decisions.

He went back to Simon. His aide looked crushed and Mangala felt a wave of fellow-feeling. They both had wives and children they would never see again. He squeezed the man's arm, and then they both picked up their suitcases and left the airport.

Outside the world was black, as black as the deepest abyss in the remote depths of the sea. They used flashlights to find their way back to the car park, and there it took them the best part of another hour to find their own car. It was a wasted effort, for when they found it the car had been smashed open and stripped.

It was not the work of senseless vandalism, but deliberate cannibalism for the means of survival. The bonnet was up and the battery had been taken. It would provide power to light a bulb for a few precious hours. The petrol cap was missing and he realized that the petrol had been siphoned out of the tank. Now that he looked more closely he saw that every vehicle in the car park had been raped in the same way.

He cursed bitterly over the lost time, and now there was no way back to Manhattan except to walk. The subways and bus services were all part of the past.

They faced a sixteen-mile hike and the batteries in their flashlights were getting weak. The beams were fading and they had to hurry to find the main road, and then hope that the street lamps would be lit. The suitcases they abandoned, leaving them in the boot of the gutted car.

Ten minutes after leaving the car they were mugged.

The street gang which caught them gave them no mercy. In one moment they were picking their way carefully along the edge of the road, and in the next they were attacked without warning. The unfortunate Simon gasped, choked and died almost simultaneously as a thin stiletto knife slammed into his chest, scraping his breastbone and piercing his heart. In the same moment a baseball bat clubbed Mangala across the shoulders and he was knocked face down into the gutter.

The big African struggled to rise and fight, but he was half-stunned and a dozen heavy boots kicked into his face and arms and ribs. The baseball bat cracked down again, almost breaking his spine, and a steel toe-cap caught him squarely over the right eye. He blacked out and slumped motionless.

The two victims were stripped of their valuables, which included their flashlights and warm topcoats and jackets, and then left to freeze by the roadside.

19

The groundswell of reaction to Allington's television interview was explosive and immediate. Throughout the United States, wherever the lines of communication remained unbroken, people from all walks of life besieged their congressmen, their senators, and their church-leaders. These in their turn clamoured to Washington for more information, and above all for urgent action.

In the White House Glenn Anderson and his crisis-room aides were both angry and frustrated.

'How the hell can I negotiate with the Russians while the whole goddamned country is yelling round my neck?' the President demanded in disgust.

No one could answer him and he cursed Allington for a meddler and a fool. Now, instead of getting on with the essential nitty-gritty of bargaining with Komarov, he had to take time off to address a joint session of Congress. They gave him another rough ride on Capitol Hill and when he returned his first move was to fire the bungling aide who had stalled and mishandled Allington. His second move was to fire Merle Forrester. He couldn't prove where the leak had come from, but he could make a shrewd guess, and his Scientific Adviser was becoming too irrational anyway.

The film of the interview had been flown to London, Paris and Moscow, and the sound broadcast transmitted to Peking. In Russia the film was not shown to the general public, but throughout Europe, wherever TV services were still functioning, the face of Richard Allington and his message of hope was screened. As a result Whitehall and the Elysée Palace came under enormous pressure, and indirectly, through Russian embassies all over Europe and North America, some of that pressure reached the Kremlin.

The appeal by the Secretary-General of the United Nations mildly impressed Komarov, and helped to convince the wavering Ladiyev. It was dismissed as mere Western propaganda by Sukhov, and received the same indifference from the rest of the old men who could not conceive of any overture from the West in any other light.

The only man on the Politburo who took it with complete seriousness was the hatchet-faced Chairman of the KGB. He knew only too well that propaganda could prove to be an extremely efficient and damaging weapon. Over the past thirty years his own Department of Disinformation had refined the use of propaganda and the subversion of man's most noble causes and ideals to a fine and insidious art. Slow poison was more mighty than the sword, and the results, in terms of the creeping advance of world-wide Marxism, were greater than any amount of military fire-power had achieved.

The Chairman of the KGB definitely did not underestimate the power of propaganda. He viewed it automatically as a danger which demanded an immediate response. When the Politburo meeting ended he hurried back to his sanctum in Dzerzhinsky Square, there to initiate the transmission of certain specific instructions to the KGB *Residentura* at the Soviet Embassy in Washington.

In the corridors of the Pentagon the levels of rage were reaching paranoia. The hawks of the Navy and Air Force were desperately trying to claw back as much of their missile arsenals as possible, and they wanted no interference or counter-balance to the powerful pressure they were trying to exert upon the White House. Their considered opinion of Richard Allington was that at best he was nothing more than a horseshit intellectual pinko, and at worst a paid tool of the Russians.

The same view also prevailed in certain hidebound ranks of the CIA where the old guard had been preoccupied for too long with the threat of subversion. The Department Chief of the Domestic Operations Division of Counter-intelligence was Sam Brubecker, a sixty-year old veteran who had fought the frontline cold war in Berlin, Vienna, Prague and Budapest, before becoming deskbound at Langley. He sorely missed his active service days of the fifties and sixties, but even though he was no longer out there in the field he still liked to think he was doing his bit in defending the home base. He had the experience, he knew how those sneaky red bastards worked, and he knew they had to be neutralized quickly.

Brubecker knew what everyone with balls was saying, and he agreed with them. It didn't matter whether Allington was some blind, screwed-up idealist, or whether he was open-eyed, bought and bent. Either way he was doing Moscow's job and something had to be done about it.

The CIA had had its share of desertions the same as everything else. Langley was only skeleton-staffed, but with most of its functions made impossible there were still a few spare agents with nothing to do. Most of them were pros, wedded to the Agency, with no home to go to. Brubecker frowned over the list of names available, and decided upon Rex Langford. He didn't want to sacrifice an old friend, and it just might come to that. He was going out on a limb, with no firm directive from above, so if there was any backfire he had to be able to ditch the agent as an incompetent who had misunderstood or exceeded his instructions.

Langford was young, hard and bright, but still slightly green. Langford fitted the job perfectly.

Brubecker called the younger man into his office. Langford was thirty-five, crisp and keen, with steel blue eyes and wearing a conservative grey suit. A stuffed-shirt, Brubecker thought, better fitted for the FBI, but he had been doing pretty well down in Mexico before the cloud had screwed up his last, unfinished assignment. He had got within spitting distance of busting up the hard drugs pipeline that was funding the Cuban DGI covert operations in America.

'Sit down, Rex.' Brubecker liked to be informal, to let the guys know he remembered their names. 'I want you to take a look at this.'

This was a video-tape replay of Allington's speech. They watched it in silence, then Brubecker asked for comment.

'It's a miracle,' Langford said with feeling. 'Until I saw it for the first time on TV last night I sure as hell thought we were all doomed.'

'We could still be doomed,' Brubecker growled sourly. 'The Secretary-General got some of his facts right, but he's gone off half-cocked and what he's doing isn't helping any.'

Langford stared at him. 'Meaning what?'

'Meaning we can get rid of this cloud, but we don't have to throw everything away to do it. If Allington gets what he's aiming for the US of A will commit every missile and rocket we've got, and afterwards the reds will blast us with the nuke overkill capacity they are sure as hell going to hold back. Uncle Sam gets wiped out. Uncle Ivan rules what's left of the world. That's what Allington is aiming for, and we have to get him off the President's back.'

'Are you telling me that the Secretary-General is a red agent?'

Brubecker nodded. 'You've got it.'

'Can we prove it?'

'Maybe, but we can't afford to pussyfoot around on this. The White House has to make a deal with the Kremlin, that's a fact, but it has to be very carefully handled. The President can get all the hard advice he needs from NASA, from us here at Langley, and from the Pentagon. He doesn't need the UN stirring up the whole country and howling for a rushed deal that can only favour the Russians. Hell, Rex, you know the UN is nothing but a hot-bed of stinking communism. They've been anti-American for the past two decades.'

'I'll go along with that,' Langford agreed. 'But Allington is an Englishman, not some jumped-up Third World left-wing politician. I can't see him in Moscow's pocket. And I can't see how we're gonna prove it.'

'I told you, there isn't time to prove it. We have to accept it as fact, and put a stop to it. We have to discredit Allington — smear him any way we can. There isn't time to investigate for evidence, so we just have to invent some. That's your job.'

Langford looked doubtful. 'But suppose —'

'Suppose nothing. What Allington is doing is working for the reds, whether he knows it or not. So plaster him down with some mud that will stick, anything to stop him pushing.'

Langford's opposite number on this particular operation was Aleksi Fedorenko, an older, stiff-necked and even more ruthless member of an even more vicious organization. He was listed as a chauffeur to the Third Under Secretary at the Soviet Embassy. The Third Under Secretary was, in fact, the *Residentura*, a full colonel of the KGB. Fedorenko held the rank of major in the same service, and was the *Residentura's* executive arm.

The *Residentura* relayed the instructions from Dzerzhinsky Square, and in essence they were the same as those Langford had received from Brubecker. Richard Allington was attempting to subvert loyal

Soviet officials in New York and Washington. His actions were a threat to the long-term interests of the USSR. Therefore he must be discredited by an effective smear campaign as quickly as possible.

Unlike Langford, Fedorenko accepted his task without question. He did not even blink when his instructions included an additional footnote. If the smear campaign failed there was a second option. *Mokrie Dela* was the grim term used. It meant 'Wet Affair', because it frequently involved the spilling of blood. It could be a messy accident or a direct assassination. It was Fedorenko's licence to kill.

It had simply not occurred to Allington and Lorna that the extremist elements on both sides would take active steps to plot against them. They were too busy planning more TV appearances, trying to repair relations with the White House, and striving to win more supporters for their cause. They were also unaware of another minor drama that was taking place in Washington, in a neat red-brick town house in the fashionable suburb of Georgetown.

It was the home of Merle Forrester, and he had returned there after he had been fired by the President. He had not argued with Anderson. He had not put up any fight because there was no fight left in him. As Senior Scientific Adviser he had carried the cloud as a personal burden right from the beginning, and now he was beaten, drained, exhausted and empty. He had tried everything possible and they had ignored him. They wouldn't listen. And now Anderson had fired him. It wasn't his burden any more, but there was no relief. The world was dark and dying and there was nothing left.

The house was empty. His wife was dead and gone, and there had been no children. He found a bottle of whisky, a glass, and the old army revolver he had kept as a souvenir of his brief term of military service when he had been drafted into Korea. He carefully loaded the gun and took them all into his study. He sat down at his desk and there drank silently until the lights went out.

It was the inevitable power cut. Domestic supplies were now only switched on for two three-hour periods in the morning and evening, and Forrester saw no point in waiting for six blind hours until the power came on again. The black cloud had seeped into the room and claimed him.

He put down the whisky glass and groped for the revolver. When he found it he pressed the muzzle gently against his right temple. He sighed bitterly, concentrated his last thought on his curled index finger, and pulled the trigger.

While Langford and Fedorenko were receiving their orders, and while Merle Forrester was taking his leave of a world he considered insane beyond redemption, the *Pennsylvania* had at last sighted the east coast of America. The ship's engineers had fashioned a makeshift compass to replace the one smashed by Diego's bullet and the westward journey had continued. In the bows Bradley had ordered powerful searchlights to be rigged, and a constant watch was kept on the radar screens. Within seconds of the radar registering the line of land ahead Bradley had rung down the order to reverse engines and the spotlights were switched on.

The huge passenger liner slowed, but she needed time and distance to come to a full stop. The beams of light lanced forward from the bows, splitting the dreadful darkness, and faintly showing a line of heavy Atlantic rollers breaking upon a black beach. Bradley ordered, 'Hard to starboard.' And the helmsman swung the wheel. The bows turned slowly north, away from the wave-pounded shore, and a few minutes later the big ship came to a stop.

Bradley ordered, 'Stop engines.' And, 'Lower the anchor.'

For this occasion all of his deck officers were on the bridge, and all of them were grinning broadly. They had crossed the Atlantic, without running aground, and with the anchor down to stop them drifting inshore they could at last relax.

However, they still did not know exactly where they were, and while the weather was holding fine Bradley could not allow them too much time to become complacent.

'Mr. Kubrick,' he spoke calmly to his Chief Officer. 'Take Mr. Grant and a lifeboat crew and go ashore. Find somebody and ask them where we are.'

Kubrick moved promptly to obey, and within an hour he was back and making his report to the bridge. They were off the coast of Maryland, midway between the Delaware and Chesapeake Bays, some two hundred miles south of their port of destination. His tone was subdued, and when he had fixed their position on the chart he told Bradley what he had learned about conditions on shore. It was a grim picture, with no light, no warmth, and no food. He and Grant had knocked on the door of the first house they had found, and had brought back the starving family who had given them their information.

'It all sounds as though we've been much better off on board the *Pennsylvania*,' Kubrick concluded. 'Perhaps we should just stay here.'

Bradley had known it would be bad. The long radio silence and the lack of response to their own urgent messages had prepared him. But the ship could only be a temporary refuge and they both knew it.

'We can't, Ed,' Bradley spelled it out with a slow shake of his head. 'We're almost out of food, oil and fuel. We have to move up to New York and disembark the passengers. We have our own floating city, but within a few more days our generators are gonna die. We'll have no more power than those blacked-out cities on land, and the longer we wait the worse the situation is gonna get.'

Most of the ship's passengers had watched the lifeboat being lowered, and later raised again, either from their cabin portholes or from the rails of the upper decks. In general they were elated and relieved that the long, uncertain voyage had come to an end. They were not yet thinking ahead to the inevitable moment when they would have to leave its comforts and security.

Barbara was one of the few who did not feel any uplifting of the spirit. For her the magic of the voyage was already over. Her fairytale romance had come to an abrupt end with the hi-jack in mid-Atlantic. Not because anything had changed between herself and Johnny Chance, but because Lou Haskins had only survived for a few hours after being shot. The bullet had passed through his lung, and the ship's surgeon had been unable to save him.

They had buried Lou at sea, and Johnny had taken it badly. It was a gut-blow to lose a friend, and something worse to consign his remains to a cold and hostile ocean. When they had not been tied up with the music business, or Johnny's family commitments, they had both been outdoor men. They had shared a mutual love of the mountains, the wild forests and the free valleys. When Johnny Chance sang his ballads of the old West he sang with a true feeling for its open skies, and Lou had been a fellow traveller. It had been impractical in the present circumstances to think of taking Lou's body home for a land burial, but even so its last resting-place smacked of betrayal.

Since the funeral Johnny had been sad and bitter. He had lost his former hearty appetite, and he no longer thought of love-making or strumming his guitar.

'It was a crazy thing to do,' he told Barbara over and over again. 'There was no need for Lou to come up on the bridge. He just wanted to be there so he could get between me and that bullet!'

Barbara knew he would get over it, but not before the voyage ended, and then he would be reunited with his wife and son. Like the moon and stars, and the precious sunlight, the golden hours of their dawning love affair had gone for ever.

The *Pennsylvania* began to move again, very slowly with half engine power. Bradley studied his coastal charts every inch of the way, and Kubrick stood with his gaze glued to the radar screen which mapped out the contours of the passing shoreline. One of the two searchlights was still beamed directly ahead, while the other had been turned to port to show up the distant line of breaking waves. Kemp and Grant were both posted on the port wing of the bridge with binoculars, searching the furtherest reaches of the two beams.

At less than ten knots the big ship nosed her bows north, passing the mouth of Delaware Bay and then keeping to deep water but as near as Bradley dared to the New Jersey coast. Kemp and Grant looked hopefully for signs of life, which meant signs of light, but America was in unending darkness and appeared to be dead. After the first few hours Bradley decided to relieve his two junior officers, replacing them in turn with sailors from the duty watch. For his own part he intended to remain on the bridge until the ship was safely docked. Kubrick had volunteered to do the same.

After some eight hours of slow, cautious sailing the first glimmers of light showed ahead off the port bow. Grant had gone below and Kemp had just returned on duty, so it was the Second Officer who called the attention of the bridge. Bradley had their position calculated on the chart and they realized that the lights were those of Atlantic City. Gone was the bright blaze of the popular holiday resort. Instead only the white blobs of the street lamps gleamed like faint strings of pearls, together with the dim red glow of flames somewhere behind the promenade.

They stared landward with mixed feelings. There was some light, and therefore some life, and that was a relief. But the pale street lamps revealed nothing of the once glittering theatres, fun-spots and cafes, and there was no cheer in the fact that part of the city was burning.

For the first time since the ship had turned northward Ed Kubrick took his eyes off the radar screen. He moved across the wheelhouse with Bradley and they went out on to the open wing of the bridge to stand for a few minutes with Kemp. All of them used binoculars to search the five miles of promenade. They saw abandoned cars, silent palm trees, and a few signs of movement. The queen of the New Jersey resorts had become a depressing place, and finally the bitter cold drove Kubrick and Bradley back into the wheelhouse.

Kubrick returned to his radar screen and glanced down, expecting no dramatic change. He received a shock.

'Jesus Christ,' he yelled in alarm.

Bradley was beside him in two strides and two seconds. The green screen made the approaching danger crystal clear. A massive, solid object had moved up to within a mile of their starboard bow and was closing fast.

'Stop engines,' Bradley snapped. He did not dare turn to port, or he would run the risk of running the ship aground. He moved up to the window with Kubrick and they stared out, but they could see nothing in the pitch blackness.

'Mr. Kemp,' Bradley shouted. 'Have one of those searchlights swung to starboard.'

Kemp carried a hand radio to communicate with the seamen operating the two searchlights in the bows. He relayed the order and after a moment the light that was shining ahead began to swing slowly to the right. It traced a path across the empty sea but there was nothing. The sudden danger was still out of range.

'Hold it steady,' Bradley instructed.

Again Kemp relayed the order. The beam of light became still. The *Pennsylvania* was drifting slowly to a halt as they waited.

A minute passed, and the light from the bows was faintly reflected. There was something out there, a vast, polished surface looming slowly closer, and with a flash of inspiration Bradley identified it.

'An iceberg!' There were no giant rocks marked on the chart and his voice was certain. 'That's the only thing it can be.'

From the size of it Kubrick had expected another large ship, perhaps a supertanker, but now he saw the frozen white cliff-face in the searchlight's beam, and he knew the captain was right.

'Oh, Jesus,' Kubrick said again, half in blasphemy and half in prayer. 'It's like the north face of the Matterhorn.'

It was a good description, for like that much-photographed mountain of the Swiss Alps the visible face of the iceberg rose in a great spiked pinnacle. It was bigger than the *Pennsylvania* and towered half as high again over the topmost mast. And it was going to pass very, very close.

Barbara saw it through her cabin porthole and it filled her with terror. She called out to Johnny and together they stared out at the awesome, monumental menace to their lives. It was sliding slowly past only a few hundred feet away, glittering in the ship's lights, and seeming to fill the whole world outside with sheer, unscaleable ramparts of frozen grandeur. It was as though they were cruising off the ice-cap of Antarctica itself, and gradually the gap was narrowing.

'Jesus Christ,' Johnny said, and like three hundred other passengers gaping through their portholes he was echoing the voice of Ed Kubrick on the bridge.

'The whole Polar ice-cap must be breaking up,' he added, marvelling at what he saw.

'Then the Earth must be getting colder,' Barbara whispered, as if fearful of being heard.

'Sure. With no sunlight it had to happen, but I didn't expect it so soon. The ice must be building up in the Arctic, and then breaking off as it gets top-heavy. Then it drifts south.' A thought struck him and he shivered. 'This can't be the only one. There must be more of these monsters drifting down into mid-Atlantic, probably even bigger than this brute. I reckon we got across only just in time.'

Barbara swallowed hard. She knew what he meant. Here they were within lifeboat range of the shore, if the ship struck the iceberg they would not be in such dire straits as if the collision had occurred in mid-ocean, but it was still an experience she could do without. She recalled one of the few things she knew about icebergs, that five-sixths of the whole mass was always submerged, and it started a terrifying new train of thought. She could barely see the top of this staggering pinnacle of ice, which meant the invisible bulk could stretch down almost a mile below the surface. If it dragged on the sea bed perhaps the whole colossal edifice would topple over, and crush the *Pennsylvania* like a falling white tombstone.

She trembled, and Johnny put his arm around her shoulders.

'It must be bigger than the one which sank the *Titanic*,' he guessed. 'Maybe twice as big.'

His arm was a comfort, but his words were not.

Slowly, infinitely slowly, the lofty ice-peak drifted past. As it drew level Bradley ordered, 'Slow ahead engines.' And again the *Pennsylvania* began to move.

It was not until the iceberg was safely behind them that the men on the liner's bridge began to breathe deeply again. Bradley gave the orders to resume half-speed, and for the two searchlights to make wider and more frequent sweeps of the sea ahead, and the ship continued her creeping progress up the New Jersey coast.

During the next eight hours they saw more of the jagged ice blocks, but nothing as close or as huge as the mountain monolith that had almost caught them unaware. Bradley had made no reprimand, but after that first experience Kubrick did not allow his attention to waver from the radar screen for a single second.

When at last they turned the *Pennsylvania's* bows into the wide mouth of the Hudson River the Captain and his Chief Officer were grey and hollow-eyed with fatigue. They were staying awake on will-power and endless cups of black coffee. Probing her way with searchlights and radar the 27,000-ton cruise ship inched her course around Staten Island, and finally passed beneath the Verrazano Narrows Bridge. The lancing spotlight beams picked out the twin, steel-draped towers, each as high as a seventy-storey building, which supported the world's longest suspension span of more than four thousand feet. It was a sight which many on board had feared they would never see again.

With the bridge and the Narrows behind them they were into Upper New York Bay, and here large ice-floes crunched and cracked like cannon shots beneath the cleaving bows. A searchlight picked out Liberty Island on their port bow, but there was no welcoming beacon of light in the uplifted torch in the statue's green copper hand. The 'Gateway to America' was at last extinguished.

They had arrived during one of the enforced power cuts, and the once familiar skyscraper skyline of Manhattan was blacked out. Bradley steered a course by instinct into the Hudson River, and found it completely frozen over. Like a great axe the bows of the *Pennsylvania* carved open the flat ice sheet and turned the splintering slabs on either side.

More than thirty years before, during a longshoreman's strike, the captain of the *Queen Mary* had performed a magnificent feat of seamanship by docking his vessel between the passenger piers of the Hudson River without tugboats, or any aid from the shore. Now Bradley repeated, and even excelled that memorable performance, for he had to dock the *Pennsylvania* unaided in pitch darkness except for his own lights. He succeeded, edging the ship gently into her berth with no more then a bump. Ben Grant and a handful of her crew scrambled ashore to take the mooring lines and make the ship secure.

Bradley ordered, 'Stop engines,' for the last time, with a sigh in his voice and an ache in his heart.

Kubrick offered his hand and Bradley took it, and they held the handshake for a long time. It had been a traumatic voyage, they were almost dead on their feet, but they had brought their ship home.

20

Rex Langford began his new assignment by making a detailed study of everything the computers could print out on the activities of the United Nations, particularly in regard to the background, track record, and political connections of its current Secretary General. It proved a mammoth task, for there was no lack of amassed data, and the bulk of it backed up Brubecker's argument that the UN was nothing but a hostile spawning ground for anti-American abuse and activities.

Both the Soviet and Cuban delegations to New York were heavily overloaded with operatives of the KGB and DGI, and the conference and assembly halls of the UN headquarters had frequently been described as a nest of spies. A former mayor of New York had called it a den of iniquity without morality or justice. The entire organization was dominated by the Third World and Communist countries who had turned it into a strident parrot house of Marxism, Maoism, and other forms of extreme left wing opinion.

Every study and every report was damning to the United Nations as a whole, but there was nothing personally incriminating about Richard Allington. Langford checked back on everything on the files and then reported his findings to Brubecker. The nearest he could get to a sex scandal was Allington's relationship with Lorna Maxwell, and the only basis for a spy scandal were various press photographs of Allington in earnest conversations with members of the communist delegations.

'Good.' Brubecker rubbed his hands together to show that he was pleased. 'We can make some mileage out of some of this. Forget the sex angle. The world's too Goddamned free and easy these days, even if she is an octaroon. Play him up as a top level red agent, another fucking Philby. This picture of him here, talking to Vasilyev. We can use it. We know damn well that Vasilyev is a tool of the KGB.'

'But maybe Allington doesn't know that,' Langford objected. 'It's pretty flimsy evidence.'

'It doesn't matter,' Brubecker said calmly. 'With the whole world in a state of complete chaos, there's no need for us to try and get too subtle or complex. We just have to find some plausible mud, or invent some, and sling it.'

'He was on TV again last night,' Langford said uncomfortably. 'And again this morning. What he's saying seems to make sense.'

'Sure, it makes sense for a lot of people. That's why we have to make them see Allington for what he is — a red agent who is determined to push the US into firing off all her weapons into space, and leave Moscow as the only remaining superpower. Stop believing what you want to believe, Rex. Believe the truth, and help make the rest of the country believe it before it's too late.'

Langford was still not happy. His face showed it.

'Look, I got contacts in the Pentagon. Most of the top Navy and Air Force guys see this the same way. Sure they want to get rid of this cloud, but at the same time they want to safeguard American interests. Allington wants us to strip naked in front of the Russians. No American with balls is gonna do that. So — we have to fix Allington.'

Langford nodded slowly. The CIA and the Pentagon together couldn't be wrong.

'So get to it,' Brubecker commanded. 'Newspapers aren't being printed any more, so we'll have to fight this the same way as Allington, through the TV stations. There are guys on the networks who owe us favours. Get the story right and feed it to them.'

Langford went back to work, but he didn't like it. He wasn't convinced that Allington was a red spy, and deep down he couldn't help wondering if Allington could be right.

Aleksi Fedorenko had no such doubts, and no qualms of awkward conscience. He had been given a directive and he obeyed it without question. In Soviet Russia no one ever argued with the high mandarins of Dzerzhinsky Square, not unless they wanted to depart as martyrs to Siberia, or join the screaming ranks of the living dead in the cellars of Lubyanka.

Fedorenko and Langford were working on a parallel course. They had the same objective, which was to get Allington off the TV screens, and they each chose the same simple method, which was to portray him as a traitor to the West. Fedorenko saw nothing devious or ironic in this. It was simply expedient. Langford had to work hard to invent most of his story, but Fedorenko had better material at hand.

Three years before there had been a tentative KGB attempt to snare Barbara Allington during her student days at Cambridge. She had enjoyed a brief flirtation with a young Palestine Arab named Karim Jalil, who was, unknown to her, a planted tool of the Russians. The handsome young Arab had received his real political education at the Patrice Lumumba University in Moscow before being infiltrated into Cambridge.

Unfortunately for the Russians Barbara had not fallen hard enough. Jalil's dark film-star looks and the mystery of a different cultural background had provided the initial attraction, but he could not match Barbara's bright, intelligent mind, and the affair had quickly fizzled out. The KGB had managed to secure a few photographs of the couple dancing, and of one innocent kiss, but that was all. The hoped-for hold on Barbara, which might have proved a lever on her father, had never materialized.

However, the details of the incident and copies of the photographs were all available and provided Fedorenko with a ready-made story. It did not require much imagination for him to see that he only had to reveal the story and the pictures, and circulate them through the media with a claim that the attempt had succeeded. In the present circumstances it seemed unlikely that Barbara Allington would ever be found to deny the story. The American public would be told that Barbara had been recruited into the KGB after a passionate love affair with Karim Jalil, and that in turn she had converted her father to the communist cause.

It was all lies, but like Langford, Fedorenko believed that he only had to stir up enough imaginary mud and some of it would stick.

Barbara and Johnny were packing their bags when Bradley knocked on the cabin door. They were surprised to see him, and shocked by his exhausted appearance. The *Pennsylvania*'s captain had brought with him a Webley army revolver which he offered to Johnny.

'I feel I owe you this, Mr. Chance. It's one of the weapons we collected from Lieutenant Diego and his group. You did one hell of a job in climbing up the outside of the hull, without your effort it would have cost a lot more lives to recapture my ship, so more than any man you've earned it.'

Johnny hesitated, but then took the weapon, and the handful of bullets that Bradley tipped into his free hand. He said slowly, 'Do you really think I might need this?'

Bradley shrugged. 'I don't know. Just now I had to

berth this ship without any help from the shore. New York is blacked out and no customs or immigration people have come on board. As far as I'm concerned all passengers are free to disembark as soon as they please, but what they are gonna find out there is anybody's guess. I hope you won't need the gun, but it's the least I can do.'

'Thanks,' Johnny said quietly.

'There's one more thing. Down in the galley the cooks are making up packs of food rations. I've ordered one for every crew member who is going ashore. I figure they'll find the food more useful than a cash bonus. My responsibilities to the passengers have ended, but I regard you and Miss Allington as exceptions. There'll be a food pack for each of you if you want to collect it before you leave.'

They thanked him again.

'What about you, captain?' Barbara asked. 'Are you leaving the ship?'

Bradley shook his head. 'The *Pennsylvania* is my home. I don't expect that she'll ever put to sea again, but I'll stay with her. I guess a few of the officers and crew will do the same.'

There was no more to be said, and Bradley was tired. He made his excuses, bid them goodbye and wished them good luck.

After the bearded sea captain had gone Johnny stared down for a moment at his parting gift. Then he broke open the revolver and pushed in six of the bullets. He snapped the chamber shut, put on the safety catch, and weighed the revolver briefly in his hand before he put it to one side. Barbara had watched him, saying nothing, and when he turned to face her they were both uncertain.

'I guess it's goodbye time for us too,' Johnny voiced it at last. 'But I can't let you go wandering about New York alone. Not the way it is now. Even if I gave you the gun, you probably wouldn't know how to use it.'

'I'll be alright. I can manage.' Barbara blinked, but she had made up her mind that in front of him she would not cry. She held her jaw tense, because she was determined that her lip would not tremble.

Johnny smiled wryly. 'Maybe you could at that. But don't make me feel a total louse. Stick with me for a little while longer. My home is an apartment suite that overlooks Central park. I want to go there first, to drop off most of this stuff and to check that Mary and John Junior are okay. Afterwards I'll take you over to the UN Secretariat and make sure you find your father.'

Barbara stalled at the idea. The thought of facing Mary Chance horrified her; she knew she would be embarrassed and ashamed, and surely the other woman would instinctively *know*!

She wanted to refuse, to turn the offer down, but the alternative was equally appalling. She would have to find her way alone through this strange and probably hostile city, in pitch darkness, with every normal courtesy of civilization vanished for ever. She would be as lost in the black depths of the Congo rain forest, and as weak and vulnerable to the jungle predators of the night.

'I don't know,' she said helplessly.

'I do.' Johnny was firm and made the decision for her. 'You're staying with me until I can hand you personally to your old man. That much I owe to you.'

They left the ship an hour later, with the food haversacks Bradley had promised strapped to their backs. Barbara led the way down the gangway with her suitcase in one hand and her flashlight in the other. Johnny carried a suitcase in each hand, and the loaded revolver was thrust into the tight belt of his black leather raincoat.

They had put on their warmest clothes, but even so the below-zero air temperature chilled them to the bone. They had been sheltered on board the ship, but now they realized that the world had grown considerably colder, and the Arctic Circle had expanded to include New York. Snow blanketed the deserted pier, visible in the ship's lights, and they could hear the harsh grating of the shifting ice-floes in the river.

They walked away reluctantly from the lighted sanctuary of the *Pennsylvania*, moving into rapidly deepening darkness as they left the pier. Barbara stopped and looked over her shoulder, wanting to run back, but Johnny urged her on. A blast of icy wind whipped across her cheek. It was too bitter to stay long beside the river, and so they plunged forward into the pitch-black canyons that were the streets of New York.

Barbara switched on her flashlight to find the glass front of the nearest building, and as fast as they were able they hurried on their way. Johnny had assured her that it should be easy to find their way around, even in these bizarre conditions. The eleven avenues of Manhattan ran north to south, and the numbered streets ran east to west, forming an easy-to-remember grid pattern. They had docked on the west side, and simply had to cross three road junctions before turning north on Eighth Avenue. It was going to be a long walk, but with care they would not get lost.

The silence frightened Barbara, but then she realized that technically it was night. Most people were probably sleeping. In the light of her torch nothing showed except snow and ice. The cars that had been abandoned along the street were misshapen igloos. Huge icicles hung everywhere, and where the shopfronts had been smashed open and later filled with drifted snow they reflected the probing beam of the torch like fairy grottoes.

Several times they had to avoid the snow-covered, solid-frozen corpses that dotted the sidewalk. Barbara did not fully realize what they were until a gust of wind swept a dusting of fresh snow from one blue marble face. The sightless, wide-open eyes stared back at her in the light of her torch and she recoiled in horror. Johnny quickly moved her on, but the image stayed in her mind and stirred a turmoil of gruesome thought. If there were dead people lying in the streets, then how many more must there be huddled in the back alleys and behind stairways where they were more likely to crawl and die?

They crossed Tenth Avenue, where the north wind travelled south, moaning and sighing between the skyscraper blocks like all the lost souls of the dying city. Barbara shuddered and almost ran to reach the other side.

As they approached Ninth Avenue they heard the crackle of burning, and smelt the tang of smoke borne on the wind. They moved more cautiously. At a warning from Johnny Barbara switched off her flashlight, for the faint glow of firelight was illuminating the next junction.

Further up Ninth Avenue a large bonfire was blazing in the middle of the road. A score or more of people were gathered around it, warming themselves. The bonfire was made up of splintered desks, chairs and office furniture, and as Barbara and Johnny watched two men emerged from the nearest building to throw more fuel on the fire. One of them hurled an armful of box files and papers. The other was dragging an interior door. He wore a length of rope for a belt which supported a large axe.

There were muted cheers as the door was consigned to the flames. The man with the axe in his belt stood back grinning; he was a negro and obviously the ringleader.

'There's not much law and order around these days,' Johnny whispered softly in Barbara's ear. 'So it might be best if these people don't see us.'

Barbara nodded, and her throat moved painfully to swallow her fear. She couldn't take her eyes away from the dull glitter of the steel axe-blade at the black man's waist. Then Johnny nudged her hard with his elbow and they began to move, hurrying fast and silently across the open avenue, and not daring to breathe until they had ducked into the black tunnel of the continuing street on the far side.

Barbara switched on the torch again to probe their way forward, and revealed more ice and snow. Wherever they passed a shopfront or a restaurant it had been smashed and looted, and now that she knew what she was looking at she saw the remnants of previous bonfires. When she recalled that this was once the greatest and richest metropolis on Earth she wanted to weep.

They came on to Eighth Avenue, and Johnny borrowed the torch to check the street sign and make sure they hadn't gone astray before they turned north. Now the bitter wind was driving full into their faces, channelled down the glass and concrete canyon like a river of cold air in full spate. They had to hunch forward and struggle against it.

At the next junction the bonfire blazing on Ninth was again visible up the street to their left, for they had walked two sides of the block. However, they were further away, there seemed less need for caution, and Barbara was tempted to linger for a moment to look at the inviting red glow. Thinking they were far enough away to be safe she omitted to switch off the pale, stabbing finger of her torch beam.

There was a sudden shout from the distant group around the fire. The silhouette figures in the shadows jerked, wavered, and then began to surge toward them. They had been spotted and for a moment Barbara froze.

'Run!' Johnny shouted at her, and swinging the suitcase in his right hand he hit her bottom hard and impelled her forward.

They ran for sixty yards before the pack leaders turned on to Eighth Avenue behind them. Several members of the group had grabbed burning brands from their fire to light the way and they were gaining fast. Johnny and Barbara were slowed down by their suitcases which they were reluctant to abandon, and they hadn't realized yet that it was their luggage which had attracted pursuit. To the starving mob there was only one burden which still had any value, and they had been mistaken for looters who had found a source of food.

The chase was short and swift, and ended when Barbara slipped and fell heavily on the ice. Johnny blundered past her before he could stop his own momentum without losing his balance in the same way, and then turned back. Barbara had lost her suitcase and her torch, but was desperately crawling towards the latter. The dim but precious beam of light was more important than anything else.

She reached the torch, picked it up and rose unsteadily to her feet. She was bruised and breathless and two of the running men with firebrands were almost upon her.

Johnny dropped one of his suitcases and used both hands to hurl the other. It struck the first man in the chest and bowled him over backwards. The second man skidded to a stop, and Johnny recognized the negro with the axe. He now wielded a flaming chairleg in one hand, and the axe in the other. With a wild yell he leaped forward, both weapons whirling.

Johnny pulled the loaded revolver from his belt, levelled it quickly and fired. The black man was blasted back on his heels. The axe flew from his hand and crashed through the windscreen of a snow-shrouded car that was parked at the kerb. The fiery torch dropped from his hand and sizzled as it rolled over the hard-packed ice.

The rest of the pack wavered and fell back, uttering savage yells of alarm and fury. Johnny couldn't be sure that there wasn't another firearm amongst them, so he grabbed Barbara's arm and hauled her away. Their lives were more important than their luggage and they left the suitcases behind.

They ran until their lungs were bursting and then looked back. Far behind in the darkness they could see the faint flickers of flame from the hand-held torches. The chase had stopped and the shadowy figures were busy forcing open the locks on the suitcases.

'Damn them!' Barbara cried, and wept with anger and frustration. For a moment she was forgetting that they were all damned already.

'It's only clothes,' Johnny tried to console her. 'A few souvenirs and some toilet gear. I guess what they were really after is still on our backs.'

He was referring to the haversacks of food which Bradley had given them, but Barbara was not thinking of her stomach. She held up her torch with its fading beam and said in anguish, 'All my spare torch batteries were in my suitcase. When these are dead we'll be blind.'

It was a grim prospect, but Johnny would not let her dwell on it. 'All the more reason to keep moving,' he told her. 'We just have to follow Eighth for the next fifteen-sixteen blocks, so we can go sparing with the torch.'

They pushed on, and this time Johnny took her arm and they followed the straight line of abandoned vehicles that appeared to run the whole length of Eighth Avenue. They moved faster without their luggage, and by feeling their way from one vehicle to the next they were able to dispense with the torch for much of the time. Occasionally, down some of the intersecting streets, they saw more distant glows of firelight.

After what seemed an age of groping blindly into the teeth of an icy wind they reached Columbus Circle at the south-west corner of Central Park. Here Johnny had to use the torch for a few minutes to find their way across. It had been one of Barbara's schoolgirl ambitions to see the lights of gay Broadway, but now, ironically, she was crossing that world-famous thoroughfare without even knowing it.

'Only a few more blocks,' Johnny encouraged her, and they struggled on.

Central Park was now on their right and more bonfires burned throughout its length to give some flickering relief to the darkness. They could hear the sound of axes chopping down trees as desperate men sought out the last stands of fuel to keep the fires burning.

Johnny moved with yet more caution now, for even before the coming of the cloud the park had earned a bad reputation as a haunt for rapists and muggers. He knew the packs on their backs would mark them down as a likely target. Barbara was stumbling wearily at his side, and he knew that she was no longer in any fit state for a sharp burst of speed. He eased the revolver out of his belt and carried it in his hand.

He was counting the blocks on their left, and was relieved when at last they could turn away from the park. When he found the apartment block that contained his New York home it was in darkness, like all the rest of the city. He hesitated on the sidewalk outside, afraid of what he might, or might not find, then drew a deep breath and plunged into the building. He kept the revolver at the ready, letting Barbara carry the weakening torch.

There was no point in trying the elevator. Instead he directed her to the stairway and they climbed up to the third floor. He located the apartment door where he hoped to find his wife and son, and then stopped dead. The door was sagging open on its hinges, and beyond it the apartment was a black cavern of silence.

Johnny was shocked. Barbara could feel him stiffen, and heard his muffled sob. He released her arm and then took the torch from her hand. In its light she saw that his face was drained white. She had seen pain there when Lou Haskins had died, but it was nothing compared to the infinite, soul-crushing agony she saw now.

Like a zombie Johnny moved into the apartment, and Barbara had no choice but to follow him. Every room had been stripped, the furniture smashed. The kitchen had been gutted, the refrigerator was overturned and empty. Barbara guessed that the looters had wanted food, and anything that would burn on the bonfires.

The boy's bedroom was recognizable from the football players on the wallpaper. The main bedroom still contained the double bed that had been too bulky to drag away. Both were empty. Johnny searched in anguish for bodies, but the dim light of the torch beam revealed nothing.

'Oh, my God,' he whispered. 'Where are they? What happened to them?'

Barbara could give him no answer. She wanted to put her arms around him, to comfort him and hold him tight, but he was seeking his wife. It was the wrong moment, and even in that way she could not help him.

Johnny closed his eyes, as though trying to shut everything out. He swayed, seeming on the point of collapse, and Barbara reached out a tentative hand to steady him. With an effort he opened his eyes again.

'The Jacksons,' he said hoarsely. He was thinking aloud. 'Mary and Selena were close friends. Maybe they'll know something.'

He stumbled out of the apartment and moved to the next door down the short corridor. It was closed and locked and he began to hammer on it with his fist.

'Selena! Frank! It's Johnny Chance. If you're in there, for God's sake answer me.'

The Jacksons, Barbara realized, were his neighbours. She waited uncertainly while he continued to shout and pound on the closed door, and it was not until he had almost given up in despair that they heard a muffled answer from inside.

Johnny stepped back from the peephole in the door and shone the torch on his own face so that he could be identified. A bolt and chain rattled and then at last the door was pulled open. A young coloured woman stared at them, her face startled, and almost as anguished as Johnny's own.

'Johnny — Johnny Chance. Oh, thank God, it is you!'

'Selena.' Johnny moved forward and gripped her arms. 'What's happened here? Where is Mary? And John Junior?'

'Your boy is here with me,' Selena Jackson told him. Her voice choked and then she burst into tears. 'But Mary is gone. She went out with my Frank three days ago. They were looking for food while I stayed here with the kids. But they never came back, John. They just didn't come back.'

21

To Barbara the next hour was eerie and dreamlike. First there was an emotional reunion between Johnny Chance and his six-year old son. The boy heard and recognized his father's voice and came running out of a bedroom in his pyjamas. He sobbed uncontrollably and it took a while for Johnny to calm him down. Finally they all found seats, and Barbara switched off the torch again to conserve the last glimmers of light while Selena Jackson explained in more detail what had been happening.

The entire nerve-wracking experience of finding their way from the ship to the apartment block had seemed unreal, but it was even more nightmarish to sit and listen to Selena's disembodied voice in the darkness. Now that they had stopped moving Barbara felt weak-kneed and sick, her head ached and her whole body trembled.

In New York things had quickly gone from bad to worse, Selena told them. Because this was the biggest city in the United States, with an already stupendous and continuous demand for electric power, it had been the first to break down. With no sunlight the demand had immediately doubled, and it had proved impossible to generate the electricity needed to keep the millions of lights burning. Now electricity was strictly rationed, and rotated between the boroughs. Power would be switched on to Manhattan and the Bronx for two hours between eight and ten a.m. Then it would be the turn of

Queens and Brooklyn between ten and twelve. New Jersey was twelve to two. The cycle was repeated, and then twelve hours of darkness that would be normal night.

'So there is some light,' Johnny said with relief.

'In another hour,' Selena answered.

'Then as soon as the power comes on I'll go out. I have to try and find Mary and Frank.'

'You won't find them,' Selena said with the conviction of despair. 'I know if they could have come back, they would have. Frank wouldn't leave me with the kids. And your wife wouldn't leave John Junior.'

'I know,' Johnny said, and there was a thick lump in his throat. 'But I have to go out there and try.'

'Maybe you do,' Selena was resigned. 'But while you're out there, maybe you can find something to eat. I got practically nothing left to feed the kids.'

'There's food in my backpack,' Johnny told her. 'Enough for a few days. You take charge of it, share it out as you see fit.'

'Take mine as well,' Barbara offered.

There was a short silence. Johnny was still confused, his mind reeling from the shock. He was holding his son tight enough to hurt, but John Junior was quiet now and did not even whimper.

'What happened in my apartment?' Johnny asked at last.

'Some people broke in there, two nights ago.' Selena sounded embarrassed. 'I heard them shouting and smashing things up, but they sounded drunk or high and I didn't dare go out. The telephones don't work any more so I couldn't call the police. And even if I did, I guess the police wouldn't come any more anyway.'

Her voice trembled at the memory. 'They banged on this door, too — tried to break in. I shouted out that I had a gun in here, and a dog. I don't have either, but they wouldn't chance it. They just went back to breaking up your place.'

'It's okay,' Johnny assured her. 'It's not your fault.'

They talked some more, but there was not much more to say, and the silences lengthened.

When the power came on it startled them. Selena had left a light switch down, so without warning the room was abruptly flooded with light. They were all dazzled, and it took a few seconds before their eyes could adjust and they could at last see each other clearly.

Selena's children were a girl of five and a boy of three, two sleepy-eyed, dusky infants who woke automatically and came stumbling in search of their mother. The introductions were made, and the food packs Johnny and Barbara had brought from the *Pennsylvania* were quickly investigated. There was butter, coffee, sugar, biscuits, and tinned meats and fruit. The children were eager and excited and Selena quickly prepared breakfast.

Barbara was not yet feeling hungry and declined. Johnny also waved aside the food. He had only two hours while there was some light, and he was determined not to waste any. He kissed John Junior and gave him a hug, and assured Barbara and Selena that he would take care. He went out with the revolver to begin his hopeless search, and they locked the door behind him.

Barbara helped Selena to wash the dishes after the children had eaten, and the conversation between them was strained as they tried to avoid worrying aloud over Johnny. When the job was done Selena switched on the large television set in the corner of the room.

'It's only on for an hour,' she explained. 'And then only for the news. We don't get entertainment programmes any more, but it's better than nothing. They keep saying the government can rip this cloud away with rockets, but it ain't happened yet.'

It was the first Barbara had heard of the controversial plan to peel off the cloud and hurl it back piecemeal into space, and she quickly pressed for more details. Selena did not fully understand all the arguments, or the technical details, but she gave the bare facts as well as she was able. Barbara listened with rising excitement. She knew the cloud was magnetic, and the rocket plan did sound plausible. She wanted to know more, and suddenly she could not wait for the TV set to come alive.

They settled down to watch. Selena had her arms full with her own children and for a moment John Junior stood uncertain. On impulse Barbara held her arms out to him. He bit his lower lip for a second or two and then came to her. He had Johnny's eyes and Johnny's tousled black curls, and like his father he immediately won her heart.

The face of the newsreader appeared abruptly on the TV screen; he was talking but there was no sound. The transmission flickered, and Barbara guessed that the studios were probably undermanned and the equipment breaking down from lack of maintenance. She was frustrated by the poor reception and resisted the temptation to get up and tune the set. Selena and the children were watching patiently, and had obviously become resigned to its erratic behaviour.

There was a buzz of interference, the picture rolled for a few seconds, and then it steadied and the newsreader's voice broke through in mid-sentence.

'... worst hit states are Dakota and Minnesota. In parts of North Dakota the blizzards have been raging continuously for five days. The Polar air mass seems to be pushing south through all the mid-west states, and heavy snowfalls have been experienced for the first time in the jungle areas of Mexico.

'Scientists are agreed that our planet is definitely getting much colder. Rivers as large as the Missouri and the Mississippi are freezing over, and ice is creeping down from the Polar regions toward the equator. The new ice age is beginning, and scientists predict that without sunlight the Earth will be a dead planet in less than six months.'

The newsreader's face was expressionless, his voice toneless, but he was not inhuman. He had to pause and swallow hard before he could go on.

'We have no world news to report. All Third World continents are silent, and although a few people may still be alive there are no longer any communications. The picture in Europe is much the same as the situation here in America. The struggle goes on in most cities to maintain domestic power and keep the street lights burning for a few hours of each day. In New York and Washington the power-rationing schedules are unchanged. For other cities and areas please watch your local TV station after the main programme. . . .'

The picture suddenly cut out, but the sound continued. The news was all bad and for all warm-blooded life forms time was fast running out. The grim nightmares that had destroyed the Third World were now being repeated in Europe and America, as people from the smaller towns and villages flooded into the big cities where there were still some hours of power and light. Even so, many power stations had broken down. Food and energy supplies were dwindling, and there was increasing mob violence, looting and burning. In all the large cities sectarian and racial gangs were roaming the streets, killing each other as they competed for the last scraps of food. In many cities great fires burned out of control, the flames fanned by the fierce, driving winds. Atlantic City, Chicago and Birmingham in Alabama were among the cities listed as being totally obliterated by fire.

The picture returned and the sound went dead, and Barbara sat in frustration again as the newsreader shifted his papers and his mouth opened and shut like that of a goldfish in a square bowl.

'. . . . From Vatican City in Rome.' The words

boomed through with increased volume. 'The Pope was speaking in answer to the many new bizarre pseudo-religious cults which have appeared with their own explanations for why God has decided to punish the world. His Holiness reaffirmed his belief that God does not intend the entire world to perish. He called again for Catholics and Christian peoples everywhere to maintain their faith and to join him in prayer. Especially to pray for guidance for the governments of Great Britain, France, China, America and the Soviet Union, in their efforts to find a solution to their dilemma.'

Barbara thought the sound had gone again, but it was only a bitter pause before the newsreader launched into his next item.

'A press statement from the White House, issued just before this programme came on the air, regrets that there is no progress yet in the difficult negotiations with the Soviet Union. However, President Anderson and his crisis team are confident that eventually an agreement will be reached.'

'God damn them!' Selena burst out angrily. She had sat throughout in impassive silence, but this was too much and the tears flooded down her cheeks. 'They say that every day but they don't do nothing. My Frank's gone and he ain't coming back. I sit here in the dark and my kids cry and say when's Daddy coming home. We cold and we hungry — and they don't do nothing!'

Barbara was embarrassed and didn't know what to say. She didn't know the other woman well enough to pick the right words. But then the children began to whimper, and Selena controlled herself enough to calm them, shushing them and rocking them gently in her arms.

'. . . . The Secretary-General of the United Nations, Mr. Richard Allington —' Barbara's attention had wavered but at the mention of her father's name it snapped back sharply to the screen. The newsreader's face was expressionless again as he continued: '— More doubts have been raised today concerning Secretary-General Allington's motives in revealing the top secret government plan for removing the black cloud with a mass launch of rockets and missiles. We learned yesterday that Allington was a close confidant of Igor Vasilyev, a member of the Russian diplomatic mission to the UN who is also known to the CIA as a high-ranking officer of the Soviet KGB. A few hours ago more facts came to light which would suggest that Barbara Allington, the Secretary-General's daughter, was suborned by the KGB while at university in Cambridge, England in the summer of 1983.'

Barbara stared aghast at what followed. First a photograph of her father in earnest conversation with another man, presumably Igor Vasilyev, taken in the foyer of the UN General Assembly building. And then a photograph of herself dancing with an Arab student whose name she could barely remember. If anyone had told her three years before that Karim Jalil was a spy intent on converting her to the communist cause she would have found the whole idea laughable. To hear the same idea presented on American television as something that had actually happened was both staggering and unbelievable.

'To answer these charges we have Secretary-General Allington here in the studio, in a live interview with Max Cornfield.'

The screen went dead for a moment, and then lit up again to show her father and an interviewer seated in facing chairs. Barbara stared, feeling a surge of emotion, and when the camera closed up on Allington's face she was shocked to see how much he had changed. The streaks of grey in his hair were thicker, and there were more of them. His face was tired and strained.

'Mr. Secretary-General,' Max Cornfield opened the interview. 'These attacks on your integrity are an outright insinuation that you are working primarily for the

Russians. What do you have to say to that?'

'I find it both amazing and irrelevant,' Allington said calmly. 'Our world is caught up in a cosmic disaster that has already brought our civilizations to ruin, and has already caused the death of more than half the planet's population. For those of us who are left to continue to argue over the fears and aspirations of individual nations is both crazy and suicidal. I am working for all the survivors of mankind, whether they be Russians, Americans, Hottentots or Chinese.'

'But you cannot deny your close friendship with Igor Vasilyev, whom we now know to be a member of the KGB.'

Allington shrugged. 'If you try hard enough you're sure to find evidence that at some time or other I've talked to every member of the UN General Assembly. I only knew Vasilyev as a secretary to the Soviet delegation. Perhaps he is also a KGB officer. I'm not ignorant of the fact that some of them are.'

'So you won't deny that Vasilyev is a KGB man?'

'Frankly I don't care a damn whether he is or he isn't. They only important thing now is to secure an international agreement between the five so-called space nations that will enable us to bring back the sunlight.'

'That's why you're putting pressure on Congress, and on President Anderson and his government?'

'Yes.'

'But you can't put that same pressure on Grigori Komarov and his Politburo, because they will censor any media approach to the Soviet people. Which means your pressure is one-sided.'

'That is something beyond my control, but I am doing everything in my power to impress the need for urgent action on the Soviet government.'

'But you don't deny that everything you do is putting more pressure on President Anderson than on Komarov?'

'No, I can't deny it. But —'

'So the fact is that in effect, if not in intention, you are working in the best interests of the Russians. If America has to go it alone to clear the cloud, then the Russians will be left as the only major nuclear superpower.'

'America cannot go it alone. That is the whole point. It is going to take every single rocket and missile on the face of the Earth to be sure of clearing the cloud. If anybody holds anything back the whole effort could fail.'

'There are experts in the Pentagon who refute that claim, but I think we've covered this ground before. The big news tonight is that your daughter was subverted by the Russians during her time at Cambridge. We have this photograph of her dancing very closely with Karim Jalil. We know that Jalil was working for the Russians, and that he had a very passionate affair with your daughter Barbara. Since then has Barbara tried to influence you in any way with her communist views?'

Barbara fumed, and if it had been possible she would have slapped Cornfield's face. The man was so smug and his mouth was full of insinuation and lies. She could see the little signs which showed that her father was also angry, although he was careful not to lose his temper.

'I've never heard my daughter mention this man by name, and all your photograph proves is that once they danced together.'

'But in approaching your daughter the Russians were obviously hoping to get a hold on you?'

'To the best of my knowledge the Russians have never had any kind of hold on my daughter,' Allington stressed firmly. 'She has never communicated any communist views to me.'

The cross-examination continued as though Allington was on trial, and when the interview ended

Barbara was both furious and frustrated. She wanted to know more about the survival plan, but every time Allington had attempted to get on to that track he had been thwarted by a fresh attack. Practically all of his valuable air time had been taken up in defending himself against the various charges the media had raked up.

There were more news items and interviews to follow, but Barbara was no longer interested. Her mind and emotions were in turmoil and she only knew that it was now more imperative than ever before that she reach her father as quickly as possible.

The power was cut again before Johnny returned, and they endured another hour of darkness before they heard his knock. Selena demanded to hear him speak before she opened the door, and Barbara was almost sick with relief to hear the familiar sound of his voice.

They found each other and Barbara held him tight. He hugged her in return and she could feel the emotion in him through the hard tension in his shoulders and arms. However, he did not kiss her, even though Selena and the children could not see them. His thoughts were still with his lost wife.

'You didn't find them,' Selena said. It was a statement, sombre and matter of fact.

'No, I couldn't find them.' Johnny tried to keep the pain out of his voice. 'I went round all the stores where she used to shop. All of them have been broken into and emptied. Some of them are burned out. I couldn't find any of the store-keepers, or anyone we used to know. I stopped a few people on the street — tried to describe Mary and Frank — but nobody wanted to listen. They're all scared, or too busy hunting for something to eat. They're like wild dogs out there, scavenging, snarling at each other, or just avoiding each other. I wouldn't have believed it possible that people could go back to being animals so soon.'

Barbara could feel John Junior trying to push his way between them. She felt guilty and disentangled herself from Johnny's embrace. She felt Johnny lift the boy up in his arms. For a while there was silence.

'So what are you going to do now?' Selena asked at last.

'Keep trying, I guess.' There was no hope in Johnny's voice and none in his heart. He knew that if his wife was alive she would have come back. 'I'll go out again when the power comes back.'

Johnny was tired; he had been on his feet and burning up nervous and emotional energy for the past three hours. He found the settee and sat down with his son. Barbara sat beside him. They heard Selena settle into a chair and begin crooning to her two children.

There was a long silence, and Barbara began to bite her lip. She didn't want to intrude into their shared grief, but there was so much she had to say. Finally she took the plunge and told Johnny everything that was in her mind, about her father, the TV interview, and the little she knew about the plan to remove the cloud.

Johnny stirred, showing interest. 'You think this crazy idea could work?'

'I think that it must be worth a try. Remember that I watched the cloud as it approached Earth. The Columbus Two comet mission satellite which brought it down weighed only a few hundred pounds, and not all of it was steel. That ought to give you some idea of the magnetic strength of the cloud. All the huge stockpiles of rockets and missiles we have available must add up to *thousands of tons* of steel that can be hurled outward from the planet. It must work to some degree.'

Johnny whistled softly in the dark. 'So maybe this old Earth isn't doomed after all.'

'Maybe not. At least my father thinks there's a cause still worth fighting for, and I have to help him. I can refute some of these stupid spy stories that are being spread about him if nothing else.'

'Okay,' Johnny decided. 'I promised to deliver you to your old man and I will. We'll go over to the UN as soon as the power comes on again.'

'Don't worry about John Junior,' Selena told him. 'I'll take care of him while you're away. Maybe if you can help that man get the rockets launched we'll get the sunlight back. Maybe then we can find out what happened to my Frank — and your Mary.'

'Maybe,' Johnny said. He hardly dared to hope, but at least it seemed a better bet than just groping in the dark.

When the time came it was hard for Johnny to wrench himself away from his son. The boy cried and Barbara felt bad too. Finally Selena took the initiative and pushed them out. They had eaten while they waited but they left Selena with the bulk of the food. In return she had provided them with two new batteries for Barbara's flashlight, the last of her own private hoard.

The wind was still bitterly cold, but now there were scattered street lights burning to reveal the glittering, ice-coated sidewalks. There were more people prowling the shadows, lean and hungry people who looked desperate and dangerous. Barbara was afraid, remembering the mob that had chased them up Eighth Avenue, but this time they were travelling light. They carried no packs that might have contained food, so they were not attacked.

They skirted Central Park and then hurried down Fifth Avenue to Forty-Seventh Street where they turned east. It was a longer walk, equally depressing, but they made fast time. The street lights helped them find their way, and they knew they had only a limited time before the whole city was plunged once more into that terrible, total darkness.

When they reached First Avenue Barbara thought that the entire complex of the United Nations Headquarters was in total darkness. Then she looked upward. High up, where the 38th floor of the Secretariat building must be, a single square of white light was showing.

'Dad must be up there,' Barbara said, and they crossed the road quickly and hurried to the base of the building.

The glass doors into the foyer were closed but not locked. They went inside. The building was blacked out and Barbara switched on the flashlight. They moved forward slowly and saw the elevators.

'Too risky,' Johnny decided. 'If the power goes off while we're halfway up we'll be trapped. We have to climb.'

Barbara nodded agreement. They found the stairway and began to climb. It was hard work and they had no breath left for conversation.

After what seemed an age of toiling upward they reached the 38th floor. Barbara played the torch up and down the empty corridors and found the office where the light was showing. It was the office of the Secretary-General and her heart soared as she ran the last few steps to push open the door.

There was a man seated behind her father's desk, but it was not her father. There was no one else and she looked round helplessly before staring into the bruised and battered black face. She drew a deep breath, but her voice faltered.

'Who — who are you?'

Julius Mangala looked weak and exhausted, like a man who had come back from the dead. He had, in fact, nearly died, and it had taken him two days to find his way back to Manhattan from the airport. A lesser man would never have recovered consciousness after the beating he had taken, but Mangala had the constitution of a bull, and an iron determination to match. He had survived and returned, and there was still some dignity in his voice when he answered her question.

'I am the Under Secretary-General for Assembly

Affairs. But who are you?'

'I'm Barbara Allington.' She frowned at him. 'I suppose my father isn't back yet from the TV studio.'

'Richard's daughter.' Mangala understood. 'I'm sorry but your father is no longer in New York. The TV interview was broadcast from Washington.'

'Washington?' Barbara was bitterly disappointed and it showed. It had not occurred to her that the TV station didn't necessarily have to be in New York.

Mangala nodded. 'Richard left a note on his desk. Perhaps for me, perhaps for you, I don't know. It was not addressed to anyone. It simply states that he and Lorna Maxwell have moved down to Washington. They are still trying to influence the White House, Congress and the Pentagon, and they hope to achieve more in the capital. The letter is dated yesterday. I'm afraid you have missed your father by twenty-four hours.'

It was a blow, but Barbara would not admit defeat. She turned to Johnny who waited in the doorway behind her.

'I have to go to Washington,' she said simply.

Johnny was torn again, thinking of his son. He had only just found the boy, and if he went to Washington he would have to leave John Junior for several days at least. Perhaps he would never get back. But if he went back now there was nothing to do except sit and die in the dark. He struggled with his inner anguish, and in the end he nodded.

'Okay, if we can find a way, I'll take you.'

Barbara nodded her thanks. Her eyes were damp and she didn't know what to say. She knew what an agonizing decision it had been, and if Mangala had not been watching she would have kissed him.

The African stood up slowly behind the desk. He had abandoned Allington once and it had been a mistake. Now he knew the world had no other hope and he was ready to give his full support to Allington's efforts. He would have to swallow some pride and admit he had been wrong in the past, but he was man enough for that.

'I think maybe the UN still has a few automobiles locked away,' he volunteered hopefully. 'If we can find one with a tank full of gas I'll come with you to Washington.'

22

Allington and Lorna had set up their new base in the Washington Hilton. With the collapse of the telephone service New York had become too remote from the hub of government, and the move had become essential. Here they were within walking distance of the White House, the Capitol, and after a three-mile hike to the far side of the solid-frozen Potomac River, the Pentagon. Washington was also blessed with more working hours of light and power. Electricity to the city as a whole was switched on between nine a.m. and noon, and again between three and six p.m. The supply to the main government buildings was still maintained round the clock.

Allington had delayed the move, hoping that Barbara would arrive in New York, but he had kept a constant check on the Amtrak schedules. The service was down to one train each day and the line could not be kept open indefinitely. When he learned that the service was to be terminated he knew that he and Lorna would have to take the last train to Washington.

They arrived with the buoyant hope that they would be able to do more on the spot, but after the first two days those hopes were beginning to fade. They could get to the guarded doorways, but more often than not the doors were closed in their faces.

At the end of the second day Allington returned to the hotel with his spirits dashed. He found Lorna stretched out on the bed, her shoes off and her eyes closed, looking as tired as he felt. For both of them it had been an exhausting day. It was a moment before she became aware of his presence and her eyelids flickered open. She smiled faintly and roused herself with an effort.

'Coffee, Richard?'

He nodded and she poured two cups from a flask. There was also a large plate of beef sandwiches which they ate hungrily. The menu at the Hilton was no longer luxurious and varied, but the simple fare provided was more than could be found on the streets and they were grateful.

The electricity had been cut for the past two hours, but the hotel was doing its best for its few remaining guests. A paraffin stove had been found to give some warmth, and the suite was romantically lit by the small yellow flames from three solid silver dinner-table candelabra.

When they had rested and refreshed they compared notes. Lorna had spent all day in the Senate Building offices and in the Capitol, and her feeling of achievement was not high.

'I think I've talked to every Senator and Congressman who is still holding on,' she said wearily. 'Most of the people I talked to are in agreement with us, but they are in the same position. They can't crack open the White House or the Pentagon. Anderson and the generals have sealed themselves off from everybody else. They can't cope with the pressure so they've shut it out.'

Allington nodded agreement. They were fighting a losing battle because they couldn't get through to the men who mattered, the men at the very top who were blind and deaf to all reason.

'I spent three hours at the Pentagon,' he told her bitterly. 'The highest Navy rank I could get face to face was a Lieutenant Commander. The Air Force wouldn't let me get above a Major. They both stone-walled like a couple of androids.'

'The Pentagon is a waste of time, Richard. The White House is the key. It must be. It seems as though it's almost a personal thing now between Anderson and Komarov.'

'I called at the White House on my way back from the Pentagon. The guards wouldn't let me through the gates. A bloody aide came down to talk to me. He brought me President Anderson's compliments, told me the President is familiar with all my views and agrees with them in principle — but the President is too busy working out the *necessary adequate safeguards* to spare me any of his time.'

Allington quoted the exact words of the White House aide with the emphasis of disgust, and his face was bitter.

'Damn the safeguards!' Lorna blazed with sudden passion. 'Surely they must see that if they wait much longer there won't be anything left.' She got up from the table and paced the room. All the frustration was boiling up inside her, but after a moment she calmed herself and apologized.

'I'm sorry, Richard. It's just that I can't help thinking of all those people who helped me out in the Far East. There was a young Indonesian army lieutenant who saved my life in Indramaju — the little *betjak* driver with six children who found me a ship to get out of Djakarta — and Chandra Singh who helped me to cross India. I suppose they are all dead now. They helped me, but there is nothing I can do to help them. It's as though it has all been a total waste of their effort and mine. I'm back here with you, but we can't help anyone. We can't help ourselves. The darkness is for ever and we're all going to die.'

Allington stood up and took her in his arms. 'We'll keep trying,' he promised her. 'Sometimes I think the world is so bloody-minded that it is hardly worth saving, but we'll keep trying. Tomorrow I've got another TV spot, after that I'll go back to the White House. You can try the Soviet Embassy. Perhaps you can persuade the ambassador to use whatever influence he may have in Moscow. We must keep trying to impress Komarov as well as Anderson.'

Lorna leaned against him, glad of his strength and the warmth of his arms. She listened to what he was saying, but her dejection made the renewed effort they would make tomorrow seem of little importance. They were quiet for a little while as she leaned her head upon his shoulder, but then she raised her head to look hopefully into his face. He understood her need and tenderly he kissed her.

Lorna was comforted, and allowed herself a selfish thought. Her long and arduous journey had been worthwhile, if only for these few stolen moments. They both knew now that they loved each other. There was no more need for tests or separations. The tragedy was that there was no more future. There was very little time left for them to share.

'Let's go to bed,' she said at last. 'The world has had enough of our time for one day.'

Allington smiled and nodded. 'I'll fix us a nightcap while you get ready. Is brandy okay?'

'Please.' Lorna kissed him again and then disappeared into the bathroom to shower.

Allington poured two balloon glasses of cognac. The Hilton was still well-stocked with liquor so there was no problem there. He tasted his drink slowly, letting the warmth flood his stomach, and trying to ease the weight of the world off his shoulders.

When Lorna reappeared she wore a filmy nightdress of yellow silk. The colour was fresh and exciting against her smooth coffee-cream skin, her eyes were soft and sparkling and her hair was luxurious and loose. Allington caught his breath when he looked at her, and thought her the most beautiful and splendid woman he had ever seen. He gave her her drink and she toasted him briefly before taking it into the bedroom.

Allington joined her a few minutes later. They lay side by side in the large bed, propped up on one elbow, facing each other and sipping the last of the brandy. Lorna's eyes seemed to grow larger, more luminous, and more gently teasing with every passing moment. When they kissed again her lips were moist and sweet.

For a long time, even after they had been reunited, they had refrained from making love. Lorna had feared that because of her skin colour a sexual affair between them could have been used as another character smear against her lover. But she needed him as much as he needed her, and as despair for the world had plunged ever deeper into hopelessness it no longer seemed to matter.

They had eaten by candlelight, and now they made love by candlelight. It was not the first time, but they were still discovering each other's special needs and delights. They were gentle at first, touching, kissing, caressing, almost in fear of offending, but swiftly confidence and passion grew together as their blood caught fire and their bodies came alive to ecstasy. Lorna felt her senses swirling, her heart pounding and her loins melting in the overpowering waves of her emotions. Her lovemaking became desperate, shameless and abandoned.

Allington tasted the sensuous hunger in her kisses and embraced her more fiercely. He wanted to take her, and give to her, and become one with her. He wanted to make her his woman, and make himself her man. His need was her need, and when they joined together need became desire, and desire became a soaring entwinement of all the agony, beauty, and rapturous fulfilment of enduring love. Their climax was an explosion, not only a physical outpouring, but a release of feeling that was too wonderful, too intense, and too exquisite to contain.

They lay breathless and silent, and slowly peace returned and a deep contentment. Lorna closed her mind, refusing to think of anything. For the moment it was enough to be warm and satisfied in her lover's arms. However, after a few minutes, Allington voiced his own troubled thoughts.

'What we just shared was beautiful, but it leaves me a little sadness. My deepest regret now is that the world isn't going to last long enough for me to marry you and make you my wife.'

Lorna kissed his bare shoulder, and stroked his cheek with her fingers. 'It's alright, my darling. It doesn't matter.'

He sighed heavily. 'Perhaps that part of it doesn't. We can dismiss it as ritual. But we hit such a peak. It was so — so excruciating.' He had to search for the word and even then he was not sure that he had chosen correctly. 'Somewhere there's an instinct inside me which just feels that I may have fathered a child for you. But it's something we shall probably never know. Our world will be dead long before it can be born.'

'Oh, Richard.' She felt his anguish and held him close. In the same moment the last stubs of the candles burned out in the silver holders and the room went black.

Time passed. Allington slept, but Lorna lay wide awake. He had started a train of thought that was spinning in endless circles in her mind. An idea was forming, but she had not grasped it yet. She couldn't forget the powerful emotion Allington had expressed when he had talked of wife and child, and like an insistent echo in the background of her brain was President Anderson's demand for necessary adequate safeguards. Perhaps somehow the two could be made to work together, combined, dovetailed — perhaps there was an answer.

She couldn't quite work it all out, and with her brain still dizzy she slipped into sleep. But the glimpse of the idea was still there, germinating in her subconscious.

* * *

On the far side of Connecticut Avenue Alexi Fedorenko was watching as the last faint flicker of candlelight expired from the fourth-floor window. The Russian was cold, shivering inside his heavy, full-length overcoat. His hands and feet were numb, and his hat was pulled down and his coat collar turned up to protect his ears from frost-bite. He was a patient man, invisible in the eternal night.

He was failing in his mission, and that would not be forgiven. Therefore it was unthinkable. It must not happen. Despite the success of the smear campaign Allington was still pushing his views and pestering Soviet diplomats. Slandering Allington had not been enough, and so Fedorenko had decided to get the whole business finished quickly and go for his second option. It would have to be a wet job.

He had decided that a knife would be best, the thin-bladed knife in the leather sheath strapped to his forearm. He was tempted to enter the hotel and get it over, but he realized that Allington was probably sleeping with the woman, and that the obvious murder of such an important man might still prompt some awkward repercussions.

It would be better if the murder fitted the pattern of a random killing. Washington was littered with the corpses of mugging victims, and the unfortunates who had simply fallen prey to senseless street violence. Allington would have to join them the next time he emerged from the hotel on one of his endless treks around the capital.

Fedorenko switched on the pencil beam of a small flashlight, located the edge of the sidewalk, and began to walk away. His vigil was ended for tonight, but he would return.

While Lorna and Allington slept, and Alexi Fedorenko made his grim, compassionless way back to the Soviet Embassy in Washington, a large black Lincoln limousine was driving carefully along the New Jersey turnpike between New York and Philadelphia. A small blue flag of the United Nations still fluttered bravely from its gleaming bonnet. Johnny Chance was at the wheel, with Barbara hunched beside him, and the solid bulk of Julius Mangala in the seat behind.

In the white swath of their headlights the highway was covered by a blanket of hard-packed ice and snow, and Johnny did not dare to put his foot down too hard on the accelerator. Tyre tracks showed that a few vehicles were still using the road and keeping it open, but many of these had come to grief. Almost every mile they passed crashed cars, or cars that had skidded off the road and plunged into snowdrifts. Before leaving the underground garage where the few remaining UN vehicles had been locked away Johnny had found a set of light snow-chains which he had fitted to the Lincoln's wheels, but even with these he had his doubts that they could make it.

'So far the worst of the blizzards have hit the midwest states,' Mangala was leaning forward and tried to encourage him. 'The news reports say there isn't a single road open in Wyoming, Colorado or Kansas. Here on the east coast it hasn't been quite so bad.'

'It's bad enough,' Johnny said bleakly. 'Let's just hope that none of these drifts are completely blocking the highway.'

Mangala nodded and said no more. He could see that Johnny needed to concentrate all his mind on his driving. The African was beginning to wish now that he had not suggested this wild and dangerous journey. He too was having his doubts that they would reach Washington.

The miles cruised slowly past as they pushed steadily south. Frequently Johnny had to ease the car down to a crawl, and sometimes to a stop, before he could figure out the best way to manoeuvre around the frozen scene of a road accident, or the white dune of a drift. Fortunately the weather was clear, there was no snow falling, although they could hear the icy moaning of the wind across the unseen polar landscape. Barbara shivered at the sound, and was grateful that the heater was working.

They had covered less than fifty miles when they ran into trouble. Johnny saw the obstacles coming up ahead and automatically lifted his foot from the accelerator. There were two police cars parked sideways on, facing each other with a row of black oil barrels in between, effectively blocking off the whole width of the road.

'Hell,' Johnny swore. 'It's a roadblock.'

He moved his foot over to the brake as he saw figures stirring in the gloom behind the police vehicles. The whole set-up looked official, and being an honest citizen with no criminal intent or record he was fully prepared to stop. Then Mangala yelled urgently in his ear.

'Keep going and crash through! It's a trap!'

Johnny was startled, but then he saw that among the half-dozen muffled and desperate men who manned the roadblock only one wore the peaked cap and badge of a police officer. All of them were armed with rifles, and in another few seconds the weapons would be aimed and firing.

'Duck,' he shouted, and his foot hit down hard on the accelerator. The big limousine gunned forward with a roar of engine power, the wheel-chains flailing as they churned up ice and snow. With one hand Johnny grabbed Barbara's shoulder and pushed her hard down in her seat, and with the other he spun the steering wheel and aimed the Lincoln square at the centre oil barrel. He could only pray that the barrels were empty.

A rifle cracked and the windscreen shattered, showering them all with broken glass. Barbara screamed and Johnny cursed as the flying splinters gashed his cheek. Then with a violent crash the big car butted its way through the barrier, sending the crumpled oil barrels spinning to either side. The men manning the roadblock went sprawling or were scattered. The Lincoln skidded to one side, cannoned into one of the police cars with a lurch and a tearing of metal, and then sped on her way. A hail of bullets followed them, but mercifully none found a target.

Johnny drove for another mile down the turnpike before he dared to slow and look back at his passengers.

'Is anyone hurt?' he asked.

'I do not think so.' Mangala picked himself up from the floor of the car and his sweat-shiny black face appeared again behind the seats. 'Barbara?'

'I'm okay,' Barbara answered without conviction. 'Just a scratch here and there. But why did we have to burst through a police block?'

'It was not a police block,' Mangala told her. 'There is no police force any more. There is just mob law, and some of these starving mobs include men who were once policemen. To them a travelling vehicle must mean that someone is surviving, perhaps with food in the car, and at the least with gas in the tank and power in the battery. These things are priceless, so it is suicide to stop.'

'You could be right,' Johnny agreed. 'As we went through I saw up to a dozen vehicles pushed off the road. They all looked as though they had been looted. Thanks for the warning.'

'I was almost too slow,' Mangala apologized. 'It took a moment for me to remember what had happened to my own car at Kennedy Airport.'

There was nothing to do but drive on, and now the wind was blasting directly into their faces through the broken windscreen. The cold was ferocious, and their only comfort was that the rifles at the roadblock had not shot out the vital headlights. The double beam still probed ahead to light the way.

After twenty minutes another obstacle loomed, and they recognized the scene of a multiple car smash. There were seven or eight vehicles tangled together in the pile-up, and the whole mess showed signs of having been engulfed by fire. In at least two of the burned-out steel tombs the trapped corpses remained frozen where they had died.

Johnny realized that for so many vehicles to be involved the accident must have happened some weeks ago when the road was still busy. But nobody had bothered to remove the bodies, or tow away the wrecks. It underlined Mangala's view that there were no police forces any more, and no emergency services of any kind. All the dignity and decency of civilization had dissipated with the apocalyptic impact of the cloud.

Grimly Johnny skirted the metal graveyard and their desperate journey continued through the frozen night. It was too late now to turn back, and no matter what horrors or ambushes lay ahead, they had to face them.

23

In all five of the superpower capitals the agonizing debates continued. The Presidents, Prime Ministers and politicians went through their own kinds of hellfire and purgatory, and Merle Forrester was not the only one to leave the conference rooms of power and commit suicide in despair.

As the days and weeks went past the endless arguments began to wear themselves out. Darkness was King, and Death, Ruin and Starvation were his Princes, and no amount of arguing could change that. Richard Allington had revealed to the world that there was a way to salvation, and the demands of the people could not be denied. The cracks appeared in the governments in London, Paris and Peking, and the government of Great Britain, taking refuge in their special relationship with the United States, was the first to give way.

From Whitehall the British Prime Minister announced that Britain's four missile-armed submarines would be placed at the disposal of the United States. The missiles would be programmed for Earth escape, and fired upon American command.

The British had, in effect, passed the buck.

Peking capitulated forty-eight hours later. Chinese oil, coal and food stocks had already been depleted. The nation was becoming extinct and its leaders had nothing left to lose. They signalled that they were prepared to follow the British example.

Haughty France, the nuclear renegade of Europe, proud of her fine independence from both East and West, was the last to climb down. Recognizing the inevitable the French government finally committed its missile arsenal to American command. However, Paris insisted that this was subject to the Soviet Union entering into the same pact.

As Lorna Maxwell had already surmised, the final stages of the conflict were being argued between Washington and Moscow. The battles of willpower were still being fought in the White House and the Kremlin, and still Anderson and Komarov could not find the essential formulae for agreement.

The one immovable obstacle which remained was the vital question of safeguards. Both Presidents now accepted that everything had to be committed, even though they still faced opposition from within their own inner circles, but neither side knew how to trust the other. All their observation satellites had been swallowed up by the cloud, their high-flying spy planes could no longer fly, and there was simply no way in which either side could monitor the actions and intentions of its long-term, cold-war enemy.

Anderson had to put blind trust in the personal integrity of Grigori Komarov, and in Komarov's ability to keep faith.

Komarov had to put blind trust in the personal integrity of Glenn Anderson, and in Anderson's ability to keep faith.

And neither of them could do it.

At Langley Rex Langford made his third progress report to Brubecker and he was still uncomfortable. He was fully aware that his low-gear smear campaign had been speeded up by some unexpected help, and he had a pretty good idea of where that help was coming from. He hadn't planted the story about Barbara Allington, so it had to be the work of the opposition.

And if their old enemies of the KGB were also working to discredit Richard Allington, then the whole business stank.

He told it all to Brubecker straight — what he had done, what was going on that he was not responsible for, what he thought, and how he felt. It was a forceful account and he finished bluntly: 'The whole damned thing is beginning to be more and more pointless anyway! Our message is getting through to the media, but Allington is still pushing his message just as hard. We've cramped his style and we've wasted some of his time, but we haven't stopped him. And nobody cares. The top people who matter aren't listening to his message or ours.'

Brubecker scowled, but he had to chew down a couple of hard facts. One was that his subordinate was close to rebellion. And two was that Langford was right, the whole damned ball game was now irrelevant. Allington had become over-exposed and in a couple of days media interest was going to fizzle out anyway. The man had nothing more to say.

'Okay,' Brubecker decided. 'We'll drop it.'

He wanted to slap Langford down. He didn't like these bright new whizz kids, still green behind the ears, who wouldn't stay in line. But he couldn't afford to get ugly. The ranks of the CIA were growing thinner every day, and he couldn't afford to waste one of the few agents still reporting for duty.

'You can forget Allington,' he continued. 'I've got another job you can handle.'

'What job?' Langford looked surprised, and still doubtful.

'At the White House. It seems that even the Secret Service is suffering from desertions. Now things are getting really bad most of the married guys are staying home to be with their wives and kids. The defences round the President need some new muscle, and we've been asked to help out.'

'Guarding the President?'

'That's right. Get yourself over there and report to the Senior Agent in Charge. From here on he's your new boss. He'll assign you your new duty.'

Langford hesitated, and then smiled. This sounded better, a job he didn't have to be ashamed of. 'Okay,' he said. 'I'm on my way.'

Brubecker watched him go out, and scowled again when he closed the door. Langford was a greenhorn, trying hard to be too big for his boots, but maybe he was sending him to the right place. He had a smart suit, his hair was cut neat and he had a pretty face. He would look okay as part of the White House furniture. Plus he could shoot fast and straight with a handgun if he had to; he had got top marks at the shooting range last month. That was all they needed for this job, a dummy who could shoot.

Brubecker curled his lip with contempt, then sighed and began thinking about the old days. Berlin and Vienna. The Cold War when he was young. God, it had been different then. In those days a guy really had to have balls to make it. . . .

The cold was going to kill them. Johnny realized that after the first couple of miles of driving with no windscreen. The wind chill factor out here on the open road had to be sixty or seventy below zero, and the full force of the wind was driving straight into the car. Barbara had climbed into the back with Mangala where they could duck down behind the seats and escape the main force of the blast, but Johnny was taking it full in the face. Wet snow whirled in on the wind, clogging his eyebrows and turning to ice. More ice was forming under his nostrils, and it felt as though soon his whole face would be a mask of ice. Even inside his gloves his hands were freezing at the wheel.

He had to stop. He was driving almost blind and the snow was getting thicker. He slowed the Lincoln to a crawl and looked for something to replace it, any kind of car that seemed in good enough shape.

He passed another head-on smash. No good, both vehicles too crumpled. Another half-mile and there was a car on its side, again no good. Then finally he saw the body of another limousine half-buried in a drift of snow. He turned the wheel and pulled up beside it.

Mangala spoke hoarsely behind him. 'You want me to drive?'

'Thanks, but not in this car,' Johnny said grimly. 'We'll be stiff as dead beef in a freezer before we ever get to Washington.'

'What then?'

'We change cars. We won't get another windscreen to fit the Lincoln, so we'll try that one in the drift. If we swap over the battery, the gas in the tank, and the snow-chains, maybe we can still make it.'

Mangala groaned at the thought of doing all that work in the murderous cold, but he knew Johnny was right. They couldn't survive much more of what they were already taking. His teeth chattered as he answered.

'Okay. I think I saw a tow-rope in the boot. We'll pull that baby clear and check it over.'

While the African climbed out and fixed the tow-rope Johnny tried to beat some warmth back into his hands. His fingers were numb with no feeling, and he was afraid his ears and nose already had frost-bite. Barbara put her arms round him from behind, wiping the ice off his face and trying to warm him up.

Mangala called out when he was ready and Johnny put the car in reverse. He eased back slowly, the snow-chains held their grip on the hard-packed snow and inch by inch the Lincoln hauled the car backward out of the drift. It was a red Cadillac, and when it was clear Johnny switched off the engine and got out to join Mangala.

The red car was intact and appeared to have suffered no damage. The doors were closed, the windows all wound up, and there was no sign of the owner. Johnny began to hope that the car had simply run out of gas and the owner had walked away and abandoned it. Maybe the guy was dead under a blanket of snow further down the road, or maybe he had found help and survived. They would never know, and it didn't matter.

They checked under the bonnet. Someone had stolen the battery, but they had a good battery on the Lincoln, and nothing else had been touched. The tyres were hard, so maybe the Cadillac hadn't been here too long. Maybe it would start without too much trouble.

There was only one way to find out and they set to work. Most of it was done by Mangala, for Johnny's fingers were still too stiff to function. The African used a screwdriver and spanner from the toolkit in the Lincoln's boot and transferred the battery to the Cadillac. It took a few minutes to cross the wires under the dashboard and get ignition. The engine turned but didn't start. The needle on the gas gauge didn't move.

'The tank is empty.' Johnny was shivering and his teeth chattered as loud as Mangala's. 'We could be lucky.'

He got into the Lincoln, turned it round and backed it up against the Cadillac. Before they had left the garage where they had picked up the Lincoln he had hunted around for anything that might come in useful, and the same foresight that had made him fit the snow-chains had made him pick up a length of rubber tubing. He expected bad road conditions and slow driving, and he couldn't be sure that they would have enough gas to reach Washington. He had thought it likely that he would have to siphon more gas into the Lincoln, but now he used the rubber tube to siphon the gas from the Lincoln into the empty tank of the Cadillac.

On the next attempt the Cadillac started. They had one more task, to transfer the snow-chains, and then they were mobile again. This time Mangala took the wheel, and Johnny huddled in the back with Barbara.

He was as cold as death and she pulled off his gloves and massaged his blue-frozen hands vigorously between her own.

They now had a windscreen again to keep out the wind and the snow, and with the heater going the interior of the car slowly thawed out. Johnny felt agonizing, tingling pains in his fingers as the blood began to flow again, but he was grateful. He smiled at Barbara and she kissed him. She opened her coat and gently pulled his head inside to warm his wind-chapped face against her bosom.

Half an hour later they reached Philadelphia, crossing the Delaware River by the Benjamin Franklin Bridge. The city was blacked out, for again they were travelling through the long hours without power that would have been normal night. It was the best time to move, Johnny realized. They had got through the roadblock further back only because the group manning it had been asleep and needed time to wake up and grab their weapons.

Their headlights picked out the direction signs and they left Philly on Interstate 95. The famous birthplace of the nation showed no signs of life, as though the cycle it had begun had already ended. That thought did not occur to Barbara and Mangala, who were not Americans, but to Johnny it was a knife-thrust to the heart.

The road continued as before, part of the white wasteland, littered with wrecks, and in places partly blocked. They made slow progress and without the snow-chains it would have been impossible. There was nothing else moving on the highway, except the thick white flakes that rushed up on the wind and splattered on the windscreen. The wipers hissed back and forth to keep the screen clear, and their visibility was cut down to a few yards. Mangala began to mutter curses under his breath, because he wasn't sure he could keep them on the road, and Barbara began to fear that the snow would build up into a full-scale blizzard and bury them.

Mercifully the snowstorm blew itself out, but even so it took another five hours before they were at last by-passing Baltimore. It was another ghost city, seemingly dead and invisible in the darkness. The power was cut and all was black silence.

Mangala was tiring now. Johnny was rested and recovered, and he took over the wheel to drive the last lap down to Washington. Finally, after fifteen gruelling hours since leaving New York, they drove across the Anacostia River and entered the capital. Johnny had been here before, on a tourist trip to show Mary and John Junior the White House and the Capitol, and now he drove direct to Connecticut Avenue. The red Cadillac coughed and spluttered and ran out of gas, rolling to its last resting-place just two hundred yards short of the Hilton.

Allington woke up to the loud knocking on the outer door of their suite. It was as black as the inside of a tar barrel, and a glance at the luminous dial of his wristwatch showed that it would be another hour before the power was due to come on. The knocking persisted and Lorna stirred beside him.

'Who on earth —?' she complained.

'I'll find out. It's obvious they're not going to go away.'

He was wide awake now and groped for the flashlight he kept under the pillow. He switched it on and got up to hunt for his dressing-gown. When he had belted that on he went to the door. The knocking was repeated and he heard movement in the corridor. He sensed that there was more than one visitor outside and he was cautious.

'Who is it? Who's out there!'

'Dad, it's me! It's Barbara!'

The joyful shout rang loud and clear, and for a moment Allington stood as though locked in an incredible dream. Like Lorna before her he had given Barbara up as lost. To hear the sound of her voice was too wonderful to be true, and suddenly he dared not move in case he broke the spell. Then she called his name again and he realized that this was no dream. Instead it was another miracle.

He forgot caution and quickly unlocked the door. The instant it was open Barbara hurled herself into his arms, laughing and crying, and hugging and kissing him with all the abandoned enthusiasm of a six-year old at Christmas or her birthday party. Allington was smothered by her pent-up relief and affection, and he was equally delighted. He, too, didn't know whether to laugh or cry.

He was vaguely aware of the two men who had accompanied Barbara, but it was several minutes before the excitement of the reunion abated and he was able to pay them any attention. Mangala he recognized and warmly welcomed.

'I was wrong,' the big African admitted gravely. 'It was a mistake for me to try and leave. If I can help you now in any way, I will try.'

Allington pumped his hand. 'Julius, I'm sure you can help us. And I'm very pleased you came.'

'Dad,' Barbara said proudly. 'This is Johnny Chance. He's been a very good friend. Without him I would never have got here.'

'I met Barbara in England,' Johnny explained. 'We came over on the same ship.'

Allington realized immediately that there was much more, and realized too that his little girl had done a lot of growing up since he had last seen her. The tone of her voice had announced a whole wealth of powerful feeling for the tall, rugged American, and he sensed that she desperately wanted his approval. It was easy to give, for he would have been grateful to anyone who had helped her, and there was something immediately likeable in the relaxed smile of Johnny Chance.

They shook hands, and then Barbara was hugging him again.

'Dad, oh, Dad — it's so good to see you. There's so much I have to tell you. And so much I want to know.'

'Whoa, now,' Allington said laughing. 'Come and meet Lorna. Then we'll get some candles alight so we can all see each other better. Then we'll pour some stiff drinks — after all that driving I'm sure Johnny and Julius can use a scotch or a bourbon. Then we'll all sit down and relax, and you can talk until your heart is content. You always did chatter like a whole flock of sparrows.'

Lorna had emerged from the bedroom and was already busy with the candelabra. Soon they had candlelight again, and for the next hour they exchanged stories and news. When the electricity came on again at nine a.m. Allington went in search of the hotel manager and ordered the best possible breakfast that could be provided. They all ate hungrily and heartily, still talking almost non-stop.

At last Allington looked reluctantly at his wristwatch.

'I have to go out,' he apologized. 'I have an appointment at the TV studio. Anyway, it'll give you all a chance to get some rest, and we can talk again later.'

'I'm coming with you,' Barbara said firmly. 'I watched your last interview with that — with that Cornfield man.' Her face became an expression of fierce disgust. 'So this time I'm going to put him straight, and everybody else who listens. Those things he said about me and that boring Arab boy were a pack of lies, and if he repeats them then I want to be close enough to smack his face.'

'Whoa again!' Allington raised his hands. 'It might be better if you didn't start a fight. But okay, you can come. Just keep it verbal.'

'If you don't mind, Richard, I guess I'll tag along,' Johnny said calmly. 'Looking after Barbara has kinda become a habit, and you just might need some help to stop her scratching this guy's eyes out.'

'Be my guest,' Allington raised no objection. 'I'm sure we'll both be glad of your company.'

One man who was not pleased to see them leave the hotel together was Alexi Fedorenko. The Russian had returned to his observation point on the far side of Connecticut Avenue just before the power had been switched on in the city, and he had confidently expected Allington to reappear alone. That had been the pattern of the past few days, for Allington and Lorna had always gone in different directions to cover as much ground as possible. Today Fedorenko had determined to follow the UN Secretary-General, and kill him at the first opportunity.

He was not prepared to see Allington with new companions, and now he could only fume and grind his teeth with frustration. He did not recognize Barbara, even though he had studied and circulated her picture. She had turned up the hood of her coat and brought it close around her face. In any case it was not the slim build of the girl that worried him. If necessary he knew he could handle Allington and his female companion. What made him back off was the presence of Johnny Chance. There was an air of tough competence about the young American, and Fedorenko did not miss the steel glint of the revolver that was still tucked in the belt of Johnny's black raincoat.

He cursed the delay, but knew he would have to wait for a better time.

24

As the crisis deepened and the Herculean task of negotiations dragged on, sleep became essential for the battle teams in both the White House and the Kremlin. Glenn Anderson chose to snatch his brief few hours in the early hours of the morning, leaving his Vice President with orders to wake him immediately if anything came over the red telephone from the Russians. However, he was back at his desk and working long before the power came on to the rest of the city.

It was too early for breakfast, but he drank his first cup of coffee while he studied the staggered launch plan that NASA scientists and their computers had prepared for his approval. Twice the steam from the hot coffee misted up his horn-rims and he had to take them off for a quick, irritable wipe and polish. He was always irritable now, the tension never left him, and he felt like a man walking a tightrope over a blind abyss. Except that the tightrope led nowhere, there was nothing on the other side, and he felt that at any moment the rope itself would just disappear.

A tremendous amount of work had gone into the 500-page document before him. The experts had immediately realized that it would be pointless to allow a series of rockets from the same launch area simply to follow each other through the same hole in space. Shooting straight up would bunch the missiles too close, so a separate trajectory had been calculated for every available launch vehicle. The most powerful vehicles with maximum thrust had been assigned the lowest and longest angles of flight, so that they would pass through the cloud at the farthest possible point from their home base.

The ideal submarine locations had been calculated, a scattered handful in the Arctic, but most of them evenly spread through the southern oceans. Again an individual target programme had been computed for each submarine-based missile, so that when launched they would radiate outward from the parent ship in the widest possible penetration pattern.

To fire everything simultaneously was the ideal, thus giving the cloud no chance to thin out and make later launchings less effective. In practice they could not risk a collision of missiles as they passed through the cloud, for most of the military missiles would still be carrying their nuclear warheads. Nobody wanted to think about what might happen if two multiple warhead nukes kissed each other goodbye in an exploding impact inside the cloud. Perhaps nothing beyond their own multi-megaton death blast, or perhaps a final holocaust that would ignite the cloud itself and roast the entire planet. Nobody knew. Nobody dared make a guess. So they had to stagger the launching sequence just a little, to make sure that there would be no collisions.

It was all there in the top secret document, a solid mass of figures listing the proposed firing order, launch data and countdown times for 7000 launch vehicles and missiles. It made Anderson's eyes blur and his head ache. He couldn't absorb all the fine detail, just the main points, and he just had to pray that NASA had got it right.

Everything that could be done, had been done. All NASA launch vehicles and the majority of the Titan ICBMs had been adapted to magnetic payloads. All United States, French and British submarines were en route to take up their computed positions. In theory the countdown to a mass launch could begin within forty-eight hours.

In practice one essential ingredient was missing. The master plan included the deployment and launch sequences for the Soviet arsenal, but there was still no firm commitment from Moscow.

Anderson had out-fought his own war-hawks to the point where he had enough support to make the deal, if he could get some sort of guarantee from Komarov. But he didn't know how close Komarov might be to being able to make the same deal, or how either of them could give any cast-iron guarantee.

There was no way, and the mutual distrust between the superpowers had them shackled between the Devil and the Darkness.

Gloomily he turned over the other reports that were piled up on his desk. They were all stark indications that this was Doomsday. America's food and power supplies were racing neck and neck in a downhill spiral to extinction. Soon they would have eaten the last crumbs, and there would be no more harvests. The oil lifelines had stopped flowing, and the last supertanker to leave the Persian Gulf was now six weeks overdue. The ship was feared sunk by one of the terrible hurricanes raging almost continuously across the Atlantic, or by collision with one of the giant, drifting icebergs.

Ice, Death and Darkness, that was all there was left, but soon the dying would be over, and only the ice and darkness would remain.

If they were to prevent it they would have to act soon.

There must be a way.

But how?

Anderson groaned and felt as though his head was going to burst. How could he trust the Russians? How could he devise safeguards or guarantees that would satisfy the generations of fear built into both sides?

There had to be a way.

*   *   *

In Moscow Grigori Komarov presided over yet another full-strength meeting of the Politburo, or perhaps it was an extension of the same meeting which seemed to go on and on for weeks without end. The adjournments had been so brief that the meetings had all blurred into one, until it seemed to Komarov that he had spent a lifetime sitting or standing at the head of this table, arguing with these ugly, stubborn old men, breathing in the foul, thick clouds of their tobacco smoke, and getting inexorably nowhere.

The world situation outside the Kremlin walls had become unreal, and sometimes he wondered if they were still aware of it. For himself and the other twelve there was just this one lighted room, the long table and their own faces. They were insulated in the cocoon of their own power struggle, still living in a past world when everything could be solved by a quote from Stalin, Marx or Lenin.

Each man had before him a copy of the fat document compiled by the American scientists at NASA, and they had listened with sour, silent faces as a series of experts from their own Academy of Sciences had filed through the room to give their considered opinions on the value and feasibility of the American master plan. Now they had assimilated all the available information and the meeting was wide open to their own argument.

'This plan is nothing but a filthy capitalist trick!' The automatic outburst came immediately from Sukhov. 'A child could see through it and realize their intention. If we were to deploy and launch our weapons as this plan suggests we would have nothing left. We would be naked to American aggression.'

'There will be no American aggression,' Komarov stated bluntly. 'No more than we could hope to act as the aggressor.'

'We must trust the Americans.' Ladiyev was the first to voice full commitment. 'Just as they must trust us.'

A chorus of denials howled him down, from Sukhov

and the majority of the old men. Ladiyev flinched but held his ground and Komarov intervened to halt the irrelevant exchange of abuse.

'Perhaps we should stop thinking of our missiles as weapons. Think of them instead as Earth-escape vehicles, and the only means of removing the cloud. Remember that we will still have our long-range bombers, our fighter planes, and our tanks and ships. We shall not be completely naked, even without the missiles.'

'America outnumbers us with conventional aircraft,' Sukhov screamed. 'That is why we must keep back a large proportion of our missiles.'

'We have been through all this before —' Komarov knew that the only way was to grind him down, even if it meant repeating the same old argument over and over again. 'Our space scientists have agreed with the Americans that every Earth-escape vehicle we have may not be enough.'

'So I will say again that I will never, never, NEVER AGREE TO THIS PLAN!' Sukhov was on his feet and shouting, his sagging jowls red with rage as he pounded on the table with his bare fist. It was a performance he had learned to ape from Krushchev in the sixties, and this time it proved to be his swan song. A spear-thrust of pain ripped through his chest and his mouth stayed open in mid-defiance with only a strangled, long-drawn death rattle coming out. His eyes closed and his face froze as he pushed himself away from the table in one last valiant effort to stay upright. He staggered to one side and collapsed in a heap.

The hatchet-faced Chairman of the KGB was the first to move. He was familiar with the torture chambers of Lubyanka and was not unduly shocked when men screamed and died gibbering at his feet. He knelt beside Sukhov and noted that the white lips were turning blue. Without haste he pulled open the man's jacket and shirt and felt for a heartbeat. He was not surprised to feel nothing. Sukhov was eighty-seven and had pushed his blood pressure far too high.

'Comrade Sukhov is dead,' he announced without emotion. 'He has suffered a heart attack.'

Komarov had left his place at the head of the table. He came closer and stared down at his enemy. The indestructible Sukhov, the Iron Man of the Old Brigade, the Guardian of Marxism, the Shadow of Stalin, the Voice of Lenin — dead at last. It was almost unbelievable.

'Send for a doctor,' Komarov said. He knew he had to go through the motions, even though it was too late. At least, he prayed it was too late. With Sukhov dead one of the major barriers was removed. The other old men were merely echoes of Sukhov. Without him they would crumble.

The Chairman of the KGB stared into Komarov's eyes, reading the President's mind.

'Comrade Sukhov was correct,' he declared harshly. 'We must never agree to this American proposal. They will betray us. Then they will destroy us. That is their intention.'

It was just before noon when Allington returned with Johnny and Barbara to the Washington Hilton. The TV interview had gone smoothly and the studio had been fair-minded in giving Barbara the opportunity to say her piece and refute the charges that had been made against her. Allington and Johnny were still smiling over her fiery encounter with the unfortunate Max Cornfield.

'I don't know if you are a liar yourself,' she had told him stoutly. 'But when you use other people's lies you should at least have the decency to examine them more closely before you pass them on as truth.'

There had been more in the same vein, and Cornfield had spent an uncomfortable five minutes in trying to attack, but most of that time fumbling in defence.

Barbara had come looking for a fight and she had no intention of losing. Her performance was not exactly a lesson in diplomacy, but it was high-spirited and effective, and she was sharp enough to keep it above the level of a mere slanging-match.

'You are a very emotional young woman,' Cornfield had floundered. He probably had a point to make about emotional instability, but he never got it out.

'That means I'm smart enough to out-talk you,' Barbara flashed back. 'Which also means that I'm smart enought to see through any amateur spy, unless they are like Karim Jalil, so boring that I didn't even bother to look. God help him, he was almost as tedious as you!'

On the sidelines Johnny Chance had burst out laughing. He had come along to give her moral support, but obviously he wasn't needed.

The studio schedules were tight and Allington had given up his own pre-arranged screen time to make room for Barbara, so they left soon after the interview was over. Allington's plans were hazy for the rest of the day. He had yet to approach the State Department and he felt that he ought to try again at the White House, but he had no specific appointments. In fact he was beginning to wonder if he was on the right track, and whether his efforts could make any difference at all to the final outcome.

However, with Barbara beside him, and still flushed with her minor victory over Cornfield, his spirits were still buoyant. He had decided to leave his next move until after he had seen her and Johnny comfortably settled at the hotel.

He was surprised to find Lorna still at the suite. They had planned that she would try her powers of persuasion at the Soviet embassy, but she had either delayed or changed her mind. Either way he found he couldn't reproach her. If she had given up then it was probably inevitable. What was surely more surprising was that she had supported him so strongly and so steadfastly for so long. Mangala was still there, and Allington assumed that Lorna had simply continued telling the African the long story of her adventures in India and Indonesia.

He was wrong. Lorna had been developing her idea, weaving together the separate strands that had begun to form before she had last fallen asleep. Mangala had stirred up the train of thought anew when he had talked of his ill-fated trip to Kennedy Airport which had almost cost him his life. He admitted it had been foolish at that late stage for him to think he could still return to Angola, and his only excuse was that he had been desperate to rejoin his wife and child.

It was there again, Lorna realized, the powerful protective instinct men felt toward their women and children. Allington had voiced it when they had made love. Now Mangala was expressing anguish with similar roots in a different set of words. It was the same thing, and suddenly in a flash of triggered inspiration Lorna saw the one way in which they might be able to provide both Anderson and Komarov with their necessary adequate safeguards.

She waited until Allington and Johnny had finished their chuckling, blow-by-blow account of Barbara's verbal duel with Cornfield. It put them all in a good humour and at the end of it Barbara had the grace to blush and look embarrassed. Finally the topic had exhausted itself, and when the conversation flagged Lorna brought it up to a more serious level.

'Richard,' she said quietly. 'I've been thinking. There is something that could solve our problem, although I'm not sure if it could be put into practice. I've sounded it out with Julius, he's not certain either, but we both think it could be worth a try.'

'What is it?' Allington asked.

'An exchange of hostages between the superpowers,' Lorna told him bluntly. 'Not just any hostages, but the people who are most dear to the top men in the White House and the Kremlin, their own wives and children.'

Allington stared at her, letting the idea sink in slowly so that he could absorb its full implications.

'It's the obvious answer,' Lorna continued. 'NASA has solved the problem of getting rid of the cloud. The only problem left is to overcome the mutual distrust between East and West that prevents them from working together to do it. So let us suppose that the wives and children of the American leaders can be persuaded to go to Moscow. What better sign of good faith can Komarov have?'

'And if the families of the Russian leadership are invited to come to Washington — ?' Mangala backed her up. 'If they will come of their own free will — then Anderson will have his guarantee in return.'

'It must be a sufficient demonstration of goodwill,' Lorna continued. 'Surely neither of them will believe that the other could be so monstrous as to destroy his own flesh and blood?'

The excitement gleamed in her eyes as she talked. The plan was a ray of hope that grew stronger each time she refined and related it. Allington could feel her enthusiasm and began to share it, but he knew they had to iron out any snags before they could take it any further.

'Flying across the Atlantic involves some terrible risks,' he said slowly. 'I'm not sure that Lucy Anderson or Irina Komarov would be prepared to take those risks — or that their husbands would either ask them or allow them to put themselves in such danger.'

'Perhaps not, but if they do have the courage, then it must be the solution. We can at least propose it.'

'Nobody has listened to us yet,' Allington reminded her. He was not being defeatist but simply stating a fact. 'Our reputations have been so slurred that anything coming from either of us is going to be suspect.

That would seem to rule out a TV approach. We have to take this direct to the President, and neither of us can get any access to the White House.'

'Damn the President!' Lorna snapped with startling passion. 'Damn his Crisis Team and damn the Politburo. If we go to any of them they'll block it automatically without giving it another thought. It's their wives we must reach! The only person who can push this through is Lucy Anderson. If we can get to her, and if she will announce the plan as her own, then, and only then, will it carry enough weight to be given any serious consideration.'

She was right, Allington realized. If he, or Lorna, or anyone else, was to ask for such a sacrifice, then officialdom would nail it down with so many objections that it would become unworkable. But no one could refuse to listen to the First Lady of America if she had the courage to speak out, and offer herself publicly as an exchange hostage with the wife of the President of the Soviet Union.

'It could be the answer,' he agreed. 'But it still hits the same initial barrier. We haven't any more hope of getting into the White House to talk to the First Lady than we have of seeing the President.'

Lorna shrugged. 'This is important, and if I can't get through the main entrance hall, then I'll just have to sneak in through the back. I know I can't do it alone, and it's not your kind of enterprise, Richard — but I do think we have just the right man to help me.'

She turned to Johnny Chance. 'Maybe I shouldn't ask, but Barbara has told us everything about what you did on the *Pennsylvania*. Even allowing for the fact that she's in love with you it still comes out as a high recommendation for your personal courage and character. That's why I'll believe that any man who can walk up the outside of a ship in a hurricane must be resourceful enough to get me into the White House. All I need is ten minutes face to face with Lucy Anderson.'

'The hurricane had passed over.' Johnny grinned a protest. 'I'm not Superman.'

Lorna smiled and waited.

Johnny shrugged in turn and became serious. 'Okay,' he said grimly. 'We'll give it a damned good try.'

25

A fierce snowstorm was howling across the south lawn of the White House when Lorna and Johnny finally made their approach to the protective railings on Executive Avenue. They had waited until the power was cut to the rest of the city, and the high, semi-circular south portico of the elegant residence of the President was one of the few partial oases of light in the subterranean blackness.

A few weeks before they would never have got within a half-mile of the executive mansion and its grounds. The whole area had been sewn up tight by national guardsmen, marines, and crack troops from the Old Guard at Fort Myer. Security then had been designed to protect the White House from siege and storm by clamouring mobs. No mass attack of that kind had taken place, and as the darkness continued and all hopes of survival had faded, the men detailed to guard the President had gradually slipped away to spend the time that remained protecting their own homes and families. The rate of desertions had slowed when the world learned that there was a way to survive, but then the whittling-down process had begun again as the days dragged on with no sign of the essential co-operation from Moscow.

Now Lorna and Johnny were gambling that the human screen around the White House had been reduced to the point where two determined infiltrators could get through. The snowstorm was an added bonus to shield their approach, but even so they were under no illusions. What they were attempting was a dangerous game which could easily cost them their lives. Breaking into the White House just to talk to Lucy Anderson held exactly the same risks as breaking into the White House to assassinate the President. The Secret Service agents still at their posts were probably tense, strained and trigger-happy. If they spotted intruders they would shoot first, and maybe ask questions later.

The darkness hid them as Johnny gripped the railings with both hands, bending his back and allowing Lorna to use him as a stepping-stone. She scrambled swiftly up over his shoulders, over the fence, and dropped inside the grounds. They were separated only by the railings but they couldn't see each other. During the three hours of the afternoon, when the street lights had been switched on, Johnny had scoured the whole of Washington to find a sixty-foot length of nylon climbing-rope and a lightweight steel grappling-hook. These he now pushed through the railings, and felt her take them from his hand. Then he hauled himself up over the fence and dropped down on the inside to join her.

He found her by touch and gripped her shoulder firmly so they would not lose each other again. They were in the south-east corner of the fifteen acres of parkland, surrounded by trees and shrubbery, and he steered her slowly toward the east wing of the White House. Lorna retained the rope and grappling-hook so that Johnny's hands would be left free.

They had planned every step in advance, so that in theory they knew exactly what they were doing. In reality they were disorientated by the driving force of the wind and snow, and by the unseen foliage whipping across their faces. They blundered into tree-trunks and stumbled over bushes, straying off-course and emerging on to the south lawn. The south portico was suddenly visible again, through a racing curtain of snow, but now it was much closer.

It seemed unlikely that anyone would see or hear them in these conditions, and Johnny took the risk of staying on the edge of the lawn as they approached the building. There seemed no real point in flailing blindly in the shrubbery, but it was almost a fatal mistake. A grumbling voice reached them faintly on the blustering wind, a flashlight glimmered, and Johnny moved Lorna swiftly sideways, off the lawn and into the bushes. He pressed her down and they crouched and waited. Lorna could feel her heart pounding like a sudden death knell.

A two-man patrol went past, either troops or White House cops, they couldn't distinguish enough of the bulky figures to tell. They counted the flashlights, and it was safe to assume that both men were armed.

It was a near miss, less than two yards, and without the noise of the storm to blanket their own approach they would have been caught. Johnny drew a deep breath and prayed that their luck would hold out. He eased Lorna up and steered her forward again, but this time they stayed just inside the trees and shrubs. The illuminated white columns vanished, reappeared and vanished again as they passed behind the intervening screens of black branches. Then suddenly they were clear of the trees, with the main building to their left, the east wing to their right, and the columned terrace connecting the two immediately ahead.

Johnny pulled Lorna back into the trees again and they moved to their right. They had no intention of approaching the main ceremonial entrance beneath the impressive south portico, and they had decided to keep as far away as possible from the executive west wing. Anderson was probably working there in his Oval Office, and the highest concentration of security men would be in the immediate vicinity of the President.

Their first target was the east wing and they reached its south wall unseen. Lorna's heart was racing again as they left the pitch blackness beneath the trees, but even up close where the building was spotlit the driving snow was cutting visibility down to a few yards. Johnny signed to Lorna to wait, and she crouched down shivering and scared as he moved cautiously round the corner of the building to scout the way ahead.

There was a man guarding the terrace, sheltering behind the columns with his back to the doorway into the east wing and watching the far entrance into the main building. He was six feet tall, solid, motionless and silent, hunched into a dark grey topcoat. The collar was turned up, but not quite high enough to conceal the small plastic earpiece of his personal radio. The radio marked him as a Secret Service agent, in two-way contact with a senior man who would tell him when and where to re-deploy as necessary to protect the premises and his President.

Johnny knew the man would have to be physically fit, well trained, alert with acute hearing and 20-20 vision, and a fast, accurate marksman with a handgun. With this kind of man there would be no second chance, no time to correct a mistake.

Johnny frowned, and now his own heart was beginning to thump as the adrenalin surged. He could try another approach, but he could only expect to find near-identical sentries on all sides of the building. Before he could break in he would have to take out one of these grim guardians, and it might as well be this one.

There were no more guards in sight and Johnny made his decision. He was carrying his revolver, but that was just a last resort, to freeze a guy, and give himself a chance to explain. He didn't want to talk to this particular guy, he just wanted him out cold. His mind went back to Vietnam and all the unarmed combat training. This would have to be a bare hands job, and he hoped that he could still do it. The only snag was that this guy was a good guy, he didn't want to kill him.

He had two big advantages. One was the roar of the storm: the wind was howling so loud he could probably have driven a tank to within ten yards before the Secret Serviceman would have heard the sound of its engine. The other was that on this kind of night the guy just wasn't expecting any trouble.

Johnny eased forward, keeping his back to the wall of the east wing. He was almost through the line of columns before the agent sensed his presence and whipped round. In that split second Johnny launched himself forward with the whole weight of his body behind the driving power of his right fist. He had another advantage he hadn't counted, the guy was numbed by the bitter cold and his reactions were a fraction slower than they might have been. The punch connected with a bone-snapping crack to the jaw and the man went sliding down the double glass doors he was guarding.

Johnny piled on top of him, knees crushing down on the other guy's chest to force the wind out of him, hand screwing down over the agonized mouth to stop a shout through the sleeve microphone that went with the radio. The agent tried to get a hand to the gun inside his coat, but Johnny's knee rode higher and pinned the struggling arm to the bruised chest. Then he slammed the writhing head hard against the paved floor. The body beneath him slumped and went limp, and he crouched over it gasping for breath.

Nothing happened. No one came rushing to the scene of the disturbance. Johnny sucked in air and then quickly pulled off the agent's radio earpiece and held it to his own ear. The little radio was silent: nobody was asking what the hell was going on, nobody had heard the brief grunting and gagging before the agent had become unconscious.

Johnny worked fast, knowing that his time was limited now because eventually somebody would come to relieve this man, or check that he was still at his post. He used the agent's belt and necktie to secure his hands and feet, and his own necktie and handkerchief to gag the mouth. He handled the guy's jaw gently, hoping it wasn't broken, but fearing he had at least cracked the bone. Finally he took the rest of the radio, tucking it inside his coat, and making sure the curved plastic tube was secure behind his ear. When all hell broke loose at least it might help to be warned.

He went back for Lorna and found her still crouched and shivering under a blanket of snow. He smiled to reassure her and took the rope and grappling-hook from her numbed hand.

'I've made a gap in the ranks,' he informed her. 'So let's get through it fast.'

Lorna followed him to the terrace. This time he didn't pass through the columns to where the unconscious agent lay bound and gagged. The private quarters of the President and First Lady were on the second and third floors of the main building, so it would not particularly help them to penetrate the east wing at ground level. Johnny had his route planned and he didn't intend to detour. His next step was on to the roof of the terrace, and he swung the grappling-hook upward.

It was only a twelve-foot throw. The hook caught and held fast and Johnny went hand over hand up the rope, leaning back and walking up the nearest column. Once on the roof he hauled Lorna quickly up behind him.

Here they were fully exposed to the howling, snow-laden wind. It almost blew them off and Lorna staggered and all but lost her balance as she stood upright. Johnny caught her arm and hauled her back from the edge. Quickly he looped up the rope again, and keeping a tight hold on her coat sleeve he led her along the terrace roof and up to the east wall of the mansion.

The stone balustrade around the roof of the White House was some thirty-five to forty feet above them. It was a longer throw and Johnny couldn't afford to miss. If the three-pronged steel hook fell back, or if the wind carried it through one of the tall closed and curtained windows, the crash would surely be heard. He bit his lip and stared upward, hardly able to see the short, blurred pillars of the balustrade through the swirling snow. He swung the hook in his right hand, slowly back and forth, keeping the coiled rope bunched in his left hand as he tried to calculate the effect of the wind, and the force he would need to put behind the final swing. Finally he decided that all his strength might not be enough, so he held nothing back. He lengthened the swing slightly, and then hurled it up into the wind with all the power of his arm. The hook sailed over the balustrade, clearing it by some three or four feet. It dropped inside and Johnny froze and waited for any indication that the muffled clang of its landing had been heard.

There was no alarm, his ear radio was silent, and after a couple of minutes he breathed again, thanking the storm and the blanket of snow that was blotting out the unavoidable noise. He pulled back gently on the rope, felt the hook bite under the top rail of the balustrade, and then with a swift smile to Lorna he again began to climb.

He was climbing past the state floors of the White House. Behind the first window he passed was the long East Room, used for state balls, receptions, and the scene of several famous weddings. Immediately above it was the Rose Guest Room. It was reasonable to assume that in the present circumstances both these rooms would be empty, but even so Johnny tried to make as little noise as possible. He didn't want to push his luck, even though the storm had now reached blizzard strength.

It was a tough climb. Twice the wind swept his feet

away and left him dangling by his arms alone, but each time he found his footing again and continued his upward struggle. The freezing cold was getting into him now, the ice was cracking across his face as he grimaced and strained, and his fingers were feeling numb. He carried the extra weight of his topcoat soaked with snow, and there was a moment when he feared that his grip might fail or his strength might burn out before he reached the top. When he tried to look up the snow blinded him. His heart pumped painfully, and the sound of the blood roaring in his head was almost as loud as the sound of the blizzard raging furiously all around him.

He slipped for the third time, and his elbows banged against the stubby columns of the balustrade. He realized he was nearly there and made the final effort. Seconds later he was dragging himself over the top and falling inside the stone rail. He felt as though he had climbed a mile up the north face of Everest, but he had made it. He was on top of the White House.

He needed a few minutes to get his breath back, and then he began the task of hauling Lorna up behind him. He gave three short tugs on the rope. Lorna had already tied a bowline around her waist exactly as he had showed her earlier in the afternoon, and immediately she returned the signal. Johnny braced himself and hauled her up. He had passed the rope round the back of his waist and then around one of the balustrade columns, so heaving first with his right arm, then taking up the slack with his left he belayed her to the top.

For Lorna it was a terrifying experience. She tried to help him by walking up the wall as he had told her, but after the first few yards the wind tore her feet away and left her suspended. She could only hang helpless while she was hoisted up in jerks, spinning in the wind with the snow rushing into her face and hair. She couldn't fall off the rope, but she was afraid that

Johnny wouldn't be able to hold her. Her ordeal seemed to last for eternity, although in fact it was only a few minutes, and long before she reached the top she convinced herself that this mad venture was doomed and they must have been insane to make the attempt.

Johnny was almost exhausted when he helped her over the stone rail, and she collapsed shuddering into his arms. They both needed a few minutes to recover their strength and their nerve, but finally when he grinned at her she smiled weakly back. They straightened up together to make their next move.

They were on the balcony outside the third floor, on top of the second-floor roof, and they walked slowly over to the west side of the building. Here Johnny looked for a point of entry and decided upon a pair of french windows. There was no light or sign of life inside and it took him ten minutes to force the windows open with the blade of a large knife. They passed inside and closed the windows behind them.

They were getting close; the First Lady had to be either on this floor, or on this side of the building immediately below them, but from here on every step would be loaded with the increasing danger of discovery.

'We'll leave our topcoats here,' Johnny said, and Lorna murmured agreement.

It was still cold even inside the building, but they stripped off the wet, snow-heavy outer clothes that would have betrayed them as intruders at first sight. Underneath Johnny wore grey flannel trousers and a smart blue blazer. He hadn't been able to get one of the ESP presidential badges which the agents of the Executive Protection Service wore on the top pockets of their identical blue blazers, but the guise could give him an edge if trouble came at him from behind or side-on. Lorna wore a neat blue jacket and skirt, the colour fashionable with this presidency for White House female staff.

They searched in the pitch darkness for an interior door, and finally found one on the far side of the room. Cautiously Johnny tried the handle. The door was not locked and he eased it open. Light spilled through the narrow crack from the lighted corridor beyond, and then a voice crackled sharply in Johnny's ear. He had almost forgotten that he was wearing the earpiece radio and he felt his heart kick with alarm. Automatically he stepped back and shut the door again.

'Update all agents,' a toneless voice was saying inside his ear. 'The President and Mrs. Anderson have just finished eating dinner. The President is returning to the west wing. The First Lady is returning to her room on the second floor. All agents deploy as standard to cover their routes. Standard cover for the Oval Office once the President is inside.'

'What is it?' Lorna hissed in alarm. She had seen and could hear nothing.

Johnny told her and finished quietly, 'We'll wait a few minutes to let security settle down, then we'll make our move. At least we know now we have to get down to the second floor.'

They waited. The minutes ticked slowly by, each one a long-drawn agony of time in a silent limbo of darkness, but at last Johnny decided the time was right to continue. He inched open the door again, the light hurt their eyes and made them blink, but the corridor was empty. They stepped out and looked for a stairway going down.

They found a staircase at the west end of the corridor and began to descend, moving slowly and carefully. Johnny led the way, signing to Lorna to stay one step behind. Lorna could feel her heart beating again and her mouth was dry. Her knees felt weak and her mind was suddenly a frightening blank. The suspense had at last drained her of any capacity for independent thought or action, and all she could do at this stage was to trust blindly to Johnny.

At the foot of the staircase Johnny paused to listen, and then risked a brief one-eyeball glance round the corner of the wall. He looked down another short corridor, two doors on either side, leading to a T junction. It was deserted and he exhaled with a soft sigh.

They couldn't hang back for ever and he moved quietly out into the second-floor corridor. Lorna followed him and their steps were silent on the plush red carpet as they moved from door to door, listening for sounds of movement inside. They were both certain that Lucy Anderson had to be behind one of these doors, or a door that was very close.

There was no sound within any of the rooms. They had reached the fourth door and Johnny paused with his ear pressed close to the polished wooden panel. He was resigned to having to check along the cross corridor and was just about to move toward it when a man walked round the corner and stared at him in amazement.

They moved together. Johnny whipped out the revolver from his waistband and brought it up level. The security man facing him was equally as fast. This one wasn't numb with cold and his hand movement was an instantaneous blur. It came out from his shoulder holster gripping a Colt 0.45. The left hand came up automatically to support the right wrist. The black muzzle of the Colt was aimed point-blank at Johnny's heart.

'Hold it!' Rex Langford snapped. He would have fired automatically but Johnny's revolver would have fired too and they would have both died. He kept his cool and added grimly, 'Just drop the gun, buddy. Just open your hand, nice and easy, and let it fall.'

Johnny smiled faintly, and hoped his hand was as rock-steady as the other guy's. 'I don't like that idea,' he objected. 'I think I'd kinda like it better if you dropped yours.'

Langford didn't blink. Neither did Johnny. They

watched each other's eyes, challenging and calculating. Johnny was realizing that at any second the other man would raise the alarm, and that he had to talk fast to stop him. Langford was wondering if he was going to have to die in a shoot-out with this stranger, and deciding that he would if he had to.

Lorna's initial reaction had been a groan of dismay, but then she pulled herself together and moved out gingerly from behind Johnny's shoulder.

'Stop there!' Langford warned her sharply. 'Don't separate on me.'

'Please,' Lorna begged. Her throat moved with difficulty and the words came out low and husky. 'We don't mean to harm anyone. I just want to talk to the First Lady. It's very important.'

'She's telling you the truth,' Johnny added quietly. 'It's the only reason we're here.'

Langford frowned. The woman's face was familiar. In fact both faces were stirring memories, but the woman's face most of all. Then it clicked and it all became clear in his mind.

'Lorna Maxwell,' Langford identified her in a flat, accusing statement of fact. 'You're the woman who has been campaigning with Allington, the Secretary-General of the UN. You're Columbian, born in Bogota, your country's ambassador to the UN General Assembly.'

'Thank God.' Lorna swayed with relief. 'If you know who I am then you must know what Richard and I have been trying to achieve. Nationalities don't matter now. We're all just people on a dying planet. That's why I have to talk to Mrs. Anderson. I can see a way in which only she can help.'

Langford was hesitating, all the guilt he had felt over working to slander Allington was rushing back. Maybe these people were on the level, maybe they had something, but he wasn't forgetting that the guy had a gun.

'So who are you?' he demanded of Johnny.

Johnny shrugged. 'I'm just a guy who is helping out. I want to see the sun shine again. If Lorna is on the right track then maybe it can happen.'

'But I know you, too. I've seen your face somewhere. You got a name?'

'Sure, most folks know me as Johnny Chance.'

'The country and western singer.' Enlightenment dawned and Langford almost smiled. 'Hell, I've got your ugly face on a dozen albums back home. I always was a sucker for your style.'

Johnny smiled and tried to relax. 'How about it? Will you take us to the First Lady?'

'Not with a gun in your hand.' Langford was grim again. 'You still have to drop it.'

For a few seconds Johnny didn't move. He knew that once he lowered the revolver the other man had full control of the ball game. The agent might yell immediately for help and they would be hustled away with no more listening or talking. But they couldn't hold the stand-off for ever. One of them had to give way or they both had to die, and although the agent wasn't quite as hostile as he had been at first Johnny sensed that he would still put his job first and die doing it. Slowly Johnny lowered the revolver and flipped it on to the carpet at Langford's feet.

'It's getting heavy,' he said wryly. 'And I guess I couldn't shoot a fan anyway.'

Langford relaxed a little more, stooped and picked up the revolver with his left hand. He dropped it into his pocket. All the time the Colt 0.45 remained steady in his right hand, its aim never wavering from Johnny's heart.

'Please,' Lorna begged again. 'Now will you take us to the First Lady?'

'You busted in here illegally,' Langford pointed out. 'Maybe Mrs. Anderson won't want to talk to you. In any case I ought to report this straight away to the Agent in Charge. It'll cost me my job if I don't.'

'What's your job worth in a dead world?' Johnny asked quietly. 'At least let Mrs. Anderson make the decision.'

Langford was torn two ways. He knew what he had to do. He had his orders to cover every situation, including this one. But he was already plagued with doubt over the misguided set of orders he had carried out for Brubecker. This woman represented Richard Allington, and he felt that he owed Allington for all the lies he had invented to bring the man down. He struggled with his conscience, and finally looked back to Johnny.

'Okay,' he decided. 'I'll stake it all that no one who can sing country music with real soul could ever turn out to be one of the bad guys. I'm sticking my neck full out, but I'll take you to the First Lady.'

While Lorna and Johnny were out of the way Alexi Fedorenko was at last making his own move. He had tired of waiting in the black, numbing cold. It was worse than being exiled to Siberia and he saw no reason to prolong his own discomfort. Allington had to die, and if Allington wouldn't come out then there was nothing left but to go into the hotel and find him. As far as Fedorenko was aware Allington had only one companion left, the young girl who had accompanied him on his last appearance. However, the Russian knew that Allington was sleeping with the Maxwell woman, so it was unlikely that the girl would also be sharing their bedroom.

The six o'clock power cut came soon after Lorna and Johnny had disappeared down Connecticut Avenue. The tough young American whom he had instinctively feared had left the building, and with the blackout to hide him Fedorenko had no difficulty in making his entry. He had already checked up on the number of Allington's suite, and made his way silently up to the fourth floor. The hotel was ninety percent empty of both staff and guests, and stealth was more a matter of form than necessity.

The Russian carried a pencil torch which he used

sparingly. The stairways and corridors of the hotel were in pitch darkness, but brief stabs of the thin, faint beam enabled him to find his way.

There was a glimmering line of very dim light at the bottom of Allington's closed door. Fedorenko checked the number and then switched off the pencil torch and dropped it into his pocket. He moved closer and listened at the wooden panel. From inside he heard the faint rustle of paper, and guessed that Allington was either reading, studying, or planning.

Silently the Russian went down on one knee and moved his eye to the keyhole. There was no key in the lock and he saw the blurred outline of Allington's shoulders. His target was sitting at a writing desk, his back to the door, his head hunched down over his work. The weak, flickering light came from the candelabra on the desk beside him.

Fedorenko guessed that the Secretary-General of the United Nations was writing his next speech, but it was one he would never deliver, not on TV or anywhere else. The Russian's mouth twisted in a wolfish smile of satisfaction, and with his right hand he drew the knife from the leather sheath strapped to his left forearm. The blade was long and thin and razor sharp. He had used it for this kind of work before. It was designed to spear through clothing, skin and rib cage, slice through the protective fat and muscle, and thrust deep into a victim's heart.

With his left hand Fedorenko turned the door handle, infinitely slowly, a millimetre at a time. The door was not locked. He eased it open half an inch. Through the keyhole he could see that Allington was still busy with his notes, unsuspecting. He had heard nothing.

Fedorenko straightened up and continued to push the door gently open, widening the crack until he could see through it. Still Allington's back was towards him.

There was no sound as the door moved back, three inches, six inches, twelve inches — and then

Fedorenko slipped through and into the room. He had three strides to cover and he had made the first stride, the knife already lunging for a point of impact just behind Allington's right shoulder-blade, when Barbara came through the open bedroom door.

She was wearing a nightdress and dressing-gown she had borrowed from Lorna. She was tired and had prepared herself for bed, but first she intended to kiss her father goodnight. Her mouth was open in a long yawn, which abruptly became a startled scream.

Allington twisted round. Fedorenko continued his lunge but Allington's flailing arm knocked the knife aside. The blade cut through his clothing and gashed a bleeding line across his lower ribs, but the point failed to penetrate.

Fedorenko cursed and aimed for the throat with the return slash of the knife. Allington ducked and reeled to one side, half-falling from his chair. The Russian would have killed him then with a downward stab, but Barbara flew in to the attack and grabbed his knife wrist with both hands.

For a few minutes all three of them fought blindly. The writing-desk tipped over with a crash and the candles went out as the candelabra spilled on to the floor. Allington hooked an elbow hard into Fedorenko's groin and Barbara continued to scream with all the power in her lungs as she hung desperately on to the knife arm. Fedorenko felt panic and kicked out viciously with his boot. He caught Allington in the chest and the Englishman went back gasping, blundering into the TV set and knocking it over with another violent crash. For a moment there was only the girl to deal with and the Russian smashed his fist viciously into her face. Blood spurted from Barbara's mouth and nose but still she hung on. Fedorenko turned his wrist, skewering with the knife, and scored deep cuts across the back of her fingers. In the same moment he kicked her between the legs. Crippled by her hurts Barbara at last let go and fell away.

Allington was on one knee, rising to his feet. There was candlelight still in the bedroom and here they were just visible to each other in the gloom. Fedorenko leaped forward again for the kill, but behind him the door he had eased ajar so softly was suddenly crashed fully open with a resounding bang.

Julius Mangala charged in, like a massive black bull in crimson pyjamas. He had been awakened by the disturbance and Barbara's screams and had come running to investigate. He saw the glint of the steel blade in Fedorenko's hand and didn't stop to ask questions. He already had momentum and his huge bulk smashed into Fedorenko from behind, carrying him past Allington and crushing him against the far wall. Fedorenko was startled, flattened and gasping for breath, but he had been trained by the most ruthless men in the world and he was still fighting. He succeeded in twisting his body round and jabbing two extended fingers into the black man's bulging eyes. Mangala backed off with a howl of pain and fury.

Fedorenko had not expected three opponents, and the presence of the big black man was a complete surprise. Rage and the rising wave of panic were combining to blur his judgement now and he saw Mangala as the most dangerous of the three. Desperately he lunged the knife at the African.

Allington threw himself at the Russian, grappling him with a bear hug and pinning his arms to his sides. Fedorenko roared and cursed as they reeled around the room, toppling more furniture and smashing every flower-vase and item of glass. Once, twice, three times Fedorenko brought his knee up into Allington's groin until finally Allington was weakened enough for him to break free. He kicked the Englishman away and tried for a killing stab, but again the girl was clawing at his back.

Fedorenko crouched; reaching behind him with his left hand he caught a fistful of Barbara's hair and heaved her bodily over his shoulder. As she hit the floor he straightened up again to look for Allington, but the diversion had given Mangala time to blink away his tears and clear his vision.

The African had no finesse. Once more he charged with all the thundering power of an enraged bull. Head down and shoulder forward he hit Fedorenko like a battering-ram and again carried him forward, straight through the open bedroom doorway and clear to the far wall. Except that at this point there was no wall, just the yielding glass of the window. There was an explosion like a cannon shot as Fedorenko went backwards through the shattering glass, screaming and falling until he hit the pavement on Connecticut Avenue four floors below.

Mangala almost followed him through. He clutched at the broken window-frame to save himself, and blood spilled from his fingers as they were gashed by fragments of the splintered glass. He pulled back and stood there panting, and began to wonder what it was all about.

All of them had collected cuts and bruises, but none of them were seriously hurt. They spent ten minutes in bathing and binding their wounds, and in puzzling over the identity and motives of their unknown assailant. Finally curiosity prompted Allington and Mangala to put on their topcoats and go out into the street.

They found Fedorenko sprawled amongst the broken glass from the window. His head was twisted to one side and his right leg was bent up beneath his body. Both the leg and his neck were broken.

Mangala shone a flashlight on the dead man's face, stared for a moment, and then said in surprise: 'I know this man. I have seen him before.'

'Where?'

'In Luanda, three years ago. He was attached to the Russian Embassy. I do not remember his name. I had no dealings with him. But everyone knew he was a KGB man.'

'So he wasn't just an ordinary thief.' Allington was confused, but then some of his past problems took on new meaning. He said slowly, 'Perhaps this explains some of the mud-slinging by the media.'

'It could be.' Mangala's tone was sombre. 'The KGB are very dangerous and devious people. They have twisted minds. Who knows what mischief they will make — or why?'

Allington shivered and they turned to go back into the hotel.

'It doesn't matter now,' Allington decided. 'It's all up to Lorna and Johnny.'

26

Glenn Anderson was mystified as he made his way up from the west wing in response to the urgent but totally uninformative telephone call from his wife. He was also somewhat annoyed. They had dined together less than an hour ago, and he couldn't think of anything that might have come up since that could be important enough to drag him away from the hot line in the Oval Office. However, Lucy had insisted it was vital.

He found her in the private sitting-room she favoured when she wanted to be alone. He guessed their two daughters would be in the main living-room, arguing over a game of chess or watching an old film from a video cassette on the TV. Lucy got up and closed the door behind him to ensure their privacy, and her face looked older and more serious than he had ever seen it before. She commanded his attention, and he listened with growing sensations of shock, anger and amazement as she told him about her long conversation with Lorna Maxwell.

'Where are these people?' the President of the United States demanded at last. His tone was curt and furious and his temper was only just under control.

'They've gone,' she told him calmly. 'I gave Langford instructions to escort them off the premises. Miss Maxwell promised me that her visit and our talk would remain a secret, and I felt sure you wouldn't want the world to know there had been such an embarrassing breach of our security.'

'Jesus Christ!' Anderson blasphemed in horror. The whole situation was unreal and he felt stunned. 'They could have come here to kill you! They could have kidnapped the girls! Where the hell is this idiot Langford? He must have been crazy to let them in. Right now he's fired!'

'He's attending to some little matter on the east terrace. Miss Maxwell's friend apologized and said he had to leave one of our security men tied up down there. Langford was going to let them out, release the man who is tied up, and then report discreetly to the agent in charge of security.'

The President gaped at her, and the First Lady continued gravely:

'But none of that is important, Glenn. It's not why I brought you up here.'

Anderson understood her meaning. 'Forget it,' he ordered. 'Some nutty dame breaks in here and sells you the idea of you going to Moscow as an exchange hostage for Irina Komarov. It's crazy! It's insane! My cabinet won't listen to it. I won't permit it!'

'Darling, this subject isn't up for discussion with your precious cabinet. I'm not asking for official government approval. This is my decision — and mine alone. And I have made up my mind. I'm discussing it with you before I go any further because you are my husband — because my children are your children — not because you are the President of the United States.'

'Lucy, don't you come all defiant with me.'

'Glenn Anderson, you should know by now that when I tell you something straight I mean what I say. You men have let this thing go on long enough. Now I intend to go on TV and say my piece. I'm going to announce this as my own idea — and I'm going to appeal to Irina Komarov to come here to Washington, while I take our children to Moscow.'

Anderson knew he had married a woman with fire, a

proud woman with a high degree of moral courage. He just hadn't realized the whole of it until this particular moment. He argued for two solid hours, and then he had to concede to her crushing, irrefutable logic. Everything else had failed. Life on the planet Earth had all but perished. And there was really nothing to lose and everything to be gained by putting the hostage offer to the test.

At ten thirty a.m. the following morning the face of the First Lady of America filled the TV screens of the nation. She had chosen to be filmed in the Diplomatic Reception Room at the White House, where Franklin Roosevelt had once made his famous fireside chats. She wore a tailored grey-blue costume, and sat in a straight-backed, elegant eighteenth-century chair. Her daughters flanked her on either side, sitting on the oval rug that was woven with the symbols of fifty of the states of America.

Lucy Anderson spoke for five minutes, to America, to the world, and to the Soviet Leadership in Moscow. But most of all her appeal was addressed directly to one woman — to the wife of President Grigori Komarov.

She stated briefly the bare facts they all knew. The world was dying inside the black cloud. There was a way to salvation but it demanded trust and cooperation between the superpowers. And there was no trust, only deadlock.

'To break that deadlock I am prepared to go to Moscow, as an indication of the good faith of my husband, and my country.' Her voice rang out brave and clear and determined. She reached down to clasp the hands of the two girls at her feet and continued, 'As a further gesture of our goodwill, President Anderson and I have decided that our daughters, Claire and Ellen, will travel with me. In return for receiving such an invitation from Moscow, we extend our own sincere invitation for Mrs. Irina Komarov to visit Washington as our guest at the White House.'

She gazed into the camera and her voice filled with emotion. 'Irina Komarov, this message is personally for you. I beg you with all my heart — trust me — believe me. Only you and I can do this, and there is no other way. I appeal to you now, not as the wife of one world leader to another, but as a mother of children to another mother of children. There is no hope for our children, no hope for the world, unless we can eliminate the fear between our two great nations, and provide the guarantees that both sides need.

'Persuade your husband, Irina. As I have persuaded mine. Come to Washington, and I will go to Moscow.'

Copies of the video tape were flown immediately to London and Paris, and all major European capitals, and from Europe additional copies with voice-over translations in Russian and Chinese were flown on to Moscow and Peking. Six copies arrived in Moscow. Five were immediately confiscated and destroyed by the KGB. Only one was retained for a private showing to the Politburo. None were screened for the benefit of the Russian people.

The hatchet-faced Chairman of the KGB would have destroyed all six copies of the tape if he had dared, but Anderson had already given advance notice to Komarov over the telephone hot line. The Soviet President knew the tape was coming. He had discussed it with Ladiyev and they had decided to put the issue to debate by the full Politburo. Even the Chairman of the KGB could not openly defy them all, although his hostility was iron-clad, and his displeasure evident.

A TV set was brought into the conference room and the video tape was screened. The twelve men watched in stony silence. The face and the appeal that had brought tears to the eyes of millions of Americans and Europeans left them unmoved. Each of the old men had a copy of the speech translation in front of him, but if it stirred any compassion in their hearts they were careful to conceal it from each other.

When the screen went blank Komarov looked slowly round the circle of faces, his raised eyebrows inviting comment. The faces stared back through the drifting fog of cigarette and tobacco smoke, most of them with sagging grey jowls, here and there a set of lips pursed in thought, the ancient, rheumy eyes all hooded by heavy, half-lowered lids. They were almost equally divided between varying degrees of contempt, and the guarded masks that wore no expression at all.

Predictably it was the Chairman of the KGB who spoke first. He had taken on the role of Sukhov, the Devil's Advocate, the new guardian of the old dream. He all but spat in the direction of the TV set.

'This is just another capitalist American trick. We must ignore it. It means nothing!'

'I disagree.' Desperation had made Andrei Ladiyev bolder. He was ready to stand up and be counted. 'Grigori, Irina is your wife, the choice is yours and hers. But if it were Natalya, and she was willing, I would let her go.'

'I have talked with Irina,' Komarov said calmly. 'I know her view, and she knows mine. For the moment I have forbidden her to make any answer to this plan.'

'You had no right to discuss this matter outside this room,' the echo of Sukhov snarled at him. 'Not even to your wife. This is a matter of vital importance to Soviet security. Any descision can only be made here in this room.'

'The decision will be made here,' Komarov conceded.

'By talking outside this room you have betrayed your position.'

'There was no betrayal. You are a fool, comrade, if you believe this issue can be kept a state secret. You can prevent the film we have just seen from being shown to the Russian people, but the full text of the speech is being broadcast constantly by the BBC overseas radio stations in Europe. It is being transmitted over our borders in all the major East European languages.'

The Devil's Advocate fumed and bared his teeth.

'Then send your wives to Washington,' he sneered. 'It will do no good. This is still just a trick and you will never see the wife of the American President here in Moscow.'

'So you give your approval?' Komarov queried. 'And if the wife of the American president does come — ?'

'No, I do not give my approval. Even if this exchange of hostages should be made, it is still an American trick. We would not allow the fate of one woman, any woman, to weigh against the preservation of the entire Soviet Union. The American leadership is no less realistic. The Pentagon generals will sacrifice the wife of their President. The woman is a fool and a pawn. Anderson himself must care nothing for her, either that or he too is a fool.'

The in-fighting continued, but resistance was waning. The Chairman of the KGB was making a last-ditch stand. Komarov gave no ground, but he seemed unusually patient, and in no hurry to put the issue to the vote.

While the Politburo was still in session in the Kremlin a large black limousine arrived at Moscow's international airport. Two women disembarked, both of them heavily shrouded in thick fur coats. The older woman was in her sixties, the younger less than thirty, and with them were three small children between the ages of five and nine. The chauffeur and an additional bodyguard escorted them into the blacked-out building, using flashlights to find their way to the office of the Airport Director.

The senior airport officials had not been warned,

and were startled by these unexpected but Very Important People. The Director recognized the wife of the Soviet President, and soon realized that the younger woman was her daughter, and the children her grandchildren.

Irina Komarov showed him a letter of authorization which appeared to have been signed by Grigori Komarov himself. It instructed the Director to provide her with the Aeroflot jet-liner that had been placed on permanent stand-by since the beginning of the crisis. The aircraft was ready to fly any necessary top-level government mission abroad. It was to take off immediately to fly the wife and family of the President to Washington.

The Airport Director read the document through twice. He was uncertain. His hand reached tentatively for the telephone on his desk.

'I must confirm this,' he apologized. 'I'm sure you understand. It will only take a moment.'

Irina Komarov reached for his wrist and pulled the outstretched hand away from the telephone. She leaned forward, her face a stern mask, her eyes fixed on those of the man in front of her.

'It will take at least an hour.' Her voice was taut but firm. 'Probably two. You know that telephone communications are no longer reliable. I tell you, comrade, that in this matter there is no time to waste.'

The Airport Director bit his lip. He began to sweat. 'It is my duty to confirm,' he said weakly.

They both knew with whom he had to confirm. Dzerzhinsky Square. Irina Komarov stared at him and said slowly,

'You know why I must go to Washington. You have heard the radio broadcasts from Europe — the words of the wife of the American President. I am the wife of President Komarov. You have the letter with his signature. It is enough.'

Before the coming of the cloud it would not have been

enough, and they both knew it. But everything now had collapsed into black confusion, and the Airport Director knew desperation and despair as much as anyone else. He swallowed the hard lump of fear in his throat and nodded.

'Yes, comrade, it is enough. I will notify Captain Zuyov, he will be your pilot, and give clearance for your flight.'

His hand trembled as he reached for the telephone again, for he knew his actions would not go unreported.

The Politburo meeting was becoming tiresome. It was the same old roundabout of obstruction and dead dogma and had dragged on for three pointless hours. Ladiyev could not understand why Komarov did not wind it up. He thought at least they would have an evenly split vote, perhaps, just possibly, a seven to five majority, and there was nothing more to be gained by prolonging the inevitable show of hands.

Then quite suddenly there was an interruption, a discreet knock on the door. A nervous secretary came in and handed a note to the Chairman of the KGB.

The Devil's Advocate read the message, his neck flared crimson, and he lurched to his feet in a towering rage.

'Your wife has just left Moscow Airport on a flight to Washington,' he howled at Komarov. 'She has taken her youngest daughter and three of your grandchildren with her. You knew this! All the time we have been sitting here, *you knew!*'

'I knew nothing.' Komarov stood up and glared down the table. 'If my wife has done this it is her own doing. I forbade it.'

'She presented a letter of authorization with your signature!'

'I signed nothing!'

Komarov was icy, angry, but perhaps not quite as

surprised as he should have been. None of them dared accuse him of lying. Most of them, even Ladiyev, were confused and unsure.

'She must be stopped.' The Chairman of the KGB was almost hysterical. 'This disobedience cannot be allowed. The plane must be turned back.'

'Of course,' Komarov agreed smoothly. 'You are correct, comrade. I will give the order immediately.'

The Tupolev TU-144, the Russian equivalent to the British and French Concorde, was streaking over Poland at a thousand miles per hour when the curt command to return to Moscow crackled over the radio. The supersonic airliner was flying at only two-thirds of her maximum speed, but because it was necessary to keep below ten thousand feet to avoid any magnetic interference with his instruments, Captain Valery Zuyov was reluctant to give the huge turbofan engines their maximum thrust.

The harsh voice in his headphones startled him, and the contradiction in his orders made him hesitate.

Irina Komarov was talking quietly with her daughter when one of the two stewardesses on the flight crew approached with a polite request. She gave the captain's compliments, and asked if Comrade Madame Komarov would please come forward to the flight deck where Captain Zuyov wished to speak to her.

Mother and daughter exchanged worried glances. The face of Alicia Komarov was pale and frightened, but Irina gave her hand a reassuring squeeze before they parted. The stewardess led the way forward, but then stood back to let the older woman precede her on to the flight deck.

Zuyov looked back over his shoulder. He was an experienced pilot in his fifties, a competent man who would normally obey his flight control without question, but now his face was dark and strained with doubt.

'Madame Komarov,' he said seriously. 'Forgive me, but it appears that your journey does not have the approval of your husband or the Politburo. I have been instructed to take you back to Moscow.'

Irina Komarov knew the bluff was over. She did not try to carry it any further, but she was not beaten yet.

'Captain Zuyov, you know why I must go to Washington.' Her voice was calm, but she was a matriarch who demanded respect and a hearing. 'I cannot force you to take me to Washington, for I am only an old woman, but I appeal to your reason. You are a married man, I think. You do not look like a bachelor. You probably have children. Do you want your children to die in a dark world without sunlight?'

Zuyov frowned and looked at his co-pilot. The other man was blank and dumb, offering nothing. Zuyov felt opposing forces tear at his heart. He had one son. The son was married. There was an eight-week-old baby. He had held the baby in his arms, he could almost feel it now, the tiny limbs kicking, the dampness in his palm. His son and daughter-in-law laughing,.

'I think not,' the voice of persuasion was driving home. 'You wish for the sun to shine again, for Mother Russia, for the world — but most of all for your children. It is your choice now, Captain. Your decision. Perhaps the sunlight, or forever the darkness. Do we turn back — or do we go on?'

Zuyov was silent for a full minute. In that time the TU-144 had covered another 150 miles, leaving the Soviet bloc behind as it entered West German air space. Then Zuyov squared his shoulders and made up his mind.

'Enjoy your flight, Madame Komarov, and let us hope your mission is successful. We shall arrive in Washington DC in approximately four hours.'

Within twenty-four hours Lucy Anderson had arrived in Moscow, to an embarrassed and somewhat uncertain reception by six members of the ruling Politburo. They had not issued an official invitation, but the arrival of Irina Komarov in Washington had been invitation enough.

The First Lady of America was not alone. In addition to her two daughters she was accompanied by the wife of the American Secretary of State, the wife of the American Secretary of Defence, and the wives of two four-star Pentagon generals. There were five more assorted children.

Before they left the airport they encountered a small group of Russian women who were waiting to board their plane for its return flight. The elected speaker for the group smiled hesitantly at the Washington wives and offered her hand.

'I am Natalya Ladiyev,' she told them. 'These ladies are all from Moscow. All our husbands are in the government. We are going to join Irina in America. We think now is a very good time to take a short holiday.'

'You'll be very welcome.' Lucy Anderson took the offered hand and gripped it warmly. She laughed and added, 'There'll be plenty of room for you all. I think every government wife in Washington has already volunteered to come to Moscow.'

Their combined good humour eased the tension and briefly cheered the gloomy airport lounge before they parted to go their separate ways. The Moscow wives trooped out to the tarmac and the waiting aircraft. The Washington wives boarded the small cavalcade of official cars that were to take them into Moscow.

Lucy Anderson found herself seated beside Grigori Komarov, her reluctant host. They were in the leading car, alone except for Ellen and Claire, and the silent Russian chauffeur.

'Irina sends you a message,' she said quietly. 'She sends you her love. She wants you to know that Alicia and the children are well. And she hopes you will not be too angry with her.'

'Of course I am angry with her,' Komarov said severely. 'She disobeyed my direct order.'

But he was speaking to the back of the chauffeur's neck, and only Lucy Anderson witnessed his faint smile, and the slow, deliberate wink of his left eye.

27

After the women had taken the initiative there was no turning back, and the final cloud crisis meeting of the Soviet Politburo ended in a seven to five vote in favour of complete co-operation with the American survival plan. More time was needed for the Soviet missiles to be re-programmed for their new task, and for the Soviet submarines to sail' at full speed to their appointed positions in southern hemisphere waters, but within six days the mass launch sequence was ready to begin.

The entire operation was co-ordinated from NASA Mission Control at Houston, although each space centre, missile complex and nuclear submarine had received in advance its own carefully timed firing schedule. Close timing was critical, and to avoid any communication breakdown during the vital two-hour launch period, each control centre had to be able to continue independently to maintain the overall strategy.

The first blast-off of sixty assorted launch vehicles and missiles was made on simultaneous countdown. At zero fifteen American Titans achieved lift-off, from Vandenberg, Kennedy, and the Air Force missile silos at Ellsworth, Whiteman, McConnell and Little Rock. Three Soyuz launch vehicles thundered up from the cosmodromes at Tyuratum, Plesetsk and Kasputin Yar, together with twelve Soviet SS-9 and SS-10 ICBMs from the Soviet missile sites. Two French S-2 ballistic missiles left the Albion Plateau in southern France, and two Chinese CSS-X4 Long March missiles hurtled up from their bases at Shuang-Cheng-Tze and Lop Nor. The balance of the first salvo was made up by the submarines in the Indian and Pacific Oceans, ten US and British Polaris, six French M-1 missiles, and ten Soviet SSN-4 Sark missiles.

At sixty widely separated points above the Earth's atmosphere the rockets crashed through the black cloud, tearing out great swirls of the magnetic gas and dust. On thrusting pillars of fire they broke free of the gravitational pull of the planet, radiating outward and sucking the substance of the cloud behind them as they plunged onward into outer space. Approximately half of the gaping holes they left behind were on the sunward side of the planet, and brilliant beams of sunshine lanced down to the light-starved world.

The cloud began to spread, healing its own wounds, and narrowing the beams of sunlight, but with less than a two-minute delay the second salvo was launched. From America, the Soviet Union, Japan, French Guiana, and three major oceans off the shores of Africa, South America and Australia, the rockets soared upward. Again the black cloud was ripped and torn asunder, and the black trailing plumes of its shredded mass were carried outward on journeys that would end no man knew where.

As rapidly as possible the staggered firing sequence continued. Each individual rocket was computer-programmed with its own individual trajectory and flight path, enabling the mission control centres to pepper the Satan cloud with evenly spaced shots over the entire surface area of the Earth. Salvo followed salvo with stockpiles declining evenly in the five armouries until every missile silo, every submarine launch tube, and every space-centre launch pad was empty.

One hundred and twenty salvoes were launched, accounting for more than seven thousand assorted rockets and missiles. With the final salvo all five of the superpower nuclear armouries were exhausted. Earth had thrown everything it had, at and through the dark, swirling nebula of the cloud.

And the sun was shining! A few black patches and wisps remained, but almost everywhere there was a new dawn and the sun was bursting through. Sanity had prevailed, and the planet Earth had survived. The miracle had happened, and the long night of the comet was at last over.

America was on the dark side of the Earth when the cloud was attacked, and so the people there had to wait for the Earth to rotate, and for the first natural sunrise to prove to them that the skies were really clear.

Glenn Anderson watched the magic glow appear from the south lawn of the White House, standing between Irina and Alicia Komarov. His guests were weeping unashamedly with emotion, and the President of the United States found it difficult to hold his own tears back.

It was still bitterly cold. Washington was revealed as a frozen city of glittering snow and ice — but soon the ice would begin to melt.

Almost the entire population of the capital flocked to the open spaces and parks along the west bank of the Potomac, cheering, laughing and crying with unbelievable joy as the first rays of sunlight crept over the solid white surface of the river. Among them were Johnny Chance and Barbara Allington, hugging each other with happiness and relief. Johnny's only wish was that John Junior could have shared this moment with them, but as soon as he could find some transport he would be hurrying back to New York, and he knew that Barbara would be going with him.

Richard Allington and Lorna Maxwell stood at the foot of the tall white marble obelisk that was the

Washington Monument. From here they could see the Greek temple of the Lincoln Memorial to the west, the White House to the north, and the magnificent dome of the Capitol on the crest of the hill to the east. They were holding hands and drinking in the wonder and beauty of the scene as the sun kissed each famous landmark.

Julius Mangala stood beside them, his black face exultant, positively radiating excitement.

'I did not expect to see this moment,' he marvelled. 'I did not think this moment would come. Now the brilliance dazzles my eyes. I feel the warmth on my face. Richard! Lorna! The Earth is reborn! We will all live again!'

'Yes,' Lorna whispered, as though she hardly dared to say it aloud. 'The cloud has been dispersed. The Earth is alive again. We have won.'

'We have won,' Allington agreed. 'But there is still a vast task of reconstruction ahead. The United Nations must and will play a vital role in the rebuilding, which means that for us there are still more battles, and plenty of hard work to be done.'

'We will work,' Mangala promised. 'Together, Richard. There are no longer Third World countries and superpowers. There is only one shattered world which has suffered incalculable damage. Now we cannot afford to fight between ourselves. All our energies and resources will be needed to rebuild.'

'And not only at the United Nations,' Allington said slowly. 'This new mood of co-operation must be continued between East and West. I suspect that the United States and the Soviet Union will have saved as many of their nuclear warheads as they can, and unless we can stop it the race will be on again to rebuild and replace the rocket vehicles to carry them. The world cannot afford to waste resources on another arms race, so it is up to us to ensure that it cannot happen again.'

'But how?' It was a new thought to Lorna and it left her perplexed. 'What can we do?'

'There's a plan in my desk at the Secretariat,' Allington answered quietly. 'It was put forward some years ago. The proposal was for the United Nations to launch its own international reconnaissance satellites in space. Three UN satellites would be able to police the world. We would be able to spot immediately any build-up of military forces, and be in a position to give advance warnings and thus forestall any military operations before they start. We would be able to monitor and verify all strategic arms limitation treaties, and thus make them workable.'

'UN spy satellites in space?' Lorna said doubtfully. 'Could the idea really work?'

'It was shelved before because of the cost and the fact that the damage was already done,' Allington told her. 'But now the superpowers have hurled all their missiles out into space we have an opportunity to justify the cost. Our first battle must be to ensure that the only rocket vehicles to be built in the foreseeable future will be those which carry our own UN satellites. With our own technological watchdogs policing the world from space, the priority task of reconstruction will be undertaken. We will be able to build a better and safer world. The United Nations will at last be able to play its true role of keeping the peace, and providing a genuine World Parliament.'

It was a dream, a vision, but it fired them all with new hope. Julius Mangala held out his hand, and Richard Allington grasped it firmly. The black hand and the white hand were met in friendship and the slim brown hands of Lorna Maxwell held them both. They said nothing, but the gesture and their smiles were a pledge of all their future endeavours to meet the bright new challenge of the way ahead.

Out of the ultimate disaster, the planet Earth had at last discovered a golden ray of hope for a better tomorrow.

THE END

A SELECTION OF TITLES FROM CORGI BOOKS

While every effort is made to keep prices low, it is sometimes necessary to increase prices at short notice. Corgi Books reserve the right to show new retail prices on covers which may differ from those previously advertised in the text or elsewhere.

The prices shown below were correct at the time of going to press.

☐	10955 X	**THE JIGSAW MAN**	*Dorothea Bennett* £1.75
☐	11982 2	**THE HASTINGS CONSPIRACY**	*Alfred Coppel* £1.75
☐	12079 0	**THE APOCALYPSE BRIGADE**	*Alfred Coppel* £1.95
☐	12145 2	**CONTRACT!**	*Chris Dempster* £1.50
☐	12007 3	**HIT!**	*Chris Dempster* £1.50
☐	11975 X	**THE TIPTOE BOYS**	*James Follett* £1.50
☐	12180 0	**THE MAN FROM ST. PETERSBURG**	*Ken Follett* £1.95
☐	11810 9	**THE KEY TO REBECCA**	*Ken Follett* £1.75
☐	12140 1	**NO COMEBACKS**	*Frederick Forsyth* £1.95
☐	11500 2	**THE DEVIL'S ALTERNATIVE**	*Frederick Forsyth* £2.50
☐	10050 1	**THE DOGS OF WAR**	*Frederick Forsyth* £1.95
☐	09436 6	**THE ODESSA FILE**	*Frederick Forsyth* £1.95
☐	09121 9	**THE DAY OF THE JACKAL**	*Frederick Forsyth* £1.95
☐	99062 0	**BALEFIRE (Trade Paperback)**	*Kenneth Goddard* £3.95
☐	11533 9	**GENESIS**	*W.A. Harbinson* £2.50
☐	11901 6	**REVELATION**	*W.A. Harbinson* £1.95
☐	12160 6	**RED DRAGON**	*Thomas Harris* £1.95
☐	10174 5	**THE ATTORNEY**	*Harold Q. Masur* £1.75
☐	10595 3	**DUBAI**	*Robin Moore* £1.95
☐	11850 8	**THE WINDCHIME LEGACY**	*A.W. Mykel* £1.75
☐	12307 2	**RED SQUARE**	*Edward Topol and Fridrikh Neznansky* £1.95
☐	11941 5	**THE TURNAROUND**	*Vladimir Volkoff* £1.75

ORDER FORM

All these books are available at your book shop or newsagent, or can be ordered direct from the publisher. Just tick the titles you want and fill in the form below.

CORGI BOOKS, Cash Sales Department, P.O. Box 11, Falmouth, Cornwall.

Please send cheque or postal order, no currency.

Please allow cost of book(s) plus the following for postage and packing:

U.K. Customers—Allow 45p for the first book, 20p for the second book and 14p for each additional book ordered, to a maximum charge of £1.63.

B.F.P.O. and Eire—Allow 45p for the first book, 20p for the second book plus 14p per copy for the next seven books, thereafter 8p per book.

Overseas Customers—Allow 75p for the first book and 21p per copy for each additional book.

NAME (Block Letters) ....

ADDRESS ....

....